RIP-ROARING ACCLAIM FOR
KERRY NEWCOMB'S *THE RED RIPPER*

"Kerry Newcomb is one of those writers who lets you know from his very first lines that you're in for a ride. And he keeps his promise. THE RED RIPPER bounds along with unrelenting vigor. This is historical fiction crafted by a writer who never loses his sense of pace, drama, adventure, and fun. Kerry Newcomb knows what he is doing, and does it enviably well."
—Cameron Judd, Golden Spur Award-nominated author of *Texas Freedom*

"With the historical accuracy of a L'Amour novel, the characters are well drawn, leaving the reader to feel the openness and harsh challenges of the Texas frontier ... Don't expect to get any sleep when you start this one."
—John J. Gobbell, bestselling author of *The Last Lieutenant*

"The ornery, pugnacious and legendary William 'Bigfoot' Wallace, a sometime Texas Ranger and full-time knife-fighter, strides through early 19th-century Texas history in this rangy, fast-moving historical novel."
—*Publishers Weekly*

Coming soon from St. Martin's Paperbacks—
New editions of Kerry Newcomb's classic works:

Texas Anthem
Texas Born
Shadow Walker
Rogue River
Creed's Law

The Red Ripper

Kerry Newcomb

St. Martin's Paperbacks

THE RED RIPPER

Copyright © 1999 by Kerry Newcomb.
Excerpt from *Mad Morgan* copyright © 2000 by Kerry Newcomb.

Library of Congress Catalog Card Number: 99-21752

ISBN: 0-312-97153-2

Printed in the United States of America

St. Martin's Press hardcover edition / June 1999
St. Martin's Paperbacks edition / August 2000

St. Martin's Paperbacks are published by St. Martin's Press, 175 Fifth Avenue, New York, N.Y. 10010.

10 9 8 7 6 5 4 3 2 1

Always for Patty, Amy Rose, P.J., and Emily
and in memory of Ann Newcomb and Virginia Reno

I'll eat when I'm hungry,
And drink when I'm dry.
If someone don't kill me,
I'll live till I die.

—LYLE SAXON,
ROBERT TALLANT,
AND EDWARD DREYER
Gumbo Ya-Ya:
Folk Tales of Louisiana

Here's a sigh to those who love me,
And a smile to those who hate
And whatever sky's above me
Here's a heart for every fate.

—LORD BYRON, 1817

AUTHOR'S NOTE

I give glory to God.

I humbly embrace in love my family.

A special thank-you to Aaron Priest, my agent and true friend on this publishing journey, and to my editors at St. Martin's for their patience and expertise.

This book owes a debt of gratitude to *Recollections of Old Texas Days*, by Noah Smithwick, and *Big Foot Wallace*, by John C. Duval, for their marvelous descriptions of life on the Texas frontier and the colorful pilgrims who hitched their dreams to a lone star.

The Red Ripper is a work of fiction, and that's a fact. I have taken liberties with time and events where it suited the yarn. If you're writing a thesis on the Texas Revolution this probably isn't the research novel for you, unless your topic is tall tales, high courage, dangerous days, and a legendary hero.

The Red Ripper

How was it in those dangerous days? Sit down here by the fire, pilgrim. Rest a spell, and I'll tell you.

William Wallace was the genuine article, a bold man, generous and full of good humor, but a real bloodletter in a scrape. He strode the frontier as tall as the tales time has nurtured into legend.

Friends christened him Big Foot Wallace and the Wild West Wind. To his enemies he was El Destripedor Rojo, the Red Ripper.

This is his story, just as he lived it. And what isn't true . . . ought to be.

1

❖

"I WAS BORN READY!"

September 1829

Iridescent bolts of blue lightning pinned the roiling clouds to a witch's brew of bone and blood and black water. A raging wind drowned the cries of men about to die.

The *Patience,* a three-masted barque with a fool for a captain and an untested crew, had tried to outrace the squall . . . and failed. With the Mexican coastline barely visible through the driving downpour, the storm pounced and caught the ship running with full sails.

At the last moment, the more experienced hands climbed into the rigging to trim the canvas before the barque capsized. Pulleys jammed. Knots tangled. In desperation, the crew aloft slashed at the ropes in an attempt to cut the swollen topsails free. Too late.

A treacherous jawline of jagged rocks seemed to rise from the ocean floor and grind into the barque's battered hull. The ship lurched violently; wood groaned. The impact snapped the weakened foremast like a chicken's neck and spilled the helpless sailors into the maelstrom. Angry swells engulfed their prey, crashed against the ravaged hull, then surged past the gunwales and raked the deck in search of more victims.

The *Patience,* in its death throes, shuddered and

thrashed as foam-capped waves buried the stern. One last time the barque fought free. Forked lightning sizzled and cracked off the starboard bow. Its lurid glare revealed a deck littered with sodden whipcord and the massive remnants of the shattered foremast.

Trapped men, passengers and crew, struggled beneath that crush of timber and downed rigging. But the weight of the wreckage was simply too great. Bound to the deck, the desperate souls were doomed to go down with the ship.

Still they fought to free themselves, exhorting one another to be brave. They called out to their shipmates and to heaven for help. But the rain beat them down, blinded them; the wind and thunder stole their prayers. And the Lord didn't hear them.

But Wallace did.

Suddenly the mass of timber and whipcord shifted, and slowly the pressure eased. For a moment the wreckage threatened to settle again; then, inch by inch, it lifted free.

"By all the saints, it's a miracle!" one of the injured cried aloud.

"William Wallace!" a merchant hoarsely exclaimed, awed by the apparition towering over them.

Thunder cracked and lightning split the dark, tracing their benefactor in phosphorescent fire. Wallace straddled the legs of a fallen seaman to prop fifteen feet of shattered foremast on his own powerful shoulder. In that moment, buffeted by wind and rain, his limbs aglow with an unearthly blue flame, the nineteen-year-old seemed born of both flesh and iron—from woman drawn yet forged by the hammer of God.

His features contorted in pain beneath the terrible weight. Splintered wood tore his shirt and dug into his flesh. Blood streaked his thickly muscled chest.

Wallace readjusted his footing on the slick deck and,

working his shoulder down the length of timber, squirmed for all the leverage he could muster. He gritted his teeth, lifted, and took one step forward, then another.

Around him the remainder of the passengers, clutching the most precious of their belongings, abandoned the ship as it reeled and tossed before the punishing elements. Torn canvas streamed from battered spars. The ship's wheel spun crazily where the captain had forsaken his post.

"C'mon!" Wallace shouted to the men crawling out from the debris. "This load has plumb worn me out. I don't know how much longer I can stand to it. Any man looking to survive this night had best be quick!" In truth his collarbone felt about to break and the lacerated flesh burned like fire. Still he held his ground, refusing to abandon the trapped men struggling to free themselves from the tangled ropes.

"William! For heaven's sake the damn ship is breaking apart!" a voice shouted from behind him. He recognized his older brother striving to be heard above the storm. Samuel Wallace, eleven years William's senior, staggered along the deck, lost his footing, steadied himself, then, leaning into the wind, fought his way to William's side. "There is still one johnnyboat tethered near the stern!"

"Help them," William managed to growl.

Samuel shook his head in disbelief, then crouched on the trembling deck and helped to untangle the remaining couple of seamen from the wreckage.

Although Samuel Wallace was a big man in his own right, William stood a head taller, and what he lacked in quickness and agility was compensated for by sheer brute strength. No matter how the ship tossed and twisted, William's legs were like twin oaks rooted to the deck.

Samuel trusted his younger brother, but every man

has his limits and he could tell William was nearing his.

"Thank God," Samuel muttered as the last passenger scrambled free. "You've done it, Will!" He gestured to the black smoke billowing from the hold. A fire had broken out belowdecks. "Looks like we can drown or fry."

Wallace nodded and shoved clear of the wreckage. He fell backward into Samuel's steadying embrace, allowing the foremast to crash onto the deck once again, this time for good. Ropes and pulleys and another pair of spars split from the rigging and came hurtling down. The two brothers darted out of harm's way and made for the last of the johnnyboats as the stern surrendered to the pounding waves.

It was a sodden pair that reached the larboard side of the ship near the bow only to discover the last of the longboats had drifted away. To their credit, the men in the johnnyboat dug their oars into the black water and fought to remain within reach of the brothers.

Samuel wiped a forearm across his eyes and stared at the treacherous-looking spray. William's hair was matted to his skull like a dark red cap; blood flowed free from his cuts and mingled with the rainwater washing his naked torso.

"Curse our captain, he's ruined us for true," William bemoaned. "But the man's fish food now. I saw him go under!"

"Courage, little brother!" Samuel shouted, glancing aside at his powerful sibling. "We aren't finished yet." He patted a pouch of gold coins secured to his belt— seed money for their grand aspirations. "Mexico's ripe for a couple of bold hearts like us." Samuel hung a leg over the gunwale and prepared to leap. "Are you ready?"

William's green eyes twinkled with a sense of anticipation that belied the perilous situation at hand. It was as if he could already reach beyond the storm and seize the dream they shared.

"I was born ready!" He vaulted over the gunwale and leaped into the savage sea.

"They say Texas is prettier than a dream in Venice," *William remarks. "It's the place for us. A whole new* *world, like a plum ripe for the picking. And if the Mex-* *ican government is willing to issue land grants to set-* *tlers, then I say we light a shuck for Mexico City before* *summer ends and claim our share. You've a golden gift* *for words, Samuel. I warrant the Mexican president will* *listen to you."*

"Seems like yesterday you were an eleven-year-old *boy. Eight years later, you're carving an empire out of* *the wilderness," Samuel dryly observes, a bemused ex-* *pression on his face. He thinks of their hardscrabble* *farm in the hills of Virginia. Even then, young William* *had the wanderlust, toiling long hours on the rocky soil* *but his eyes ever on the horizon.*

"Not alone. We can divide our land grant into smaller *tracts and sell them off to colonists and make a profit."* *William is positively beaming. He's got it all figured out* *and is quite proud of himself. "Lawyering may be fine* *for you, big brother," he adds, "but I've got a hankering* *for something that can't be found in books."*

Samuel crosses the law office to stand at the window *overlooking Bourbon Street. The thoroughfare below is* *crowded with street vendors and pushcarts, townspeople* *ambling along the stone walkways, gentlemen planters* *in their carriages, merchants, ladies in velvet dresses* *gossiping in the shade of gaily colored parasols.*

Leaving Virginia hadn't been easy. Moving south to *New Orleans and apprenticing himself to a lawyer and* *living hand-to-mouth only made Samuel's success that* *much sweeter.*

"I promised Mother on her deathbed I'd look after you, Will. I have raised you as best I could. We've made a life for ourselves here. Are you so eager to risk it in the wilderness, fighting redsticks and bandits, hard winters and drought?"

William moves to his brother's side. For the first time that he can remember, they are talking as equals. He knows Samuel is tempted by the vision. But how to make him commit? . . .

"I intend to make my mark," William begins, "to match myself against whatever the world throws my way. Call me fortune's fool, but I would rather fall trying to fly than wait for a wind to knock me out of the nest."

Samuel Wallace smiles. "Now who has the golden tongue? So be it. We'll go together." He extends his hand to seal the pact.

William reached out to his brother but found himself alone, immersed in a blackness no light could penetrate.

"Samuel!"

His brother had to be alive. That was part of the dream.

"Samuel!"

The only reply was the thunder of the waves crashing against the rocks.

2

"WELCOME TO VERACRUZ."

On the gray morning after the sea tried to kill him, William Wallace staggered up from the water's edge, bruised, battered, but alive and determined to stay that way. The storm had taken its best shot at his hide and failed. He glanced over his shoulder at the incoming tide. The gulf was tranquil now, sated from its feast of ships and men.

Wallace raised his fist to the waves and in a hoarse voice croaked defiance: "Still here!" The effort nearly drained him. He cautiously appraised his condition, attempted to brush the sand from his naked chest and shoulders, then doubled over and retched the seawater from his gut.

His head hurt. Reaching up, he gingerly prodded a lump on his forehead. The pain stirred a vague memory. A section of mast or perhaps the bow of the lifeboat or a sea trunk looming out of the darkness had crashed against his skull as he fought to keep the current from pulling him under.

The world reeled for a second, the dull blue sea blurred with the gunmetal gray sky, a dark brown smear of coastline, and the lush green foliage of the palm forest sweeping back into emerald hills. He fell to his knees, propped himself upright, and willed the world into place. A lazy spiral of gulls circled overhead, as if studying the wreckage for something of value. The sandy shore was littered with debris from the ship: sodden sea chests, shattered timber, and sections of shattered spar were all that remained of the *Patience.*

William struggled to his feet, heard a groan, and for the first time realized he wasn't alone upon the shore. Other survivors were scattered along the beach, surprised to find themselves alive and too overjoyed for the moment to share grief for the dead. Wallace recognized some of the seamen he had rescued. He counted four traders, a Creole cattle buyer, and a wealthy silk merchant and his wife, all of them passengers aboard the ill-fated vessel. The johnnyboat that had carried them to safety lay on its side a few yards up from the water's edge. The longboat had provided a makeshift shelter from the elements. William remembered fighting for breath and sinking beneath the waves. All but unconscious, he had fought the clutches of the undertow. How had he kept from drowning? Only an instinct to survive, deep-rooted in the Wallace clan, had brought him through.

Samuel!

Even as William thought the name, a familiar face lifted from the mud and flotsam. Samuel Wallace rolled over on his back and stared at the white smear of sunlight hidden beneath a veil of ashen streamers. William ran to his side and helped him to stand.

"We made it, little brother," Samuel said in a rasping voice as he clapped the larger man on the arm.

"I never doubted," William gruffly replied, pulling his brother upright.

"You look like you've been keelhauled," Samuel muttered.

William dismissed his lacerated shoulder and bruised head with a wave of the hand. "Just a scratch." He dismissed his brother's appearance with an offhanded observation about how Samuel more resembled a derelict than a distinguished barrister. Along the shore, some of the other survivors had already begun to browse among the wreckage the waves had deposited on the shore. The merchant's wife began to weep from shock. Her husband, a wealthy exporter, was relieved to find an oilskin packet of valuable papers and a coin chest still aboard the johnnyboat. Sailors and tradesmen hurried to drag an assortment of chests up from the sea and claim their salvage rights. Trade goods were searched for and inspected.

"I don't think anything of ours made it to shore," William remarked, surveying what he could of the shoreline. "Perhaps further up the coast, beyond that point . . ." Wallace pointed toward a spit of land that stretched out into the bay. He looked at his brother for confirmation and found Samuel staring past him at the line of palm trees. William turned as a man and a woman astride a pair of skittish bay geldings emerged from the shadow of the palm trees. The couple were soon flanked by eight dragoons, Mexican light cavalry, looking somewhat stern and quietly officious in their blue tunics, white breeches, and horsehair-plumed helmets. Judging from their appearance, the soldiers had found shelter from the recent storm.

Samuel started toward the horsemen. William fell in step a few paces back. His boots dragged in the moist sand, slowing his progress. In the aftermath of the gale, the whole setting seemed quite unreal.

The couple, both in their early twenties, bore a close resemblance to each other. Indeed, they looked to be brother and sister. They were simply attired in loose-fitting cotton shirts and matching white breeches, black boots, and wide leather belts. The woman wore a yellow bandanna that covered her head and kept her long black hair from blowing in her face. Her brother sat straight as a ramrod, his hands crossed on his saddle's high pommel, a man of station, sure of himself.

They were a handsome pair, disdainful, impassive, with a disturbing way of peering at and through the two men approaching them. William had the disturbing feeling that the couple might have been watching a pair of curs lumber up from the beach for all the warmth they projected toward the *norte americanos*. Closer now, William noted how the dragoons surveyed the stretch of sand and the salvage that had washed ashore.

"*Buenos dias,* my friends!" Samuel called out. "The sea has claimed our ship, the *Patience*. But God in his mercy spared us and brought us safely through the storm." He indicated the others with a wave of his hand.

"I am Juan Diego Guadiz!" the aristocrat called out. His eyes were dark and revealed little of the inner man. "And this is my sister, Señorita Paloma Turcios Guadiz." The woman's expression remained unchanged, eyes like chips of black glass, her mouth a tight pink slash above a pointed chin. "Welcome to Veracruz." Guadiz pulled a flintlock from his saddle holster and shot Samuel Wallace dead.

William froze as Samuel's body shuddered on impact, lifted, flew backward like a broken doll into his arms. As in a dream where all the players move with leaden grace, William lost his footing and fell like a toppled oak as the line of horsemen opened up with their rifled muskets and charged the water's edge. William shielded his brother from the flashing hooves and flame-stabbed powder smoke. He caught a glimpse of yellow bandanna as Paloma Guadiz rode him down and emptied her flintlock at the big man beneath her charging steed. The pistol ball missed by inches, searing William's cheek with its trajectory, then thudding into the moist sand.

The dragoons galloped past, drawn sabers gleaming through the powder smoke, intent on cutting down the survivors as they fled down the shore. Seamen, merchants, the trader and his wife, it mattered little whether they ran for their lives or remained to plead for mercy. Death had come to claim them on the storm-swept shore.

William lifted himself from the sand and grabbed his brother by the shoulder and rolled him over and nearly gagged. A fist-sized chunk of Samuel's skull had been shot away. His once kind and gentle features were hidden beneath a mask of blood and brains, disfigured beyond recognition.

William retreated in horror and scrambled toward the palm trees. He plunged through the foliage, stumbling blindly, as green fronds slapped his face and torso. Parrots, regal in their plumage of scarlet and vermilion, exploded into the air, causing him to trip over a tangle of vines. William kicked free and ran from the cries of the dying, from the gunfire, from the murderous wrath of Guadiz and his sister, from the dreadful image of his brother, forever seared in his memory. He glanced off one tree, regained his balance, swerved to avoid a lightning-shattered palm, and stepped over the side of an embankment. Wallace cried out and tumbled head over heels down into a wheel-rutted path that cut through the forest.

He lay there, minutes dragging past while he struggled for breath. *Samuel!* Palm branches intersected overhead, shading the road, fracturing the sunlight where it peeped between the clouds. A shaft of golden illumination heightened the colors, intensified the different shades of green, the flash of scarlet in the trees, the deep brown soil upon which he lay.

Samuel!

Shame assailed him, stormed the fortress of his resolve, and put his pride to flight. He had abandoned Samuel and fled for his life, run like a whipped pup while Guadiz killed his brother. William lowered his head. The Wallaces did not forsake their own. No matter his ordeal of the night before. Bruised and battered flesh was no excuse. He had dishonored the family name.

William closed his eyes, his mind replaying Samuel's death. A tear squeezed between his eyelids. *No! No!* He allowed the anger to fuel him, felt it course the length and breadth of him, reviving his spent strength. *Damn them! And damn you, William Wallace. Get up!*

William heard a rustling in the underbrush and forced himself to stand as two of the dragoons, dismounted now, broke from cover and scrambled down the bank to confront their prey. The men grinned and brandished their sabers. Slowly, as if relishing the moment, the soldiers advanced on William, who stood unarmed with fists clenched, summoning the last of his resolve, knowing he didn't have a chance in hell but determined not to leave this earth without taking one of his attackers with him.

"Here I am, you bastards. *Tengo prisa!* I haven't got all day." William slowly retreated, playing for distance, biding his time, determining which man would strike first, gauging his own fading strength and the reach of those steel blades.

Suddenly the two soldiers halted in their tracks. William sensed movement behind him, panicked, and turned to protect himself against some new threat. A man of slender build and wind-seamed features dismounted from a mouse gray mare and advanced down the path. He was older by three decades than any of the other men standing in the path. His bald bullet head, hawkish nose, and sharp-eyed stare beaming beneath thick brows made for a remarkable appearance. The man was attired all in black, from his loose-fitting ruffled shirt to his breeches and boots. A gold ring dangled from what was left of a gnarled, chewed-upon right earlobe.

Farther up the path, the mare whinnied, then chose to

ignore the confrontation and begin to crop the grasses
sprouting beneath the ferns. William took note of the
animal. He was going to have need of that horse. Then
he returned his attention to her owner.

To William's surprise, the newcomer calmly passed
him by, ignoring the larger man's show of defiance, and
continued on toward the dragoons blocking his path.
"Black Shirt" called out in a gravelly voice, "Enough
blood has been shed. Return to your master!"

"Strange talk, coming from a man like you," replied
one of the soldiers. "Juan Diego ordered us to bring back
the gringo's head. Do not interfere, old man."

Wallace felt his legs grow weak, willed himself upright and cast a wary glance in the direction of the mare,
then focused on the confrontation. The man in black
dropped his hands to his belt and drew a pair of knives.
Even in his beleaguered state, William could appreciate
the weapons: one was a twelve-inch double-edged short
sword, the width of four fingers at the hilt, fluted for
bloodletting, tapering to a finely honed point. Its
companion, a dirk, had a blade shorter by a few inches,
slender and wicked-looking, like a tempered steel razor-
sharp stinger. No hunting knives these, both weapons
were made for war.

"Old man? We'll see," purred the knife fighter. With
his fingertips he flicked a silk scarf from his belt. The
cloth draped across the blade's keen edge and parted.
"Old Butch punishes," said the man in black as the two
swaths of silk fluttered to earth. Then, with a swipe of
his right hand, the short sword sliced through a nearby
sapling the thickness of a man's wrist. "Bonechucker
destroys." He hooked a finger in the short sword's
curved hilt and spun the weapon. With a repeated flick
of his wrist he kept the heavy blade twirling until the
staghorn grip slapped the palm of his hand with a loud
smack. At the same instant he tossed the dirk into the

air, timed his catch, and snared it again without severing his fingers.

The dragoons exchanged nervous glances. One of them audibly gulped. But they were too proud or stubborn to retreat, each man unwilling to be the first to flee, so they grudgingly held their ground. The soldiers were full of fight, vain and eager to prove themselves to Juan Diego Guadiz. They recognized the man in black but discounted his reputation.

The knife fighter shrugged and waved them forward. He had given the two a chance to walk away intact. "Come and take it," he purred.

With sabers raised, the soldiers attacked in unison, intending to hack the older man to death and proceed on to *El norte*. William dizzily searched for a branch or rock with which to defend himself. He was determined to fight alongside his benefactor.

The man in black was a blur of motion. He parried the slashing swords, whirled and stabbed, darted back, parried again, attacking and defending at the same instant. One soldier collapsed, clawing at his severed jugular. The second soldier garbled a scream as Old Butch stung his rib cage. Riding a rush of fear and pain, the soldier lunged for the old knife fighter. The saber he held was no match for Toledo-forged steel. Bonechucker batted the saber aside, shattering the soldier's blade. The man in black followed up with a left-hand thrust, plunging the dirk into the soldier's chest. The dragoon dropped against the embankment and slid to a sitting position, the light dying in his eyes.

"Black Shirt" did not take time to observe his handiwork. He softly whistled and called out, "Manuel ... Josefina!" A muscular young native couple, their tattooed arms and faces the color of coconut shells, emerged from the underbrush, gathered up the dead men, and carried them off among the jacaranda trees and wild orchids.

"My servants, Tainos Indians," "Black Shirt" explained, cleaning his weapons in the dirt. The couple were lithe and strong. By the time the man in black sheathed his knives, all trace of the fight had been removed. "Juan Diego will probably assume his soldiers deserted after being unable to find you. It won't be the first time men have fled his wrath. Guadiz won't tarry long to look for them. He and his sister are due at the governor's palace by tomorrow night. Domingo Guadiz is their uncle."

William had heard enough. He couldn't allow his brother's murderer to escape. The big man turned and started toward the mare; if he could just reach the animal and pull himself into the saddle, he'd ride back to avenge Samuel. . . .

The ground rose up and slapped him between the eyes.

Rough hands grabbed Wallace by the shoulders and helped him to stand. William struggled at first. "Black Shirt" steadied the wounded man and brought him over to the mare. With assistance, Wallace climbed into the saddle. The knife fighter grabbed the reins and led horse and rider up the path. A last ripple of gunfire carried to them from the shore. William glanced toward the trees obscuring the bay.

"We must go back," he said, benumbed by his brother's murder. His voice sounded distant, unrecognizable. "Samuel. My brother . . ."

"I can do nothing," the older man replied matter-of-factly. He gestured toward the path where it climbed the side of a steep hill, rising up several hundred feet from the shore, and indicated the colonial two-story house nestled in a grove of jacaranda trees, flowering shrubs, mangoes, and bananas. "Now we must hurry lest Señor

Guadiz come calling as he did last night at my hacienda. He was a most unwelcome guest. I do not enjoy the company of unpredictable men."

William tried to pull the reins from the older man's grasp. "I won't leave my brother's body for the beasts."

The man in black sighed and shook his head, then changed course and guided the mare into a nearby thicket, following a narrow, dimly visible game trail that ended in a shallow cave, a fissure in the volcanic rock left by the turbulent forces that shaped the coast in ages past. "We must wait out the soldiers."

William grudgingly agreed, dismounting as he passed through a curtain of thickly knotted green vines. The cave was barely deep enough for the mare to turn around in. The walls were smooth and glassy-looking, the floor littered with leaves and brittle vines and the skeletal remains of small animals. The air was musty with spoor. The men were obviously intruders in some beast's lair.

"Jaguar," the older man remarked, as if reading Wallace's thoughts. "She's probably hunting back up in the mountains, lucky for us."

William nodded. "I am in your debt, sir . . . whoever you are."

"I am Captain Jacques Henri Flambeau."

"Mad Jack? The Butcher of Barbados?" William's pulse began to race. Had he fallen into the clutches of another villain?

The man leading the mare gravely nodded and bowed. "And the Scourge of the Antilles," he dourly boasted.

"I don't understand," William said, staring in wide-eyed wonderment at the brigand whose brutal exploits were legendary along the Gulf Coast. The bloodthirsty rogue had not been heard of for years. Rumors of his death were common talk among the denizens of New Orleans. Acts of kindly intercession were hardly in keeping with the cutthroat's character. "What are you doing?"

"Saving your life."

"My name is William Wallace. I am no one you know," William said, guardedly watching the smaller man. "Why save my life?"

Mad Jack shrugged, then quietly laughed as if amused by a private joke known to only himself. Suddenly he brought his fingers to his lips, grew quiet, and listened. William strained to hear. His head throbbed; he felt nauseous. Voices drifted on the breeze. Someone was looking for the soldiers who had failed to return.

A red wasp, wings droning with a faint burr, flirted with the cave's concealed entrance before gliding off to inspect a wild bouquet of jasmine. William saw Mad Jack drop his hands to his knife hilts. Then silence followed. Wallace could hear his own heart hammering. Each beat was a deafening thud inside his skull.

The mare shook her head and began to stir. Wallace caught the bridle and stroked her velvet pink nose, calming the animal. He lost count of the sluggish minutes.

My brother is dead. And I have fallen among thieves, murderers, and black'ards. What next?

Capt. Mad Jack Flambeau, tense as a cornered pit viper and just as dangerous, glanced in William's direction and winked. What next indeed. Fate and this wiry little killer held the answer.

Down by the water's edge, medallions of pale sunlight glimmered on the gray surface of the sea like dead men's eyes peering from the briny depths. The plunderers had finished their grisly business and moved on, leaving an empty beach crisscrossed with tracks. William could only surmise the dragoons had dragged the bodies of their victims back into the bay, leaving behind nothing of value and no one to link Guadiz to the crime, except Wallace.

"My God. I talked him into this. It's my fault," Wallace said aloud, in a voice thick with self-recrimination. His dream of Texas land grants, of empires and high adventure, had become a nightmare. The big man closed his eyes as the horizon reeled. His legs started to buckle. Mad Jack stepped forward to steady him.

"I don't understand. We weren't looking for trouble," William told him.

"Life *is* trouble. Only death is not," Flambeau replied.

"Who is this Juan Diego Guadiz?" William clutched the pirate by his ruffled black shirt. "Where does he live? No matter how long it takes, I'll find him."

"Juan Diego is the nephew of the governor, Domingo Guadiz. Cool your vengeance, my young friend. The man is beyond your reach." Mad Jack pried loose of William's grasp. "Even if you were to somehow get past his dragoons and lancers, Guadiz himself would slice you to ribbons. He is a celebrated swordsman, a marksman without peer, and has personally claimed the lives of seven men on the field of honor."

"You could help me kill the bastard," William told the pirate. "I have never seen such skill."

Mad Jack's expression changed. "Me?" He shook his head no. "I have sanctuary here by the grace of the governor's favor. His friendship runs as deep as my purse. Killing his nephew would undoubtedly wear out my welcome." Flambeau sighed. "I am too old to put to sea again. Nor do I long for the roll of a deck beneath my feet and the skull and bones fluttering overhead. Besides,"—the buccaneer lowered his voice, his gaze narrowed—"Diego killed your brother, not mine."

"Indeed he did," William growled.

"Vengeance is like a wine—it's better sipped slow and savored," Mad Jack observed. "Wait then. Bide your time. And if you must strike, choose the moment carefully when it will not result in your capture and execution."

The old brigand spoke the truth. Wallace realized he was in no shape to search out Juan Diego Guadiz and avenge his brother's death. Not yet. But one day. Everything had changed with Samuel's death. William's future was a slate wiped clean and marked with a single word: *revenge*. And if he was unprepared for such a course, well then, who better to chart his way than a cutthroat like the Butcher of Barbados?

"Teach me," William said.

"What?"

Wallace stretched out his right hand, pretending it was clasped around the staghorn grip of an imaginary knife. "One punishes . . . the other destroys."

Capt. Mad Jack Flambeau paused a moment, then gravely nodded. He guided the rawboned young giant up from the beach, where his Tainos servants, Manuel and Josefina, waited to help William up once more astride the mare. Wallace offered no resistance. He was too weak, too dizzy, and full of grief. Manuel held the reins while Mad Jack forged ahead with quick sure steps, following a game trail through the palm trees and onto the road where it began to climb into the hills.

William struggled to remain alert. He tried to focus on the road but could not see their destination for the trees. "Where does this lead?"

Mad Jack replied, "To the rest of your life."

3

"COME AND KILL ME."

November 1830

Mad Jack roared with laughter, intending to infuriate his younger, larger opponent. Knife blades flashed in the sunlight, glittering like steel fangs as the two men warily circled each other. "That's it. Here now. Do I strike here ... or there? Watch out!" the buccaneer said, his right arm extended. He jabbed and William stumbled back. "Big and slow, like an ox. Easy to slaughter." Both men were streaked with sweat and sand from their exertions. Flambeau kept up a stream of insults and chatter, hoping to goad his hulking twenty-year-old opponent into a foolish move. The ploy had always worked.

Until now.

"Now, now, that's a good lad. Come and kill me. If you can...."

It was a game they played, like children, with knives sharpened to a razor's edge. A man must be honed like the blade he holds.

A year had passed, a year of watching the ever-changing sea and reliving the nightmare of his brother's murder, a year learning the wild ways from the Tainos natives, a year spent devouring the volumes of stolen books in the Frenchman's library, a year of the *game*.

The hackles rose on the back of William's neck, and

his cheeks flushed with anger. But this time he ignored the insults. For once he refused to be baited into a mistake that might cost him his life.

This time the game continued, for William had a good teacher. The Butcher of Barbados had forged and tempered the substance of Wallace's youth and inexperience and taught him to rely on more things than his great size and strength. Even a rawboned giant of a man could be quick and cunning. Even a heart sworn to vengeance could discover the value of patience.

So William waited, bided his time, feinted, darted back, and then lunged forward as he had done in the past, hoping to bull his way past the buccaneer's guard. The move tricked Mad Jack into a costly response. Mistaking this second feint for William's attack, Flambeau committed himself. He darted to one side and thrust forward, but William danced from harm's way with catlike grace, batted the short sword from the buccaneer's grip, stepped in past the Frenchman's guard, and placed the tip of his own knife under Flambeau's chin.

Mad Jack froze. Death was a pinprick away. And then it slowly dawned on the knife fighter that he had been bested.

Manuel and Josefina Tamayo good-naturedly applauded their master's downfall from where they watched on the porch of the whitewashed house on the hillside above the bay. The Tainos couple, though loyal to a fault, were not above taking pleasure at William's victory. The gentle rawboned youth had become a part of the family, someone for Manuel to instruct in the ways of the forest and for Josefina to mother.

"You're dead," William drawled, staring down at the smaller man he held at his mercy.

"Hhrumph!" Mad Jack scowled and pretended to be disgruntled at the outcome. He eased himself from knifepoint, rubbed his throat, glanced in the direction of his servants, who continued to demonstrate their delight at the contest's outcome. Then he grinned. "You'll do."

"You're damn right," William replied.

The rawboned young man turned his back toward Mad Jack as if to walk away. Why be satisfied with one win, he thought, when he could have two? Mad Jack always exhorted him to be constantly vigilant. William decided it was time to test the teacher. In mid-stride he shouted, "Mad Jack!," whirled, and lunged, hoping to place the point of his dagger against the freebooter's chest and cry, "Touché!" But in a blur of motion Mad Jack spun on his heels, parried the thrust as he danced past the big man. Something slapped William across the neck, leaving a welt on the flesh. Wallace froze, his knife blade sawing the empty air, his neck stinging from the blow he had received. He seemed momentarily stunned. And then Mad Jack spoke.

"In case you're wondering, I just slit your throat." He looked at his knife, which was free of blood, and then tilted William's chin upward. "Damn, I used the flat of the blade. I must be getting soft," he added with a chuckle.

Wallace tucked his knives away, the lesson brought home. He also filed Mad Jack's maneuver away in his memory—it just might come in handy one day.

"I might have taught you everything you know," Flambeau said, grinning, "But not everything I know."

"I'll remember," William said. He waved toward the Tainos servants, then caught Mad Jack by the arm and led him over to a stone table set on a knoll above the mountain road. Manuel arrived bearing a tray with a brown glass bottle of rum and two pewter tankards.

"He beat you fair and square," Manuel said, his nut-brown features split by a broad smile.

"And you loved every minute of it," Mad Jack grumbled threateningly.

The Tainos servant wasn't afraid. "Yes, I did." He ambled off, chuckling to himself and mimicking the contest, much to Josefina's consternation. She had chores to tend to and could no longer be bothered with the foolishness of men.

William poured the freebooter a drink. Clouds drifted above the tops of the trees and out across the bay, dotting the hillside and cerulean sea with patches of shadow. Mad Jack thirstily accepted the grog, drained his cup, and slammed it down on the tabletop. William instantly refilled the vessel. A breeze stirred and he glanced back toward the house with its wide, deep porch and inviting shade. Palm trees shuddered and fanned the clearing with their bright green fronds. Thinking back, William remembered his first impression of the place.

Sanctuary.

William had worked hard to heal his physical wounds and recover his strength. Flambeau's house on the hill had been William's retreat from the hard world that had claimed his brother's life and their dreams of adventure and wealth. He weathered the nightmares and prepared himself for the day when he would go forth to set things right.

"I want to accompany you to Veracruz tomorrow," he said.

"See here; you weren't invited."

"No one will question it if you bring me."

"I'd question my own sanity," Flambeau chuckled and gulped down the rum. He smacked his lips. "Better'n mother's milk to a man of the sea." He wiped his mouth on his coat sleeve and held up his cup. "Anyway, you've been to Veracruz."

William had the bottle ready. He paced himself and only took a sip from his own cup. This was the dark Jamaican rum, brewed from sugarcane cut at midnight, pressed by lantern light, and fermented by the dark of the moon in kegs buried deep in island caves.

Mad Jack eased himself onto one of the stone benches near the table. He rubbed his eyes and tried to focus on the horizon. "These old lights of mine are growing dim." Perspiration beaded his shaved skull. Sea and sky stretched on forever, farther than any man could see. But Mad Jack did not need fresh eyes to read the course William was charting for himself. "Do you take me for a fool? This is the governor's ten-year jubilee. I hear even President Bustamente will attend. No doubt the governor's family will be on hand. And that means Juan Diego Guadiz."

"I never gave it a thought," William said, pouring the weathered old sea rover another measure of rum.

"There's no way I'd bring you along. No man needs that kind of trouble. You are not going. And that's all there is to it." Mad Jack cleared his throat and nodded as if to indicate his final position on the matter. Then he drank to his decision.

And William kept pouring.

4

"SHE WALKS IN SHADOWS."

Two rode together along the Spanish road where it followed a ridge of low hills overlooking the sun-washed city of Veracruz, gleaming like a pearl in the emerald haze of noon. Heat waves rippled from whitewashed haciendas, storefronts, and the red-tiled roofs of walled estates scattered amid a profusion of humbler jacals capped with brown thatch, dried brittle by the warm winds sweeping in from the Gulf.

Mad Jack Flambeau and William Wallace paused before descending to the outskirts of the city below. The wiry old freebooter, flamboyant in his ruffled yellow shirt, nankeen trousers, and dark blue broadcloth, dabbed away the perspiration from his weathered features and glanced longingly over his shoulder at the distant snow capped summit of Mount Orizaba a hundred miles to the northwest.

"Citlaltapetl," he softly remarked, squinting. Try as he might, the peak remained a familiar blur in the distance. "The Star Mountain . . . home of the gods." It would be cool up there, wreathed in pink clouds, where the air was thin and a man could hear his soul sing in the wind.

Mad Jack adjusted the scarlet scarf protecting his shaved skull from sunburn. Flambeau shifted his weight in the saddle, glanced in William's direction, and tried to remember when he had agreed to bring the big man along. His memory was a rum-induced haze.

Wallace tilted his sombrero back on his head and mopped the perspiration from his youthful features with a long white scarf knotted carelessly about his throat. He threw a long shadow. His powerful frame strained against the laces of his coarsely woven cotton shirt, the carefully restitched seams of his embroidered coat, and the earthen-dyed trousers he'd tucked into his oversize boarhide boots. The big man gave silent thanks that Josefina had proved to be a deft seamstress.

Wallace tied back his shoulder-length red hair with a leather string, then, at Flambeau's bidding, grudgingly removed the pistol and dagger from his belt and tucked the weapons away in his saddlebags. He held up his empty hands and grimaced as if to ask, "Satisfied?" Sea breezes carried the pungent fragrance of low tide to the hillside. Gulls rode the blue wind from the shore and traced their shadows in lazy arcs upon the grassy slope.

"Every inch the gentleman," Mad Jack remarked, examining his younger companion. Old Butch and Bone-chucker had already been concealed in a leather pouch dangling from his saddle horn. "And see you remain that way. We are sailing into harm's way, *mon ami*. The good graces of Governor Guadiz are not to be taken lightly." He started his mount down the well-worn trail that years of travel had cut through the wind-rippled leaves of grass.

Wallace followed a few paces behind the pirate, a sense of expectation tightening his gut. He was no stranger to Veracruz. They had visited the port several times during the past year. But today was different. Today there was a good chance Juan Diego Guadiz had returned to attend his uncle's anniversary celebration. And that made all the difference in the world.

*   *   *

A maze of streets fanned outward from the city's crowded central plaza. The *mercado* was ringed with cantinas, hotels, and a stately cathedral whose bells tolled the noon hour, summoning the faithful into the friendly shade of the sanctuary. Wallace and Mad Jack secured lodging for the night at Casa del Gato Negro. The hotel overlooked the busy marketplace and had its own stables off the alley behind the rear kitchen. The owner, a gray-haired spinster with a face like a hatchet, asked no questions and insisted her guests do the same. The two men took a room, stored their few belongings, then continued across town.

The massive gray battlements of the Castillo de San Juan de Ulua, bristling with cannonades, guarded a placid aquamarine bay. The busy pier and shipyards were a forest of mainmasts as brigs and sloops, heavily laden barkentines, and stately frigates vied for placement on the piers. A swarm of laborers ferried the cargo from the ships to the warehouses lining the wharf.

The port's sights and sounds quickly assailed their senses as the riders immersed themselves in the heart of the city. Storekeepers and street vendors haggled with their customers in animated contests over prices and trade goods. Children and dogs darted among carts, carriages, and horses, escaping disaster by a hair's breadth. Quarrels and gossip mingled with the harangue of over-eager merchants and the music from the cantinas. On one avenue, a peg-legged man with a cage of speckled parrots played a merry jig on his concertina to the delight of several smudge-faced children. Elsewhere, a passionate musician strummed his guitar while a pair of young dandies, strutting like peacocks, danced to impress a senorita who seemed oblivious to their courtship as she dried her long black tresses in the sun.

The excitement over the president's visit and the governor's anniversary had spread through every street and alleyway, for a holiday had been declared, debts were forgiven, even a handful of prisoners had been freed from the jail.

William was aware of the curious glances they received. He noted when a passerby recognized Captain Flambeau and watched with a mixture of envy and guarded respect as the Butcher of Barbados rode past. Having spent a year beneath the Frenchman's roof, William was hard-pressed to equate the buccaneer's grisly reputation with the man who had saved his life and befriended him.

Mad Jack turned to his companion and pointed toward the governor's palace lording over the city from atop the mounded ruins of Aztec temples plundered and razed by the Spanish who landed on the shore centuries before. Outer walls festooned with bouganvillea and flame vines and patrolled by sentries protected the main hacienda—a spacious two-storied structure built of pink granite and surrounded by a splendid array of gardens, gazebos, and walkways of crushed conch shells.

"President Bustamente's already arrived," Mad Jack laconically observed as they left the vicinity of the *mercado*. "The dragoons in green coats and flat-crowned hats are his personal guard." The pirate stroked his chin as he assessed the bivouacked soldiers. "Looks like General Antonio Lopez de Santa Anna has come to show off his troops as well."

"Why not? Isn't he the governor's man?" William remarked, observing the familiar garrison of soldiers in blue tunics trimmed with scarlet epaulets and blue sashes. Despite the guarded animosity of their commanders, Santanistas and Nationalist troops could be seen casually fraternizing with one another on the outlying parade grounds surrounding the estate.

"This has got to stick in the governor's craw, having to play host to *el presidente* even while backing General

Santa Anna for the same job," Mad Jack chuckled. "And Bustamente, the crafty old fox, has no doubt shown up to gauge the opposition."

"Santa Anna . . . Bustamente . . . it is of no concern to me," said Wallace. He steadied the roan stallion and quickly surveyed the gathering of soldiers. He recognized a third cluster of dragoons by the sunlight glinting off their plumed helmets. Juan Diego was not among them. William counted fifteen carriages and three times as many horses lining the circular drive in front of the governor's palace and wondered which, if any, belonged to Juan Diego and his sister.

Suddenly an old fear began to gnaw at William's gut and forced him to question his resolve. A familiar nightmare had plagued him since the murder of his brother. Something in William had snapped that fateful morning, little more than a year ago. With his brother's blood fresh on his hands, William had abandoned the survivors and run for his life. He had fled like a frightened rabbit from Juan Diego and his lancers. How many times had he relived his failure, how many long nights of restless sleep?

The city's dignitaries were congregated in the front gardens, engaging *el presidente* and his entourage of medal-bedecked generals and civilian guests. As Mad Jack and William Wallace halted their mounts before the wrought-iron gate, the old freebooter pointed out President Bustamente. This robust, stocky individual, resplendent in his medal-laden uniform, was no stranger to the banquet tables and kept up an animated conversation while filling his plate with delicacies from the various buffets. Servants scurried among the landowners and the city's elite, bearing trays of cut crystal wineglasses and bottles of Sangria, platters of tarts and honeycakes, puffed pastries filled with clams, oysters, and spicy morsels of pork, bowls of tiny orange carrots sweet as sugar, and melons and avocados carved into pink, orange, and luscious green crescents.

Mad Jack rubbed his rumbling gut but eyed the feast with certain misgivings. "I don't know why the governor should have invited me to this soiree. He doesn't like to mix my visits with the landed gentry. His friends are particular about who they sip sherry with."

"If you're worried, let's heave to and put our sails to the wind," William replied, dismounting and tethering the roan to the first post they found free. He looked long and hard at his saddlebags and the bulge of his pistols and knife against the flap. *I don't like it.* However, he really had no choice; guests did not go armed past the governor's gate.

"We stay. After all, I was personally invited. And Domingo owes his position to me as much as anyone. Best I not stir the waters." Flambeau quietly appraised the big man at his side. The buccaneer's chest swelled with paternalistic pride.

During the past year, William had never refused a task. He had toiled in the gardens and learned the ways of the wild places from the Tainos themselves. As for his deadlier skills, they had come natural. The blood of Highlanders, that dark, fierce fuel, flowed in his veins. Mad Jack had only polished William's skills.

"What's on your mind, you old cutthroat?" William asked.

"Only this. The governor has ordered me to present myself to him in his study as soon as I arrive. I've got to leave you alone down here. Keep a tight rein on your temper. Steer clear of Juan Diego Guadiz. Start trouble and we'll be dangling by the neck from the governor's gate before sunset. I don't aim to hang just so you can settle a debt of honor. Remember what I taught you."

" 'Vengeance is best savored.' " William nodded. "Go

on. I can look after myself." He stared at the guarded entrance to the palace grounds. Despite the warm Gulf wind scouring the avenue, a chill settled in his soul. Beyond that gate, something wicked waited. "Don't worry," the big man added. But his words had a hollow ring.

Half an hour later found William still standing just inside the front gate, somewhat taken aback by the scope of the gardens and the press of people ambling among the fall flowers. It appeared all of the city's dignitaries, not to mention the *haciendados* from outlying ranches, had come to pay their respects to the governor and show support for either President Bustamente or his rivals. Although the soldiers and guests might have given way for the likes of Capt. Mad Jack Flambeau, they held the big *norte americano* in much less esteem.

Señoritas, all decked out in their finest dresses, gathered in giggling clusters to gossip and peer teasingly past the veils of their elegant mantillas as they argued the eligibility of their latest paramours. Would-be suitors, the sons of wealthy merchants, shipbuilders, and the landed gentry, passed beneath the watchful scrutiny of stern-faced *mamucitas* determined to make the best possible arrangements for their daughters. Husbands and fathers, officers and dandies, marked their future by attending to President Bustamente. Others avoided *el presidente* like the plague and chose to court the favor of the Santanistas.

It already seemed like hours since Flambeau had marched off into the governor's palace. William maneuvered his way along the shaded perimeter of the main courtyard, searching the sea of faces for the one man he had come to find.

Perhaps this was a bad idea after all. Every fiber of his being screamed for him to beat a hasty retreat, yet

Wallace held his ground, steeled himself, and continued to scrutinize the crowd. He had weathered a shipwreck and storm-tossed seas; he could endure this.

And then the unexpected happened. Call it fate, or chance; choose a name. *El destino,* destiny, will do. A chorus of wandering mariachis struck up a sweet sad melody upon their guitars; a chorus of pleasing voices interpreted the lyrics of a lover's lament. The din of laughter and gossip, invention and artifice, bold talk and subterfuge became an indistinguishable blur of noise overpowered by these unseen singers who spun a tale of romance and lost love, of passion and death and the ache of yesterdays.

William's heart stirred for a song, and in that moment, for a brief instant, he forgot his reason for being, the trail of blood and retribution he followed. He was here in a garden of faded blooms, a sentinel spirit in silent observation. For a moment, revenge faded from his mind, unclouded his vision, and allowed him to see the woman who crossed his path.

She moved with catlike grace as if gliding across the stone paving beneath her feet. Hair as glossy black as a raven's wing framed her sensuously oval face framed by a delicately trimmed veil. She glanced demurely in his direction and stopped time, or so it seemed. Her smile was warm as the days of heaven, but a hint of the devil's disciple lurked in those sloe brown eyes. The woman saw him, and for a moment the connection was made. Although she was a stranger, William's spirit soared, lifted on the wings of that immediate joy one feels who has discovered a long-lost friend.

One brief moment . . .

Then the vision continued on her way down a path that led through a narrow gate and into a more secluded side courtyard. The world wagged on, leaving William Wallace to catch his breath.

"She's a fair one," a voice drawled from a few yards away. A sandy-haired *norte americano* ambled over to the big man. "Her name is Esperanza Saldevar." He could tell Wallace did not understand. "It is said she has the gift of sight beyond seeing. I don't know about that being a good Christian soul, but the Texicans up north swear by her. They call her Ella anda en las sombra. 'She walks in shadows.' "

William was surprised to find another Southerner from the States. The reference to Texas fueled his curiosity, awakened painful memories. "I thought I would be the only gringo here," Wallace replied, finding something oddly familiar about the stranger.

The newcomer chuckled. He made his way through the dust and sunlight with a glass of wine in one hand and tucked a scrolled map under his arm as he held out his hand. "Stephen Austin of--"

"New Orleans," William finished, recognizing the name.

"Texas . . . now," Austin corrected, glancing up at the *americano* towering over him. "Formerly of New Orleans. Do I know you?"

"My brother was a lawyer and used to share a drink with you from time to time. That's how I heard how you were setting up a colony in Texas. Samuel and I had a similar dream."

"That's it! Samuel Wallace. And you're his brother— Will, isn't it? I thought I placed you," Austin remarked, a friendly grin reflecting his easygoing nature. "A long drink of water your size is hard to forget. William Wallace." Austin glanced around. "And how is ol' Sam? Is he here with you?"

"He's dead," William bluntly replied. Austin's expression grew stern as he listened to the big man's brief account of his brother's murder.

"Juan Diego Guadiz and his sister, Paloma," Austin

repeated with a wag of his head. "I don't doubt it. All the way down from Mexico City I had the feeling those two could not be trusted."

"You have seen them?"

"I spent several days in their company," Austin replied. "Diego is a loyal nephew to his uncle, the governor. I had hoped to sway Diego's allegiance and win his support for Bustamente's policy. But I failed. I fear the governor and General Santa Anna will cook up mischief for us Texicans if either of them ever gets the chance. Fortunately, I am under the president's protection."

"Diego is here?"

"And his sister. I left them in the side garden. Paloma is a pretty thing, but I'd sooner sidle up to a viper. I warrant she and her brother were born on a dark and windy night and suckled on the breast of a blue norther; that's as cold a pair of hearts as you're likely to come across. You seldom find one without the other."

"Just so long as I find them," William muttered. He touched the brim of his sombrero and excused himself from Austin's company and stepped out onto the path that Esperanza had taken out of the front courtyard. The crowd thinned. The music faded as he forced his way along the crowded path toward the entrance to the side garden. If he didn't find Juan Diego, at least he might encounter "She walks in shadows." *Ella anda en las sombra.* Even the name sang. She had the kind of beauty that could turn a boy into a man and an old swayback into a young stallion. Kings had fought wars to possess such a woman. And she had looked right at him, through him, and with a glance stolen the heart right out of his chest.

William glanced over his shoulder at the pink adobe walls of the governor's palace and considered waiting for Mad Jack. But Wallace was too full of his own purpose to worry about his friend. Anyway, the old buccaneer had a silken tongue and could charm the nettles off a prickly pear. Why worry about Mad Jack?

"Captain Flambeau . . . I am placing you under arrest. Guards! Escort this freebooter to the stockade. Perhaps a few days on parched corn and water will loosen his tongue." Governor Guadiz hooked his thumbs in the pockets of his frock coat as beads of perspiration dotted his round, wide forehead. The man's great belly shook as he spoke. "If you do not choose to cooperate, I shall personally introduce you to the jailers in the Castille."

"Now see here, Domingo; we have been friends a long while. How can you think I would lie to you?" Flambeau purred.

Generalissimo Antonio Lopez de Santa Anna stood with his back to the study. His hands were tightly clasped against his backbone, his shoulders squared and spine stiff in his black frock coat and woolen trousers. "Bring the pirate over here," he said. His bearing and tone of voice was that of a man who must be obeyed.

Guadiz led his unwilling guest to the double windows overlooking the front courtyard. Santa Anna did not bother to look in Flambeau's direction. His attention was fixed on President Bustamente below. El presidente was surrounded by his fawning admirers. Mad Jack had the distinct impression the general would remember each and every one of Bustamente's supporters.

Governor Guadiz shooed the flies away from a clay pitcher, then filled a tall crystal goblet with sweet cream buttermilk brought fresh for the general's pleasure. He covered the pitcher with a damp cloth and handed the glass to Santa Anna.

"The president has grown soft and weak," Santa Anna began. "There is a rebellion in Coahuila. While in Texas, this man Austin continues to bring colonists down from the north under Bustemente's protection. I do not trust the *americanos,* these Texicans."

"I will have Diego see that Austin is removed from his hotel and placed under custody," Guadiz said. "His absence ought to stem the tide of settlers."

"A new president with a new policy is the only way to deal with it," Santa Anna quickly retorted. "I can throw Bustamente out of office if need be. But everyone will have to support our effort."

Mad Jack didn't like the sound of that last remark. The soldiers by the door were hardly comforting. "Unfortunately, I am a poor man—," Flambeau began. His pitiable reply was quickly interrupted by the governor's laughter.

"Come, come, you old cutthroat. We are not so easily swayed as your Tainos savages. I know you did not declare all of your ill-gotten gain when you bought your freedom long ago. But I didn't mind; half of what you offered was enough at the time."

"And now?"

"Times have changed." Guadiz did not wish to be humiliated in front of Santa Anna. The governor was determined to have his way. "Now you will describe what you held back. Is it buried up the coast? Beneath your house? How much can we expect?"

"You misjudge me," Mad Jack said, retreating into the cool interior of the study. The room smelled of leather-bound books and tobacco. Dust motes danced in the sunlight streaming in through the windows and French doors. "I am a simple man, an honest man, and your most loyal advocate." He continued to make his way toward the door. "But I will make an inventory of all my possessions. Perhaps some of them can be sold on your behalf. My friends, it is the least I can do."

He bowed and started through the door that opened into the hall. One of the soldiers, at a signal from the governor, brought his musket up and struck Flambeau just above the right eye with the butt of his gun. Mad Jack groaned and fell to his knees, grasped his head, and toppled forward to sprawl upon the cool tile floor. The governor sauntered over to stare down at the fallen figure.

" 'The least' isn't good enough," he muttered and motioned for the guards to gather the unconscious freebooter and carry him to the guardhouse. "Perhaps our bird will sing a different tune tomorrow."

Santa Anna shrugged. "If not, let it be his last." He continued to glare at Bustamente from his vantage point above the president. "Enjoy your moment in the sun," he quietly said. There was a change coming. One day soon he would sweep up from the coast like a hurricane and rattle the walls of the presidential palace, driving Bustamente from power. He paid no heed as the pirate was dragged away. Nor did he notice the redheaded *norte americano* making his way through the dignitaries below. The general's eyes were fixed on the future, and in so doing he failed to see the fly in the buttermilk right under his nose.

5

"EL DESTRIPEDOR ROJO . . ."

Paloma, what would I do without you?" Juan Diego purred, his head tilted back against his sister's cushioning bosom, his eyes momentarily closed as her fingertips massaged his forehead. An animalistic sigh of pleasure escaped his lips as pain flowed from the throbbing center of his skull and into the conduits of her hands.

Paloma replied, "Without me, you would be—"

"Lost," her brother finished. Juan Diego patted her wrist, then winked in the direction of a pair of nubile señoritas who were obviously hoping to catch his interest. They giggled and waved while whispering demurely between themselves. A warning glare from Paloma cooled their ardor. The two women switched their affections to the homely but wealthy son of a local merchant.

Paloma's lips drew back in a tight smile. She stroked her brother's close-cropped black hair, relishing the sense of control she had over her volatile sibling. Juan Diego was quick to anger and as unpredictable as a spring storm, but Paloma stirred the clouds.

"And now the cards," Juan Diego said, piquing the interest of his entourage. The privileged sons and daughters of Veracruz's own aristocracy and a few of his fellow officers began to congregate around Diego's table. Some feigned indifference, others nervous curiosity. Esperanza's talents had been the subject of much speculation throughout the morning. Now Juan Diego and his friends intended to judge for themselves whether or not the woman possessed supernatural talents.

The captain of lancers drew a silk kerchief and made a show of nervously patting the moisture from his forehead and cheeks, an act that elicited a round of laughter from his peers. Then pretending to compose himself, Guadiz glanced in the direction of the woman seated across the table from him, cleared his throat, and said, "Señora Saldevar, at your convenience."

Paloma, standing off to the side now, resented Esperanza for her beauty and, worse, her lack of breeding. Everyone knew the señora came from peasant stock. No doubt Esperanza had bewitched her way into her present circumstances. Men were such fools, always eager to trade position and wealth for the scent of a silken cheek, stolen kisses, or love in the afternoon.

Paloma had no time for the nonsense of courtship. Juan Diego needed her. And what man could compare with her brother? Capt. Juan Diego was destined to accomplish great things. His loyal sister intended to have her share of the spoils, if only she could keep him focused. What was Juan Diego up to? Did he believe the hearsay concerning Saldevar's skills, or, worse, could he actually fancy the señora?

"Señora Saldevar?" Juan Diego repeated her name. But the woman appeared dazed or distracted. For whatever reason, her eerie silence had an unsettling effect on the people around her.

"Card tricks and fortune-telling are nothing but slick pretense. Why waste your time?" Paloma remarked, filling the void left by the woman's silence. Her comments went unnoticed. Maybe there was something to the rumors after all. The world had its share of mysteries. Paloma scowled; she had no use for the supernatural, or for anything that was beyond her ability to control.

Juan Diego glanced around, confused. He shrugged, then leaned forward on the sandstone table and studied Esperanza Saldevar's brown oval features, her full red lips, black eyes, and pert nose. She was a beauty all right. He indulged his own fantasies, undressing her in his mind, and impatiently gulped the last of his wine.

Esperanza seemed to be daydreaming, her eyes focused on the worn deck of cards in her hands. It was her own fate, not Juan Diego's, that held her entranced. She was haunted by the image of a man, a rugged real face in a crowd of pretty strangers. Sensing his presence yet again, she lifted her gaze and saw him duck beneath the arched entrance to the side garden.

Who was this red-haired *norte americano* towering in the shadows beneath flame vines, a figure of raw power in repose? And why this sense of kinship? He seemed so out of place. An innocent glance bridged a gap between strangers and left her with the disturbing premonition life would never be the same. *Madre de Dios,* maybe she really did have a gift.

"So, woman, I have heard of your talents," said Juan Diego, clearing his throat. "Come and show me. Walk in the shadows and see beyond seeing and tell me what you find." Diego glanced from his sister to his circle of friends, bluebloods one and all. Sunlight glinted off the medals dangling from his blue jacket and the plumed helmet he had placed on the table. He shrugged and sipped wine from a long-stemmed crystal glass. "Sergeant Obregon, perhaps you should nudge the señora with your saber and see if she is still with us."

Cayetano Obregon, the captain's subordinate, grinned and rolled his eyes as if to indicate the woman must have taken leave of her senses. A burly, balding old warhorse, the sergeant was a familiar sight hovering protectively around Juan Diego and his sister. Obregon mopped the moisture from his bald pate; beads of sweat collected in his brushy black sideburns as he stared at Esperanza. Despite the carnal hunger etched in his pock-marked features, the sergeant was loath to disturb the young woman. Obregon came from peasant stock and carried a healthy fear of the unknown. The soldier had heard enough rumors concerning Esperanza and was not about to test her powers by openly antagonizing the woman. The sergeant shifted nervously, rattled his saber, but remained alongside the twins.

Juan Diego slapped the tabletop. *"Señora!"*

The young woman jumped where she sat, startled from her reverie, jolted back to the present. The eighteen-year-old mystic tore her gaze from Wallace and focused on the gathering of men and women who had come to see the "shadow walker" ply her trade. Their doubts were plainly visible. Was she a fraud or was there something to the cards and the powers she had inherited from her mother? She didn't care whether or not they believed, just so long as they feared.

"What do you see in the shadows for me?" Diego asked, leaning forward. His black hair was swept back from his angular features. His mustache was a mere suggestion, a dark line tracing his upper lip. Eyes like chips of obsidian judged her every move. Rare was the woman who did not swoon over the governor's eligible nephew and fantasize being swept off her feet by the swaggering captain of lancers. No officer was more daring in battle or dashing on the dance floor. And yet Esperanza Saldevar was immune to his charms. She wasn't fooled. In her judgment, Juan Diego and his twin sister were like ravens—sleek, disdainful creatures to whom most people were so much future prey.

Esperanza studied the faces of the people gathered around her. They wanted a show. She would give them one. Taking up the gypsy cards that had been her mother's legacy, Esperanza stood and slowly made her way through her audience. She expected the disdain in their eyes, but there was also misgiving, a primal fear of something beyond their ken.

She paused before Sergeant Obregon and blew softly on the deck. Her eyes rolled back in her head, and she began to softly laugh, in a voice that seemed not her own, deeper in tone and issuing from another's throat. Obregon gulped, derision faded from his expression, and he blessed himself with the sign of the cross.

"I am she who walks in the shadows between what is and what will be." She spun on her heels and passed the deck beneath the very noses of those who had come to be amused. "Would you know the very hour of your death? Draw a card and I will number your days. What of love or betrayal? Ask, place your hand upon the cards, and all will be opened unto you. Seek and you shall find."

The colorful array of gentlemen and their ladies shrank back from Esperanza's outstretched hand. No one wished to play. Suddenly the afternoon's diversion had lost its appeal, the basking sun its warmth. The chill of the grave clung to the shadows of the madrona trees. Insects and birds avoided the side garden altogether. The woman focused on Juan Diego. She glided toward him over the stone-paved path.

"And you, sir, your heart's desire is an open book." Esperanza paused for effect, a trick of her mother's, then flipped a card or two upon the table. One image was that of a drake rising from a wellspring; the next, against a backdrop of a star-filled night, that of two nudes draped in garlands emptying a cornucopia upon plowed earth. A third card depicted a majestic stag standing upon a ridge and, below the beast, scattered bones.

"What man does not hunger for wealth and power, for all life's riches, and glory, too?" Esperanza continued. "Señor Guadiz, your ambition soars. Abundance awaits you. A triumph where others fail."

"Well spoken, señora, but I could have—"

"But every victory has its price," the woman continued, cutting him off. "All things are possible. Draw the final card and see for yourself. There is always a card between you and your desires. Fate is the prince of tricksters. Tempt him, if you dare. Draw the last card and see for yourself what must be overcome. Beware, though. Once it is drawn, the card can never be returned." Esperanza blew gently on the deck. The governor's side garden fell silent. All eyes were on Juan Diego. The governor's nephew licked his lips, ran a tongue around his dry mouth, and tried to swallow. It might be a good thing to know what to expect. And yet the woman intimated that by drawing the card Juan Diego could set in motion a disastrous chain of events he might come to regret.

Esperanza's eyes were mere slits. Her hand never wavered. The deck was an extension, almost a part of her, but with a life of its own, a serpent waiting to strike the man foolish enough to risk disaster. Knowledge carried a high price.

He reached out, hesitated, stared at the deck, then withdrew his hand. Leave well enough alone. The cards on the table were enough for him. Wealth and power and glory were his for the taking. And nothing was going to stand in his way. He glanced around at his friends and then, smiling broadly, applauded.

"Bravo, señora, a most enjoyable performance. But the future is in my hands, not yours. And right now"—he held up his long-stemmed glass—"it needs more wine."

A chorus of relieved laughter filtered through the crowd. Juan Diego motioned for his friends to follow him back into the main garden. Turning, the captain of lancers almost blundered into the *norte americano* blocking his path.

Wallace stared at his brother's killer, waiting for some glimmer of recognition to alter the captain's expression. Guadiz hesitated for a brief second, then brushed past the redheaded stranger without so much as a "by your leave."

"Señor Guadiz," Wallace blurted out. The officer swung about. William's hand, on reflex, dropped to his belt, where a knife or pistol might have been; then, altering its course, he reached out and snatched the top card from Esperanza's grasp. He showed her the image, then held it face out to the officer. "You forgot your card."

Juan Diego was taken aback by the impertinent stranger. He advanced with Sergeant Obregon and cautiously eyed the faded image stolen from the hand of fate by the redheaded stranger. The card held the likeness of a man, bathed in crimson flames and brandishing a lethal array of knives. Other blades littered the ground at his feet, thrust into the earth like so many grave markers.

"It is the Prince of Daggers," Esperanza solemnly intoned. "El Destripedor Rojo . . . the Red Ripper. A difficult card to ignore. Be wary, Captain."

Juan Diego ignored the woman and the card. His eyes turned stone cold as he studied the man towering over him. "Who are you?"

"He is no one," said Paloma, dismissing William with a flick of her wrist. She caught her brother by the arm. "A waste of time that could be better spent enjoying our uncle's wine cellar."

Juan Diego nodded, gave Wallace a last lingering look, then with a great sweep of his hand motioned for his party to follow him off toward the main courtyard. As they passed beneath the arch and entered the throng of well-wishers, Juan Diego motioned for Sergeant Obregon to approach him. It was a struggle to be heard above the din.

"Cayetano, have the gringo followed. Learn his name and who invited him to my uncle's celebration. I think later tonight we may need to teach the impudent rascal to respect his betters."

"With pleasure, my captain," said Obregon. A cruel grin crawled across his features. Now this was something he could understand.

William watched his brother's killer saunter out of the garden, then stared down at his empty, trembling hands and wiped them on his coat. It wasn't supposed to have happened like this. For months he had envisioned an encounter with Guadiz, grabbing him by the throat, wringing the life out of him. The moment had come and gone without incident. But there was comfort in the fact Juan Diego was in Veracruz. Let night fall and the soldiers drink themselves into sweet oblivion. Juan Diego would not live to see another sunrise. William glanced in Esperanza's direction. Damn, it was hard to keep murder in his heart while in the company of such a pretty señorita.

"Who are you?" the woman asked. "And what business do you have with the captain of lancers?" She returned the cards to her deck and tucked them away inside an ornately beaded bag of white buckskin brushed soft as a baby's cheek.

"William Wallace," the big man softly replied. Ice worms burrowed into his spine. For a moment, he was transported back in time, forced to watch Samuel die, to look into the eyes of his killer. He experienced the same fear, became the same hunted animal running for his life. And, worse, Juan Diego didn't even remember the incident. The deaths of a few strangers meant nothing to the governor's nephew. "And I have come to kill Juan Diego Guadiz."

Esperanza's reaction was instantaneous. Her eyes widened, her jaw dropped slightly, mouth framed a silent *oh,* while she caught her breath.

"But enough about me," William said. "Miss Esperanza, perhaps you would do me the honor of allowing me a dance or two."

"You know my name?"

"A fellow named Stephen Austin pointed you out. I'd say he did me a favor."

"Señor Austin is a friend—"

"Then I never envied a man more," William interrupted.

"Wait," she said and placed her slender brown hand on his arm. The effect was instantaneous, as if he had been struck by lightning. Electricity crackled through his body. William was caught between stalking off after Juan Diego and swooning at this woman's feet.

"Ma'am, beauty like yours is a fatal gift. Makes a man want to kill off his worst habits," he said. "I reckon if you were to hold a rose, it would bloom all year." William tried his most winning smile on her. But his tactic failed. She was looking past him toward a white-haired gentleman of average height, his features burned brown by the sun. He approached with short quick steps, an aura of wealth and quiet confidence preceding him.

"So there you are, my dear!" the older man exclaimed, closing with Esperanza. "Did you hold the governor's nephew spellbound?" He took her by the arm and faced Wallace. "She does me." The *haciendado* looked regal in his silver-stitched waistcoat and trousers. A black sash and throat scarf matched his attire. "I see you have found a friend. I am Don Murillo Saldevar."

"Pleasure to meet you, señor," William replied. He glanced in Esperanza's direction. "I grinned a fox out of its den once. She walked right out into the sunlight and into my grasp. I was hoping to do the same to your daughter."

"Daughter, señor?" the gentleman crisply responded, eyes twinkling with merriment. Esperanza was an attractive, nubile woman, and Don Murillo was accustomed to the envious stares of younger men. "She is my wife."

Wife!

The word struck William like a slap in the face. He almost recoiled from its impact. For the first time Wallace noticed the triple rings on the fourth finger of Esperanza's left hand. The blood rushed to his cheeks. How could he have missed the rings and made such a fool of himself?

"I was trying to say that Señor Austin is a friend of my husband's," Esperanza interjected with a winsome smile. She seemed more amused than offended by the situation.

"Yes, ma'am," William stammered. "I understand. Please . . excuse me. . . . My behavior was . . . Uh, anyway, I apologize."

"For finding my wife beautiful? Come now," Murillo said, clapping the big man on the shoulder. "I do the same." The old *haciendado* laughed and leaned in close, lowering his voice, and continuing to speak in a conspiratorial tone. "So you know Stephen Austin, eh? And has he told you of our plans for Texas? We have earned the disfavor of the governor and General Santa Anna. I fear if either of those two come to power, it will make for heavy seas and rough sailing."

"In all honesty, sir," William said, "I only talked briefly with Austin. I knew him a long time ago, in another life. Much has changed."

"I understand change. We are at the mercy of time and fate." He placed his arm around Esperanza's shoulders. The gesture had a curiously painful effect on William. He felt guilty for envying the landowner. "Once I was a grieving widower. I was like a ship, cast adrift. But Esperanza opened my heart to the wonderful possibilities of life." His chest swelled as he beamed with pride.

"I, too, was rescued," William told the *haciendado*, wryly adding, "but it was by the beast, not beauty." He gave a brief recount of his arrival in Mexico. Esperanza's features were an open book to her soul. He could tell she was genuinely moved by his tale. Don Murillo listened with interest. He was more reserved but reacted noticeably at the mention of Mad Jack Flambeau.

"You know him?" William asked.

"Only by reputation," Murillo conceded. "However, I fear your colorful benefactor is in trouble. Only a few minutes ago I saw him carried from the governor's mansion. He had been placed under guard. He looked ill-used from what I could see."

"Where did they take him?" William glanced toward the governor's palace. His pulse was racing now, adrenaline rushing into his bloodstream.

"To the prison stockade behind the barracks, I should imagine," Don Murillo suggested. "My wife and I are staying with my sister. If I can be of help—"

"And place you at risk? No, señor, you are kind, but no," William said.

"You might appeal to the governor on behalf of Captain Flambeau. You are a well-spoken young man. He might hear what you have to say." Don Murillo stroked his goatee as he studied the redheaded *norte americano*. This "William Wallace" was a big brute of a man, yet forthright, articulate, and obviously given to sentiment and passion. He was the kind of man the Texas frontier needed.

"The governor will 'hear' me; I can promise that."

William bowed to the couple and excused himself from their company.

Watching the big man stalk off with a long-legged stride that soon carried him from the estate, Esperanza experienced a twinge of regret. His farewell saddened her.

"What can he say to change the governor's mind?" Esperanza asked her husband.

"I think perhaps talking is at an end," the landowner sagely observed. Don Murillo stared at the empty gateway Wallace had so recently filled and, in the seclusion of this side garden, sensed the passing of some great force. This encounter had been like the prelude to a storm and only hinted of the fury to come.

6

"... YOU MIGHT LIVE
TO SEE THE SUNRISE."

Back alleys and narrow streets cut a serpentine course through moon-washed plazas where pastel-painted shops, cantinas, and houses marched up from the Bay of Campeche. Ocean breezes, scented with decay, set window curtains aflutter, stirred the branches of the palm trees lining the Avenida del Puerta, and hinted an age-old warning to the dried husks of summer: time is the hunter.

The *mercado* at midnight was a quiet, lonely hunting ground. Stray cats, their gleaming yellow eyes ever watchful for intruders, prowled among the shuttered stalls and paused to focus on the patrol as it worked its way across the marketplace and entered the Avenida del Puerta. Sgt. Cayetano Obregon halted the three men behind him and cautiously approached the sentry he had posted outside the Casa del Gato Negro.

"So, Emilio, what of the gringo?" the sergeant brusquely inquired, eyeing the front of the hotel.

His subordinate, a quick dark malcontent with a penchant for cheap whores, showed a row of crooked teeth as he grinned and cocked a thumb toward a side alley. "He just left, carrying his saddlebags to the stable. I think he is pulling out."

"And abandon his friend, the Butcher of Barbados?"

"Sharing a room does not make them blood brothers,

my sergeant," Emilio replied, leaning on his musket. The soldier removed his short-brimmed hat and ran a hand through his sweat-slick thinning black hair. The breeze felt cool on his head. Unlike the rest of the patrol, who were anxious to conclude this night's business and return to the celebration up at the governor's barracks, Emilio relished the prospect of a fight. He had no use for *norte americanos.* "I think he intends to leave Veracruz under cover of night and travel hard and far. I don't blame him. Juan Diego has a long reach. I followed him to the widow's stable. Then I came back to wait for you. He is one big bastard."

The other men heard and began to shift nervously where they stood, regretting the business they were about. No one wanted trouble on the governor's night, when the women were willing and the tequila flowed freely.

"Big trees make the most kindling," Obregon said, appraising the men he had brought with him. These were the most sober men he could find. Five seasoned veterans should have no trouble cutting Wallace down to size.

William Wallace.

The proprietress of the hotel had provided his name but claimed to know nothing of her boarders save the fact that Wallace and the Frenchman had arrived earlier in the day. The widow took care to stress she had no part in whatever crime the gringo had committed.

But of course there was no crime, only a personal affront. The sergeant harbored no particular ill will toward Wallace. Sergeant Obregon was only following Juan Diego's orders. That was the way of things, life's chain of command.

"Come along then. Step easy now," Obregon muttered to the patrol. Juan Diego Guadiz wanted Wallace in leg irons by sunup. The sergeant intended to carry out those orders to the letter. A few weeks in the governor's jail would dull the edge on Wallace's pride.

Obregon tugged the pistol from his belt and checked to see if it was primed, then motioned for the patrol to follow him down the alley toward the stables at the rear of the hotel. A pair of tomcats, jealous over territorial rights to the alley, began to howl and hiss at each other. Emilio cursed and tossed a pebble in their direction. The felines scattered in opposite directions, abandoning their contested terrain to Obregon and his patrol. Emilio chuckled and glanced over his shoulder at his companions and saluted.

The rear of the alley was faintly illuminated by lantern light spilling through the main door, which had been left ajar. A breeze stirred and the door began to sway and creak on its rusted hinges. Obregon placed a finger to his lips in the universal sign for silence and quickened his pace. One of the men behind him inadvertently stepped on the broken remains of a tile that had slipped off the roof. The brittle clay crunched underfoot seemed deafening in the midnight stillness.

The sergeant whirled about, eyes blazing with hostility. Even Emilio knew better than to comment. No one moved for fear of directing the sergeant's anger toward himself. Unable to discern the guilty party, Obregon silently indicted them all. There would be hell to pay come morning and extra sentry duty for the lot of them. The sergeant continued on over to the front of the stable. As he placed a hand on the door, the light vanished, returning the interior to darkness. Obregon shook his head. So much for surprising the gringo. The sergeant stiffened his backbone, shoved the door open, and darted inside.

The moon's pale glare filling the entrance helped to illuminate the front stalls but left two-thirds of the interior in darkness. *This is not good,* Obregon thought. He motioned for Emilio and one other to take up a position on the left. The other two soldiers angled off to the sergeant's right. A horse whinnied and pawed the earth at the rear of the stable. Obregon sensed someone waiting, watching beyond the reach of the moonlight.

"Well, what do we have here? Mad Jack's young squire?" said the sergeant, hoping to trick his prey into revealing himself, then continued in a stern tone of voice. "You are to come with us." Obregon was accustomed to intimidating strangers. "Captain Guadiz wishes to speak with you again, about cards and the proper conduct of a gentleman and the price one must pay for impertinence. You can join your friend, the pirate, in the governor's jail."

"Let me pass in peace, *cabrito*." The words drifted out of the gloomy interior, the voice gentle yet ripe with warning.

"You call me an animal." The sergeant's eyes narrowed. He would have given a week's pay for a lantern. Emilio found one, shook the chamber and discovered it empty of oil, and tossed the lamp aside. The glass chimney shattered on the hardened earth floor.

"You smell like a goat," Wallace continued, unseen. "Be off. Dunk yourself in the ocean. And burn the uniform. You've lived in it too long." Wallace sniffed the air, loud enough for all to hear, a gesture that only heightened his insult.

"Bastard! I'll teach you respect for the governor's guards." Obregon shifted his pistol to his left hand and with his right unsheathed his saber. "Show yourself!" The soldiers pointed their bayonets toward the darkness.

"Put those toad stickers away. If you kill me, you'll still smell like a goat. And if I kill you, you'll smell even worse."

Obregon's features contorted with rage. Unable to contain his anger, he loosed a stream of epithets and charged down the center aisle, sawing the air with his curved steel blade. Behind him, the patrol advanced in a pack, muskets primed and ready, bayonets to the fore, each soldier convinced Wallace was cornered and helpless. That was their first mistake . . . and their last.

"Heeyahh!" A sombrero slapped across horseflesh. A pair of horses charged down the center aisle, scattering the soldiers. A pair of muskets belched smoke and flame and shot holes through the back wall of the stable. In the glare of the muzzle blasts Obregon glimpsed a great and terrible silhouette sweeping past him. He lunged forward with his saber. Wallace thrust a leg out and tripped the man, then hammered him across the back of the neck with a powerful forearm that sent the sergeant sprawling into a stall. Obregon hit hard; his pistol discharged, setting fire to the straw.

"Bastard!" one of the men shouted out, attacking with his bayonet. Shadows flew out to attack him. He skewered a bag of oats, a bridle, another bag of oats. A wooden bucket of slops materialized out of thin air and crashed over his head. Wallace spun the man about and planted a foot in the soldier's backside and propelled him toward his companions. Blinded, the soldier ran headlong into a post, splintering the bucket and knocking himself unconscious.

Emilio and his *compadre* glimpsed movement and fired simultaneously. "Got him!"

But Emilio's elation vanished as one of their own, framed in the glare of the muzzle blasts, stumbled forward, his hands outstretched, his expression "Why?" as he collapsed against a stall gate, then crumbled to his knees and curled over on his belly.

Emilio held his ground, but his *compadre* had lost his taste for battle. The soldier threw his musket aside and dashed to safety. Emilio pointed the bayonet at Wallace's belly as the big man loomed out of the dark. Sergeant Obregon struggled to his feet and, wielding his saber, charged the *norte americano* from behind. Juan

Diego's orders were forgotten now. This was personal.

Knives appeared in Wallace's hands, the dirk in his left hand, the short sword in his right. How many times had Flambeau tested him? Every day, rain or shine, come wind or high water, Mad Jack had prepared him for this moment.

Emilio lowered the bayonet and charged. Wallace, despite his size, proved to be an elusive target. He parried with his right, twisted about, ducked as Emilio tried to club him with the butt of his musket, plunged the dirk into the soldier's thigh, then knocked him senseless with the flat of his broad blade. Wallace heard the saber behind him as it sliced through the air. He spun on his heels.

Steel crashed against steel. The saber clanged against the short sword. Wallace stepped inside the sergeant's guard, opened a gash along the sergeant's cheek, sliced him down the length of one shoulder, and plowed a furrow in Obregon's flesh deep enough to hurt like hell but not enough to kill him. The sergeant was no match for the knife-fighter. He stumbled over the bodies of his fallen command, toppled backward, and crashed through the side of a stall. Howling like a wounded bear, he crawled hand over foot toward the front door. Glancing over his shoulder, he saw Wallace advancing on him. The gringo's red hair, in wild disarray, looked like flames beneath the moon's baleful stare; the blades in his hands flickered with cold fire as he twirled them in his grasp.

"El Destripedor Rojo! He is here!" the sergeant moaned, crawling into the yard, trying to sound an alarm. The last of his patrol, the one frightened soul who had fled the barn, had no intention of confronting the Red Ripper. He clutched the holy medal he wore about his throat and vanished around the corner of the hotel.

"*Ahorre qui vida!*" Obregon blurted, holding his

hands out before him and trailing blood in his wake. "Spare my life."

Wallace slowly advanced, breathing hard, limbs trembling with blood lust, the blades of his knives stained with the crimson residue of battle. The two horses he had saddled waited near a trough a few yards from the barn. The animals whinnied and pawed the earth. A nighthawk soared past on its nightly foray, the rush of its wings in kinship with the beating of a warrior's heart. Wallace lifted the knives in his hands, glanced down at the sergeant, then slowly exhaled, cooling the fire within.

"Do as I say and you might live to see the sunrise," he calmly advised.

Obregon nodded. He had no problem with that.

Dolores Medina, the camp laundress, waited while the two men gambled for her favors. She did not care which went first, just so long as both were quick. The woman was tired, her gums hurt, there was a nagging ache in the small of her back that no amount of pulque seemed to deaden, and she wanted to be on her way. But the jailers continued to argue over each other's seniority. The men were almost as drunk as the soldiers asleep throughout the barracks. The whole powder magazine could explode in a ball of fire and Dolores doubted any of the troops in the compound would rouse from their stupor to investigate.

But here in the guardroom her paramours were still on their feet. She was so tired of their quarreling yet knew better than to interfere. All the yelling had given her a headache. The laundress drained the last of the milky white pulque from her jug and set it on a shelf above her head. The cot creaked as the woman shifted her weight. She yawned, stretched a moment, and closed her eyes. Sweat trickled down the roll of fat under her neck as she turned her face to the wall. Moisture beaded the inside of her thighs. She fluffed her cotton dress to fan her lower limbs, then left her clothing bunched at the waist and exposed the ample delights of her brown derriere to the lamplight while she tried to catch some rest. A few minutes later she began to snore and dream of being a young girl again, wild and fresh and dancing on the fringes of the sea.

"*Más tequila, mi amigo*," said Felix Salcedo, older by a fortnight, a wiry little man with bloodshot eyes. "More tequila, my friend." He stabbed a thumb in the direction of the woman on the cot. "Another glass of tequila and she'll be pretty enough to lie with, eh?"

Carlos Pilar came from the same village as his friend. They had run whores from Tampico to Yucatán and chased Apaches until they learned better. There was no man Carlos trusted more than Felix, but there was no way he was going to bed a woman still wet from another man's juices.

"Another glass of tequila and it won't matter what she looks like. I'll not be able to find my pole."

"Then I'd better hurry up and tend to her while you still can manage," Felix said, attempting to rise from the table.

Carlos reached across and caught him by the arm and forced him back into his chair. "I'll be the first to plow that field."

"The hell you say," Felix replied, frowning.

Silence filled the guardroom as the two men tried to stare each other down. Frijoles hardened in the skillet atop a wood-burning stove. Coffee and a stack of tamales wrapped in corn husks had yet to be distributed to the prisoners in the cells beyond the heavy oaken door at the rear of the guardroom. Tobacco smoke drifted between the two friends as Felix reached over and tapped a stack of cards on the tabletop.

"I guess this is the only fair way, old friend. High card takes first poke."

Carlos stared at the deck before him. He mopped the perspiration from his features on the wrinkled sleeve of his uniform. It was either cards or pistols at close range and a trip to the local sawbones. "Why not?" He shrugged and cut the deck, turning up a nine of diamonds. He scowled and waited for his companion to make a move. Carlos glanced at Felix, who looked alarmed and was staring past his partner toward the doorway leading out to the parade ground and barracks. Carlos turned and discovered for himself what had captured his friend's attention.

Sergeant Obregon, his uniform streaked with blood, stood off to the side, allowing the individual behind him to fill the doorway. William Wallace towered over the men at the table. He tilted his hat back from his features, flipped aside his serape to reveal a brace of heavy-bore pistols trained on the jailers. The lust of battle had left him; what remained in that sun-bronzed face was an expression of implacable resolve and deadly purpose. Then he spoke.

"I've come for Mad Jack Flambeau. Any problems from either of you boys and I'll blow your damn arms off."

The door at the rear of the guardroom opened onto a cheerless hall whose thick adobe walls radiated the dank coolness of the tomb. Indeed, the prisoners here had suffered a kind of burial. Behind rows of barred doors the miscreants, criminals, and others unfortunate enough to earn the enmity of the local authority endured long hours of punishment. Perhaps some had earned their fate. Wallace didn't care. He only brought release to one prisoner. Carlos Pilar needed little prodding from the pistol jammed between his shoulder blades to walk the gringo right to Flambeau's cell. The jailer's hands trembled as he worked the iron bolt and slid it free. The door swung open, and lantern light spilled into the narrow confines of the cell.

Mad Jack Flambeau eased himself from his cot. Shielding his eyes, he stumbled toward the light. His finely tailored coat was stained with his blood. He had torn away the front of his shirt and bandaged his head where one of the guards had struck him a vicious blow. Despite his blurred vision, he could make out the identity of his rescuer. The hulking physique and red hair were impossible to mistake. The voice helped, too.

"You gonna stay for breakfast?" Wallace asked. His friend had suffered a grievous head wound. Mad Jack's features were caked with his blood. He looked dazed and unsure of his steps. Color crept to Wallace's cheeks. Now he had another score to settle with the governor and his kin.

Flambeau grinned, winced as pain stabbed through his skull, then gingerly felt beneath his crude bandage and prodded the lump above his right eye. "I think not," he said, staggering from the cell, "much as I appreciate the governor's hospitality."

Once the freebooter was clear, Wallace motioned for Obregon and the two jailers to take the Frenchman's place. The guards hurried inside. Obregon hesitated and started to object. A glance from Wallace warned him against such a mistake.

"You'll never leave Veracruz alive," the sergeant muttered, his own wounds giving him grief.

"Say hello to the devil, you tub of guts," William snarled and shoved one pistol into Obregon's side.

The sergeant hurried inside the cell. "And if you do escape, Juan Diego will come for you. Hear that, you old butcher? Captain Guadiz knows where you live, and he will come."

"I am counting on it," Mad Jack replied.

Wallace slammed the door shut and slid the bolt home.

"Free me, señor," someone pleaded from one of the other cells. A chorus of entreaties echoed the muffled cry: "Free us. Don't leave us, amigo!"

Wallace ignored the outcry. He caught Flambeau as the man sagged against him and allowed him to sit for a moment to catch his balance. The delay permitted Wallace to hear his name called from the rear of the dismal corridor.

"Is that William Wallace?" a familiar voice called out, struggling to be heard above the other prisoners clamoring to be released.

"Austin?" William called out.

"Afraid so." came the reply.

Wallace's long-legged strides brought him to the far corner of the governor's jail. Moments later a second door was flung open to permit Stephen Austin to emerge, somewhat disheveled but none the worse for his ordeal.

"I was on my way back across town to rejoin Señor Saldevar at his sister's hacienda when I was set upon by men who I believe are in the governor's employ." Austin stopped next to an olla half-filled with cool spring water and drank his fill. "Santa Anna resents the fact I have the ear of *el presidente*. I should have never allowed myself to become separated from Murillo and his escort. He, too, has many powerful friends."

Wallace was only half-listening to Austin. His focus was on Mad Jack Flambeau. The Frenchman's head wound needed a proper dressing. And Wallace knew just the place to go for help.

"Can you take us to Señor Saldevar's?" he asked. They might be able to find help for Flambeau. And there was always the possibility of a chance meeting with Don Murillo's lovely "child-bride," Esperanza Saldevar.

"I know the way. And there will be safety in numbers."

"When the governor and his nephew discover what has happened this night," Flambeau muttered, "no one will be safe in Veracruz. Guadiz will never forget you now." He placed his hand on Wallace's arm and followed the younger man out of the darkness and into the light.

The lanterns in the guardroom did not offer much illumination, but it was better than where Flambeau had been.

7

"I RECKON THE ANSWER TO THAT IS IN THE CARDS."

My sister is an excellent nurse," said Don Murillo, standing in the doorway of the hacienda. "It is one of the reasons I have asked her to join us in Texas. She can be meddlesome, but there comes a time when it is good to have family close by. Dorotea is alone now, since her husband's death. A change might be just what she needs." Don Murillo was enjoying a flour tortilla wrapped about a link of spicy chorizo sausage. Indulging his appetite, he took a moment to dwell upon the past. Dorotea's husband had been a physician, a generous man who treated his practice as a ministry, much to the detriment of his finances. The house by the sea, this plot of land along the shore, some livestock, and the trade goods the mestizos had left in exchange for his services were all the legacy of a decent life cut short.

"We sail within the week. I should like to see my sister settled at the ranchero before the end of the year." He unwrapped a second tortilla from a cloth bundle and invited his guest to partake.

William was more thirsty than hungry. He gulped down his third dipper of spring water from the olla. Fighting might be a dry business, but inaction was the more difficult burden. It was impossible to relax. Wallace continually shifted his stance and paced the porch like a caged animal, his features a restless mask of shadows and light.

Humidity was on the rise. A damp mist drifted across the obsidian surface of the bay and stole ashore on silent cat feet to prowl the distant streets. Wallace nervously checked the road into town, what he could see of it. A groan from the house distracted him. He glanced past Señor Saldevar and caught a glimpse of Mad Jack slumped in a cane-backed settee being tended to by Don Murillo's sister, a tall, big-boned woman whose stern visage and gruff demeanor were hardly becoming to a sister of mercy.

Dorotea Saldevar y Marquez and Don Murillo's willowy young wife were a study in contrasts. Esperanza, kneeling at the Frenchman's side, was warm and sultry and full of life. Dorotea wore her bitterness like a shroud around her heart. It was clear she begrudged even this simple act of kindness toward a stranger. As William looked on, Esperanza dabbed a cool cloth across the Frenchman's cheeks, eyes, and throat. She spoke in soothing tones and stroked his face and hands. William had to envy his injured friend. It was worth a bludgeon to warrant such a ministering angel.

As much as he enjoyed observing the *haciendado*'s nubile bride, William forced himself to look away. He made his way along the front porch until he found a better vantage point from which to watch the shore road leading off toward town. The hacienda had been built on the outskirts of Veracruz, set apart from town like an unwanted child, nestled amid a cluster of palm trees with a panoramic view of the moon-dappled bay and, farther along the point, the sinister black fortress that guarded the seaport.

The hacienda's pink adobe walls had endured sea and sand, hurricanes and blistering heat. It was resilient as its mistress. Dorotea Saldevar y Marquez had lost her world with her husband's death. But like the sea, she remained.

"Someone's coming," William observed, staring off toward the dimly lit streets of the city. A horseman rode toward them at a gallop. He sat low in the saddle, hunched forward, his serape streaming behind him like the wings of a hawk. Wallace drew his pistol, dropped his left hand to the knife hilt at his waist, straightened to his full height, and resolved he wouldn't be taken without a fight.

Esperanza spied him through an open front window. Despite his common garb, the red-haired *norte americano* was obviously born of a brave heart. He seemed almost regal in bearing. The back of her neck began to tingle, and she glanced around to find Dorotea studying her. The widow obviously disapproved of her sister-in-law's interest in the redheaded stranger.

"This Wallace has captured your fancy." Dorotea frowned disapprovingly. "Your conduct is unbecoming the wife of a man like Don Murillo. Besides, the gringo is as common as you were before you married my brother."

"Mon Dieu," Mad Jack drowsily corrected. "You are no student of history. He is a Wallace and sprouts direct from a branch of Scottish kings." Mad Jack adjusted the bandage circling his forehead.

Esperanza flashed her sister-in-law an "I told you so" look and then returned her attention to the man looming large in the window. She felt a kinship for William in that the two of them shared Dorotea's censure.

"Ahem!" Mad Jack cleared his throat. "A little more of that brandy wouldn't hurt."

Esperanza returned to Flambeau's side and poured a measure of brandy into a cup and offered it to the old freebooter. Mad Jack grew pale, shook his head, rubbed his eyes, and stared blankly past the cup. He blinked several times; then a helpless expression came over him. Esperanza placed the cup in his outstretched hand. He closed his eyes, took a couple of swallows, grimaced, massaged his closed eyelids with thumb and forefinger, then chanced a second look and found he could focus on her sweet face. She started to speak. He placed a finger to his lips.

"Don't tell him."

Wallace steeled himself for what was to come. The lust for battle still smoldered within. What had he read among the pirate's stolen tomes? "If it be not now, yet it will be," he whispered, remembering the Bard. "The readiness is all."

"I see him, too," Don Murillo spoke up. "Excellent, my young friend. You have eyes like a Comanche. And a spirit just as wild, I think." The *haciendado* joined Wallace at the corner of the porch and placed a restraining hand on the big man's gun arm.

"*Descanse*. Relax, my young friend. It is only my *segundo*, Chuy Montoya. I sent him into town."

William returned the pistol to his belt but kept a watchful eye on the shore road, half-expecting to see a troop of Juan Diego's lancers in hot pursuit. Montoya reined in his mount before the front of the hacienda, showering the steps with sand as he alighted and slung the gelding's reins through an iron ring on the hitching post. The *segundo* was a short, stocky individual, with sunburned features the color of tanned leather, shaggy black hair, and a goatee that masked his scarred jawline. There was a swagger to his walk and a reckless energy given to men of purpose. He was armed with a pistol and carried a short-barreled rifle slung over his shoulder. There had to be a dagger hidden on his person.

Montoya removed his sombrero as he approached

Don Murillo. Beads of sweat spilled down from his receding hairline. He mopped his brow on his sleeve. Bushy black sideburns framed his guarded expression. A heavy mustache hid his upper lip.

"Que noticias?" Murillo said, anxiety creeping into his tone of voice. "What is happening in town?"

"An alarm has been sounded at the governor's palace. Many soldiers are milling about. I saw the governor's nephew through my spyglass. He looked furious." The vaquero grinned and shifted his gaze to William Wallace, recognizing a *simpático* in the big man. The *norte americano* was armed to the teeth. A brace of pistols were holstered in a bandolier draped across his broad shoulder. The Castilian blades were nestled in their buckskin scabbards at either side. "You may have worn out your welcome in this town, señor."

"An easy thing to do these days," said Don Murillo. "God help Texas if Santa Anna ever becomes president. It is only Bustamente who stays the general's hard hand. Chuy, continue your vigil. Be our eyes in town."

"As you wish." Montoya nodded to Don Murillo and started back to his horse. "I will keep watch along the road. If you hear a pistol shot—"

"I know it'll be time to root hog or die a poor pig," Wallace said.

Montoya chuckled knowingly. He touched the brim of his sombrero in salute, then took the porch steps two at a time, gathered the reins in his left hand, and leaped astride his horse. The gelding responded to his touch, backstepping, pawing the earth, and then, obedient to his rider, charging off into the night.

"There goes a man with the bark still on," William reflected aloud. Don Murillo and his vaqueros were a capable bunch of men but few in number and hopelessly outnumbered this far from home. William did not wish to bring any harm down on Saldevar for harboring Mad

Jack and himself and was preparing to voice his concerns when Stephen Austin emerged from the hacienda. With a whiskey under his belt and a full belly to settle his nerves Austin was ready for whatever came next. He had washed the dust from his features, donned a fresh shirt borrowed from Murillo's wardrobe, and helped himself to the tortillas and beans in the kitchen.

"Any news?" the Texican asked, rounding the corner of the porch. He looked none the worse for his recent ordeal and was obviously grateful to have been released so soon after his incarceration. William Wallace had been a godsend.

"We haven't long. Juan Diego will probably come," Murillo said. "However, you are under my protection here and, through me, *el presidente*'s. No doubt Guadiz will claim your arrest was all a mistake. He will offer you his sincerest apologies. That is his way, and General Santa Anna's." Murillo stroked his silvery goatee, sighed, shook his head, and shifted his gaze to William. "However, I cannot offer you sanctuary, my young friend. Captain Flambeau is a pirate. Your loyalty to him has placed you outside the law and earned the governor's enmity."

"You have done enough for us already, Don Murillo," William said. "And if fortune permits, one day I will repay your kindness."

"Well, there is something I can do," Stephen Austin replied, drawing an oilcloth packet from his coat. "If it wasn't for you there's no telling how long I would have been the governor's 'guest.' Here is a map of my land grant. I've set aside a tract of land along the Brazos River for you." Austin placed the map in William's hand. "It'll be waiting."

The big man opened the packet and stared down at the hastily scrawled deed with its crude but legible de-

lineation of the property granted him. A place in Texas
. . . the dream Samuel had died for.

"Quit this fracas. Join us. We are building something
in Texas and have need of men like you. And you'll be
beyond the governor's reach and among friends." Stephen held out his hand. His was a tempting offer. But . . .

"My thanks. But I still have business in Veracruz,"
William replied. "Perhaps one day." He tucked the
packet inside his coat pocket. "Tell Captain Flambeau
I'll bring the horses around. When he's finished with the
ladies he might choose to join me, before he winds up
with his head decorating Juan Diego's lance."

Wallace stepped off the porch and rounded the hacienda, leaving his tracks in the sand all the way to the
weathered corral where they had left their mounts. Saldevar's own animals, including Esperanza's sleek black
mare, began to nervously circle as Wallace approached.
William spoke in a low, soothing tone that served to
quiet the skittish animals.

In the corral Wallace lost track of the minutes as he
prepared his own and Mad Jack's horse for the long ride
home. He checked the cinches on each saddle, appor-
tioned the gear, and, as an afterthought, cleaned the
hooves of each animal with the tip of one of his knives.
Despite his preoccupation, Wallace caught a scent of jasmine and rosewater and, wrinkling his nose, glanced up
from his labors as Esperanza entered the corral. She
wore a pale blue dressing gown and a voluminous russet-
colored cape that concealed her slender frame.

The woman's black mare immediately hurried to her
side and received an appropriate treat from her outstretched hand. Esperanza stroked the animal's pink
muzzle and the white blaze between her eyes. Then with
a push and gentle pat on the mare's neck she sent the
horse on her way.

William crossed his long arms, relaxed, and just drank

Esperanza in. Moonbeams became her, playing soft on her delicate oval features, highlighting her long black tresses with quicksilver. Esperanza was poetry and passion, ice and desire, all in a single gliding silhouette. And she was someone else's.

"Ma'am?" Wallace nodded, touching the brim of his sombrero. He glanced over her shoulder and spied Dorotea watching them from a side window. In her black veil and widow's weeds, Murillo's sister resembled a brooding raven bathed in the glow of lamplight but untouched by its warmth. Wallace indicated the stern sentinel with a glance. "Your sister-in-law disapproves of me."

"And my behavior," Esperanza said. "She thinks I bewitched Don Murillo into marrying me so soon after the death of his first wife." The woman cradled a leather packet in one hand and with the other stroked the muzzle of Wallace's roan gelding. "My mother was a servant in his house. I grew up in his hacienda. For a time he looked upon me as a daughter. Then he began to think of me as something more." Esperanza lowered her face and looked up at Wallace. A man could willingly drown in the twin pools of her eyes. "Dorotea thinks I should have no life but to serve my husband. Fortunately, Don Murillo does not share her beliefs."

"He is a kind old gentleman," William replied, working in a reference to Murillo's age. It seemed unseasonably warm.

"Not as 'old' as you think," Esperanza corrected, with a nervous laugh. She blushed and was grateful for the night shadows.

"Maybe not," William said, bemused. "That is, if you played 'his' cards right."

"Now you are making fun of me. But there is power in the cards. A man like you has no time for mystery. You think me a charlatan, a pretender."

"No, ma'am. Folks are welcome to believe what they want."

"But you doubt my skills?"

"Señora, I think if you said up was down and left was right I'd probably believe you to my grave."

"Do you always put such trust in strangers?" Esperanza asked, unsettled by his response and what it might mean.

"No, ma'am." he answered. "You're the first."

"Why me?"

"I reckon the answer to that is also in the cards," William said, resisting the forbidden urge to reach out to her in the night. What the hell was he thinking? Didn't he have enough enemies without making another in Don Murillo Saldevar? Wallace retreated a few steps back, as if distancing himself from a fierce blaze. "Watch your step, señora." He opened the gate and led his two horses out of the corral. Beyond them, the waters of the bay rolled in upon the shore in unceasing cadence.

Esperanza was left momentarily bewildered, caught off guard by his candor. She had never met a man like him and doubted she ever would again. The curious affection she felt for this man confused her. It was as if she had known him in another time and place, when the world was young. She couldn't explain it away. There was a reason their paths had crossed. Perhaps they were children of fate. She feared what Wallace had awakened in her, but not enough for her to leave him alone.

Suddenly remembering the reason she had come to him in the first place, Esperanza lifted the hem of her dress and darted after Wallace, whose long-legged gait quickly covered the distance to the hacienda. He slowed his pace when she called him by name.

"Señor Wallace! This is for you," Esperanza breathlessly said, removing a bulky leather bag from beneath the folds of her cape. "I packed tortillas and cheese and dried beef for the ride back. Perhaps, after you have brought Captain Flambeau to his home you might think to join us in Texas?"

William gratefully accepted the gift. "Mad Jack hates to ride on an empty belly. I'll pack it away with his gear. I still have business in Veracruz. But he'll be most appreciative."

"You aren't going with him?" Esperanza's eyes widened with astonishment. "But what about Captain Flambeau?"

William shook his head. "He'll manage."

Better to leave now and allow the pirate his chance to escape. As for Juan Diego, all William needed was a chance encounter in the street, a bold strike, and a reckless charge to scatter the lancers and bring him face-to-face with his brother's killer. Simple, yes, and possibly suicidal.

"You don't understand. Captain Flambeau cannot reach safety without you."

"Don't let that salty sea dog fool you. He's tougher than he looks," William chuckled.

"You don't know . . ," Esperanza said, realization slowly dawning. *"Madre mia,* you have not been told."

The big man at her side slowed and turned to face her. He didn't like her tone. "What?"

"Your friend, the captain, his eyesight is rapidly failing. I think soon he will be completely blind and at the mercy of his enemies!"

Juan Diego and his lancers arrived in the early hours of the morning. Don Murillo had been absent for the past hour. Only the two women and Chuy Montoya remained to greet them. Dorotea Saldevar v Marquez clung to the folds of her shawl and stared ruefully at the barred front door as Juan Diego shouted her brother's name.

"What do you see?" she asked as Esperanza peered through a crack in the shuttered windows.

"Soldiers with torches and guns and lances," Don Murillo's young wife calmly described. "They have surrounded the house."

The next time Guadiz spoke it was to demand the surrender of William Wallace for assaulting the governor's own guard. Mad Jack had been added as an afterthought.

"We have come for the *norte americano* and the Butcher of Barbados!" Juan Diego announced, after one of his subordinates had read the warrant aloud.

Esperanza watched with interest as Paloma Guadiz, dressed in black pants and a gold-stitched short coat, maneuvered alongside her brother. Juan Diego's twin sister was flushed with excitement. She handled her mount better than any of the troopers. A pair of pistols jutted from saddle scabbards on each side of the saddle pommel.

"I will take some of the men and search the barn," Paloma told her brother, her voice carrying to the house.

Juan Diego nodded and dispatched a few of his lancers to follow her lead. Esperanza chose another vantage from which to observe the intruders. She could observe Paloma by the corral. On her orders her escort began to search the barn and surrounding area. Paloma waited astride her charger, hands folded upon her saddle's pommel glinting silver in the mist sweeping in from the bay.

"My brother's generosity has brought trouble to our door. I warned him! And this big gringo, your new friend. I saw you two. A man under warrant from the governor—"

"Hush!" Esperanza snapped, stilling her sister-in-law's remarks. She walked across the room and unbarred the door. As an afterthought she took a quirt, a foot-long whip with a weighted handle that one of her husband's vaqueros had left dangling from a wall peg.

"Señora?" Montoya warned, moving to intercept her.

"Stay here," the young woman firmly ordered and stepped out onto the porch.

Juan Diego and the remainder of his command had arranged themselves in a half-circle in front of the hacienda. At his command, three of the troopers dismounted and started up the steps to the porch, only to be met by Esperanza, who emerged from the house and turned them back with several stinging blows from the braided rawhide. The soldiers yelped and retreated down the steps. Chuy Montoya revealed himself in a front window, his shotgun balanced on the windowsill.

"What is the meaning of this!?" Esperanza exclaimed.

"I am about my uncle's business," Juan Diego replied. "We are looking for a pair of fugitives. It would be helpful if you did not interfere." He motioned for his soldiers to remount. Juan Diego glanced aside at his sergeant. Cayetano Obregon was bandaged and had replaced his uniform. His features were bruised and he sat stiffly in the saddle, his close-set eyes narrow and full of malice. "Tell me, Sergeant Obregon, what kind of man chooses to hide behind his wife's skirts?"

"An 'old' man, Captain."

"Too old for such a pretty wife," Juan Diego added, dismounting.

"Stephen Austin is no longer here. My husband had brought him to President Bustamente, who will be most displeased at the way you have treated one of his guests."

"We have not come for Señor Austin. His arrest was a terrible mistake. My uncle has already conveyed his personal apology. Rest assured the soldiers who arrested Señor Austin will be punished," Juan Diego explained. "I have come for the *norte americano* and the pirate, Mad Jack Flambeau. I think you have seen them." He climbed the steps to the porch. Esperanza raised the quirt, but Juan Diego was too quick and caught her wrist. Then, try as she might to resist him, Guadiz forced her hand to his lips and kissed the back of her fist. His tongue flicked across her knuckles. "Is this how that unwashed gringo kissed your hand? Did it excite you, señora? Maybe that is why you hide him." He opened her fingers and took the riding whip from her hand. Juan Diego stepped past the woman and prodded open the front door with the quirt's wooden handle. Dorotea stood in the hallway, wrapped in her shawl, eyes wide with apprehension. The room was empty. But he noticed the basin and bloodstained bandages on the floor near the hearth.

"Those whom you seek are no longer here," Esperanza said, her voice trembling as she struggled to suppress her anger.

"Ah. Honesty at last." Juan Diego turned back toward the woman. "Now we can be friends. And I make a much better friend than enemy." He continued to crowd the woman, forcing her back until her shoulders were against the wall. A chorus of muted laughter rippled through the horsemen in the yard. Juan Diego brought his face close to Esperanza's and whispered, "Why don't we take a walk to the barn? You can personally show me you have nothing to hide. What do you say to that?"

Esperanza smiled; a flirting, come-hither expression brightened her features and fueled his hopes. She leaned forward, her breath fanning the captain's cheek. "I would rather lie with the pigs."

It took a moment for her words to sink in. It was as if a dark veil had been suddenly drawn across the captain's confident facade. His look of expectation soured into a cold, hard glare.

"Wallace is gone. Mad Jack has gone. And you will not catch them."

Juan Diego nodded. "We'll see about that." He started back toward the horses as Paloma rejoined the troops, then, as an afterthought, returned to Esperanza's side. "Until we meet again, señora." He bowed quite graciously, but his words were more threat than farewell.

The captain remounted, smartly swung his horse about, and led his troops away from the hacienda. Paloma was the last to follow her brother onto the road. She lingered before the hacienda, a dimly glimpsed wraithlike figure wreathed in the mist and one with the shrouded moon and black water.

"You have no authority in Veracruz except by my uncle's good graces!" Paloma called out. "And my brother's whim. Be warned, little 'bride.' Do not cross us. You aren't in Texas now." A softfall of hooves in the moist earth and Juan Diego's sister disappeared in the gathering gloom.

"Fortunately for you!" Esperanza retorted. She remained in the doorway, bathed in the light that shone from within, unnerved perhaps, but defiant all the same.

Two rode together along the Spanish road where it followed a ridge of low hills overlooking the moonlit city of Veracruz, shrouded in sea mist and low clouds driven landward on the silent wings of the wind. On the skyline, one of the men looked back upon the port below, where armed patrols prowled the streets.

The wind rushed upslope, caught the folds of his serape, sent his long white scarf and unruly red hair streaming as he leaned forward in the saddle and stretched forth his hand in a blessing of blood red vengeance. Eyes ablaze in the belly of the night, he directed his pride and his passion toward the torchlit silhouettes below. The wind moaned and mocked his silent litany: And there will come another day.

8

"WHO IS THIS WALLACE?"

A caved-in roof.

Fire-gutted walls.

Charred earth.

Juan Diego Guadiz, astride his winded gelding, slowly circled the remains of the house on the hill. The column of lancers, twenty men strong, fanned out to explore the clearing and search for tracks. They found plenty, leading off in every direction, too many to follow.

The gelding balked at entering the wreckage. Plumes of charcoal dust billowed up beneath his hooves. The animal tossed his head and fought the bit. Guadiz directed his wrath upon the poor beast, savagely whipping the steed with the reins and raking the animal's side with his spurs.

The gelding reared and bucked. Juan Diego lost his purchase astride the military saddle, tumbled from horseback, and landed in the ashes. Guadiz rose from the soot like a vengeful phoenix.

"Son of a bitch!" exclaimed the officer; his blue coat and cream-colored trousers were smeared black. Guadiz drew his saber and began to hack at the offending debris; misshapen hulks of furniture, the remains of books, a ruined bedstead bore the brunt of his wrath. His boot heels ground the skeletal wine racks and shattered bottles of stolen wine underfoot. He slashed away at shipboard relics, kicked and crushed the brittle husks of sea chests. His sword blade clanged off the stone fireplace. The chimney, burned black by the savage blaze, made a fitting tombstone.

He dragged his pistol from his belt and leveled the weapon at the treacherous mount that had thrown him.

Paloma rode across his line of fire, placing herself in harm's way. "Brother, it is a long walk back to Veracruz."

"Get out of my sight!" he roared.

Paloma dismounted and strode toward him, keeping herself in front of the flintlock. Juan Diego's hand wavered as he sighted on his twin. Paloma remained calm and continued up to him. She reached out and lovingly began to massage his temple and jawline, drawing his pain and fury into her hands. Juan Diego lowered his head until it touched her shoulder. She stroked the back of his neck. After a few moments of her tender mercy, he took control of himself, began to breathe easier, then straightened and walked from the ruins, dragging his saber in the dust.

Paloma surveyed the damage with regret. She had wanted to leave Veracruz the morning after the pirate's escape and take up the pursuit. But her brother and the other men had overruled her advice. They tarried in the port to conclude their search of the town and surrounding hills. The whole day had been wasted when it was plain to the woman that the freebooter would head directly to his lair. These ruins proved her point, but she knew better than to remind her brother of that fact. She did not want to instigate another outburst.

"It is done," she sighed.

"The hell it is," Juan Diego replied.

"For now," she added.

"They mock me," Guadiz said, gesturing to the blackened site, "with this." He walked to the edge of the clearing, past the dueling ground, and across the narrow winding road until he overlooked the distant shore and the blue sea below. The breeze smelled of brine and moist sand and decaying shells washed ashore by the tides. Mad Jack was an old fool, but this gringo, Wallace, the big bastard, was trouble, a thorn in Guadiz's side. Paloma's shadow fell alongside his.

"Who is this Wallace? He plagues me."

"No one," Paloma replied, recalling her earlier assessment of the redheaded stranger.

"No one," Juan Diego ruefully repeated. He studied the surrounding forest and for the first time noticed they were being watched by a pair of Tainos natives. The Indians had appeared at the edge of the forest farther up the hillside. Juan Diego recognized the two, remembering them from Flambeau's household. They had been the pirate's servants.

Juan Diego had no sooner barked an order for Manuel and Josefina to be brought to him than the pair were joined by the men of their village, over fifty dark-skinned Tainos warriors armed with bows and arrows and conch-shell clubs. The lancers balked at following the orders. Manuel and Josefina weren't going anywhere they didn't want to go.

"Where is your master?" Juan Diego called out.

"The captain is gone," came the reply.

"I can see that, you bastard," Juan Diego softly muttered. "And the *norte americano* . . . where is he?"

"Ask the wind," Manuel answered.

"That isn't good enough," Guadiz said.

"I have his words."

Juan Diego glanced at Paloma, who shrugged and nodded in accord with her brother. The captain gestured, and his lancers pulled in to form a defensive circle alongside the remains of the house. Sergeant Obregon retrieved the captain's horse. Juan Diego climbed into the saddle and pointed his mount toward the warriors gathered at the edge of the clearing. The forest seemed to swallow them up. Suddenly they were gone.

"Wait. Tell me his words. I must find Wallace."

A voice, in reply, drifted out from walls of foliage and emerald gloom: "He will find you."

9

"I SURE AM ALMIGHTY TIRED OF BEING CHASED OUT OF PLACES."

It looks like more of Mexico to me," Mad Jack glumly observed, squinting behind the thick lenses of his spectacles. Texas waited across the river, beyond the shallows of the Rio Grande, its surface aglow with shimmering patterns of reflected light.

"That's because you have no eyes," William Wallace replied, breathing in the crisp, clean desert air. They finished the last of their coffee and broke camp, pausing now and again to watch the morning sun escape the bonds of earth, lift above the horizon, and chart its timeless course above the great river and the arid landscape. Now it hung like a beacon of hope in the mid-December sky, guiding them to the future, into the heart of a wilderness dream.

Wallace's mount, a long-legged roan gelding, seemed anxious to get on with the journey and not the least bit worried about fording the river. Thankfully, the Rio Grande was at its ebb, months away from spring flooding.

"My lights aren't dimmed yet, *mon ami,*" the pirate grumbled. The farther from the ocean, the more he complained. The headaches that continued to assail him were a painful reminder of Governor Guadiz's treachery. Ironically, for once in his life the irascible old freebooter had been telling the truth. All that remained of his treasure was a couple of leather pouches of Spanish gold coins, one of which he had left with Manuel and Josefina for their village. The second bag was tucked away in his saddlebags. The bulk of the pirate's wealth lay among the ashes, the mementos of his wild and lawless life, leatherwork, books, fine furniture to rival any of the governor's, all of it burned and melted beyond recognition to ensure that Juan Diego and his lancers would find nothing of value when they came calling.

Wallace and Mad Jack had traveled hard and fast, avoiding contact with government troops, exchanging horses when necessary at isolated ranches, skirting Mexico City, and always watching their back trail. As the days stretched into weeks, the two grew confident that they had escaped pursuit. Wallace was under no illusion, however. Juan Diego was a proud man and not one to overlook the humiliation he had suffered at Wallace's hand. "Guadiz will never forget you now," Mad Jack had grimly observed the night they escaped from Veracruz. William Wallace wouldn't have it any other way.

Throughout the first long week on the trail, William brooded over his failure to avenge his brother's death. Eventually he came to terms with his guilt, knowing full well he could not have allowed Flambeau, his friend and benefactor, to fall into the clutches of the governor. With his eyesight failing, Mad Jack was no match for his enemies. Flambeau continued to experience frequent headaches, and the vision in his left eye was severely clouded. Although the freebooter could still see well enough to function for himself, his swashbuckling days were history.

"C'mon," William said, grinning beneath his broad-brimmed sombrero. He swung up astride the roan and waited, quietly bemused, as Mad Jack grudgingly re-mounted. The sea dog preferred the rolling deck of a ship to the brown mare with her jolting gait and let the world know of his displeasure.

"We're burning daylight." William's long white scarf fluttered in a breeze that hinted of colder climes to the north. Winters were seldom harsh here on the Rio Grande plain. But like all of Texas, if a person didn't like the weather, he only had to wait a minute. "Time to get wet," William added, with a glance toward the river.

"Wait," the Frenchman said, and, reaching out, caught the younger man by his iron hard forearm. A black-throated sparrow scolded them from the thorny branches of a nearby ocotillo. The bird's signature dark ruff of feathers was similar in hue to the pirate's somber attire, black shirt and breeches beneath the gray, and brown folds of his serape. Mad Jack dressed as if he were in mourning for the life he had left behind. "These are for you." He tugged Bonechucker and Old Butch from his belt and passed the sheathed blades to his towering companion.

William looked perplexed. "I don't understand. Captain, I cannot accept—"

"Hang 'em from your belt."

"But they're yours," William protested, staring at the pair of weapons.

"No," Flambeau said. "I stole those knives off a Spanish grandee, and they have served me well. But I think maybe I have been keeping them for you all along." The freebooter refused to accept the weapons back. "Take 'em, my friend, and cross the river."

"Not without you at my side." William tucked the scabbards into the broad leather belt circling his waist. "See that path yonder. I reckon there's the Camino Real. The royal road. According to Don Murillo it cuts clear across Texas, practically all the way to San Felipe. Let's go."

Mad Jack warily studied the opposite bank, so far from everything he had known. A desert was hardly the place for a sea wolf like himself. "I don't know. Where does it lead?"

And William, recalling another time and place when he had asked a similar question, replied, "To the rest of your life."

Texas opened to William Wallace like a willing new bride at the first blush of morning. Texas seduced him with stark vistas of desert mountains and limitless sky and air fragrant as the first sweet breath of creation.

Day after day the beautiful country revealed its wonders. Vast and lonely peaks in the purple distance gave way to stark, eroded canyons and winding ravines that seemed to resonate with the echoes of all who had passed before.

Pine trees thrived at the higher elevations but quickly surrendered to frost-dusted cottonwood and post oak, to elegant madrona trees with smooth pink bark and twisted limbs, to cactus and mesquite, bunchgrass. Here was an ancient plain, a dry, serrated terrain where the wind moaned and whose harshness was only diluted by the infrequent encounter with a welcome spring.

The first week of Texas was a courtship; it was the land's own wisdom, its way of weeding out the weak and foolhardy. Those who persevered in the rómance were rewarded with a wealth of grasslands, thigh-high bluestem and Indian grass, then the limestone escarpments of the Balcones Fault, battlements of pink granite, broken hills teeming with wildlife and a thousand springs and creeks bubbling cold as melted ice out of the earth.

They reached San Antonio nine days into the new year and found a bustling community sprawled along the banks of the Rio San Antonio de Padua. The adobe buildings were a familiar sight with their natural brown or whitewashed walls.

William paused to appreciate the town, its haciendas, shops, shaded courtyards, mesquite fences for corrals, thatched jacals, hotels, and a thriving central market, orderly arranged streets bustling with wagons and horsemen, where children darted like swarms of angry bees among the merchants, farmers, laborers, and soldiers. . . . an all too familiar sight.

The troops stationed in the town were hardly the cream of the Mexican army. There was an unmistakable aura of dissolution to the scene. Men marched with less precision; the garrison housed in the abandoned mission on the edge of town appeared to be languishing within its crumbling battlements.

William scowled as he made a quick assessment of the soldiers garrisoned in the Alamo Mission a mile from town. A military presence was to be expected, but he didn't like it.

The two trail-weary travelers left the main road and approached San Antonio by keeping to the riverbank. News from Mexico, perhaps warrants for their arrest could have preceded their arrival, brought by boat and dispatch riders from the coast. Wallace and the pirate entered San Antonio as surreptitiously as possible, concealed by the willows and post oaks lining the river. They avoided the main streets and kept to a footpath that ran alongside Acequia Principal, one of the many aqueducts built by the early Franciscan friars who had settled the area and Christianized the local *tejanos.*

Mad Jack was leery of the soldiers lazily patrolling the streets. William retreated when necessary and kept to the alleys to keep from attracting the attention of the military. The two men reached the Calle Dolorosa and, with the helpful directions of a local goatherd, found the hacienda of Don Murillo Saldevar.

It was a handsome, solid-looking two-storied structure. A balcony with a rust-patched wrought-iron railing overlooked the street and a walled garden where the winter months had taken their toll. The hacienda's windows were shuttered and closed. A knock on the heavy oaken door failed to rouse anyone from within. No animals disturbed the serenity of the empty corral at the rear of the house. William shrugged. It had been worth a try.

Mad Jack sniffed the air and squinted up the street. "We passed a cantina over by the river." His stomach growled. Someone was cooking chili and beans.

"Let's find a place without any soldiers. I think that goatherd might have mentioned our arrival to the local troops."

They selected a ramshackle *pulqueria* on the outskirts of town. A reed-thin barkeeper filled a couple of clay mugs with pulque, the fermented juice of the agave cactus, and set out a couple of bowls of chili. The pulque helped to cut the trail dust. A meal of eggs, chili, and tortillas was simple but nourishing.

The *pulqueria* seemed to have its share of patrons— mestizo laborers, herders, a couple of vaqueros in from the range, a man who sold firewood. All of them seemed willing to gossip, and William soon learned the name of the local commandant, General Cos. The general had only recently arrived with the news that Bustamente had been deposed by Santa Anna. As the new president's personal representative, General Cos was held in particularly low esteem by the populace, who regarded him and the dictator as no friends to this far-flung Mexican state. Texicans had been fending for themselves without much help from the central government and resented the recently installed taxes and levies collected by the local authorities when the government in Mexico City provided them so little in return.

However, Don Murillo was well-known throughout

the community and much respected. The patrons of the cantina were quick to inform Wallace that the *hacien-dado* had been spending more and more time on his ranch along the Brazos near San Felipe. No one could blame the landowner, now that he had such a pretty young wife.

One of the cantina's patrons, a bewhiskered saddle maker with a generous demeanor, approached Wallace and Mad Jack and in a low voice informed them that General Cos had orders for any strangers in town to be brought before the general for questioning.

Mad Jack bought a round of drinks for everyone in the *pulqueria* and double for the saddle maker, then followed William out into the street. A column of soldiers in faded white uniforms hailed them from up the street and ordered the newcomers to remain by their horses. Deciding they had enough provisions to last until they reached San Felipe, William and the freebooter ignored the troops, mounting up and galloping out of town, leaving the startled dragoons in the dust.

A few miles from San Antonio, the two men slowed their horses to a walk and headed back onto the Camino Real. Mad Jack declared the encounter a bad omen. The fact that Santa Anna's influence penetrated this far north filled him with misgivings. To make matters worse, the saddle maker had cautioned Mad Jack to ride carefully, for the Comanche were raiding this winter and one of General Cos's patrols had fought a skirmish with a war party up on the twin forks of the Guadalupe.

"I sure am almighty tired of being chased out of places," William grumbled. The idea of *President* Santa Anna left a bad taste in his mouth. With the general's ascension to power, Juan Diego's fortunes could only continue to rise. "I think that's the last time."

Mad Jack sensed his partner's changing mood. "Watch yourself now, my boy. Defiance is a luxury neither of us can afford right now. We're sailing in uncharted waters. A wise man keeps his sail to the wind, a spyglass to the horizon, and his powder dry."

"Don't worry, Captain; I'll steer clear of trouble," William replied.

"I want your word!" Flambeau exclaimed. San Antonio receded in the distance, and the rolling landscape embraced them, lush with wildlife and great stands of white and red and blackjack oak, cedar and cottonwood, pecan trees and small-leafed maples. "I haven't come this far to have my scalp lifted by savages."

"Yours would be a poor trophy," William laughed, indicating his companion's smooth, hairless skull.

"That red mop of yours would be treasure enough for any heathen and see us both sent under the brine." Mad Jack gave the big man a sharp-edged look. "We sail clear of trouble, I'll have your word on it."

William shrugged. The Butcher of Barbados had turned sheepish in his old age. But assurance wasn't all that hard to give. Wallace hadn't come to Texas looking for a fight. "You have my word," he said.

It was the only promise he ever broke.

10

---◆---

"I GOT A BAD FEELING
ABOUT THIS."

Two days later, along the San Felipe road, "winter" found them. It rode the wings of the north wind over the bent earth, blanketed the sky with battlements of heavy clouds, dropped the temperature below freezing, and painted a sheen of frost on tree trunks and thistles. Despite the cold, William broke camp with renewed enthusiasm. Texas was a nourishment to his soul. His spirit feasted on the thick leafless stands of live oak, blackjack, pecan, elm, and walnut, on rolling meadows carpeted with yellow bunch grass and creeks teeming with sand bass, perch, and catfish.

Twice that morning Wallace cut the tracks of a white-tailed deer, and later the same day he spooked half a dozen wild turkeys from a tangle of bramble bush and deadfall. He rode easy through the morning, and his heart soared with the circling hawks. The future for him was the next stand of trees, the next meadow or broad open valley or brush-choked creekbed to cross. Everything was new and all things were possible if a man was bold enough. And didn't get himself killed.

For the better part of an hour the lowering clouds had threatened snow. Now the air was thick with a flurry of sodden flakes. Wrapped in his serape, with a wintry gust whipping across his left shoulder, William reined in his gelding beneath the spreading branches of a pecan tree.

He blew in his cupped hands to warm them, then pulled out his spyglass. Beyond the timber, where the land sloped down on a long gradual decline to a distant line of live oaks that concealed the sluggish undulations of a creek, a covey of quail had just exploded into bleak daylight from the underbrush where the trees thinned. That coupled with the distant rumble of hooves reverberating in the muffled air made ample reason for the spyglass.

Mad Jack walked his mount alongside William, who handed him the spyglass. Flambeau rubbed the moisture from his spectacles, hooked the wire rims over his ears, and squinted to clear what he could of his hampered sight. The sound of approaching horses was unmistakable.

"I got a bad feeling about this," he muttered. With his good eye Mad Jack grudgingly studied the far side of the meadow, dimly visible through the snowfall. A particularly soggy flake spattered against the back of his neck and worked its way down between his shoulder blades. The freebooter grimaced and bunched his shoulders and wriggled in his shirt. But the ice trickling along his spine didn't chill him near as much as the sight of a Comanche war party driving their stolen horses and prisoners out onto the grassland. Mad Jack stifled a gasp and lowered the spyglass.

"Remember, my brash friend. We do not look for trouble."

Wallace tossed his rifle to his companion, slid from horseback, and began to gather as much dried kindling as he could find, bunching it together with a length of his hemp rope. The big man refused to be distracted, working with a sense of purpose and righteous resolve.

"William? Remember . . . ," Mad Jack tried. But it was a waste of breath.

*   *   *

"They'll bust in your head if you don't stop your crying," Roberto Zavala told his nine-year-old sister. Isabel rubbed her eyes and glanced around at her brother, who shared the saddle. He was five years older, and it seemed as if he had been ordering her around all her life. Right now she was grateful for his comforting arms about her waist. They kept her weary little body astride the mare. A wet snowflake slapped against the girl's cheek and sent her burrowing deeper into her woolen coat.

"I can't help it," Isabel whimpered, struggling to stifle her sobs. Hours earlier she had seen her uncle killed, watched him tumble from horseback, clutching at the feathered shaft protruding from his chest. Her cousin had tried to make a stand, hoping to give the children a chance to escape. She had heard him cry out as the Comanche rode him down. Within minutes, the war party had surrounded the herd and captured Isabel and her brother. Now every mile took them farther from San Felipe and home. She thought of her father, the settlement's strong, sturdy blacksmith, whose heart would break when he learned of his daughter's capture. She thought of her mother, whose warm, shielding embrace couldn't save her children now.

"My sister needs to rest!" Roberto called out.

The Comanche warrior riding alongside the children gave them a withering look. His dark brown face, streaked with bands of crimson and black, held no softness. Like his four companions, the horseman's expression was as implacable as the gunmetal gray sky. Complain to the storm, to the winter wind, to the plump, wet flakes of snow.

There would be no camp until the raiding party had put a considerable distance between their captives and the stolen horses and pursuit from San Felipe. If the Comanche were lucky it would be several hours, possibly another day, before anyone learned of the raid. The snow, falling steady now with a mixture of pea-sized hail, worked to the Comanche's advantage, covering their tracks beneath a blanket of frozen precipitation. By the time the Texicans in San Felipe could mount a pursuit the five young braves intended to be safely across the Trinity and heading northwest to the caprock country.

The warrior alongside the children cried out to his companions, "My brothers, it is a good day!" The two men at the front of the stolen herd and the two men at the rear echoed his sentiments. They were fierce and proud, made invulnerable by their youth. Any farm they passed was fair game. The warriors were always willing to add to their stolen herd.

Roberto watched the brave alongside them turn his face to the elements and proudly appraise the horses that had made up the Zavala family fortune—a stallion, a few colts, and several good brood mares. There was not a nag in the bunch. As for the Comanche's prisoners, the girl would be raised by the older women until she was of age, then given to a warrior who had proved his worth to take to wife. The boy was still young enough to learn the ways of the People. In time he would walk like a Comanche, ride like a Comanche, think like a Comanche. Their enemies would be his enemies. And he would make war upon the very settlers he had been captured from.

"I want to go home," Isabel sobbed, struggling to control herself.

"Hush, Beth. Don't let them see you're afraid." Roberto considered making a break for it, a mad dash for freedom. He weighed his chances. The Comanche looked to be natural horsemen, born to ride and fight. Indeed, this short, stocky, bowlegged race preferred to view the world from horseback. The fourteen-year-old stared at the feathered war lances, their scalp shirts and bois d'arc bows that could send an arrow whistling through the pale light. His spirits sank. No. There was no escape. But the next second he convinced himself he had to try.

The warrior reached over and tugged at Isabel's coat sleeve. The girl tried to pull free; Roberto batted the man's hand away. The Comanche laughed and attempted to slap the fourteen-year-old boy across the face. Roberto dug his heels into his mare, caught the warrior's wrist, and held on as the mare bolted forward. The Comanche lost his purchase and toppled forward. He hit the ground, grunted, and rolled over on his backside.

"Hold on!" Roberto managed to shout into his sister's ear. The mare was a high stepper and blessed with a great deal of natural quickness that carried them past the herd and the two lead raiders before they could react to stop the captives.

"Roberto," Isabel rasped, clutching the pommel. The mare plunged blindly through the snowfall. Roberto glanced over his shoulder at the war masks of his pursuers. Three of the Comanche had abandoned the herd and taken up the chase. And they looked angry as bees on a bear.

"We aren't going to make it," Roberto moaned. He prayed to the Blessed Virgin as his father always had taught him to do. He prayed for courage, a strong right arm or a faster horse. What he got was deliverance.

"Roberto!" Isabel screamed, a new panic in her voice. Her brother forgot the Comanche gaining on him and turned his attention to the hillside and the great and terrible figure charging toward them from out of the sullen snowfall. He seemed more beast than man, a mountainous, monstrous creature shrieking at the top of his lungs and trailing fire.

"Watch out!" Roberto shouted as the mare stumbled and tossed the children onto the snow-covered slope.

Roberto shielded his sister with his own body. The boy noticed as the beast-man passed them what had appeared to be wings were the folds of a serape flailing the air. He glimpsed a long-limbed roan dragging a thick bramble bush by a length of rope. The dried vines and branches had been set ablaze. Gunshots filled the air. Off to the left, a rifle roared, then another. The towering stranger's voice echoed down the long hill. Roberto hugged his sister and buried his face alongside hers in the snowy field, hoping to shrink into the soil and find safety in the earth's bosom.

War cries, gunshots, hoofbeats drummed in every direction. Horses neighed in terror. Roberto covered his ears and still heard the screams of startled men, steel clanging against steel, the crack as a spear shaft splintered, the grunting and groaning and the thud of a body as it struck the ground. And then, at last, only silence save for the settling snow, which to the fourteen-year-old boy sounded like cats dancing on the brittle bluestem and the buffalo grass.

"Merde! Is that what you call riding clear of trouble?!" a voice shouted out, the speaker obscured by the snow. He seemed very upset.

"It's all right, young'uns," said Wallace. "Those devils have business elsewhere."

Roberto lowered his hands and lifted his face and found himself staring up at the tallest, broadest man the boy had ever seen. Flame red hair, powerful arms, a wide wicked knife glittering in one hand, powerful chest heaving for breath, legs like tree trunks, and his feet . . .

"*Usted tiene pies grandes*," the boy dryly observed. Yes, big, big feet.

11

"BIG FOOT WALLACE!"

Smoke curled from chimneys, drifted low over shingled rooftops, left soot gray patches in the snow. It was late in the day, but the inhabitants of the town were already in the streets, churning two inches of fresh snow into a muddy brown morass. A farmer had discovered the bodies of the blacksmith's kin a few miles outside of town and brought word of the attack. In response the lone mission bell of San Felipe sounded its message of disaster from the church tower on the southeast corner of Constitution Plaza, alerting the entire settlement to the tragedy.

It roused the populace from the warmth of the home and hearth, alerted the merchants and shopkeepers, emptied the taverns and the town hall where Stephen Austin, Don Murillo, and a handful of the colonists had been making plans for the settlement's expansion along the banks of the Brazos.

Men and women flocked to the plaza to learn the reason for the alert. They found Valentina Zavala beside herself with grief. Jesus Zavala, still in his blacksmith's apron, took up his rifle and asked for volunteers to help rescue his children. In a settlement of over a thousand people there was more than one opinion of what should happen and how best to track the Comanche.

Cooler heads argued against charging off "half-cocked," Austin suggested that a proper defense of the town needed to be addressed in case there were more war parties about. Zavala only knew his children had apparently been taken captive and with every minute wasted the odds increased that he would never see them again.

Don Murillo offered his vaqueros but cautioned against leaving so late in the day. Blundering about in the freezing darkness was a recipe for disaster.

Within the hour, the grim news had spread from every jacal, log cabin, and stone house. Merchants abandoned their stores and shops around Commerce Square, turned their backs on the drab, sluggish waters of the Brazos to descend on the center of town. A rescue attempt was certainly called for, but the town's safety also had to be taken into account.

Meanwhile the guests at the Farmer's Hotel and across the Calle Comercio at the Whiteside Hotel debated the merits of both arguments. Some of the newcomers chose to remain uninvolved; others loaded their guns and took to the streets ready to follow Jesus Zavala on his desperate mission.

Into the center of this commotion rode William Wallace. With Mad Jack and Roberto to help with the herd, they entered San Felipe by way of the settlement's main street, the Calle Vincente Guerrero. Isabel snuggled against Wallace's chest, burrowed into the folds of his serape, finding comfort and safety in his great size.

The horses smelled water and quickened their pace, traversing the streets at a smart clip that parted the crowd in the street. Men and women scurried out of harm's way as the missing herd burst into Constitution Plaza and formed a circle around the town well.

"Isabel . . . Roberto!" A dark-haired, big-boned woman broke from the ranks of the populace and, lifting the hem of her dress, hurried across the mud-churned snow, slipping and sliding, her eyes streaming tears of joy.

"Mama!" Isabel squealed with delight. Roberto echoed his sister. Both children leaped down from horseback and scurried into their mother's embrace.

Then the crowd gathered around the newcomers. More than a few regarded these new arrivals with suspicion. Wallace searched the gathering for a familiar face as Roberto began to tell everyone within hearing distance about the raid and how the Comanche war party had captured him and his sister and, when all seemed lost, the *norte americano* came charging out of nowhere and single-handedly drove off the raiders. Mad Jack grumbled beneath his breath about his contributions being overlooked.

Jesus Zavala came forward. The blacksmith was a man of average height with broad shoulders and powerful forearms, a simple, decent man whose expression spoke volumes. He held out his hand. "I owe you a debt that can never be repaid, señor."

William dismounted and took the blacksmith's handshake. "Glad I could be of help."

"Who are you?" someone asked from the crowd.

"A friend," Stephen Austin replied, making his way through the colonists with Don Murillo at his side. "He's Wallace."

"Big Foot Wallace!" Roberto exclaimed. The people around him chuckled.

And William said with a good-natured grin, "That'll do."

YOUNG WILLIAM WALLACE TOOK TO TEXAS LIKE A DEERHOUND TO BUCK SIGN. For nigh on to five years he roamed the beautiful country, from the Sabine River westward across the Pecos and down the Rio Grande.

But he always returned to his land on the Brazos. He called his ranch Briarwood, built a strong house, and ran cattle and horses out on the pasture. There were times when wanderlust got the better of him, when, restless as a bobcat with a burr under his tail, William would have to go.

Those were full years, I'm telling you, a time for chasing the wind over the next hill and following the sun. Now don't get me wrong. If the Comanche were raiding, bandits struck, or a child was lost, Bigfoot Wallace always answered the call and rode to the sound of the guns. William met every challenge head-on, with cold steel in his hands and fire in his eyes. That was the only hand he played. He knew no other way. William Wallace gloried in the land and in the life.

But times were changing and troubled waters were on the rise. . . .

12

"HE ALWAYS TURNED UP WHEN YOU LEAST EXPECTED HIM."

There was power in the cards, sight beyond seeing in worn and faded images, and magic in the childlike wonder of their keeper. Some called her a seer and came to her with open minds and hearts filled with questions. Others accused the woman of deluding her neighbors and herself with trickery. One day, perhaps while staring into the fractured darkness of her own demise, Esperanza might come to realize the truth of her mother's legacy. But for now, Señora Saldevar could not explain the gift she had inherited, nor did she try. After all, a life without mystery was hardly worth living.

Time and fate had raised her from servant to mistress and made her a woman of substance—tending her sun-washed gardens, riding the piney woods and pea green meadows of East Texas astride a sleek mare, learning the ways of the Rancho Rio Brazos—yet the vaqueros and servants still considered her one of their own. Throughout the first five years of marriage her husband, Don Murillo, had never been anything less than kind and generous and trusting.

"Are you content?" he would ask.

"Of course I am."

"Are you happy?"

And she would lie. "Of course I am."

*   *   *

Esperanza sensed she was being watched and glanced up from the cards on the walnut table to find herself being observed by a fastidious desk clerk who sat slouched forward, elbows propped on the scribbled pages of the hotel's leather-bound ledger. The clerk, Jack Tuttle, coughed nervously, closed and set the ledger aside, then tried to busy himself by polishing the pecan wood desk from which he watched the lobby and the street. Tuttle took care to dust beneath the inkwell and along the beveled edges of the heavy-looking counter-top. Like many of the *norte americanos* who had begun to flood across the border during the past couple of years, the clerk was new to the settlement. Tuttle was a lonely man eager to earn enough money to bring his wife over from New Orleans just as soon as he had a proper place for her to live.

Earlier that morning, Tuttle had recognized Don Murillo and his wife when they first entered the lobby. And like everyone else in the community, the clerk was acquainted with Esperanza's reputation as a diviner who could read a man's future.

The bride of Don Murillo considered dealing the cards and putting on a show for her audience of one. She might tilt her head back and roll her eyes up under her lids until only the whites showed and then draw a card and audibly gasp and stare in the poor man's direction as if she had just received some dire communication from those who had gone before, a prediction of some terrible doom about to befall him. But a glimpse of her husband through the front window changed her mind and curbed her impish nature. Don Murillo would not wish her to make a scene. These were sobering days. She didn't need the cards to tell her the time for games was at an end. Esperanza only had to look at the deserted plaza to know that the summer of 1835 promised to be a long, hot season to remember.

Don Murillo Saldevar and Stephen Austin had finished their walking tour of the settlement and were approaching the hotel in the company of the visiting official they had guided through the streets. Esperanza recognized John Bradburn, a heavyset Englishman and the alcalde of Anahuac, who struggled to match his companions stride for stride as they returned to the lobby of the Whiteside Hotel after their troubling sojourn through the dusty streets of San Felipe. It was rumored a hangman's rope awaited the alcalde should he ever return home to London town. England's loss was Texas's ill-gotten gain. Despite that fact that San Felipe's population had swelled to nearly two thousand colonists over the past couple of years, the settlement had fallen on hard times, and Esperanza knew the reason why.

Burdensome taxation and wholly unjustified levies had stifled growth and interrupted the flow of goods coming in from the States. Shipments destined for the settlement had been confiscated by Bradburn and stockpiled in Anahuac's warehouses. Bradburn, as a representative of the Mexican authority governing East Texas, had bravely consented to attend the town meeting to discuss the impasse and clarify the government's position. Colonists from the outlying areas had been drifting into the settlement throughout the morning, drawn by the desire to make their feelings known: most everyone mistrusted Bradburn's motives and considered him a turncoat for accepting Santa Anna's money. Esperanza thought the unpopular alcalde tended to act as if his mantle of authority were a crown. Bradburn might be a scalawag, but the man was no fool. He had wisely brought a troop of Mexican dragoons to enforce his edicts and ensure his protection should any malcontent attempt to cause him harm.

The three men entered through the front doors of the hotel and paused to allow their eyes to adjust to the shadowy interior. Bradburn glanced hungrily in the direction of the dining room. Don Murillo led the official over to the sitting area by the front window with its view of Commerce Square. The front doors had been propped open and the windows unlatched and swung ajar to permit a breeze. Blue checkered curtains stirred with a breath of wind. A few of the guests, itinerant traders, journeymen, and a couple of colonists and their families lingered over coffee and johnnycakes in the adjoining dining room. Esperanza wasn't hungry and preferred the lobby for its cross breezes and its view of the plaza.

To her dismay, only a handful of stalls had been erected in the square. An old man sold firewood and artfully woven birdcages; another stall had a tinker with a paltry assortment of enameled tin pots and pans. The señora noticed a Texas Indian woman selling poultices and hand-sewn moccasins and, nearby, a widow patting *masa* flour into tortillas and tossing them on a flat sheet of iron propped over a slow-burning fire. A family of mestizos displayed an array of multicolored blankets, clay jars, and braided lariats, hoping to attract the attention of a pair of disinterested dragoons, some of the very same men who had escorted Bradburn from the coast. Children, as frisky as puppies, chased one another across the marketplace, leaving in their wake a dusty brown haze to tint the streaming sunlight.

"The marketplace is almost deserted," Don Murillo remarked, stating an obvious fact. Esperanza, seated at her sunlit table, smiled and with a flick of her hand brushed back a few strands of her lustrous hair; shiny black as the mane of a new foal. Don Murillo sighed. He was much too old for such a vibrant young wife; at least so his sister had told him. But watching Esperanza in repose like this, he didn't care what anyone said.

"But then there is little to attract the farmers and ranchers into town. There are more empty shelves than full at Kania's Mercantile," the white-haired *haciendado* continued.

Though the years had added a few extra wrinkles to his features, he stood ramrod straight and carried himself with dignity. He brushed the dust from the embroidered sleeves of his gray jacket and trousers, then adjusted the silver clasp of his bolo tie. The smooth silver-embossed grip of a flintlock pistol jutted from the black sash circling his waist. He placed a hand on Esperanza's shoulder. "You must be bored. No doubt you are sorry you came along. San Felipe holds little of interest"—he glanced in Bradburn's direction—"these days."

"I welcome the change," Esperanza said.

"And the opportunity to escape my sister's company," Don Murillo chuckled. "Dorotea can be a burden at times." He gestured toward the two men with him. "You remember the alcalde."

"But of course. Señor Bradburn was our dinner guest last year. I remember he had a healthy appetite and a fondness for *albondigas*." Esperanza had personally prepared the meal, from her mother's recipe for a stew made from coarsely ground beef rolled into balls with rice and jalepeño peppers, seasoned with sprigs of mint, and simmered in a thick, fiery broth. The Englishman had devoured three heaping bowlfuls. As Esperanza recalled, the magistrate had also displayed a thirst for wine, but that wisely went unmentioned.

The alcalde was a man of average height, broad-shouldered, with a gut that drooped over his leather belt like a bay window. Sweat collected in the folds of his cheeks and drained along his thick neck. His scalp was pink and peeling beneath his thinning brown hair. The Englishman extended his meaty paw and clasped her delicate fingers in his fleshy grasp. He bowed and brought his thick lips to the back of her hand. She resisted the urge to recoil as the tip of his tongue flicked against her skin.

"I am charmed to see you again. Beauty such as yours does not exist in Anahuac. Perhaps you will visit with your husband and brighten up our little port. The coast is not without its attractions."

"The least of which are the shipments that languish in your warehouses," Austin interjected with a nod in Esperanza's direction. The founder of the colony carried himself like a man who had never been taught to smile, his pained expression but an outward display of the man's inner turmoil.

Esperanza sympathized with Austin. In the beginning, his word had been law in the settlement. He had personally picked each and every colonist who came to Texas. But all that had changed in just five short years. The *norte americanos* swarming into Texas came without Austin's personal invitation, lured to the frontier by the promise of open range, free land, and better lives. She could recount a litany of the newcomers, men like the Tennessee politician Sam Houston and Bill Travis, a lawyer from Mississippi, and a wild mélange of adventurers, poets, farmers, and families of dreamers, who owed no allegiance to Stephen Austin.

The locals welcomed the burgeoning population. With the influx of settlers, Comanche raids had become less frequent as the tribes withdrew to less populated areas of Texas. What had begun as one man's dream had become impossible to contain, and Austin, his prestige and powers reduced, could not help but be bitter.

"Ah, my friend, you wrong me. I am only following the directives of his most excellent president, General Antonio Lopez de Santa Anna." Bradburn shrugged and his chubby round cheeks split with a smile. "Come; there is no need for us to be adversaries. Indeed, you will find I can be most accommodating." The Englishman waved a hand toward the dining room. "Be my guests. Join me."

"I need to make some preparations for the meeting this afternoon," Austin said.

"But not at the town hall," the alcalde replied. "That log house is too smothering. I suggest the cantina by the river. There are plenty of tables outside, and everyone can socialize. I will avail myself to each man. Or woman."

"As you wish," Austin said and, touching the brim of his palmetto hat in salute, excused himself. It was clear to all he had complete disdain for the alcalde. But there were other ways to get these policies changed. Perhaps a boldly diplomatic move was called for.

"Surely you and your lovely bride will keep me company," said Bradburn, turning toward Don Murillo as Austin stalked across the lobby and disappeared through the front door. "And will I at last make the acquaintance of this man Wallace . . . Big Foot Wallace? I have heard the stories about him. I daresay they are entertaining."

The alcalde removed a clay pipe from the pocket of his bobtail black coat and clamped the stem between his teeth. His gaze feasted on the ranchero's comely young wife. He took her arm in his. "With your husband's permission, my dear Señora Saldevar." He moved with surprising quickness and the overbearing confidence of a man convinced of his own invincibility. The familiarity of his unwanted gesture caught Esperanza off guard. The deck of cards slipped from her grasp and landed on the hardwood floor. An errant breeze chose one and flipped it over, face up on the hardwood floor.

El Destripedor Rojo.

Esperanza smiled in silent observation. He always turned up when you least expected him.

*   *   *

The sun burned high noon over Briarwood as a warm breeze stirred the branches of the live oaks and pecan trees, sent pearl white clouds scudding across the heat-glazed sky, and set the sunflowers and firewheels dancing where they bloomed, in bouquets thick and lovely, sprung from the good earth.

"Well, Samuel, what do you think?" asked William Wallace, in conversation with his brother's ghost. The big man spoke in hushed tones, his voice a whisper on the wind. The frontier had etched his weathered flesh, left his craggy features a war map of seams and crow's-feet. He wore his skin hard as the steel blades he carried. The sun had burned him brown as Texas clay. Only the easy humor behind his green eyes tempered his appearance. Time and Texas had transformed muscle and bone into the stuff of legend.

Esperanza often teased him about how the ladies of the colony romanticized his exploits. She delighted in making him squirm with her descriptions of women she knew who would sacrifice everything, even their own honor, to stand at his side. Alas, not so Señora Saldevar. Despite her sister-in-law's suspicions to the contrary, the only woman who meant anything to William Wallace remained a faithful wife.

The big man slipped his nankeen shirt over his broad shoulders and tucked the hem into his brushed buckskin trousers. He pulled on his boots, armed himself with Bonechucker and Old Butch, grabbed his sombrero from a wall peg just inside the door, then ambled out into the warm air. He stalked across the veranda of the great stone house he had built with his own strong hands, fitting it with wide doorways large enough for a "man-sized" man to comfortably enter.

Wallace emerged from the ranch house and stepped out into the sunlit yard; his towering physique cast a long shadow upon the hard-packed earth. A large, shaggy hound bestirred himself from the shade beneath the porch and wandered over toward the knife fighter, who ignored the dog and headed for the horse he had tethered by a trough. A number of wasps hovered above the glassy surface of the water. Wallace steadied the hammerhead gray with a gentling hand. He began to tighten the cinch on his saddled mount.

The hound waited patiently for an acknowledging scratch on his shaggy brown head. The animal, part blue heeler and part sheepdog, had arrived at Briarwood during Wallace's second winter in San Felipe and had remained on the place ever since. To William's thinking, there was no poorer canine specimen in all of Mexico. He was minus half of his left ear. A patch of fur had been singed from his shoulder. Scar tissue ridged the dog's muzzle and curled his lip in an unnatural grin.

William checked the loads on his saddle pistols and replaced a flint. Before placing a foot in the stirrup he turned around and gazed upon the land, *his* land, forty-five hundred acres of prime pasture and fertile ground that stretched from the banks of the Brazos to the San Felipe Road. In five years he had built a small but substantial herd. The smokehouse was nearly full. Corn ripened in the field, row upon golden row. Half a dozen foals romped in the meadow.

You've done well, Samuel's ghost whispered in his brother's ear. Or was it the rustling of the tall grass, the whisper of a hawk's wing on the heated wind, the creak of a garden gate? *But . . . Juan Diego Guadiz still lives.*

William closed his eyes and traded the incriminating observations of his murdered brother for the guilty pleasure of a woman's face, her smiling eyes, sultry mouth, and raven black hair. *Esperanza can never be more than a friend,* he reminded himself. The bride of Don Murillo had been the knife fighter's weakness from the first day he had set eyes on her down in Veracruz.

He conjured an image of Esperanza on the balcony of her hacienda, alone in the gathering dusk, watching and thinking and wondering, till her husband called her to bed. Ah, can a man help the ramblings of his restless heart? Where is the harm in a dream?

Roberto Zavala hailed him from across the meadow. The nineteen-year-old, astride a skittish gelding, chased a headstrong calf up from the tall stands of cane that edged the riverbank. Behind the horseman, the sun-dappled surface of the river beckoned between thickets of cottonwood and willow. Cattle sampled the pasture grasses and continued on their daylong trek across the bottomland. William had chosen a building site well back from the floodplain and just a hail and holler from the San Felipe Road. Turn east and San Felipe was a half hour's ride. Ford the Brazos and the land belonged to Don Murillo Saldevar.

"You fixing to leave, Señor Wallace?" Roberto asked, riding up into the yard. William's own hammerhead gray stallion began to crop the bluestem shoots growing in the shade of the steps.

"Bradburn's supposed to have come up from Ana-huac. I reckon it is high time I met the man and heard him try to justify all these blasted taxes and explain why our goods haven't been released from the warehouses on the coast." William slapped the saddle pommel in disgust. The more he thought of the alcalde's tactics, the angrier he became. "I bought those goods in New Orleans and intended to sell them in town. Damned if I'll ransom my profits for taxes just because Santa Anna needs money to run his government."

"No doubt Señor Austin will counsel patience. Don Murillo will probably side with him," Zavala said.

William caught the reins and swung up into the saddle. "Bless my soul, but I'm scraping the bottom of the barrel when it comes to patience."

Roberto nodded sympathetically. "Whatever you decide, me and the boys will look after the place." At nineteen years, Zavala was a top hand and well respected by the other vaqueros, who called him Segundo and knew he spoke for Wallace in the man's absence.

"I wouldn't leave Briarwood in the hands of any other man," William said, glancing in the direction of the bunkhouse where the other two caballeros were hammering cedar shingles in place on the roof. He waved to the men. "Keep Angus and Ramon busy."

"With pleasure. And pass along my regards to my sister." Roberto grinned. "Isabel has her eyes on you, señor, now that she has passed her fourteenth birthday. Be warned."

"I'll ride clear of her, much as I admire your mama's cooking."

A breeze sprang up and stirred the leaf-heavy limbs of a knobby old sycamore, regal as a royal galleon adrift on a rippling sea of pink and white primroses and yellow buttercups. Home was a fair and lovely place that Wallace always seemed to be leaving. Roberto understood, but then he knew firsthand the kind of man he rode for. Texas had a habit of needing "Big Foot" Wallace: when the Comanche raided, when bandits struck, when a child was lost or a barn needed raising, or when the local military authority in the port of Anahuac confiscated shipments that were rightly the colonists' and all but dared someone to come and take them back.

Wallace said his farewell, tugged on the reins, and pointed the hammerhead gray in the direction of the road. "Stay put," the big man ordered, glancing down at the hound nearby. The dog lingered in the yard for a few seconds, whining, hesitant, its eyes on the man in the distance. Then, unable to resist its own wild urges, the hound took off after Wallace and followed him around the first bend in the road, barking and carrying on until both were out of earshot, the baying hound and the horseman, riding at a canter into the shimmering haze.

"Vaya con Dios," Roberto softly said, watching the silhouette of his friend shrink in the vernal distance and vanish like a legend in the dust.

13

"... THE WILD WEST WIND ..."

It was a rowdy collection of Texicans who came to the Flying Jib and gathered around the great oaken tables Mad Jack Flambeau had placed beneath a canopy of pine trees and cottonwoods on a bluff overlooking the banks of the Brazos. For the better part of the afternoon rum flowed like dark courage, fueling one brave speech after another. When the rum played out, tequila and Mad Jack's own concoction, a home brew referred to by the locals as "Slaughter of the Innocents," served to further loosen the bonds of civility. Before long, friends were verbally clashing with one another as handily as strangers. Tempers flared hot as the coals in the cook pit where cornmeal-breaded catfish fried in a cauldron of boiling grease. The fire pit was surrounded on all sides by quarrelsome men and a few long-suffering wives who braved the raucous cantina in a desperate attempt to lead their flush and flustered husbands into moderation.

John Bradburn was easy to recognize. The alcalde held court on a long, wide bench flanked by a half-dozen dragoons whose presence only served to rouse the ire of the colonists. The soldiers stood propped on their rifles, languishing in the shade as they watched the rum flow and licked their dry lips, eyes lit with envy, scowling, forbidden to imbibe by the alcalde, who set a double standard by swilling as much tequila as his round belly could hold.

Ah, but these Texicans were a boisterous lot whose tempers could only be diffused by the quick wits and tall tales of their irascible one-eyed host. But Mad Jack Flambeau would have to try a different tactic this afternoon. When men argued matters of justice and honor and taxes it was best to stand aside, pour the drinks, and keep the masses fed. Men with full bellies weren't as likely to riot and break up the place.

Blinking against the sweat that trickled down his naked skull and stung his eyes, Mad Jack maneuvered his way among the tables as he delivered a stoneware bowl of cornmeal to the cook, Hanneke Van Wey. This buxom widow had been unable to refuse the freebooter's charm or his purse of Spanish gold during the bleak days following her first husband's death. Years ago, shortly after arriving in the settlement with William Wallace, Flambeau had stopped in at the cantina for a "flagon of rum" to ward off the chill of a February night. The old buccaneer had stayed to warm Hanneke's bed. With the winds of a blue norther howling like banshees through the streets, the couple had romped with abandonment, oblivious to the cold and the dark. Come morning, Mad Jack found himself owning a half-interest in the Flying Jib.

It had been the freebooter's idea, with the advent of spring, to throw open the doors and windows and bring the tables and benches outside so his customers could appreciate the scent of hyacinths, honeysuckle, and wild strawberries and breathe pine-scented air while they drank themselves into a stupor. The Brazos wasn't the ocean and never would be, but the sweet flowing river had a song all its own as constant as the rolling tides.

Mad Jack estimated the size of the crowd and quietly appraised the heaping platter of dressed catfish fillets

Hanneke balanced on the lip of a shallow cast-iron pot filled with hot grease. "You reckon we've enough fish?"

"Do we have any more?" she asked. The Dutch woman was short and soft and ripely curved, with her blond hair tucked beneath a lace cap and her plump red cheeks dabbed with cornmeal. Her fingers were dusted gold from breading the fillets.

"Nope."

"Then it will have to be enough," she nonchalantly replied.

Esperanza, seated on the fringe of the crowd, excused herself from her husband's table, and made her way to the fire pit. Ladies seldom visited the cantina, and her presence did not pass unnoticed. But then, she had a reputation of being just a little "different." Those who knew her well were quick to add "compassionate" and "kind" when describing the wife of the *haciendado*.

"Señor Flambeau. Every time I try to help, Hanneke shoos me away. This is too much for one person to worry with."

"My little one, what would people think? You're a fine lady and shouldn't even be amongst all these blow-hards, much less serving them," the widow replied in a loud, brassy voice. The woman glared at the townsmen and settlers, many of whom had broken up into smaller, contentious groups. "Talk, talk, talk, that's what men do best," Hanneke observed with the wisdom of one who had seen men at their worst and loved them despite their imperfections. She lowered a handful of coated catfish into the pot. The grease sizzled and splattered the widow's apron as the cool pink-white fillets entered their hot bath of melted lard.

"I labored alongside my mother long before Don Murillo Saldevar took me out of the kitchen and gave me his name," Esperanza explained. "As for what people think, I no longer care. You have an extra apron. Let me help, *por favor.*"

A tall, powerfully muscled man in his early forties broke off from a heated debate over the merits of disobeying Mexican law. Because of the warm afternoon, Sam Houston had discarded his broadcloth coat. A watch on a beaded leather fob dangled from a pocket in his black cotton vest. He kept the long sleeves of his loose-fitting shirt rolled up past his thick forearms. "Good afternoon, ladies. That fish smells fitting, Hanneke." He lifted his clay mug in Mad Jack's direction. "But I say, Cap'n Flambeau, has the well dried up?"

"You and Travis and these other bucks have clean drunk up the last of the rum, Sam. But I've tapped a barrel of my home brew that ought to light a fire to your tail." Mad Jack gestured toward the interior of the cantina. "I'm just about to bring out a keg or two . . . or ten."

Sam Houston clapped Flambeau on the shoulder, nearly knocking the Frenchman off his feet. "Bring it on. Since talking won't do, maybe we can drink some sense into the alcalde here and Austin, too."

Stephen Austin was standing within hailing distance and heard his name mentioned. He frowned and glanced over at his rival. The founder of the colony regarded Sam Houston as a troublesome latecomer to Texas and resented the influence the man had begun to wield.

"Best you douse your own fire before it burns us all, Mr. Houston," Austin offhandedly remarked, approaching the fire pit. He trusted Mad Jack's home brew to quiet the Tennessean down. "No man can accuse me of being afraid of a scrape. But you and your friends are too blasted inclined to take matters into your own hands. Times are hard enough without picking a fight with the local authorities." Austin nodded toward the alcalde, who noticed the two influential colonists standing together. Bradburn rose from his table and circled the cookfire. Austin added in a low voice, "Remember, Santa Anna runs him."

"What plots are you hatching, my friends?" Bradburn glibly exclaimed. "Mr. Houston, you would be wise to seek Stephen's counsel. He knows the value of obeying the laws."

"And changing them," Austin said, angered at the way the alcalde was portraying him, almost as a lackey of the Mexican authorities.

Bradburn shrugged and gazed eagerly at the frying fish, his stomach rumbling. "The laws are there for all of us. If you find them unpleasant or onerous, by all means, take the matter up with President Santa Anna."

"I intend to do just that," Austin retorted, much to everyone's surprise.

"You cannot be serious," Esperanza blurted out.

"Indeed I am, señora," Austin told her, patting her hand. "Diplomacy got me this far. Years ago, I pleaded my cause before the government in Mexico City and received permission to colonize Texas. I can be successful again."

"But General Santa Anna wasn't in power then," Esperanza countered. She glanced around for her husband, but Don Murillo was deep in conversation with his *segundo*. Chuy Montoya had accompanied the ranchero to San Felipe. The two men tended to talk horse breeding and the condition of the stock and the range whenever opportunity permitted. "Weigh your decision carefully. Discuss it with my husband. Have you forgotten Santa Anna's hospitality?"

"He gave us both a taste of the Mexican dungeons," Mad Jack added.

"I don't know if that was all his doing," Austin said. "But the general is president now. It has been five years. Time changes men. I think he can be made to listen. I have already discussed the matter with Don Murillo, and he has expressed his own doubts. But I must make the attempt."

"Well, if you are determined to try," Bradburn said, "there is a schooner, the *San Gabriel,* leaving for Veracruz at the end of the week. You can catch a coach to Mexico City right from the port." The alcalde cleared his throat, adjusted his coat and flat-crowned hat, then offered his arm to Esperanza. "Señora Saldevar, perhaps you will walk with me for a few moments down by the river. My ears are ringing from all the confrontations I have had to endure today. Just a brief respite in the company of such a lovely lady as yourself would place me in a decidedly better humor."

"As you wish," Esperanza grudgingly agreed. The colonists needed the official as cooperative as possible. A brief stroll along the river with the alcalde was a small price to pay.

"Good. You can tell me about this fellow Big Foot Wallace. Our paths have yet to cross; still I feel as if I know him after listening to the local gossip." Bradburn's voice turned silken smooth as they walked. "I am holding a shipment of his for taxes. There are barrels of nails, apples, salt pork, even a load of pig iron for the forge. I am sure a reasonable man will want to reach an agreement."

Esperanza bit her tongue. Reasonable? She could recite a litany of words describing the Texican: bullheaded, stubborn, and brave to a fault, but reasonable? Hardly.

Mad Jack Flambeau watched the alcalde and Don Murillo's wife disappear along the path that wound down through the trees and brush toward the banks of the Brazos. Austin and Houston continued to verbally spar with each other, each man convinced as to the merits of his arguments and unwilling to budge from his position. Mad Jack sighed and shook his head and went about his business. The freebooter didn't care two hoots in hell for politics, as long as he turned a profit. Men like Austin would try to keep the Texicans in line, while Houston seemed bent on pushing the colonists into a rebellion. Flambeau wondered where a man like William Wallace would stand. Flambeau returned to the cantina. Enough of this tame whiskey. It was time for a little Slaughter of the Innocents.

William Wallace entered San Felipe by the river road, skirted the Calle Guadalupe de Victoria, a stone's throw from market square. There were few vendors these days, for Santa Anna's policies held the colonies in a stranglehold. William recognized Don Murillo's carriage in front of the Whiteside Hotel and was tempted to investigate whether or not Esperanza had accompanied her husband into town but resisted the urge for now. He had business elsewhere. He'd only gone another block when a woman called out his name. Wallace turned in the direction of the voice and saw three comely young señoritas crowding the upstairs window of Zavala's Stable and Blacksmith, just a block off the Calle Tercera. The dog found a patch of shade to curl up in while William walked his mount over toward the smithy.

Isabel Zavala waved to him. What a difference the years had made from when he had rescued her from the Comanche. At fourteen she was filled out in all the right places and had a wide, sweet smile a man would die for. Her two friends looked a little older, but not by much. They giggled and chided the blacksmith's daughter for calling out, although they had dared her to do it.

Wallace rode up to the front corral where Jesus Zavala often kept the horses he was preparing to shoe. The girls were in the hay loft, up to mischief no doubt, but they were as pretty as peaches and carelessly flirtatious, and the brawny redheaded Texican decided there were worse ways to spend a few minutes.

"Good morning, Big Foot!" Isabel called down.

William bowed and swept his sombrero across his chest in a grand salute. His long white scarf trailed across his shoulder. The girls noted how the muscles rippled beneath his shirt. "I believe you three are the fairest flowers in all of Texas."

The girls blushed. Isabel found her voice. "This is Consuela. And here is Elizabeth."

"I am pleased to make your acquaintance," Wallace said. "And I hope this day finds you well."

Isabel pouted and shook her head. "Everyone has gone over to meet with the alcalde. I suppose you have come to do the same." She leaned forward, revealing her bare shoulders and the frilled low-cut bodice of her blouse. Strands of straw and dust fluttered down from the window.

"Directly," William said. "But seeing three such love-lies has made my day."

"Father is over at the Flying Jib. He won't be back for hours. You could climb up here and *visit* awhile." Isabel folded her slender fingers beneath her chin and smiled.

William coughed and cleared his throat. "Well now, I don't think that old ladder to the loft would bear my weight."

"Don't worry," Elizabeth said. "If Consuela could climb it, anyone can."

Consuela, round and ripe, thick at the waist, with almond-colored eyes, reached over and slapped at the other girl. "Hush, Elizabeth!"

"If you have any trouble we'll help you get up," Isabel said, bright-eyed and eager.

The desire emanating from that loft was enough to

burn the barn down. That kind of heat it was better to
ride clear of.

"I have business today. But I shall look for you girls
at the dance."

"What dance?" they blurted out, almost in unison.

"The one we'll have about three years from now,"
Wallace said with a grin. And, bowing again, he rode
off toward the Brazos in search of safer company.

The hammerhead gray turned his ugly head toward
the river. Both the stallion and the trailing hound knew
the way to the Flying Jib and headed straight for the
sandstone façade peering from a grove of willows overlooking the Brazos.

Several Mexican soldiers, the rest of Bradburn's escort, were lounging on the benches that had been left in
the shade of the front porch. The dragoons looked on
with a mixture of curiosity and grudging respect for the
big man. Those who hadn't seen him before knew him
by his size. One of the soldiers, a young man named
Jose Oñatè, anxious to prove his mettle, shouldered his
rifled musket and placed himself squarely in the entrance
to the cantina. Wallace ignored the man as he dismounted and looped the reins of his horse over the hitching rail. The hound came slouching out of the dust, his
tongue protruding from his scarred muzzle. Oñatè noticed the animal's mutilated ear and singed flank.

"The alcalde requests no guns be brought into the
cantina," the soldier said, distracted by the hound. "Hey,
gringo, that's the ugliest dog I have ever seen."

"That ol' hound's got a stone arrowhead lodged beneath that lump of skin over his rump," Wallace dryly
observed. "He's been shot at, nicked by a Comanche war
lance, survived a tangle with a pack of red wolves, and
had his snout slit open in a tussle with a wild boar."

"What do you call such a dog?"

"Lucky," Wallace replied. He brushed the soldier

aside and continued on into the cantina. Oñatè started to call him back. But then the hound began to growl deep in his throat and his hackles rose. The scarred muzzle curled back to reveal a ragged row of teeth. Oñatè felt his belly turn cold, and he backed away, returning to the safety of the porch and his companions, who were having a good laugh at his expense.

William took a moment to allow his eyes to adjust to the shadowy interior. The cantina was empty save for its owner and a few solitary drinkers, most of whom were slumped forward, snoring. Angry noises drifted in from the crowd on the patio. One man in the back of the room glanced up from the jug he was trying to empty. He looked to be a good fifteen years older than Wallace, built thick and tough-looking, with stringy brown hair and bushy sideburns down to his jawline. The stranger seemed to take an interest in Wallace. His gaze followed the Texican as he crossed the room and came up behind Mad Jack. The Frenchman stood behind the counter, filling a clay jug from a recently tapped keg of his home brew. Flambeau glanced over his shoulder; a look of recognition softened his expression. He set the aside the jug and, with fatherly affection, hurried over to embrace William.

"Figured you'd come dragging in here after most of the hotheads were plumb argued out." Mad Jack grinned. He looked much the same as ever, save for the black patch that covered his now-sightless left eye. His shaved skull was concealed beneath a yellow scarf that kept the perspiration from rolling into his good eye. His brown waistcoat and loose white shirt seemed a trifle threadbare, but other than that Capt. Mad Jack Flambeau looked much the same as when he had rescued William from the Mexican troops. Partnership with Hanneke Van Wey suited him.

"It appears you've found your proper calling." William removed his sombrero and set it upon the bar. His red hair was matted with sweat; moisture streaked the side of his face. He mopped his forehead and cheek with the long cotton scarf casually knotted about his throat. Wallace glanced around the cantina, noticing a few additions to the seafaring relics that adorned its log walls. Mad Jack had acquired a ship's figurehead, a pair of crossed cutlasses, a small deck gun, and another flag of the brethren—a skeleton balancing an hourglass upon the palm of its bony hand. "You are a sly old sea dog."

"This arrangement started out as strictly business. I cannot help it if my own natural charm smoothed the path to the window's bedchamber."

William suspected Hanneke had played the freebooter like a fiddle right from the onset. Nothing had happened that she hadn't planned. But William would never say as much to the Frenchman. A man needed his illusions.

Most of the people here didn't know Flambeau's past, or if they did, it wasn't held against him. With the passing of the years Mad Jack had established himself as a valuable member of the community. Men from the fields, merchants and shopkeepers, colonists of every station and social bearing had sampled the Frenchman's hospitality. The Flying Jib had become a favorite gathering site.

A river breeze constantly fanned the clearing. The aroma of fried fish drifted in through the open back door. William tossed his sombrero aside, breathed deep, and heard his stomach growl. But judging from the angry voices striving to shout one another down, many of the cantina's patrons were in no mood for a fish fry. Most of the lot sounded as if they had a belly full of indignation.

"Listen to them. It's been all me and Hanneke can do to keep them supplied with drink. I've gone through every river-cooled jug of ale; the rum and tequila are gone. I'm down to home brew. And Bradburn hasn't moved from his position." Mad Jack leaned against the bar. "The alcalde insists on receiving twenty percent of the value of each shipment, in gold or goods, before any one of us sets foot in his warehouses. He claims these orders come direct from Santa Anna."

"What do you say?" William asked.

"Mon Dieu! I know a pirate when I see one." Mad Jack scowled and stroked his chin. "He's *el presidente*'s hireling. I'll warrant he reports on every *norte americano* coming and going in these parts. He's always sending dispatch riders to Cos in San Antonio. And I doubt a boat doesn't leave Anahuac without some message aboard for Santa Anna himself."

William chuckled. "Bradburn, huh? I've not met the man. How are the others taking it?"

"Austin's the voice of reason and restraint, like always," Mad Jack told him, moving toward the doorway, a pitcher in his hand. He knew the colonists had legitimate grievances—unjust taxation stuck in his craw as much as any man's. But he was older now. Sailing against the prevailing wind was a young man's game. "It's a peculiar bunch. Men like Señor Saldevar and some old-timers follow Austin's lead. But this new breed: Houston, Travis, Lamar, some of the others . . . well, you've sat down with 'em. They're . . . well . . ."

"Full of piss and vinegar." Wallace grinned. These were interesting times. He rubbed the back of his neck and glanced around at the stranger who continued to stare at him. William was not a man to stand on ceremony. He ambled across the room and came to a halt a few feet from the man. William wrinkled his nose at the smell of tequila and body sweat. The man had been on the trail for a good while.

"Well, pilgrim, take a good look," Wallace said, holding his arms out from his side.

The man's eyes drifted to the knife hilts of Old Butch and Bonechucker, the only weapons Wallace favored in town.

"You must be him, the only one they call the Red Ripper," the stranger said. "Folks said look for a man tall as timber, hair red as spilled blood, and packing a pair of knives forged in Spain."

"I am William Wallace."

The stranger drew a lethal-looking blade from his belt and placed it on the table. It was single-edged steel, about the same length as Bonechucker and almost as wide. The blade was curved at the tip—a simple but effective design for disemboweling a man in a fight. Bonechucker's fluted tip served the same purpose. "I am Jim Bowie. Perhaps you have heard of me?"

"Some," William replied. Bowie was drunk, but that didn't make him any less dangerous. The man had a reputation as a duelist throughout the South, although he was said to have left that violent life behind and moved somewhere in central Mexico.

"No man is my equal with a knife," Bowie said. He patted the hilt and then returned the weapon to its sheath.

"If you say so."

Bowie stroked his chin as he considered this reply. "I heard you throw a long shadow when it comes to 'close quarters.' " He lifted a glass to his lips and tilted his head back as if to toss down a shot of tequila. Realizing the glass was empty, he cursed and tossed it aside and watched it roll across the floor until it clinked against the stone hearth. "As long as I was in Texas, I figured to come on up to San Felipe and see for myself." Bowie grinned. "I figure you'd want to have us a little scrap, just for fun like, and find out who is the better man. Of course it would all be just a game."

Wallace studied Bowie's features, didn't like what he saw lurking behind the corridor of those cold, dark eyes.

"What do you think?" Bowie asked.

"I think you've drunk enough," said Wallace, retracing his steps across the room.

Mad Jack was waiting for him at the rear of the cantina. Wallace could feel Bowie's drunken stare boring into him. But Flambeau nodded his head approvingly. "Best you come outside." The Frenchman carried a jug of his Slaughter of the Innocents in each hand.

"Take care you don't slosh any of that home brew on your knuckles. It'll take the hide off clear to the bone," William dryly observed, rubbing the back of his neck and trying to forget his brief exchange with Jim Bowie.

"Ain't heard no complaints," Mad Jack noted, unamused. "I see Lucky's found him a place by the fire." The scarred old hound lay at Hanneke's feet, happily devouring a morsel of catfish that the woman had "accidentally" dropped.

"Hanneke's a fine-looking woman," William took care to mention. "You're blest to find a lady with such poor taste in men."

"At least I waited till her husband was dead and buried before I gave her a look," Flambeau retorted, instantly regretting his remarks the moment they left his lips. "Sorry, lad; that was below the waterline."

"But right on the mark," William admitted, a note of guilt in his voice. He spied Don Murillo and Chuy Montoya hunched together at one of the tables outside. The *haciendado* noticed the big man and waved. Wallace returned the gesture.

At another table, Austin was so embroiled in an argument with Sam Houston and the lawyer Bill Travis that he failed to notice the towering frontiersman he had once befriended. Houston and Travis, a twenty-six-year-old Mississippian, were men in search of their destinies. William Wallace understood them, for he, too, was a proud dreamer, with his own vision of empire.

Austin might have been the first of the *norte ameri-canos* to come to Texas, but it was clear he wouldn't be the last. Despite his long-standing friendship for the founder of San Felipe and the colonists who had welcomed him, Wallace couldn't help but take a liking to these newcomers. There was more going on here then a group of colonists trying to accommodate the Mexican authorities. Like a change in the weather, something was in the wind that Wallace couldn't put a name to yet, but he'd damn well know when the storm hit.

"Where's Esperanza? Back at the hotel?" William asked, half-expecting to see her at Don Murillo's table. The señora had a stubborn streak. She wasn't the kind to sit by a fire knitting when the world around her was fixing to change.

"Not hardly." Mad Jack nodded toward the path leading down to the riverbank. "She went for a walk down by the Brazos. She just left with—"

"A walk, eh? Well then, the alcalde can wait," William interrupted with a wink and started down the river path at a quick pace.

Jesus Zavala called out to Wallace, who waved as he skirted the crowd with his long-legged stride, moving silently, quickly, like some great panther on the prowl. The blacksmith had never forgotten that Wallace had rescued his children from the Comanche war party. Zavala would carry his debt of gratitude to the grave. It pleased him that his son was Wallace's *segundo*.

"I wonder if I should have told him Bradburn's with her," Mad Jack muttered beneath his breath. "Mais non. He'll find out soon enough." Flambeau would have started off among the tables, but a low rumble of a voice spoke to him from the interior of the cantina.

"So that's El Destripedor Rojo. I've come up from Guadalajara to see him for myself. He's big enough." Bowie spit in the dirt. "Think I could take him?"

"Not likely," Flambeau said. "I heard that Wallace was taught by a master knife fighter—no man was his peer." Flambeau turned and faced Bowie. "They had an outbreak of smallpox down Guadalajara way. Was it bad?"

Sadness fell on Bowie like a stone. Pain momentarily contorted the duelist's expression. The man steadied himself against the doorsill and wiped a hand across his stubbled chin, placed a hand over his eyes for a moment, then dropped it aside.

"Pretty bad," Bowie said. His blousy shirt was stained and in need of mending, sort of like the man himself. Bowie hooked a thumb in his belt near the hilt of his knife. A small-caliber flintlock pistol jutted from the top of his left boot.

"Maybe you'd better forget your business with Wallace and move on?" Mad Jack guardedly asked.

"He is a man of some renown," Bowie said. "I am no stranger to reputation myself."

"And who might you be, monsieur?"

Bowie told him, his drink-heavy breath fanning the Frenchman's face. He almost lost his balance as he spoke. His vision blurred, then focused on the world once more. He steadied himself against the door frame. "I've come a far piece to meet him. Looks like I found me a revolution, too."

Mad Jack's eyebrows raised. "Nobody's said a damn thing about a revolution; there's been no such talk."

Bowie chuckled. At his age, the veteran of several duels, he considered himself a keen judge of human nature. He had heard enough of the local gossip. Folk were talking themselves into a sure-enough shooting war. "No. But there will be."

He grabbed a mug from a nearby table, and Mad Jack poured him a measure from the jug. Bowie swilled it down, his eyes widened and bulged, his grizzled cheeks turned red, and he gasped in a great lungful of air. "What the hell's in that jug?"

"Boar piss and branch water. I cut the head off a water moccasin, toasted it, tossed it in the brewing barrel, and covered it over with cactus juice. Snake poison gives the drink its staying power," Mad Jack chuckled.

"Tastes like it," Bowie rasped. His eyes began to water as the world took a step backward, then rushed toward his face. "By heaven, there's a drink for a man."

"I boil it off over behind the smokehouse," Mad Jack told Bowie, pleased with himself. The freebooter was an easy mark for a compliment. "I let it age for a few days and toss in a pinch of jalapeños just to give it a kick."

Bowie tucked a coin into Flambeau's pocket and helped himself to another drink.

"I'll keep a marker for you, if you figure on staying around these parts." Flambeau gave the famed knife fighter a wary look. Bowie sounded like he meant trouble for William. If that was the case, Mad Jack intended to "read him from the book." "On second thought, pay as you go. If you cross the line with William Wallace you won't be around long enough to pay your bill." He filled the man's cup to overflowing.

"We'll see, Cap'n. We'll see." Bowie's speech was already slurred. He gulped the home brew, shuddering as another ball of fire coursed the length of his gullet and exploded in his belly. He clapped the older man on the shoulder and stumbled back into the cantina, disappeared around the edge of the door, and promptly vanished into the gloomy interior. Bowie slumped into the nearest chair before his legs gave out from under him.

Mad Jack backtracked and glanced inside. Jim Bowie sat with his arms outstretched on a tabletop near the back door, his eyes blank as spoons, staring into the heart of his own personal darkness.

"Careful; it sort of sneaks up on you," Mad Jack warned.

Esperanza guided Bradburn along the well-worn trail that led down from the high prairie to the banks of the Brazos. By the water's edge they continued beneath a drapery of black willows, their branches heavy with vines and gray-green leaves flirting with the silty surface of the river. The meandering current bubbled over submerged stones, troweled a trench in the mud underneath fallen timbers, and lapped against the muddy embankment, gradually shaping the earth to its own design.

The señora kept up a constant flow of information, made uncomfortable by the way the man undressed her with his hungry gaze. She had immediately recognized her mistake and suggested they return to the cantina, but the alcalde would not hear of it. Resigned to his company, Esperanza recounted the history of the settlement and her husband's own belief that Texas had for too long been treated like a poor orphan state and ignored by the government in Mexico City. Don Murillo had welcomed the settlers, she told her companion— the colonists from the north brought energy and a spirit of renewal; they came as builders, not invaders. But surely the alcalde understood all this. After all, he was one of them.

Bradburn smiled at her remark, and his thick hand reached up to brush a wisp of black hair from the woman's cheek. She retreated from his side, put off by this gesture of familiarity. He laughed as his pale eyes surveyed the riverbank, darting toward the back trail, then to the opposite shore. He mopped the sweat from his sunburned scalp and the folds of his flashy jowls.

"I am Santa Anna's man, appointed by the president himself," Bradburn said. "I am loyal to only one thing, and that's the money the Mexican authorities put in my pocket. I know what I'm here for: to keep tabs on all these blasted visionaries. *El presidente* and General Cos understand a man like me. And I understand you, se-ñora." He approached the woman, who continued to step backward, trying to keep a proper distance. "A woman like you cannot have too many patrons, eh?"

"What do you mean?" Esperanza icily replied.

"I have heard the stories. The kitchen girl whose beauty bewitched a lonely *haciendado*. You went from hauling water and stirring *menudo* to the bedchamber. Very good, my dear. See? We think alike. We do what needs to be done."

"Señor, you do not know me at all!" Esperanza snapped, her features reddening with indignation, dark eyes flashing fire.

"I am the alcalde. I have the power and authority. And before long, I'll have the wealth. A percentage of every shipment arriving in Anahuac." Bradburn followed the woman through the branches of the willow and trapped her against the tree trunk, his big belly like some massive barrier. "Don Murillo is an old man. I'll warrant you'll have his entire estate before long. When that day comes, you will be needing a friend. Someone who has the ear of the government. I can be that friend. Together we could control half of Texas." The man smelled of rum, of sour perspiration and greed, a volatile combination when mingled with lust.

"How dare you speak to me in such a manner," Esperanza said, blood rising to her cheeks.

"Save your indignation, *por favor*." Bradburn grinned. "We both know it's misplaced. You were a scrub girl until the old man caught a scent of what's underneath that skirt. I'd like to nest there awhile myself. But I can wait." His gaze swept up her willowy frame and settled on her lush red lips. "Well, maybe just a taste."

"No," she hissed and tried to shove past him, but the alcalde's bulky torso was too much for her.

"Yes," he said. And the alcalde was always right.

Cardinals and robins and raucous blue jays flitted among the branches of the pines and post oaks overhead. A pair of brown squirrels scampered out of harm's way. They leaped to the nearest tree trunk before turning back to scold the intruder who had interrupted their search for last year's pecans. Butterflies hovered like lazy rainbows, wings aflutter, brief glimpses of bright bouquets poised between heaven and earth, suspended on diaphanous wings. Wallace sucked in a lungful of air fragrant with a mixture of wild honeysuckle and cedar. He stepped over vines strewn upon the earth like green entrails, rotting in the afternoon. The siren call of the river and the promise of a chance meeting with Esperanza lured him onward.

The cantina, with its sounds and smells, fell behind as the trail wound through a patchwork quilt of sunlight and shadow. He heard a fish, possibly a bass or catfish, break the surface of the river to snare one of the many insects that dipped close for a drink. He settled into his long-legged stride and was about to softly call Esperanza by name when he heard her voice ring out, raised in protest. Wallace frowned and quickened his pace and, rounding a thick wall of cane, lady fern, and a thicket of scrub oak, broke from cover in time to see the señora being accosted by a wide-shouldered, rotund man, his belly straining the his sweat-soaked ruffled shirt. The man's finely stitched trousers were spattered with mud. The cut of his clothes befitted a gentleman, but hardly his actions.

There beneath the branches of a black willow at the

water's edge, Esperanza struggled to free herself from the heavyset man's grasp. She spun on the heels of her riding boots and almost broke free, but her companion objected, reaching out and catching her by the arm and hauling her back. His cheeks were beet red and streaked with sweat from the struggle. The woman might have worn him down and escaped. But Wallace never gave her a chance. He didn't need to see any more. The cur had laid his meaty paws upon her. He had forced Esperanza against her will to remain in his company. Nothing else was of any concern.

Wallace charged the remaining distance, legs pounding, long red hair streaming behind him, his square-jawed features ablaze with a Highland rage. Esperanza saw him and her eyes widened, her mouth forming a silent, *No.*

Too late.

A twig snapped underfoot. Wallace caught Bradburn as the man half-turned at the sound. Bradburn cried out and fumbled with the pistol tucked in the sash circling his waist. Wallace caught the man by the front of his shirt, lifted him off the ground, and tossed him into the river as he would a big sack of mealy grain. Bradburn splashed in the shallows and rose sputtering and fuming from the muddy waters. His clothes were plastered to his body, the skimpy strands of his hair matted to his skull.

"I am William Wallace. Remember the name. I shall escort this lady to her husband; then I must meet with the alcalde. That gives you time to crawl out of that river and leave these parts. Or, by heaven, it will not go well for you."

Esperanza tugged on the big man's sleeve and when she had his attention said, "This is the alcalde: John Bradburn."

"Lay hands on me, will you?" Bradburn fumed and sputtered, livid with rage. "*Wallace,* yes, I will remember all right. Remember to have you arrested for assaulting a lawfully appointed official!" Bradburn exclaimed, staggering up from the river's edge.

"And I will tell my husband that you forced yourself on me," Esperanza said, interrupting the official. "And it will not matter what rank you hold. Don Murillo will order our vaqueros to hunt you down and kill you in the slow way, the Apache way. Mark my words. Let this matter be quiet or your soldiers will not be able to save you."

Bradburn balked at her threat. He spit out a mouthful of brown silt and wiped the moisture from his face. His gaze shifted from the woman to the man, gauging her determination. At last he nodded and, brushing past both parties, made his way up the embankment, his breath coming in short, heavy rasps as he fled the scene of his embarrassment.

"There goes a man hotter than sixteen yards of hell," Wallace dryly noted. He shook his head.

"Look what you have done," Esperanza scolded him. "Now everything is ruined. I did not need your help. I have handled men like him before."

"It didn't look that way from where I stood."

"Señor Wallace, you are like the wild west wind; you do not think. You just act. You blow here, there, everywhere. Oh, the alcalde behaved boorishly and I am grateful to you. But this is serious. My husband is worried about what will come. San Felipe is our home now. Our roots are here. I fear your rash conduct will bring us to ruin."

"I only meant to help," William offered. He hadn't expected a scolding. Women were harder to figure than a Chinese box.

"You can't help it. You are a man of many names

and titles. Some days you are a rancher and a farmer; then you are gone from Briarwood and Roberto tells us you are off chasing the sunset. Months pass and we hear of Big Foot Wallace or El Destripedor Rojo, stories of Indian fights or chasing wild horses, grinning a panther out of a tree, which I do not believe for a minute, always building your legend. You have the land grant and the house you built, but I think you are as much a visitor there as anyone. Tèll me, señor, where *is* your home?"

"Texas," William said. "I have always liked the sound of the word. Texas is my home."

"But no man can claim it all."

"Wanna bet?"

"Be serious."

"The minute I crossed the Rio Grande I knew where I belonged. I was whole again. Look at the Brazos; what do you see?" He drew close to her and grabbed her by her shoulders and turned her toward the flowing water.

"A river," Esperanza meekly replied, taken back by his intensity.

"I see my life's blood."

William glanced up toward the trail. The alcalde was out of sight, but he could hear the man crashing through the underbrush. The big man glanced around at the river, the swaying branches of the black willow, kicked a rock into the current, shrugged, and did everything he could to avoid Esperanza's eyes.

"I reckon there's not much point in asking Mr. Bradburn about that shipment of mine he's holding in Anahuac," Wallace muttered. "If you'll permit, I shall escort you back to the cantina."

Esperanza studied him a moment, displeasure slowly melting, giving way to the affection she felt for this redheaded wonder. Gradually a smile brightened her face.

"Ah well, my benefactor . . . *mi amigo* . . . what am I to do with you?" she asked.

"Walk with me, señora. Just walk with me," he said.

And Esperanza held out her hand.

14

"AND I DON'T PLAY GAMES."

"She dances by the light of the desert moon;
she sings her songs where wild roses bloom.
Sad songs on the lovely wind remind me of Corrinna.
O Corrinna mi se levanté de la noche, canta para mi."

Chuy Montoya had a pleasing voice, made slightly
coarse from too much drink and too little sleep. But he
played the guitar passably well, and on this soft summer's night the ballad seemed to fill the night with memories of love lost or unattainable. William Wallace
relaxed and let the conversation wane allowing himself
a moment of the heartache he had learned to live with.

Fire consumed the last of the timber. Dying flames
lapped at the night air. Coals cracked open, and miniature explosions sent a column of fiery embers coruscating from the pit to the starlit sky. A small group of hardy
souls remained to appreciate the beauty. Most of the
crowd dispersed soon after Bradburn gathered his escort
and rode out of town with nothing more than a curt
farewell to the local dignitaries.

But the troublemakers are here, Wallace noted, somewhat bemused by the recent turn of events. One thing
was certain: he had forged no friendship with the alcalde
this day. Wallace eased back against the ladder-back

chair and stretched his long legs out before him as he contemplated the remaining Texicans and listened to the melancholy lyrics of the lone guitarist seranading the dancing embers.

"O Corrinna mi se levanté de la noche, canta para mi. O Corrinna, my rose of the night, sing for me."

Chuy's calloused fingers flew across the strings. There were moments when he fumbled a fret, but not many. And when it came time for a rousing "Ai-ai-ai-yi," Wallace and Jesus Zavala were only too happy to chime in, leaving the *segundo* to grin and nod with satisfaction. Mournful love ballads were a communal experience.

Wallace studied the colonists and adventurers circling the fire. He felt at home in the company of men such as these. Sam Houston carried himself like a man running for office; his voice had a stentorian ring. But the ex-congressman from Tennessee and the rakish barrister, Bill Travis, both seemed like men who could be counted on if push came to shove.

Zavala, the blacksmith, raised a jug of home brew in salute to Wallace. Here was a man with a deep sense of loyalty. The day Wallace rode in to San Felipe with the children he had rescued from the Comanche had forged a lifelong friendship. Neither Jesus nor his wife would ever forget. The blacksmith might be a simple man who lacked a proper education, but he had no use for corrupt officials and nothing but contempt for the likes of John Bradburn and the government that had appointed him.

Wallace shifted his gaze to another unlikely pair of insurrectionists. Even the usually conservative owners of Kania's Mercantile, Kenneth Albert Kania and his son, Robert, had begun to advocate the colonists' taking matters into their own hands. The hardship of dusting the empty shelves of their mercantile while their trade goods languished in Anahuac waiting for them to bribe Bradburn had transformed these two unassuming clerks into firebrands. Like many of the colonists, their politics were formed from personal experience.

Don Murillo, seated to Wallace's right, produced a bottle of Madeira from a cloth bag he'd brought with him to the cantina.

"Mon ami," said Mad Jack, "you have been holding out on us."

Don Murillo poured a measure for himself and then passed the bottle around to his companions. "I was going to use this to bribe the alcalde. But Señor Bradburn left in such a bad temper I never got the chance." The *haciendado* had sent Esperanza back to the hotel while he remained at the Flying Jib to support Stephen Austin, who had continued to defend his decision to return to Mexico City. Although Don Murillo echoed Austin's sentiments, diplomacy was needed now more than ever. It seemed even Señor Saldevar lacked the conviction of his beliefs. "Bradburn's conduct was most peculiar," Don Murillo added, with a glance in Wallace's direction. "To come all this way and leave so abruptly."

"Yes, it was most peculiar," Travis added, helping himself to the wine, his darkly handsome features keen with interest. "I guess the alcalde has never fallen into a river before." He looked around at the other men, then offered the bottle to Austin.

Stephen Austin, feeling more isolated then ever, declined to drink with a wave of his hand. "Bradburn was a poor choice for magistrate. I cannot fathom why he was appointed to the post."

"Perhaps because he was such a poor choice," Houston replied, not one to pass up drink.

"Santa Anna is trying to back us into a corner, where

we have no choice but to resist," Travis added.

"It really isn't fair," Kenneth Kania said. "My son and his family, all of us, have settled this land. We have built something here."

"Pa's right," Robert interjected. He was a large man, heavyset, a fair-haired individual with a mind for facts and figures. "But where do we go from here? Do we bring our protests to General Cos in San Antonio or trust in Mr. Austin's audience with Santa Anna? How do we proceed? Do we dare force the matter in Anahuac? What would be the consequences?"

"Clever people and shopkeepers," Wallace said with a grin, "you weigh everything." The big man turned to Austin, who was preparing to retire for the night. "You have no business putting yourself within Santa Anna's reach, old friend."

"I will do what has to be done. I can catch a ship out of Anahuac and be back no later than August." Austin stood, shook hands with Don Murillo, then stared at Wallace. "I want you to promise me you'll wait until I return before deciding on a course of action."

"Bradburn might not let us."

"Keep away from Bradburn. Santa Anna is no fool. I can make him listen to reason. Promise me there will be no trouble between you and the alcalde until I return." His gaze swept over Houston and Travis, the Kanias, and Zavala, the blacksmith, before settling on William Big Foot Wallace. The brawny frontiersman was the key; folk had a way of following his lead. He could be the catalyst for war or peace. "I'll have your word on it."

Wallace scowled and tried to look away, then grudgingly came around. "So be it. Bradburn will get no trouble from Big Foot Wallace."

Austin nodded, satisfied. "You'll see I'm right. All of you." He glanced in the direction of the lingering flames.

Shadows mottled his features, contorted his expression, gave him the appearance of a man in torment. Then he left the circle of light and walked off into the darkness.

Don Murillo found Esperanza awake, seated in a chair by the window, reading by the light of an oil lamp. The room was upstairs, on the northwest corner of the building overlooking a back street and a grove of pine trees that blocked a view of the river. A gentle breeze made the hotel room bearable. The *haciendado* closed the door to the hall and crossed the room, shrugged off his coat, and, with a sigh, stretched himself out onto the bed.

"Even the best room at the Whiteside Hotel is no better than our servants' quarters. Forgive me, my dear."

"I am no stranger to servants' quarters," Esperanza replied. The room was sparsely furnished with a hand-hewn dresser and a smaller table with a washbasin and pitcher. The chair she was seated in was solid but unadorned; like the bed, it was serviceable and comfortable enough.

"But you are not a servant," Don Murillo replied, a note of chill in his voice. Any reference to her past offended him, even more so when it came from her. "You are my wife."

"Yes. I only meant—"

"I know what you meant. For the past five years I have known what everyone meant," the man snapped. He rubbed his eyes and sighed. "I am sorry. These old bones are tired, and I fear I have had too much to drink. You are such a good girl. You brought life to a heart wrapped in mourning. But, my child, these are troubled times. This is man's work. Do not concern yourself."

Esperanza bit her lower lip to keep from speaking the first reply that came to mind. She calmed herself, breathed deep, considered her response, then spoke. "Texas is my home, is it not?"

"Of course, my dear. Now lie here beside me. Sleep, *pobrecita*. Rest your pretty head." Don Murillo yawned, then laughed softly. "But first help me with my boots, eh? Por favor."

Esperanza rounded the bed and with a tug and a pull managed to free her husband's feet from his boots of Spanish leather. Her husband held out his hand, and she crossed to his side and placed his hand in hers.

"Chuy had nodded off. So our friend Señor Wallace walked with me from the cantina," he said. "William was worried for me, making my way across town at night. He says I drank too much. Maybe I did. But when we were alone I asked him and still he would not tell me. What happened with the alcalde?"

"Nothing."

"I watched you leave with Señor Bradburn. I should not have let you go. I have never liked the alcalde. But he must be tolerated. And humored. Your charm has a way of bringing out the best in such men." The *hacendado* searched his wife's expression. "And maybe the worst."

"Nothing happened," Esperanza said. To confess Bradburn's inappropriate behavior could place her husband in danger. She was loath to instigate a feud between Don Murillo and the authorities. Her husband had enough enemies in Mexico City what with his support of the colonists.

"I think this is the only time you have lied to me," her husband remarked, caressing her hand. "You walk to the river with Bradburn; he returns soaked to the skin and in a foul mood. Shortly after, you appear, but this time in the company of William Wallace. I think maybe the alcalde had help falling into the river." Don Murillo closed his eyes. His breathing grew even, steady, smoothing his way into uneventful sleep.

Esperanza placed her husband's hand under the sheet.

She stepped around the bed, glanced at the open window. Something drew her across the room to brush aside
the curtains and glance down toward the rear of the hotel.

Against the velvet shadows of night stood William
Wallace, etched by moonlight, white scarf streaming in
the wind. The tall, rangy Texican removed his sombrero
and bowed, placing the broad-brimmed hat upon his
chest. Esperanza smiled and, hesitating, waved, then
pulled the curtains closed. She shed her dressing gown
and climbed into bed alongside her husband.

Don Murillo stirred, rolled on his side, his arm draped
possessively across the woman's bosom. Esperanza grew
still. Don Murillo was a good man who had treated her
with nothing but kindness. If he woke and wanted her,
he would find her willing and affectionate. Because she
loved her husband.

She did love him.

She loved him.

Better to stare at the ceiling and try to sleep and force
herself not to think forbidden thoughts of how it might
be, of how it should never be.

Her husband stirred. His hand sought hers in the
night, and she clung to him for fear of what might happen if she let go.

Lucky stirred and glanced up at Wallace as he approached the front door of the cantina. The dog, refusing
to budge, wagged his tail and then tried to get comfortable. William glared at the hound. "Move, you lazy sack
of bones. You aren't the only one who's tired around
here."

The dog held his ground. William nudged the animal
with the toe of his boot. Another man would have lost
his foot up to the ankle. In this case, Lucky seemed to

issue a long-suffering groan and dragged himself out of the doorway, permitting Wallace to enter.

Mad Jack had the place to himself. Hanneke had already retired for the night, leaving the old sea dog to sit in his rocker by the cold hearth and have a last cup of coffee appropriately laced with dark rum from the Frenchman's private stock. He held a cup out to Wallace, who sat in an identical rocker across from his friend.

"You, too, have been holding out." Wallace took a sip and eased himself against the ladder-back frame. He glanced around, checking the room for Jim Bowie.

"He's out in the barn, sleeping it off."

"Nice of you to be hospitable."

"A man like that, I want to know where he is at night. Especially if he's on the prod."

"I've heard of him, never met him. But it seems like there is bad blood between us all the same." Wallace shook his head. Some men were hard to figure.

"It has nothing to do with you, *mon ami*," Flambeau said. "I heard from Chuy there's been a smallpox epidemic down south, below Veracruz. Bowie sent his wife and children to Guadalajara for safekeeping. He thought the mountains would be safe. The fever spread and they died. He blames himself, been drinking and fighting ever since. Maybe he sees calling you out as a way to escape what's eating at him."

"Damn." Wallace shook his head, rubbed his eyes for a moment. Sweat trickled down the side of his cheek. He wanted no part of a man like that. But he understood the man. After all, William Wallace was no stranger to ghosts and self-recrimination.

"Think you can talk sense into Austin?"

Wallace softly laughed. "Are you kidding me? Stephen's determined to try his luck with Santa Anna. *El presidente*'s a 'one-eyed jack,' but I've seen the other side of his face." Wallace drained the contents of his cup, set it aside, and leaned forward, elbows on his knees as he hunched over and stared into the soot-blackened fireplace.

"Too bad about our supplies. That blasted alcalde's got us by the *cojones*. He can claim our goods for taxes and sell them back to us."

"Not likely," Wallace replied, his quiet voice seeming to fill the empty room.

"Nothing you can do, lad. You went and gave your word there would be no trouble between Bradburn and you."

"But I didn't say anything about Comanche," Wallace said.

Mad Jack studied him, brows knotted as the sea dog struggled to understand the workings of the big man's mind. Wallace knelt by the hearth, spit in the ashes, rubbed his fingers in the soot, and streaked his features with black war paint. His green eyes twinkled and a grin wide as a quarter-moon split his features.

"Oh!" Mad Jack exclaimed.

Bowie was snoring loud enough to wake the dead. The knife fighter was easy to locate in the dark confines of the stable; one only had to follow the sound of the rumbling steam engine that passed for breathing. Wallace lingered near the front door and allowed his eyes to adjust to the darkness, then moved with caution down the center aisle. Bowie might be a light sleeper. On the other hand, Mad Jack's home brew had a way of deadening a man's senses. Indeed, Bowie had drunk enough Slaughter of the Innocents to warrant sleeping with the angels.

Wallace stole down the center aisle and passed close to the hammerhead gray he had raised from a colt. The gray caught his scent and whinnied, shook his head, and stretched his nose beyond the gate. William reassured the stallion with a pat on the muzzle signaling all was well. He was relieved to find Jim Bowie sprawled on his saddle blankets in an empty stall, deep asleep on a bed of hay. Wallace dropped a hand to his side, slid Bone-chucker from its scabbard. Steel whispered on leather as the blade slipped free.

Bowie mumbled something, engaged some unseen foe in a dreamlike conversation. He frowned and called out again. His arm flung out and clutched a handful of straw. Then the turmoil subsided. Wallace knelt along-side the sleeping man and placed the cold steel blade against the sleeping man's throat.

Bowie came awake with a start, eyes wide; realization struck a few seconds later—any false move would find him slit from ear to ear. He gulped. The reaction of his Adam's apple forced his flesh against the razor-sharp steel blade and drew a thin trickle of blood.

Wallace leaned in close. "I am Wallace. I am the Wild West Wind, the Prince of Daggers, El Destripedor Rojo. I am the Red Ripper. And I don't play games."

"Sure you do," Bowie managed to croak without so much as even batting an eyelash. "Else I'd be knocking at St. Peter's Door right now."

Twirling his knife, Wallace caught the weapon by the hilt and stabbed downward. Bowie gasped as the blade sank to the hilt in the dirt floor, missing his ear by a fraction of an inch. Wallace tugged the weapon free, cleaned the blade on his sleeve, and returned the weapon to its buckskin sheath. William cursed softly, stood, and started back down the aisle.

"I know one thing about you, William Wallace," Bowie said. He managed to stand despite his wobbly legs. "You sure as hell know how to sober a man up." He stretched forth his hand in friendship. Wallace re-turned to claim it. "Reckon I let the tequila get the better of me."

"You wouldn't be the first," William said. He stepped back. "Or the last."

"Some mornings I wake up and can't even tell where I am."

"This is Texas," Wallace said. Storm clouds were brewing on the horizon, and sooner or later they were all going to get wet. "If a man wants to get himself killed, he's come to the right place."

"And if a man wants to live . . . ?" Bowie's voice drifted out of the darkness.

Wallace softly laughed. A breeze pushed against the door and stirred the straw underfoot. He hooked a thumb in his belt and took a deep breath of the night wind; it smelled of men and horses, of fires and the good land and dreams of empire. "*He's* come to the right place, too."

15

"A LITTLE SLAUGHTER OF THE INNOCENTS IS JUST WHAT THOSE BOYS NEED."

In the dark of a soft summer's night, the horsemen came riding by the light of a Comanche moon, with a drum of hooves and a rattle of wagons, wheels churning the rutted, weathered surface of the coast road, grassland and seashore beckoning as they broke from a memory of trees and hurtled down past the bayous and lowlands. Blackgrass muffled their approach, and no one in Anahuac was the wiser.

Wallace ordered a halt with the scent of sea salt heavy in the air and the moon-dappled waters of the Gulf of Mexico stretching out beyond the collection of cabins and barracks, warehouses, piers, and waterfront taverns that made up the settlement. He was stripped to the waist, his features streaked with war paint, red hair streaming in the wind. His naked torso glistened like rain-soaked granite in the moonlight.

Jim Bowie reined in alongside him and, next to Bowie, William's own *segundo,* young Roberto Zavala, breathless with excitement. Sam Houston led a second column of Texicans, all of them dressed in buckskin leggings and breechclouts, each man's identity hidden beneath a hastily smeared mask of tar black or concoctions of white and red clay.

A scrawl of clouds drifted across the face of the moon like black blood. These men shared a common bond. No innocents here; they knew what brought them. A week had passed since Stephen Austin had departed for Mexico City, a week in which John Bradburn had proved intractable, a man unwilling to compromise.

A turncoat like Bradburn smelled ill-gotten profits. The scent of money was up, and the alcalde was after his share like a hound after a hare. But tonight William Wallace and his companions intended to set the matter aright. Thirty-two men with seven empty freight wagons had followed Wallace out of San Felipe. They took their time, intending to arrive at Anahuac under cover of darkness. Astride their restless mounts they gathered in a circle to finalize their plans.

"Senator," Wallace said, addressing Houston, "I'll give you and the boys a head start. There's the corral yonder by the barracks. When I signal, drive the horses back up this road. If Bradburn wants his dragoons to follow us, he'll have to send them on foot."

Houston chaffed at being ordered about; after all, he was a good deal older, nearly two decades. The man had tasted the governorship and found it difficult to play a subordinate part in the drama about to unfold. However, this was Wallace's party. The Tennessean was confident his time would come later.

"Looks to be two dozen, maybe thirty horses," Roberto said, peering through a spyglass. "Me and Chuy and Señor Houston can handle them easy."

"Good lad," Wallace said, clapping him on the shoulder. "Just be sure you keep out of some dragoon's gunsight."

"I'll ride low and hard, like always."

Wallace's mongrel hound came slouching out of the shadows and snapped at the horses closest to him. A mare shied and forced Bill Travis to struggle to keep the animal under control.

"Don't lose those reins, Señor Travis," Chuy Montoya spoke up. He reached down and caught the skittish animal by the bit and steadied the mount. "This mare will run on you, mark my words." Montoya took his quirt and slapped the dog across the rump. The corded leather stung like a scorpion, and the dog yelped and darted out of harm's way.

"I thought Señor Murillo said the beast was saddle-broke," the lawyer grumbled. Travis had bought the mare from a string of mounts Don Murillo had brought into town. The wretched animal had been fighting him for two days solid. He was saddle-sore and his back ached like blue blazes.

"She's not quite lawyer-broke is all," Montoya chuckled. "This here mare will sit a saddle all day long once you let her know who's boss."

A ripple of nervous laughter made its way around the circle. Wallace stilled them with his raised hand. "Jim, you know what to do?"

Bowie looked like he needed drink. He licked the inside of his mouth; the flesh felt dry and prickly. He wiped a forearm across his eyes and lips and nodded. Several of the men carried ax handles and makeshift clubs. "Me and the lads will handle the guards. And there'll be no gunplay. I doubt we'll have any trouble. I've been watching that patrol and seen them passing around a jug of 'who hit John.' "

"Maybe we could save ourselves some trouble and just spike their liquor with a drop or two of Mad Jack's home brew. A little Slaughter of the Innocents is just what those boys need," said another of the Texicans.

Again the laughter, easier now, more confident. Wallace knew it was time. He broke from the circle and walked the gray up alongside one of the wagons.

"Well, Mr. Kania, are you ready to receive shipment of your goods?"

Kenneth, the elder, glanced over at his son perched

on the bench seat of an adjacent flatbed freight hauler. Robert Kania was focused, though obviously nervous. His gaze never left the barracks and warehouse. No two men ever looked less like Comanche than the two Poles with their pale blond hair unkempt and their faces streaked with crimson and white clay. Only their courage and commitment gave them dignity.

"My boy and I won't let you down."

"Movement at the warehouse, Big Foot," Jesus Zavala softly warned. The swarthy blacksmith kept his voice low. The men turned to watch as a pair of sentries rounded the corner of a long pitched-roof stone building where the alcalde kept the shipments under lock and key.

The soldiers were engrossed in conversation. One of them paused to gesture toward the trio of schooners riding easy at their moorings. Moonshadows played along the masts and spars jutting skyward from the maindecks. Music and the noise of revelry drifted on the night breezes blowing in from the gulf. Fortunately for the raiders, Bradburn's warehouse had been built apart from the central waterfront and placed under the watchful scrutiny of the soldiers in the barracks.

With any luck we won't even alert the troops until it's too late, Wallace thought. He shifted his own spyglass and studied streets, which for the most part were empty, then scrutinized the rambling stone house set on a narrow strip of land stretching out into the bay. The alcalde had chosen to reside in a place apart from the settlement proper, perhaps for the view of the restless sea; then again, maybe he did not trust the denizens of the port. William counted four sentries tending a campfire that blocked the approach to Bradburn's headquarters. No one was going to reach the alcalde without first identifying himself to the armed guard.

Wallace glanced around at the men who followed him, men who were inspired by his zeal and bristled with excitement because of where they were and what they were about to do. They were waiting for a word, a statement, a catalyst to send them on their way. He kept it brief.

"Well, boys, reckon it's time to root hog or die a poor pig."

Jose Oñatè complained about the lateness of the hour and bemoaned the fact that he would have never been assigned to the warehouse guard detail if the *alcalde* hadn't coveted Oñatè's girlfriend, the lovely Consuelo Rodrigo. Oñatè rounded the corner of the warehouse and paused to lean on his musket and glare jealously at the house out by the bay, secluded on its narrow peninsula, protected by men he knew. He watched and waited in the darkness, sweat stealing along his neck and soaking the stiff collar of his uniform of dark blue wool trimmed with brass buttons and held snug to his belly by a wide leather belt from which hung a pouch of paper cartridges for his rifled musket.

Oñatè kicked at the dirt underfoot and amused himself by plotting a variety of fates, all of them involving a painful demise for Bradburn. He tried not to picture Consuelo on her back, plump derriere glistening and moist, her legs kicking at the ceiling while the alcalde pumped his seed into her.

"What is it, young one?" a second guard asked, approaching along the path Oñatè had worn into the earth on his rounds. Pablo Gomez was a chunky dark-skinned man with close-set eyes and a prominent nose protruding from his flat face. The blood of Aztec princes flowed in his veins. But he was unaware of his lineage; generations of poverty had erased any latent tribal memory. Now he was a soldier. The military was the only world he knew. Life was reduced to a simple equation of food and drink and obeying his commander's orders. He didn't care who his officers were as long as they didn't try to get him killed with any regularity.

Anahuac was excellent duty. Nothing happened in this remote corner of Texas. A soldier could spend the entire day escaping work and enjoying the simple pleasures of the waterfront cantinas where the women were always willing but rarely beauties. Not that he was a picky man. "Ah, I know; you pine for the lovely Consuela. But she is the alcalde's *puta*. Do not punish yourself, my young stallion; there are other whores in Anahuac."

Gomez's breath reeked of pulque and his stance wavered, forcing the dragoon to prop himself against the outer wall of the warehouse whenever he stopped his forward progress.

"But none like Consuela," Oñatè replied, disdaining the old trooper's company. "She is the fairest flower in the garden."

"Trigo's whorehouse is hardly a garden," the older man chuckled. "And it's the worst place to find true love."

"What would you know of love, *viejo*?" Oñatè snapped. "That fire below your belt burned out years ago."

"There's still an ember or two among the ashes," Pablo said, adjusting his crotch. "All it takes is the right woman to blow on 'em." He cackled aloud at his own wit and continued on his rounds. Oñatè scowled and fell in step alongside the soldier. He tried to think of some clever retort to put Gomez in his place and was about to fall back on impugning the old man's masculinity when he spied an animal slinking toward them through a thicket of mesquite bush nestled against a cluster of outhouses.

"What have we here?" Oñatè muttered.

"Just a dog, wandered up from the shore no doubt,"

Pablo replied. The mongrel left the underbrush and padded toward them, passing through a patch of cold moonlight. Oñatè had the disquieting notion he had seen the animal before. Pablo fumbled in his pocket and found a twist of jerked beef. He gnawed one end until it softened enough for a morsel to break off in his mouth. He placed the remaining few inches in the palm of his hand and offered it to the dog. The animal cautiously approached the soldier, unaccustomed to the kindness of strangers, scarred muzzle to the wind, catching scent of the meat.

"I see you're an ugly old bastard," Gomez chuckled. "Just like me. Only it looks like you came near having your hide burned off some time ago, and that ear looks as chewed as this beef. That back leg of yours looks crippled. Where have you been, amigo? Some hard-luck place, I say."

Oñatè brushed past Gomez. "I have seen this dog before." The animal was indelibly etched in his mind, linked to a towering frontiersman with the eyes of a devil and tall as the mountains, desert mountains where the bones of the ancient ones haunted the arroyos and the dry, lonely washes. Jose Oñatè had confronted El Destripedor Rojo once and lived to brag of the event and embellish his account until it was Wallace who had backed down. But Oñatè knew the truth. He knew the kind of icy fear that crinkled a man's backbone and left him weak-kneed and looking to retreat. He knew danger when he saw it and didn't need a signpost to warn him off.

If the mongrel was here, then what of the Texican? Maybe it was time to send a runner to the barracks and bring over a few extra men. And the alcalde ought to be alerted. Oñatè scowled, conjuring an image of his woman in bed with Bradburn. That was a picture he had no wish to see. The hell with asking Bradburn's permission. Oñatè would take it upon himself to summon more men to the warehouse. Six bleary-eyed sentries hardly seemed enough.

The clatter of wagons caused his heart to jump to his throat. He glanced at Gomez, who shrugged and shook his head. Oñatè heard the creak of axles, the muted commotion of men's voices, and the drum of shod hooves on the packed earth. Before the two men were halfway to the corner of the building, it was obvious a frantic struggle had ensued by the front door. Oñatè heard one of his *compadres* cry out as the scuffle continued. No shots had been fired. Oñatè grabbed Gomez by the shoulder as the older man began to fade back. He shoved Gomez forward and snapped, "*Vamanos!*" The older man nodded, an alarmed expression on his leathery brown features. Gomez stumbled forward, shaking off the effects of the pulque as the adrenaline did its work. The two men unslung their rifled muskets and charged the corner.

The dog bounded out of the darkness and across the path, cutting Oñatè off from his older *compadre*. Dog and man tangled with each other. The dog yelped as the soldier kicked him in the side, his legs tangled with the musket, and Oñatè went sprawling. He bruised his shoulder, cursed, grabbed his musket by the barrel, and tried to crack the animal's skull. Lucky darted in and caught the musket by its shoulder strap. Oñatè found himself in a tug-of-war with the blue heeler when he most needed the weapon.

Gomez's cry for help was cut short. Oñatè tried to wrest his weapon free, but the blue heeler's jaws were locked onto the strap with a viselike grip. The dragoon cursed and surrendered the gun and dragged his saber free. He turned on his boot heels and hurried off to confront the intruders.

In the moonlight he could see a Comanche war party milling about the warehouse. "Madre de Dios!" the dragoon exclaimed. It was a raid! The red savages were raiding the warehouse. Several braves had already subdued the guards while others hammered at the padlock with their axes. Oñatè could make out several uniformed men sprawled on the ground. So much for the guard detail. Jose was left to consider his options. It didn't take long. A suicidal attack was out of the question. His death would serve no purpose and deny Consuela the fruits of his passion. Oñatè chose to alert the rest of the command in the barracks, rousing them from their slumber, and return with reinforcements to drive off the Comanche and proclaim himself the hero of the hour.

With his mind filled with thoughts of glory, Jose Oñatè reversed his course and headed for the barracks but only covered a few yards before finding his escape route blocked by what had to be the largest Comanche ever to ride the warpath. Oñatè gasped and stumbled backward in surprise. Despite the man's garishly painted features, this heathen seemed familiar.

The soldier raised his saber and charged. "I'll cut you down to size!" he shouted.

But William Wallace had other ideas. The Texican darted forward, faded to the right, brought Bonechucker up, and parried the dragoon's sword. The dragoon's saber shattered on impact with the knife blade. Oñatè stared dumbfounded at the remains of his weapon; an inch-long shard of jagged steel jutted from the brass guard. While the dragoon was distracted, Wallace flipped his short sword, caught the blade against the flat of his palm, and, using the brass knob at the base of the grip for a bludgeon, clubbed Oñatè unconscious. The dragoon caught the blow between the eyes, groaned, and rocked back on his heels. His legs buckled and he dropped like a rock, his head bouncing off the hard-packed earth.

Wallace returned the foot-long blade to its sheath,

quietly thanking the Spanish swordsmiths of Toledo who had forged both his knives. The weapons had saved his life on several occasions.

Worried, he glanced in the direction of the dark and silent barracks. Luck was with them. The brief skirmish had failed to arouse the garrison. Good. The colonists had come for their property, not a shooting war. Lightning bugs twinkled on the night air. Mosquitoes were a nuisance. Faint strains from a fiddler drifted up from the waterfront. One could hear the gently rolling sea as it spilled onto the shore, the distant clanging of a ship's bell as a seaman resumed his watch, and, overall, a tranquillity Wallace had no intention of disturbing. Lucky trotted past, tail wagging, dragging the musket behind him in the dirt.

"Careful you don't blow a leg off," Wallace said and, abandoning the hound to his fate, rejoined the Texicans congregated at the front of the warehouse. The remaining dragoons littered the ground, each man knocked senseless. No wound was fatal, but there would be some aching skulls come morning.

Jesus Zavala lost no time in prying the lock from the doors. Soon the way was clear for the colonists to scurry in and begin the process of loading the wagons. No attempt was made to identify the trade goods other than what was rightfully theirs to begin with. Bowie stood back and observed the activity, grinning for the first time in a long time. He looked up as William emerged from the interior of the longhouse with a bundle of iron rods balanced on his shoulder. He had paid to have the pig iron shipped all the way from Pittsburgh. There was no way Wallace was going to allow the alcalde to keep the iron or any of the other goods.

He surveyed the interior of the warehouse, peered past the boxes and barrels, and watched with satisfaction as the colonists took matters into their own hands. Austin would complain. But the alcalde had not given them a choice. By the time Austin returned from Mexico City, Bradburn would have emptied the warehouse and sold the goods in San Antonio or shipped them to Veracruz.

"I never stole anything before," one of the slight-built colonists remarked as he staggered up the center aisle, weighed down by a fifty-pound sack of flour and his own conscience.

"You aren't stealing," Wallace corrected. "You're just delivering a shipment." He winked at Jim Bowie, who stood with his back against the wall.

"You were right," Bowie told the big man as he shouldered a burden that usually would have taken two men to lift. "This is living."

"In that case," Wallace replied, "why don't you try carrying something?"

Robert Kania materialized out of the gloom and dumped a barrel of crackers into Bowie's arms, turned around, and stalked back inside the warehouse without uttering a word. Wallace chuckled and continued on over to the back end of one of the wagons. "You need help with that?" he asked over his shoulder.

Bowie snorted in disgust and made his way to the wagon. By the time he reached the back end, Wallace had already manhandled his load onto the wagon bed. Bowie unceremoniously tossed the barrel on top of the iron rods.

Another colonist maneuvered past them, a keg of spirits bound for the Flying Jib balanced on his left shoulder. The Pennsylvania whiskey merrily sloshed from side to side within its oaken canister, no sweeter music on earth to a thirsty Southerner.

Wallace was on his way back for another load when Bowie caught up to him.

"Your plan's working like a dream, with nary a snag. How long till someone sounds the alert?"

"We'll be loaded up and heading for San Felipe in an hour with any luck, and Bradburn none the wiser," Wallace replied.

"Yes indeed, a fine plan," Bowie reiterated, licking his lips. "But it seems the least you boys could do is let me carry the whiskey kegs."

Wallace had to laugh. Up to now there had been no casualties on either side. The easiest way to change all that and start a war would be to allow Bowie to tie one on. "Now, Jim, I may have been born at night, but it wasn't *last* night."

16

"... THEY HAD THE RIGHT MAN TO LEAD 'EM."

What is this?" Bradburn stood staring at the open doors of the empty warehouse. Dawn rode the rising tides; above the bay, seabirds drifted on the Gulfwind, the first blush of sunlight on the pink horizon melted like icing over the rim of the earth. "Who has done this?"

The alcalde hardly looked the picture of authority with his nightshirt hastily tucked into the waistband of his nankeen trousers, one suspender undone, the remnants of his hair in disarray. He was tired and sore, and walking was an effort on this tense humid morning.

He wheezed with every few steps and felt betrayed by the men under his command. Bradburn glared at the irresponsible soldiers he had posted to secure the warehouse. To a man they were in terrible shape, with bloodied bandaged heads and bruised limbs. Yet no one was going to be sent to the infirmary until a full account was given and the culpable parties punished.

"Comanche," one man said.

"They were on us before we knew it," another added.

"We were outnumbered, Señor Bradburn," old Pablo Gomez spoke up in his own defense. "We did not have a chance."

"But we fought like devils."

"Sí. Even harder than devils."

"No, not hard enough," Bradburn exclaimed. "You're

alive, aren't you? Then you did not put up much of a resistance as far as I am concerned." He paced in front of the battered soldiers propped against the stone wall.

From a distance, several of the townspeople watched with interest. Word of the raid had spread like a brush fire through the settlement. The inhabitants were grateful that the war party had refrained from striking the settlement itself. Bradburn had never attempted to be popular, and now that it appeared the Comanche had thwarted his plans the good people of Anahuac could afford to be amused. The alcalde's ranting and raving at first light provided quite a show.

To Bradburn's left, the remainder of his command arrayed themselves for battle, armed and determined but forced to scour the town for every available horse. Meanwhile the obsequious sentries who had failed to defend the warehouse braced themselves, uncertain whether their companions had arrived to support them or act as a firing squad. Bradburn's thick neck glistened with sweat; his shirt already clung to his chest and armpits; tiny veins formed along his cheekbones and seemed about to burst beneath the skin. Public humiliation made him dangerous and brought out the worst in him.

A few hours ago he had been asleep, nestled against the warm backside of his latest paramour, secure in his authority and confident of the handsome profit he would turn once he sold the supplies he had confiscated for taxes. In a single evening, everything had come crashing down. Someone was going to pay for this outrage.

"Comanches with wagons?" the alcalde growled. The notion seemed incredible. It was curious that only the goods bound for San Felipe were taken. But the raiders may have run out of time and simply refrained from looting the rest of the settlement. And they did steal the horses. Comanche always took the horses. "Maybe" he added. "But why did they let you idiots live? The quality of mercy does not beat in that savage breast."

Bradburn ceased his pacing and stared at the bleak expressions of the men arranged before him. They were a sorry lot. This was General Cos's fault for not sending him a full contingent of soldiers. Bradburn had proved his mettle over the months and deserved better treatment. Hadn't he diligently collected taxes, confiscated trade goods when necessary, and kept General Santa Anna informed as to the political climate in the colonies? Now when it came time to feather his own nest, a bunch of howling savages had spoiled everything, making off with the entire lot. It wasn't fair.

The alcalde was about to restate his displeasure when the orderly column of dragoons behind him parted. Bradburn sensed the motion and glanced over his shoulder as Jose Oñatè stumbled through their ranks and, seemingly oblivious to one and all, continued on to the front of the warehouse.

Moments earlier, Oñatè had regained his senses and found himself lying flat on his backside in a thicket of beach heather; crushed yellow blossoms and a dusting of sand clung to his uniform. The soldier's head throbbed, his nose was broken, but despite the pain, Oñatè had a deeper appreciation of life, having come so close to losing his own. It took him a while to find his legs, but when he did manage to rise, like Lazarus, he knew of only one direction to go, and that was toward his uniformed companions. Oñatè's throat was too dry for him to manage more than a croak.

After stumbling past the column from the barracks, the injured guard headed straight for the olla hanging to one side of the entrance. He gulped a dipper full of water, spilling the liquid down the front of his disheveled uniform, and when he had cut the grit from his throat the soldier stumbled forward to take his place among the battered guards. He was prepared to confront the alcalde.

"Comanche, hell," Oñatè managed to say, barely loud enough for Bradburn to hear. "It was those damn Texicans from San Felipe." He wiped a forearm across his mouth, smearing his coat sleeve with spittle and blood.

"You're wrong," Bradburn protested. "That bunch wouldn't dare."

"They would if they had the right man to lead 'em." Oñatè was a mess, no longer handsome, his princely features a memory now. There was caked blood from his broken nose to his shattered cheekbone, and he had a swollen right eye. The soldier looked as if he had tangled with a panther. "And I recognized him." He coughed up some mucus and spit out a mouthful of saliva and blood. "I won't forget him any time soon."

"Who?" Bradburn frowned in anticipation.

"Wallace!" Oñatè shouted the name in a great rasping bellow for all to hear, as if to say, "Look at my face, the wounds, the red wounds." "Big Foot Wallace!" He stared down at his hands, which came away from the wreckage of his face all sticky and crimson, and didn't need to add the name everyone was thinking: El Destripedor Rojo.

The raiding party had made good time from Anahuac, covering the distance in under two days, a feat that was accomplished by switching teams of horses on the wagons, keeping the animals fresh and strong throughout the long hours. William Wallace and the column of Texicans, whooping and hollering like the savages they had pretended to be, reached San Felipe during the middle of the night. Their arrival did not go unnoticed. Indeed, the men were watched for and the populace ventured into the streets so that anxious wives and neighbors could see if there were any casualties in their ranks.

A collective sigh of relief went up from the crowd as word spread that everyone had returned safe and well

and with the much-needed supplies. Some of the colonists, most of whom were staunch defenders of Stephen
Austin, began to immediately express concern about re-
taliation. Wallace was joined by his companions: Houston, Travis, Jesus Zavala, Chuy Montoya, and the rest,
who flatly rejected the notion. Houston declared such
fears to be groundless and went on to say that free men
should not have to live in fear. William had to admit it
was the prettiest speech he had heard all day. He agreed
with Houston, Travis, and the rest of the "rabble-
rousers." After all, the dragoons only had a brief glimpse
of the disguised colonists by moonlight. What could the
soldiers do? Whom could they identify?

"San Felipe is alive again, thanks to you," Mad Jack
said, saluting his friend's health with a glass of whiskey
from a freshly tapped keg. The two friends sat across
from each other at a table back near the kitchen. The
Frenchman's storehouse was loaded with barrels of rum
and kegs of whiskey. The freebooter sloshed the contents
around in his glass and then swallowed it down and
beamed as the heat spread from his gullet to his gut and
limbs. "Not bad. I can taste the keg, but not bad. Tame
but worth a sip. Still, it isn't Slaughter of the Innocents—"

"But what is?" William interjected, a grin lighting his
features.

"*Mon ami.* You're beginning to worry me," Flambeau
said.

Hanneke had prepared a hearty breakfast of ham,
eggs, biscuits, and gravy, as this was William's last
chance for a decent meal until the next time he rode
back in from Briarwood. Because of the morning hours,
the Flying Jib was devoid of customers, the front door
closed while the owners supposedly rested. But within
the confines of the place Hanneke was singing to herself;
her lilting voice drifted in from the kitchen where she

was kneading bread with her strong hands and frying up a second helping of ham for her two hungry men. Who could sleep? Not now; there was too much excitement to rest. The woman enjoyed playing hostess to William and tended to mother him whenever he stayed at the tavern.

"Don't worry. I'll leave you a couple of eggs." Wallace took an entire ham steak for himself, dropped it onto his plate, broke three biscuits, and covered them with pan gravy. His green eyes radiated merriment.

"Well, aren't you the 'cock o' the walk'? But I must warn you. Do not underestimate Bradburn," Flambeau remarked, eyeing the food on Wallace's plate. The old sea dog had a prodigious appetite. Wallace was toying with him, trying to aggravate him, to provoke his indignation, then have a good laugh at the Frenchman's expense. Mad Jack was wise to the game, after all, he had taught it to William. So the Frenchman sat back and watched William wolf down the meal and pretended not to care.

Mad Jack stroked his chin, began fidgeting with the ring in his gnarled lump of an ear. In the corner near the kitchen door, the blue heeler happily gnawed a ham hock Hanneke had left for the animal. "Hrrumph," Mad Jack complained. "Seems like even the mongrels around here eat better than the master of the house."

Hanneke appeared with another platter of biscuits, fried eggs, another fried ham steak, and a ladle for the gravy bowl. "Mind your tongue, Husband, or I'll add it to the stew." She removed his whiskey glass and replaced it with an earthenware mug of coffee. "You've had your taste; now save the rest for your customers." She ambled back into the kitchen, her full, round bosom jostling with every step. Mad Jack reached out and smacked her ample bottom. The woman giggled and disappeared through the doorway. "You old goat, don't think to start something you won't have time to finish."

"Now where was I?" Mad Jack chuckled, then grew serious. He could concentrate now that he had had some food. "Oh, yes, heed my words about John Bradburn."

"That sack of guts doesn't have the will or the men to cause us trouble. I think we taught him a lesson."

Mad Jack shook his head in despair. The lad was beginning to believe in his own invulnerability. Wallace had conceived the raid and led the men to Anahuac and back again, returning with the merchandise and trade goods that were the mainstay of a thriving community. To be sure, others had ridden with him, stalwart comrades at arms like Jim Bowie, Sam Houston, Chuy Montoya, Jesus Zavala, and Bill Travis.

But William Wallace had been the catalyst. The Texicans followed him. An event like the raid would only add to his growing legend. And that's what had Mad Jack concerned. A man could get killed trying to live up to someone else's expectations.

"Just the same, watch your back," the Frenchman warned. He leaned upon the table and stabbed a fork into a ham steak and dropped it onto his plate.

"You've become an old mother hen," Wallace laughed, patting the freebooter on his bald head. "I am not afraid of John Bradburn."

"Well then, do me a favor, young blade."

"Name it."

Mad Jack Flambeau leaned forward, his expression deadly serious. "Be afraid of someone."

17

"...LIBERTY AND FREEDOM... OF WHAT USE ARE SUCH NOTIONS TO THE PEONS?"

General Cos didn't need any more bad news. He damn near had an insurrection on his hands as it was. The populace of San Antonio continued to think of his troops as an occupying force, placed in the town to suppress their freedoms. Santa Anna expected the general to govern with a firm hand, and to that end he had outlawed political dissent; anyone expressing dissatisfaction with President Santa Anna was subject to arrest.

Meanwhile the garrison had to be supported, and that meant sacrifice on the part of the townspeople and the local *haciendados*. These Texicans were nothing but rabble-rousers who avoided paying their taxes whenever possible—miscreants, all of them ungrateful to a fault.

The general glared at his visitor, John Bradburn, the alcalde, who had abandoned Anahuac. "Haven't my troops driven off the Comanche and Kiowa?" Bradburn remained silent, allowing the general to vent his anger before confronting the man. "That I choose not to extend the patrols is my business. At least the town itself is safe from depredations. If only Indians were the worst of my problems."

Trouble was brewing in the backstreets, behind barred doors, in the shadows of night. Their resentment clouded the air, thick as smoke from a signal fire. Cos understood the warning. A shouted insult from the safety of a darkened alley or shuttered window might soon become a hurled dagger or brandished club. Unless he received reinforcements, it was only a matter of time before the Texicans began to openly defy him. All they needed was a catalyst, a spark of civil disobedience, to ignite the fuse of rebellion.

And here was John Bradburn. The foolish Englishman had allowed an act of sedition to go unpunished and placed them all at risk.

"Now you bring me news this *norte americano*, Big Foot Wallace, and a mob of Texicans, none of whom you can identify, have emptied your warehouse, stolen property belonging to . . . me!" Bradburn cringed before the smaller man.

Cos paced his office like a strutting rooster, a self-righteous little officer who had achieved his governorship by virtue of a distant kinship with the president. Cos had the authority to have Bradburn imprisoned or even hung for his recent failure. So the former alcalde stood contrite, with head bowed, and accepted the tongue-lashing without uttering a word in his own defense.

What was the use? Cos was beyond reasoning with, perhaps because he shared the same fears. His command was fragile at best. Bradburn knew the governor's entreaties for reinforcements had not been answered. Perhaps it was time to cut bait and run to fight another day. Things were getting out of hand. It might take Santa Anna himself to set things aright.

"These Texicans are growing bolder by the day. And the *norte americanos* are the worst. They poison the minds of our own people with words like *liberty* and *freedom* . . . of what use are such notions to the peons?" Cos said, sweat spilling down his cheeks like tears. The interior of his headquarters in the Alamo Mission was becoming unbearable, in part due to his exertions. Rivulets trickled down along the side of his neck; moisture glistened in the silver thickness of his sideburns. Despite the heat and his own discomfort, he remained in full uniform, determined to maintain his appearance. A governor must always look and act the part.

Behind him on the wall was a map of Coahuila y Texas that had been hand-drawn and copied by the good Franciscan friars who had crisscrossed the area on foot, baptizing the local mestizos and seeing to their needs, spreading out from San Antonio like the spokes of a wheel from the hub. Below the map he kept an assortment of books—lives of the saints, writings in English, French, and Spanish, tomes he would never read.

"Give me a hundred men and I will return to San Felipe and close down every cantina and store," Bradburn interjected, sucking in his belly and hitching up his pants.

"A hundred men? With another hundred horses, no doubt? I cannot afford to lose a hundred horses. And besides, I dare not weaken my own command. I am already outnumbered." Cos brushed past Bradburn and walked to the door of his headquarters, a room that had once housed a priest, before the mission had been abandoned and occupied by Cos and his troops. The sentries outside the door snapped to attention as Cos emerged into the sunlight. Heat waves danced in the courtyard. Other sentries paced the outer walls, heads bowed, muskets held in the crooks of their arms.

Why was he discussing his problems with Bradburn? Granted the alcalde's mother had been Mexican and Santa Anna found some use in a man who could pass for one of the *norte americanos*, but Cos did not trust him. The man had no sense of honor. He was an adventurer who would no doubt sell all of them out if given the chance to realize a profit.

Cos proceeded to march across the yard, through the

dust and the glare and the strength-sapping heat. He could feel the soldiers watching him, the pitiful column Bradburn had brought down from Anahuac and his own men, those who weren't out on patrol or drunk in the bordellos. He continued on to the entrance of the mission. The gates opened as he approached. He stood beneath the north wall, his imagination fueling his fears with images of fire and plunder, armed mobs of Texicans sweeping through the streets and surging toward the Alamo, wave after wave of crazed rebels, crashing against these crumbling battlements and engulfing all of Texas in fire and blood.

Even as the general experienced his premonition, several horsemen materialized in the distance. It was an unruly collection of individuals, coming on at an easy gait, confident, unhurried. Forty men, maybe a few more. Were they buffalo hunters? Perhaps they were just passing through on their way west. On the other hand, these strangers might have come to start trouble. It wouldn't be the first time.

The general studied the men as they drew closer. The drum of their horses' hooves sounded like a cavalry charge. The ground shook beneath his feet. The horsemen cut across the brush country and intersected the mission road, passing close enough for Cos to make out a few phrases of their banter. The men were obviously in high spirits and anxious to enjoy the pleasures of the town. He overheard a few names called out as the Texicans swept beneath the shadow of the north wall and guided their well-lathered mounts onto the San Antonio Road. They pointed the animals toward the town.

Cos eyed them with suspicion. More recruits for the coming insurrection. Suspect everyone; be surprised by no one. "If *el presidente* wants Texas held, he will have to do it himself. I do not intend to leave my bones in this damn place," he muttered. No valiant, hopeless struggle to the death for him.

Cos promised himself, then and there, at the first sign of trouble he would lead his command south. Maybe that would get the attention of the government in Mexico City. Something had to. When it came to Texas, Santa Anna and his officials were blind. But General Cos intended to make them see.

18

"... A HARD CHOICE."

Summer passed.

Weeks of endless blue skies with only a suggestion of clouds, faint brush strokes from the hand of God, diaphanous wisps, barely glimpsed by shaded eyes. From time to time men chanced a glance toward heaven and prayed where they toiled beneath the merciless sun. A few showers fell, just enough to save the crops, though there wouldn't be abundant yields, barely enough to hope for better days next year. The long days wore on, ever the topic of conversation being the heat.

"It's never been this hot."

"If it doesn't rain soon, we'll lose the crops."

"Ain't never seen the Brazos so low."

"I don't know about you, but I feel like a loaf of bread left too long in the oven, burned hard and hardly fit for sopping."

In Texas, in the summer of 1835, dry bread and thirsty men would have to do.

About the time colonists from San Felipe to Nacogdoches to Washington-on-the-Brazos and all of East Texas began to doubt it would ever rain again, September ushered in a change. The wind shifted; a storm whirled in from the gulf and flooded Anahuac, washed away the streets, blew in through the unshuttered windows of the abandoned barracks, and howled through the open empty warehouse. A high tide even threatened the house on the strand, but John Bradburn was no longer there to care. Folk rightly assumed the alcalde had abandoned his dreams and his whores and departed for San Antonio, where General Cos kept a worried command.

The storm swept inward, clouds roiling like a witch's brew, gray thunderheads piling one upon the other, billowing over the horizon, and drenching the parched pines of the Big Thicket. The rain was a blessing. But what followed it into San Felipe was anything but a godsend. A friend returned, cloaked in a mantle of war, and many who saw him would not live to see another spring.

Thunder woke him, booming like a broadside and rousing the Butcher of Barbados from dreams of sea battles and pillaging. He was Capt. Mad Jack Flambeau aboard the *Sea Swift,* ringed with fire and smoke and the clash of cutlasses. "Fire one last broadside; rake her hull; clear her decks, Mr. Smalley!" he shouted. And the gunner did as he was ordered, priming the last of the ninepounders and ordering the surviving members of his gun crew to discharge their weapons.

Karaboom!

Chain shot cut a swath across the maindeck of the *San Ignatius,* ripping through the mass of soldiers surging toward the side rails of the pirate ship. Spanish blood and chunks of flesh flowed in rivers along the gunwales and spilled into the sea. Bonechucker drank its fill of the unlucky musketeers who had the misfortune of being in the first wave to charge over the gangplanks and engage the brethren of the black flag at sword's point. Spanish musketeers died as fire engulfed their ship and explosions tore holes through the hull.

"Bring us clear!" Flambeau shouted. A bullet creased his right ear. He fired off a shot from the pistol in his left hand. Though his shot went wide, his intended victim, in darting from harm's way, impaled himself on a freebooter's blade.

"Hard to port. Cut away those lines, damn you, or the blasted Spaniards will drag us under." Even as Mad Jack barked his orders, a second explosion rocked the deck of the prize ship, hurling its Castilian captain into kingdom come.

"Heave to. Heave to!" He sat upright in bed and the thunder rattled the shuttered windows.

Hanneke woke and caught his arm, her round face pale from surprise. She patted his shoulder and whispered his name. Flambeau wiped the sweat from his brow and glanced wildly about the room, taking in his surroundings as if seeing them for the first time, as if he had somehow only this instant been transported from the violent waterways of the Caribbean to the bedroom above the tavern.

"You're safe," Hanneke said.

"What? What are you saying, woman?"

"You're safe."

"Safe," he repeated as if the word were new to him, something the old sea dog had no knowledge of. "Yes," he added, patting her hand.

"It's just the storm," Hanneke said. "It woke me as well." She leaned over and kissed his grizzled cheek. "But as long as we are both awake, maybe we can think of some way to pass the time." She ran her fingernail down his arm and then under the sheet and blanket. Her naked thigh eased over his bony knee.

"You are a saucy little cauliflower." Mad Jack grinned, rising to the occasion. "What exactly did you have in mind?"

Hanneke caught hold of his erect flesh. "Hmmm. Let me think. That's a hard choice."

Lightning shimmered beyond the shuttered windows,

this time followed by a hammering on the tavern door below. It was well after midnight. Flambeau glanced at the woman as she lowered her bodice, revealing her ample bosom, ripe for the kissing. Again the summons from below. The late-night visitor was persistent and would not be denied. "By God, who would be out on a night like this?"

"You could stay here?" Hanneke suggested. "Let them find drink elsewhere."

Not hardly. The noise below continued unabated. It was obvious no one else would do. And perhaps it wasn't a thirsty patron after all. Maybe someone was injured. There were any number of reasons to spread an alarm.

"I'd best see to it," Mad Jack growled, swinging his legs out from under the covers. He stood in his stocking feet and pulled on his nankeen trousers, slipped a linsey-woolsey shirt over his head, and started toward the stairs. "All right! All right! You've ruined my sleep, and there had better be a good reason!" he shouted downstairs. He lit an oil lamp near the washbasin and then, with a reassuring wink toward his paramour, descended the stairs.

Hanneke rolled onto her ample derriere and sighed. She stared up at the hand-dyed canopy over the four-poster bed. The print was faded now. She could barely make out the swirls of color in the weave. The bed had belonged to her grandmother and been part of Hanneke's trousseau. It was a comfortably familiar piece of furniture, one that endured like the woman herself. Grief was a part of life, but it wasn't all of life. She had lost one husband and found another and loved them both, but in different ways. She yawned and closed her eyes. "Come on, monsieur buccaneer."

Hanneke woke with a start. Oh dear, she hadn't meant to fall asleep. How long? Too long. She rose up on an elbow to apologize to her lover and found the covers still turned down, just as he had left them. She glanced at the Seth Thomas clock on the hearth across the room. More than an hour had passed. And Mad Jack had yet to return. She climbed out of bed and covered herself with a dressing gown and walked to the head of the stairs. She hesitated, listening for voices. She could hear the wind howl and the front door bang against the side wall in reply.

"Captain Jack!" she called out. Nothing. Hanneke frowned. Unsettled now, she crossed the bedroom and retrieved a short-barreled blunderbuss from its rack above the hearth and then headed for the stairs. Anything amiss and there would be hell to pay. The gun she carried was loaded with nails.

The interior of the Flying Jib was empty, devoid of any sign of life. The tables were blank black shadows, the casks behind the bar squat battlements. Lightning flashed and filled the open doorway with its lurid brilliance, and in the glare she could make out the oil lamp in the mud, its chimney shattered where it had been dropped.

Hanneke hurried to the doorway, her heart in her throat, and peered out into the black night and the driving downpour that stung her cheeks. "Captain Jack! Monsieur Flambeau!" But the wind gusts stole her voice as sure as her beloved, for the darkness had swallowed him up without a trace

"He should have closed the door," a ragged voice said from behind her. Hanneke gasped and spun about on her heels and nearly lost her balance. A reed-thin man clothed in a tattered, sodden coat and threadbare trousers, his sandy hair plastered to his skull, slumped forward onto a table where he sat, resting, too weak to move or even make an effort to feed himself. Hanneke gathered her courage and cautiously approached this derelict. "I have summoned many of the others. They must hear what I have to say . . . while I still have the strength."

Now she knew him. Even as the wind moaned through the room like a portent of doom, her lips framed his name: "Stephen Austin."

The news of Austin's return spread through San Felipe. During a lull in the storms, riders fanned out from the settlement along the roads and back trails to alert the outlying farms and ranches. Bill Travis made a special trip to Briarwood bearing word that Austin was waiting at the Flying Jib and wanted to speak with William Wallace.

That was all the big man needed to hear. In the time it took for Roberto Zavala to saddle fresh horses, William Wallace had rubbed the sleep from his eyes, dressed, and armed himself and was ready to ride. Travis suggested they wait out the storm, for it had renewed in intensity and become a full-fledged gullywasher. "You're welcome to wait out the downpour," said Wallace, "but I have business elsewhere."

Bill Travis took pride in being an excellent horseman, but he was hard pressed to keep up with Wallace on the road to San Felipe. The Texican rode like a Comanche, as if man and beast were a single entity with an uncanny sense of the earth underfoot.

Lightning crashed and split the predawn sky and thunder rolled as the elements unleashed their fury, seeking to dissuade the horsemen from their course. Wallace took the lead and charged down the road, the folds of his serape flapping like the wings of a hawk, red hair streaming, eyes like slivered emeralds. He looked the tempest in the eye and never wavered. *Stop me if you can.*

During that desperate ride, Wallace relived the events of the summer; the raid on Anahuac, the growing tensions in San Antonio, days and nights of speculation, and the absence of news from Mexico City. Three months was a long time to be in Santa Anna's company. William doubted *el presidente* was any sort of decent host.

Trees arched in the wind, their branches like talons clawing the air, dry leaves plucked away by the storm. Gray sky, gray forest, deep shadows behind a curtain of rain, ghosts in the mist, all of them a blur. He didn't have time to stop and contest the past.

An hour passed. When the storm couldn't break him, the downpour subsided in defeat. Wallace realized he was alone on the road and glanced over his shoulder. Travis was about thirty yards back, clinging to his mount for all he was worth. He waved Wallace on and promised himself never again to undertake such a perilous ride.

The unruly collection of shops, stores, and cabins clustered along the banks of the Brazos was a welcome sight in those early-morning hours as the sun slipped a gray smear through a rent in the overcast sky and gave them all a brief respite from the deluge. The unsettled clouds promised more of the same. It was only a matter of time.

Wallace and the lawyer made a sodden, mud-spattered pair of pilgrims as they tethered their mounts before the longhouse that served as the town's meeting hall. But they weren't the only ones. Several of the colonists had made the journey into town, including Don Murillo Saldevar and his *segundo,* Chuy Montoya. William could not resist searching the crowd for Esperanza, but alas, she was nowhere to be found. He recognized just about everyone, and word of his arrival spread through the gathering. Big Foot Wallace was here, a man of few words who cast a long shadow. Ranchers, farmers, townsmen, *norte americanos,* and Mexicans continued to drift into the town hall for the better part of the hour.

Sam Houston "held court" in the center of the hall. When it came to speechifying, the Tennessean was a natural. He harangued the crowd with opinion after opinion and peppered his oration with a salty story or two just to keep his audience listening. Wallace had to admire a man who could talk so long and hard. Several times he was invited to the center of the room, to address the crowd. Each time he cordially declined. Until they heard from Austin, he had nothing to say.

Jim Bowie was notably absent, having left for San Antonio a few weeks back in the company of several of his fellow Louisianans who had come to Texas in search of fortune and adventure and were about to find both. Rumors were already circulating that General Cos had failed in his attempts to tighten control of San Antonio and the outlying ranches and was practically besieged in the town. For too long he had feathered his nest with unjust taxes; now the "chickens had come home to roost"—people simply refused to obey his decrees. The more he tried to enforce his will, the greater the resistance. Wallace didn't envy Cos if the general had managed to antagonize Jim Bowie. The knife fighter was still on the prod and had no use for dragoons, lancers, or any other men in uniform who tried to tell him what to do.

The room was becoming too crowded for Wallace's liking, and when the moment was right he slipped outside for a breath of air. On a whim he started across the muddy plaza and headed for the Flying Jib, drawn by his thirst and desire to see Austin before the crowd got a hold of him.

"We are of the same mind, my friend," Don Murillo said, having observed the big man from the corner of the town hall. The white-haired ranchero fell in step alongside Wallace while Chuy Montoya, his ever-present shadow, remained a few paces behind the wealthy landowner.

"Sam Houston could talk a noon breeze into a twister," Wallace said.

"The man is eloquent." Don Murillo grinned. "He has a great future, in either politics or the theater. Both dramas suit his style." The *haciendado* stepped around a mud puddle. He had already been in town and was waiting out the thunderstorms when he heard of Austin's return and decided to remain in the settlement to hear what news the man brought from Mexico City. "You'll catch your death if you aren't careful," he cautioned.

Wallace glanced down at his disheveled appearance. There was nothing to be done. Maybe Mad Jack still had some of his clothes. It was worth a look.

They reached the Flying Jib a few minutes later. Wallace hammered on the door with his ham-sized fist until it creaked open and permitted him to enter.

"Well, look what the cat dragged in," Mad Jack remarked. "Hanneke! Best you go upstairs; William's got to strip down and dry his duds by the fire."

Hanneke stepped out of the kitchen, flour up to her elbows. "I will do no such thing. William Wallace, I took care of five younger brothers; believe me, you ain't got nothing I haven't already seen before. Sit by the fire and I'll have more biscuits and coffee directly."

"Yes, ma'am," Wallace said.

She disappeared and then poked her head back out. "Nice to see you again, Señor Saldevar. You, too, Chuy."

Don Murillo and his *segundo* removed their sombreros and bowed in her direction and thanked her for her hospitality.

"He's over there," Mad Jack said, gesturing toward

the hearth. "I've kept the others from storming the place and plaguing him with questions before he gathers his strength."

"Stephen will need it if he intends to face Houston's crowd," Wallace replied. "Sam can plumb work up a crowd." He stripped off his shirt, muscled torso gleaming in the firelight, hard flesh puckered here and there with a scattering of scar tissue.

Hanneke brought out a platter of biscuits and an enameled tin pot of fresh coffee. She glanced approvingly in Wallace's direction, her gaze lingering on his bronzed torso.

"I take back what I said," she lasciviously mentioned in passing. No, her brothers weren't anything like him.

William grinned and accepted the coffee and headed for the fireplace only to halt in his tracks at the emaciated figure warming his bones by the fire. Austin by nature was a lean and wiry individual. But he looked as if he had dropped twenty or thirty pounds. His cheeks were sunken, eyes hollow as twin cups, arms like twigs—at least what William could see jutting from the robe he was wearing.

"Poor thing. Came in here wearing rags. I tossed them on the logs," said Hanneke.

"Santa Anna sets a poor table," Austin ruefully explained. "But then, his dining room is a long reach from the palace dungeon."

"He did not listen to your proposals?" Wallace asked, taking a seat at the table closest to his friend. He was not a man to hide his emotions, so his concern was plain to see. Austin shook his head no.

"Not one grievance, my friend?" Don Murillo added, joining them. He placed a hand on Austin's forearm.

Austin mirthlessly smiled. "He had me thrown into jail. I believe eleven, no, more like twelve weeks passed. Then I was released and given that proclamation to take back to the rest of you." He indicated a folded water-stained document next to a bottle of whiskey on the table.

"And it is some piece of work," Mad Jack said, standing with his arms folded across his chest. The ring in his ear gleamed in the lamplight. "Hanneke read it to me."

"I know it by heart," Austin remarked. "I read it every night on the voyage home. I never thought I would last the ride from Anahuac. Never." He grabbed the bottle of whiskey and tilted it to his lips, nursing the burning brew, warmth spreading to his limbs.

"Easy," Wallace cautioned.

"Nothing will be easy again. Except getting shot," Austin testily replied. He stared at the document. "By decree of His Imperial Majesty, President Antonio Lopez de Santa Anna, the following edicts are become law." He took another drink from the bottle. In the silence, Chuy Montoya moved into the circle of light, staring at the paper, studying the neatly arranged words that had the power to take his life.

Austin slammed the bottle down on the tabletop. "That's why I wanted to see you alone, William. I wanted to know what you would think of all this."

"What does the paper say?" Wallace asked. "Go on."

"We cannot govern ourselves. Any talk of forming a congress is forbidden. There will be only military rule, set up by Santa Anna."

Don Murillo scowled. "Other states have the right to elect their own magistrates; why not us? What is he afraid of?"

" 'The men responsible for the raid on Anahuac' "—Austin's gaze bore into the big man seated across from him—" 'shall be placed under arrest by General Cos and dispatched to Mexico City for punishment.' "

"Ah hell, Stephen, we only took what was ours. And

we dressed up as Comanche . . ." Wallace shifted uncomfortably. Austin continued. "Santa Anna has forbidden *norte americanos* to own land or property in
Coahuila y Texas. The government has revoked all land
grants." Austin eased back in his chair. "He'll allow us
to stay in Texas, but we have no land and no rights."

"No rights for any of us," Don Murillo echoed, staring
glumly at the proclamation. "We have the right to a civil
government, not some military tribunal." Every official
Santa Anna had appointed was corrupt. The army seldom protected them. They existed only to fatten the cof-
fers of an uncaring and remote government.

"Sounds like *el presidente* is telling us to get out or
suffer the consequences," Mad Jack remarked. "Well,
there's always room for another cantina someplace else."

"What are you saying, Captain Flambeau?" the old
haciendado remarked. "You would leave?"

"Full sail to the wind," Mad Jack replied. "Santa
Anna is just looking for a reason to bring his whole army
down on our heads. A wise man knows when his bluff's
been called. Isn't that right, William? The young blade
and I rode away once before. We can do it again." The
freebooter patted his friend on the shoulder, a paternal
gesture toward one who was like a son to Mad Jack
Flambeau.

"Let him speak for himself," Austin said, his deep-
set eyes aglow with renewed energy. "Come on, William. People will want to know where you stand.
Houston may be the mind of what is to come, but you're
the heart. What say you?" He patted the proclamation.

Wallace stared at the carefully worded document. He
could sense Santa Anna staring at him through the proclamation, confident, leering, supremely corrupt. *El presidente* wanted him to run, like he had from his brother's
murderer. The list of people after his hide was getting

longer and longer. Juan Diego Guadiz, John Bradburn, and now Santa Anna himself.

You can run again, he heard his brother Samuel, whisper, a ghost in the corner, silent observer, unable to rest. *Or make your stand.*

Suddenly Wallace shot to his feet, his right hand a blur as it dropped to his waist, then swept up and over in a violent arc, Bonechucker firmly clasped in his fist. With a loud crash, William skewered the proclamation, pinning it to the tabletop. The foot-long steel blade slit the parchment and passed through the oak surface like a heated knife through butter.

It was an old adage, but in this case never more true. Actions did speak louder than words.

19

DECLARATION OF INDEPENDENCE OF THE REPUBLIC OF TEXAS

WHEN A GOVERNMENT HAS CEASED TO PROTECT THE LIVES, LIBERTY, AND PROPERTY OF THE PEOPLE FROM WHOM ITS LEGITIMATE POWERS ARE DERIVED ... WHEN THE FEDERAL REPUBLICAN CONSTITUTION OF THE COUNTRY THEY HAVE SWORN TO SUPPORT HAS BEEN FORCIBLY CHANGED, WITHOUT THEIR CONSENT, TO A CONSOLIDATED CENTRAL MILITARY DESPOTISM ... IN SUCH A CRISIS IT IS THE RIGHT OF A PEOPLE TO TAKE THEIR POLITICAL AFFAIRS INTO THEIR OWN HANDS AND ABOLISH SUCH GOVERNMENT AND CREATE ANOTHER IN ITS STEAD.

A storm blew into San Antonio on the fifth of December 1835. A storm blew in on the wings of a "wild west wind." It hounded General Cos from his bed and unleashed a thunder of guns, the screams of the dying, fire and sword and the purifying rage of battle.

Beneath the sun's blind glare, beneath a blue sky cold as the grave, muzzle blasts like lightning flashed in windows and alleys, from behind walls, and along hotly contested streets where an unruly force of Texicans fought their way from the outskirts of San Antonio toward the center of town ...

A few hours earlier, William Wallace, Jim Bowie,

Don Murillo Saldevar, Bill Travis, and a few hundred brave souls from San Felipe and Anahuac had been joined by a motley collection of San Antonio's inhabitants. Frontiersmen and merchants, blacksmiths, caballeros, fishermen, and farmers, weaned on the harsh realities of the big country and believing they had suffered injustices, took up arms and formed an alliance with this rowdy bunch of rebels gathered on the outskirts of the town.

· Columns of men broke off into smaller groups, approaching from a dozen different directions. Mexican patrols warily observed these disorganized-looking mobs of armed colonists but were unable or unwilling to understand their motives. The dragoons and grenadiers mistook the rebel advance for just so much posturing. It wasn't until the first shots rang out that the patrols realized they were under an attack.

Every rebel had his reason that day.

Many of the Texicans were hungry for a political change. Men like Stephen Austin and Don Murillo were anxious to resolve their grievances and saw themselves with no other options but force of arms. Sam Houston and Bill Travis were not alone in seeing an opportunity to wrest Texas from Mexico; they saw themselves following in the footsteps of Washington and Jefferson. Then there was Jim Bowie, who was always looking for a good fight.

William Wallace lacked animosity and a grand vision of empire. He wanted nothing more then to be left alone to live his life, build what he could, roam free whenever he wished, to be treated fairly and justly, to walk the proud land with honor. Of course he knew a fair number of his hard-case companions had joined the attack because they had a hankering for a drink or two or ten in the cantinas and perchance a romp in San Antonio's "fabled" brothels. What the hell . . . whiskey and sex were as good a reason as any to start a revolution.

The advance went without incident for the first few
blocks. Then as the Texicans broke up into still smaller
groups a troop of Mexican cavalry intersected Wallace's
column and attempted to block their path near La Villita,
a collection of mud houses, jacals, and cantinas near the
south bend of the river.

Someone fired a shot.

Another round of gunfire followed the first. Men
pitched from horseback or crumpled to their knees,
clutching their wounded limbs. Suddenly a battle was
joined and there was no turning back. The storm must
play itself out.

THE MEXICAN GOVERNMENT HAS SACRIFICED OUR
WELFARE . . . IT HAS UNJUSTLY INCARCERATED
ONE OF OUR CITIZENS . . . IT HAS REFUSED TO SE-
CURE THE RIGHT OF A TRIAL BY JURY . . . IT HAS
SUFFERED THE MILITARY COMMANDANTS STA-
TIONED AMONG US TO EXERCISE ARBITRARY ACTS
OF OPPRESSION AND TYRANNY . . . IT HAS DE-
MANDED THE SURRENDER OF A NUMBER OF OUR
CITIZENS AND ORDERED MILITARY DETACHMENTS
TO SEIZE AND CARRY THEM INTO THE INTERIOR.

A couple of miles downriver, on the west bank of the
Rio San Antonio de Padua, Esperanza heard the rattle of
gunfire and emerged from her tent to stare off toward
the cluster of cottonwood trees concealing the town in
the distance. She knew the attack had started and
glanced around at the families of the men who had come
from San Felipe to join in the fight. They were all neighbors here, friendships forged by a common bond of concern for husbands, lovers, and sons.

"You should have stopped my brother, forbid him to
go," Dorotea said, arriving at the younger woman's side.

"Murillo seeks only to impress you, to prove to you he is still the man he once was."

"He has never had to prove himself to me," Esperanza replied.

"No? You cannot see it? And I thought the cards told you everything."

"Not everything," said the young woman. "My gift cannot fathom the workings of a bitter heart."

Dorotea's expression changed. She seemed wounded by the remark, and for a moment Esperanza regretted the utterance. But words failed her. She was troubled by the gunfire in the distance and lacked the will to continue their argument. "You have resented me since the day we met in Veracruz. I know you do not think me worthy of your brother and that the first Señora Saldevar was your friend. But she is dead and buried. Now I am the mistress of my husband's house. Although you will always have a place with us, whether it is as family or a mere guest I leave up to you." She left the older woman's side and made her way across the encampment to the cookfire around which several women had gathered in a circle of misgiving and concern.

Pamela Kania was there, blue enameled coffeepot in hand. The wife of the shopkeeper was busily serving the other women. Valentina Zavala kept her rosary entwined between her fingers, her thumb moving along the beads. She was able to pray and keep up a conversation at the same time. Her daughter, Isabel, a beauty at fourteen who considered herself of marriageable age, stepped out of her mother's shadow to greet Esperanza as she approached.

"Do you hear the guns, Señora Saldevar?"

"Yes." Esperanza nodded, embracing the girl.

"Mama is so worried. Both Papa and Roberto are there."

"I know."

"But I told her not to brood or lose hope. Big Foot is there. My Wallace."

"Yours?"

"Sí. He does not know it, but one day I will marry him. And we will have many children. And they will all have red hair and be very brave."

"And have you told him this?" Esperanza asked.

"Many times," Isabel said. She could remember the first time she had seen Wallace, riding like the wind, hair streaming, arm outstretched, a pistol blazing as he swept her out from the clutches of the Comanche and spirited her away to safety. In her nine-year-old mind, they were betrothed that very day. She just needed to do a little growing up is all.

"And what does Wallace say to your plans?"

"He laughs."

"Isabel, do not bother the señora," Valentina said.

"She isn't," Esperanza replied. "We are talking about people who mean so much to us." She gratefully accepted a cup of coffee from Pam Kania. The liquid was black, hot, and strong enough to float a horseshoe.

"Kenneth is safe," Pam said, brushing a few gray strands of hair from her features. She was a plainspoken, kindly woman whose warmth and gentle demeanor in many ways reminded Esperanza of her own mother. She glanced around at the other women, Anglos, mestizos, pureblood Mexican, all of them Texicans and, with the advent of battle, all of them traitors to the central government in Mexico City.

Children darted among the trees. Esperanza watched a group of young boys with drill sticks in hand enact what they perceived to be the battle. The melee was touch-and-go. Their numbers shrank as children fell wounded, dying, expiring only to leap to their feet and complain that it was someone else's turn. Along the riverbank, soldiers and rebels fell but lived to fight again.

It would be different in the streets of San Antonio. She thought of her husband, and try as she might, her thoughts, however guilty, turned to William Wallace.

Please, Lord, not them. Not today. Let it be someone else's turn.

Gen. Martin Perfecto de Cos paced the confines of his quarters as his soldiers waged a desperate retreating action from house to house. One of his lieutenants rushed in to report that the troops had grudgingly yielded the outlying streets and were falling back toward the Alamo Mission. Cos immediately dispatched the young officer with orders to bring the Englishman John Bradburn to the governor's makeshift quarters. He'd been living in the garrison for months now, preferring the safety among his troops to the finery of the governor's palace in town.

Cos sighed and threw open a window so he could listen to the clash of arms. He recognized the din for what it was: the beginning of the end. The official wondered how much longer before the mob was at the gates. It was anyone's guess. He hoped there was time for a civilized drink. Damn if he was going to allow the rabble to get their dirty hands on the last of his brandy.

Bradburn reached the governor's quarters in a state of panic. His worst nightmares were coming true. The raid on Anahuac paled in comparison to what was happening. Thievery unpunished had become an act of open rebellion. He began to say as much, but Cos silenced the rotund Englishman with a perfunctory wave of the hand. The governor did not need a lecture from the man.

"See what my brother-in-law has done? Santa Anna has placed me in a most impossible predicament. How am I to hold Texas when I don't even have enough men to defend this garrison?" Cos managed to fill a couple of glasses with tepid brandy. His hands were trembling. Cos scowled and glared at Bradburn. "See to your dress, señor," he snapped. The Englishman struggled to tuck in his shirt. He secured a broad leather belt around his swollen belly. When Bradburn was properly attired, Cos handed him a drink. The alcalde accepted the brandy. Another day he might have enjoyed himself. Today he had the worried expression of a condemned man savoring his last meal. The governor stretched forth his arms, issued an order, and an aide, bearing a uniform, darted in from a side room and finished dressing the officer. The aide took care to smooth the coat about the general's shoulders.

Bradburn glanced down at the brandy in his hand. "Is this why you sent for me, to share a salute?"

"No, señor, I have a most important task for you to perform."

Bradburn hoped it involved fleeing the town before the Texicans were at the gates. He wanted nothing to do with that mob storming through the streets. He knew where there was a carriage and team of matched geldings just waiting for a man with enough sense to stay out of harm's way. Unfortunately, Cos had other ideas. Bradburn's carriage would have to wait.

THESE AND OTHER GRIEVANCES WERE PATIENTLY BORNE BY THE PEOPLE OF TEXAS UNTIL THEY REACHED THE POINT AT WHICH FOREBEARANCE CEASES TO BE A VIRTUE. THE NECESSITY OF SELF-PRESERVATION, THEREFORE, NOW DECREES OUR ETERNAL POLITICAL SEPARATION.

Gunfire lit the shadows where men crouched and fought and died—gunfire rumbled like thunder; deeper explosions roared and shook the adobe walls as grenades spent their swift fuses and unleashed a ball of flame in the confines of a shop, house, or fortified jacal. Shuttered windows disappeared in a hail of splinters; once-solid walls crumbled outward from the force of the blasts. Rifles and muskets and flintlock pistols spewed gray-black clouds of powder smoke that clung to the air like burial shroud and carried the stench of death.

A column of vaqueros and Louisianans led by Jim Bowie and Don Murillo Saldevar surged down the Calle Dolorosa, scattering patrols of grenadiers who made but a token effort to resist their attack. Seeing the Mexican infantry in retreat fueled the rebels' lust for battle. They hounded the fleeing troops into the market square, charged across the Plaza de las Islas like an onrushing tide only to break against a redoubt bristling with fresh troops and a nine-pounder cannon firing grapeshot. The Mexican defenders had fortified the front of "Mama Gavin's" Casa del Oro Hotel, a solid sun-washed structure overlooking the market. Its balconies and raised veranda provided excellent placement for the troops.

The attackers dived for cover, realizing too late they had plunged headlong into a trap. The *mercado* soon ran red with blood, as the first volley left half a dozen colonists wounded and writhing in agony. A second blast sent lead shot ripping through flesh and bone, silencing some, wounding others.

Don Murillo didn't need to order the men around him to abandon the attack. The column scattered and sought the meager protection of the market stalls and two-wheeled carts strewn about the square. Chuy Montoya scampered across the plaza, dodging a hail of round shot to join Don Murillo, Bowie, and a half-dozen other men behind a spring-fed well that served as a watering tank for man and beast. The well was about twenty feet in diameter. But even its yard-tall stone walls could not save them. Texicans immediately found themselves peppered from all sides by regular infantrymen placed in the shops, on the rooftops, and lining the balcony of a hotel that overlooked the makeshift redoubt.

Bowie and the others returned fire as best they could, though it was difficult to reload their flintlock rifles from a prone position. There were no other options unless a man wanted to sit up and risk having his head blown off as he rammed home powder and shot.

Despite the odds against them, the doomed column put up a valiant fight. Musket balls and round shot decimated their ranks. As the intensity of the gunfire increased, the men in the *mercado* clutched their weapons and curled beneath what little protection they could find while a pall of powder smoke stung their nostrils and fouled the air.

The abandoned marketplace had become a death trap. Lead slugs whirred like angry bees, thudded against the well, pockmarked the hard earth. A man next to Bowie clutched his throat, gasped, and curled over on his side. Bowie fired at the rooftop to his left and sent a marksman darting out of sight. The knife fighter began the arduous task of ramming another charge down the barrel of his long rifle. Don Murillo removed his black sombrero and ran a hand through his white hair. Sweat beaded his dark brown forehead. He checked the loads on his silver-plated dueling pistols, rose up and fired first one round, then a second, and sent a man tumbling from the rooftop of a silversmith's shop. Chuy Montoya tried to pull the *haciendado* out of sight as Mexican grenadiers turned their guns on the landowner.

"Padrone. You will get yourself killed!" The *segundo* grimaced as one of the lead slugs found its mark, striking the landowner in the thigh. Don Murillo shuddered and fell backward into Montoya's outstretched arms, a patch of dark crimson spreading outward from the puckered wound.

"No . . . Señor Saldevar . . . no!" Chuy gasped. He removed a scarf from around his neck and fashioned a tourniquet to stanch the flow of blood.

"The soldiers are no longer running from us, my old friend," Don Murillo said through clenched teeth.

"So I noticed," Montoya grumbled. The musket ball had glanced off the stone wall and plowed a furrow across the older man's flesh but failed to lodge itself in the muscle.

"Now that we got those dragoons treed, what are we gonna do with 'em?" Bowie sourly added, watching the grizzled vaquero tenderly minister to the landowner. He quickly surveyed the *mercado*. Where was Wallace? Bowie couldn't remember if the big galoot had followed them into the market square.

"I would prefer to be herding cattle or breaking wild mustangs," Chuy said, hunching forward as several more shots rang out and the cannon boomed again.

"As would I," Don Murillo agreed, gritting his teeth. He'd been hurt worse and wasn't about to let the wound slow him down. He intended to lead these men out of this trap or die trying. For the first time in a long while he actually considered his own demise. He had expected to die in bed, an old man, tired of life and eager for rest. Up until now it had all been like some play, a stage set for a drama in which men died for the benefit of the performance. Nothing was permanent; life was always just another rehearsal. "Ah, Chuy, one is never too old to play the fool."

"No, *padrone*," the *segundo* protested. "You are a good man, a just man, and your word is much-respected throughout the region. The men and I will always follow you. We ride for the brand, come what may."

After he finished tending Don Murillo's wound, Montoya slipped a pistol from his belt and fired at an open window in a shop across the square. He couldn't hear the yelp of pain, but a brown hand dropped a musket and clutched the windowsill before sinking out of sight.

"Well done," Don Murillo said, straining to stand. He

groaned as he put weight on his leg and tightened the tourniquet another turn. He rammed another charge down the gun barrel, then sank back and closed his eyes.

"You hit bad?" Bowie asked.

Just then the nine-pounder roared and sent a round of explosive shot into one of the wooden carts. Solid wheels and a wood frame exploded into fragments. Two vaqueros went flying into the air, arms and legs unnaturally bent; the men flopped lifelessly upon the earth like discarded rag dolls.

"Not as bad as some," the *haciendado* glumly replied, glancing in the direction of his fallen ranch hands. He had known them both and watched them grow to manhood on the ranch. They would be missed.

"Damn, I hate to see that," Bowie remarked. He eased up, raised his rifle, and fired at the redoubt as the soldiers scrambled to reload the cannon. A few of the Louisianans tried to advance before the nine-pounder could spit another charge, but the riflemen behind the makeshift barricade laid down a brutal volley that claimed one of the attackers and sent the rest scrambling back to their meager protection.

"The bastard's placed his men well," Bowie grudgingly admitted, watching as the artillery officer tightened the ranks.

The Mexican infantry kept up a steady gunfire from redoubt in the shadow of the hotel. Rifle balls thudded into the adobe bricks and riddled the greasewood sign dangling above the front doorway. They thudded into the shuttered windows and bolted door and pinged off the wrought-iron railing of the balcony. The name on the sign, MAMA GAVIA, had been practically shot away. With the amount of rifles fired in its direction, the House of Gold was fast becoming a "House of Lead." The gaily painted wooden shutters splintered. Chips of wood littered the shaded walkway. The thick clay walls were soon pockmarked from the rifle fire.

Marksmen on the hotel balcony controlled the avenue of approach from several directions with their line of fire. The nine-pounder, loaded with grapeshot, could sweep the market square with a single blast. Below the balcony, infantrymen loosed volley after volley. The bayonets on their muskets gleamed in the sun. These desperate and determined men were prepared to repel any advance.

Bullets thudded against the well and forced Bowie to duck down before he could completely assess the situation. "They tricked me like a greenhorn," the knife fighter fumed. "I should have known better."

"We'll be slaughtered if we stay here!" one of the Louisianans called out.

"Then we won't stay," Don Murillo snapped. He refused to die on his belly like a reptile.

"They'll cut us to ribbons if we try to run back the way we came," Chuy observed. He fired at an open doorway, then hastily reloaded.

"You got a better idea?" Bowie said. A musket ball missed him by inches and spattered him with limestone chips as it ricocheted off the wall and plopped into the water. His throat was parched. The sun was a soot gray smear dimly glimpsed through the powder smoke. His eyes were watering now. But maybe the pall was a blessing, it served to ruin the aim of the soldiers surrounding them. He studied Don Murillo's expression and read the older man's iron resolve. "I got a bad feeling about this, señor." He knew as well as the ranchero there was only one way out of the *mercado*.

"I will not die with my face in the dirt. Nor will I suffer my wife to think her husband was a coward." The landowner lifted his dueling pistols, loaded and ready.

"See here, I don't mind dying so much; it's dying in

pieces that gives me the willies. I don't cotton to charging into grapeshot," Bowie muttered. He could see the handwriting on the wall clear as any man. "Ah, what the devil." Bowie cupped a hand to his mouth. "Pierre Dufau, are you still alive?"

"For now!" a squat, jut-jawed Cajun shouted back from across the marketplace. "But I cannot guarantee for later, monsieur."

"Sound that trumpet of yours soon as I step out. I reckon we'll be charging those 'mescans' over yonder."

"If yer jokin' I'm chokin', *mon cher*." The Cajun sounded as if that were the worst suggestion he was going to hear all day. "You want me to summon an angel or two while I'm at it?"

"Call down who you will," Bowie retorted, "as long as they bring their own powder and shot."

Chuy blessed himself while all around him men cowering in the *mercado* steeled themselves for a frontal assault on the makeshift redoubt. The *segundo* was gamely resolved to do his share of the fighting. As for Don Murillo, the man was much too proud to stay behind. It was a matter of honor.

"Lord," Bowie ruefully recited. "For what we are about to receive, may we be truly thankful." It was a time for prayer. Charging into grapeshot at close range was akin to suicide, and every man knew it. But they would follow out of pride, out of fatal resolve, out of a last brief hope that a miracle would save them.

Sometimes the impossible happens. Prayers have a way of getting answered. Faith can triumph in the darkest hour. Sometimes there are legends in the dust.

Bowie patted Chuy on the shoulder and started to rise up. "See you over yonder." A blaring call sounded from the trumpet lost in the haze of the *mercado*. It lingered on the air, balanced on an undercurrent of gunfire and death.

"Wait, *Señor* Bowie," Don Murillo blurted out and caught the knife fighter by the arm and dragged him back under cover. "Look. There on the roof of the hotel!"

Bowie rubbed his eyes and squinted through the acrid haze that stung his eyes and lungs. "What in blue thunder?"

A familiar figure balanced his long-legged frame on the red tile roof of Mama Gavia's Casa del Oro Hotel as if summoned by the Cajun's clarion call. He was broad and tall, and his long red hair streamed in the wind while a black haze of brimstone and gunsmoke swirled about his mighty limbs. Here was no seraph, not by a long shot, but the devil at noon, unleashed from the bowels of the earth, a red-maned avenger conjured of smoke and fire and all-consuming flame.

"Wallace!" The name rose in the throats of the doomed men in the market below. His name was a benediction of thunder and fiery death.

"Wallace!" It erupted like a cheer defiantly hurled into the teeth of the Mexican troops.

He held aloft a keg of black powder two men would have struggled to raise. A fuse sputtered from one end and showered his shoulder and neck with sparks as it burned away, growing shorter with every precious second.

"Throw it," Bowie said beneath his breath.

Soldiers in the buildings surrounding the square noticed the man on the roof and tried to pick him off. Wallace took a step toward the edge of the tiles. The big man seemed impervious to the musket balls that filled the air around him like swarming mosquitoes.

"Throw it, my friend!" Don Murillo shouted, but the gunfire drowned him out.

Wallace glanced down at the upturned faces of the soldiers below him. The men on the balcony were too surprised to fire their muskets. Wallace launched the keg toward the powder kegs stacked near the nine-pounder. The soldiers on the balcony broke their trance and unleashed a volley in his direction. William threw himself backward, avoiding death by inches as the musket balls fanned the acrid haze.

The big man scrambled back up the roof and flattened himself against the crumbling tiles. Broken fragments of fired clay slid out from under his boot heels and disappeared over the edge. He began to lose his purchase and inexorably slide down the roof. Wallace spread out his arms, dug his fingers beneath the tiles, splayed his legs to gain traction, and slowly regained his hold on the rooftop. But just as he breathed a sigh of relief, the ground below erupted in a mighty blast. The earth shook; the hotel trembled; a second and third detonation followed the first as the powder kegs exploded in a flash of fire and thunder.

The shuttered windows of the hotel blew inward; the adobe brick supports cracked and collapsed. The balcony and several feet of roof came tumbling down. The walls of the redoubt crumbled outward. Several of the defenders went flying through the air to land in the *mercado,* where they lay writhing on the ground, cradling their broken limbs and gaping wounds. Some of the troops gamely charged the insurrectionists driven out by the igniting powder kegs and shrapnel, but this time the advantage belonged to the Texicans, who met them with a withering volley.

Jim Bowie leaped to his feet and emptied his rifle into one man, charged a second soldier who impaled himself on Bowie's formidable blade. Chuy wounded one grenadier, then fired point-blank into the chest of a second Mexican soldier who sank to his knees, clutched at the front of his coat, managed to stand and take a few steps, then slumped forward with his upper torso breaking the surface of the well.

The remaining soldiers surrendered after a few brief seconds of skirmish or darted toward the alleys in a desperate attempt to escape. Some made their way through these narrow avenues and headed straight for the main garrison at the Alamo Mission.

"Oh, shit!" Wallace muttered as the front of the hotel collapsed. He tensed as the roof gave way and dropped him in a rain of mortar, clay, adobe bricks, and shattered wood. The wounded and dying broke his fall. Hands clawed at him in a macabre display; men groaned, pleaded for mercy or tried to encircle his throat to drag him under as they died.

It was rough going for a few brief minutes. Wallace had knocked the wind out of himself. He fought free of his assailants even as he struggled to breathe. Dazed and blinded by the dirt and debris, he rose from the wreckage. Bodies were strewn about him along with the shattered carriage of the nine-pounder cannon and the ruins of the redoubt. Several of the defending soldiers seemed oblivious to the stranger in their midst while others recognized him as the man who had brought them to ruin. From out of the carnage a soldier lunged at him with a bayonet and broken musket. Wallace batted the gun barrel aside and caught the man by the throat as the soldier stumbled past. William lifted the man into the air and hurled the unfortunate grenadier in the direction of another group of soldiers who were about to riddle the Texican with lead. The soldiers broke ranks and as their comrade at arms collided with them, Wallace drew his knives and charged the soldiers as they attempted to regroup into a skirmish line. He was a fearsome apparition with his great size, his features caked with white dust from the wreckage, his burning wild-eyed gaze. Menace clung to him like a cold sweat.

"I am the widow maker! El Destripedor Rojo! Come and reap the whirlwind!" William pounced upon them like some great hunting beast. Old Butch and Bone-chucker were his fangs and claws. They tore through flesh, carved bone, until Wallace was crimson to the elbows. A man died from a slashed throat, another from a thrust to the heart. A soldier cursed and fired a shot that William dodged; then he ran the man through and left him dying on the hard earth.

The remaining defenders broke and ran. They had seen enough of the Ripper to last them a lifetime. Wallace in his blood rage would have followed the survivors had not Mama Gavia emerged from the ruined facade of her hotel and swatted the Texican across the backside with a long-handled broom.

"See what you have done! My beautiful Casa del Oro. You clumsy oaf! Be off with you. All of you!" The silver-haired *mamacita* batted one of the grenadiers who stumbled out of the wreckage and sent him reeling on his way. Then she turned her wrath once more upon William, who managed to parry a couple of irregular blows from the broom. He wiped the grit and powdered rock from his features and retreated out of harm's way.

"Your pardon, señora. It was, sadly, necessary. But your sacrifice will not go unrewarded."

"Ohhhh!" She charged him, broom raised like a club, her black dress catching on the rubble as she swatted and thrashed the air inches from his nose. Wallace leaped the remains of the redoubt and collided with Bowie and Chuy Montoya and the advancing rebels. More than one man stopped to clap Wallace on the shoulder. They owed him their lives. He forced his way clear and put some distance between himself and the irate proprietress. Mama Gavia continued to harangue anyone within broom's length.

"What are you running from, Big Foot?" Bowie grinned.

"Reinforcements," Wallace replied, indicating the diminutive señora. "She's as feisty as a game hen, too."

"Well done, my young friend!" Don Murillo Saldevar called out as he limped forward from the battleground that had been the market place. The remainder of the rebel column continued to roust the soldiers from the surrounding buildings. Most of the defenders had lost their stomach for the fight once the redoubt had been destroyed and were filing out of the buildings with their hands raised.

The *haciendado* read the concern in Wallace's eyes. "Just a little scratch." He indicated the crude bandage about his thigh. "Nothing to worry about."

William nodded, relieved.

"Where to?" Bowie asked, unsheathing his own famous blade.

"Cos ordered me brought to the garrison gate," Wallace said. "I'd hate to disappoint the general."

And so began a most peculiar parade. Wallace led the way, but he did not walk alone. Don Murillo, Chuy Montoya, and Jim Bowie were with him, then the rest of the men from the *mercado*, and the ranks swelled. The column doubled in size as they proceeded down the Camino Real driving the remaining troops before them. Bill Travis, Ken Kania, and Roberto Zavala at the head of another column joined them at the banks of the San Antonio River. Kania no longer resembled a mildmannered merchant. His shirt was torn, his cheeks powder-burned, and his knuckles raw and bleeding. He had endured his baptism of fire and looked every inch a warrior.

Travis brandished his cavalry saber. The blade was red-stained and nicked from use. Zavala hurried to stand alongside his friend. William acknowledged him with a nod of the head, but the amenities would have to wait.

By the time the great column of Texicans forded the San Antonio River and arrayed themselves along the ‖Calle de la Mission, the ranks had swelled yet again, doubling in size. People from town and the surrounding ranches sensed the beginning of the end and wanted to be present at the finish.

As William Wallace continued up the slight incline, his long-legged strides carried him ahead of the pack. Sunlight glittered off the knives he gripped in both hands. The wind set his red hair streaming like the flames of a wildfire.

Behind him, smoke trailed from scenes of battle and fire-gutted jacals set ablaze during the house-to-house struggle. Ahead, the crumbling walls of the Alamo, once the Mission San Antonio de Valera, beckoned like fate. His lumbering gait soon brought him to the main gate, where he stopped under the guns of the sentries on the walls. Brown faces shaded by short-brimmed red hats were inscrutable masks at this distance. He glanced up at the soldiers outlined against the cerulean sky. They watched him through their gunsights.

William knew the kind of target he made.

"Cos has issued orders for the raiders of Anahuac to be brought before him. Best one of you send someone to alert him."

"And what shall I tell His Excellency?" a voice drifted down from above.

William smiled, his chest swelled, and he raised his arms, his long knife in one hand, the dirk in the other. "Tell the general William Wallace is here!"

A cheer rolled up like an onrushing tide, crashed against those fragile walls, swept over the battlements, and lost itself in the garrison beyond. And then a most peculiar thing happened. The bolt slid back on the barred gate, the wooden door creaked open, and John Bradburn emerged from the shadow of the Alamo into the glare of the winter light. He shuffled forward with timid steps, a white flag of surrender dangling from a cane in his hand.

The roar of triumph that followed sprang from the throats of the victorious Texicans who had fought their way up from town to stand at Wallace's side. Their cry reverberated across the rolling landscape, where the wind in the buffalo grass whispered to the bristling yellow stalks, a warning that today went unheeded. In nature as in life, all things are fleeting.

WE DO HEREBY RESOLVE AND DECLARE THAT OUR POLITICAL CONNECTION WITH THE MEXICAN NATION HAS FOREVER ENDED AND THAT THE PEOPLE OF TEXAS DO NOW CONSTITUTE A FREE, SOVEREIGN, AND INDEPENDENT REPUBLIC.

20

"SEÑOR WALLACE IS IN LOVE WITH MY WIFE."

Cos was gone. The general and his troops had been allowed to march out of town by way of the Camino Real—paroled with the understanding that they would never again set foot in Texas. By evening, a troubled peace had settled over San Antonio.

It took a few hours for the populace to realize something important had been accomplished this day. San Antonio once more belonged to the people of Texas. But in the aftermath of victory few had the energy to speculate what the future held. For now, the townsfolk were content to heave a collective sigh of relief and begin the task of clearing away the signs of battle.

Luminaries encircled the plazas; by night their flickering light transformed the scene of the day's fighting and cast the streets and alleys in a magical glow. The *mercado* was again inviting; it beckoned the milling congregation, the tide of restless men who had freed the town and driven out the corrupt officials and their military court. Stalls were hastily rebuilt to house the dried produce, salted and cured meats, bolts of hand-spun cloth, woven baskets, gallon tins of goat milk, colorful serapes and sombreros, stacks of firewood, wooden trays of medicinal herbs. Everything and anything was offered for sale. The familiar aroma of tortillas and beans flavored with enough peppers to make a saint curse permeated the air.

Like weeds, life has a way of regenerating itself. Even the humblest peon will continue to reach for the stars from the rubble of his dreams. That day in San Antonio, men and women discovered strengths they never knew they had. Houses gutted by fire, their naked walls smeared with smoke, were reclaimed by their owners, determined to restore the pockmarked walls and wash away the bloodstains.

The Spanish governor's palace in the center of town, across from the Plaza de las Armas, had become an infirmary housing all of the men wounded during the street fighting. Within those walls, the wounded and suffering were tended by the local physician, an overwhelmed man by the name of Ned Dillingham. The doctor had help. Anyone with a smattering of medical knowledge was welcome at his side. It was there among the rows of injured Texicans that William Wallace discovered Esperanza and her sister-in-law, Dorotea.

William was preparing to leave the palace when he heard Esperanza's voice coming from another room. He followed the trail of her words down the long hall to a double doorway that had once opened onto a spacious dining room. The space was crowded with cots and a number of wounded townspeople as well as some soldiers who had been too injured to make the march to the coast.

William watched from the doorway as Esperanza rebandaged the bloody shoulder of one of her husband's vaqueros. Dorotea applied a foul-smelling poultice to the injured man's wound, which Esperanza quickly covered with fresh linen strips. She bathed the man's forehead with a cool cloth and stroked his hand and cheek until he fell asleep. Only then did she look up and meet Wallace's gaze.

She smiled.

William retreated and continued toward the front door of the palace. He found a spot shrouded in evening shadows beneath the twisted branches of a madrona tree and waited, his breath a faint vaporous cloud upon the December air.

His patience was eventually rewarded when the two women emerged from the building. He left his perch and started forward only to see the women joined by Chuy Montoya and another man who were obviously there to escort the ladies through the night streets. Chuy noticed William and hailed him, stroking his goatee while he talked. Montoya's eyes, like Wallace's were deep-set and puffy-looking from lack of sleep. Chuy touched the brim of his sombrero in a salute to the man who had saved his life earlier in the day.

"You ladies have been angels of mercy this night," William said.

"And now we are overdue at my brother's hacienda," Dorotea replied in a no-nonsense voice.

"I had hoped I might escort you back to the Calle Dolorosa," William said, glancing in Esperanza's direction.

"Senor Montoya is perfectly able to protect us," Dorotea snapped. She did not trust Wallace's intentions for a second.

"Indeed. No one could ask for better," William replied. "I confess my motives are selfishness. I would enjoy the company of a friend."

"And you shall have it," Esperanza replied. "Chuy, take Dorotea on ahead. I shall follow along with Señor Wallace. Tell Don Murillo I will not be long."

"As you wish, Señora Saldevar," Chuy said. He indicated the way for the widow.

Dorotea continued to protest. "It isn't proper behavior, for a married woman to—"

"What? Have a friend?" Esperanza calmly told the woman, "Chuy has told me how Señor Wallace saved my husband—your brother's—life today. I am grateful for such a friend. Perhaps you should be as well."

The young woman's remarks caught her sister-in-law off guard. Before Dorotea could figure out another point to argue, Chuy and the other vaquero all but spirited the widow off across the plaza. Dorotea continued to harangue her escort until they were out of sight.

"I did not mean to cause you trouble," William said, offering his arm.

Esperanza turned to the big man at her side. "Dorotea would find something else to complain about—if not this thing, then another."

"It was good of you to come and care for the wounded."

"I wish I were a man, so that I could shoulder a gun and take part in the struggle."

William quietly appraised the señora. She was a pretty little thing, wrapped in her wine-colored shawl, with her full red lips and dark eyes, the rustle of her riding dress as she walked, the smell of soap and lilac water that clung to her despite her visit to the infirmary, the way her long black hair parted to reveal a glimpse of her slender neck. "I'm glad you're a woman."

Esperanza blushed and averted her gaze.

"Now I will walk you home, señora," William said.

"Take the long way," Esperanza suggested. "Por favor."

Twenty minutes later, Chuy Montoya dismissed his companion and opened the wrought-iron gate for the widow to pass through into the dry, dessicated garden of Casa Saldevar. The flower beds were choked with weeds. The sandstone walkway was littered with the detritus of other seasons, the leaves and gray twigs and the dirt that had run off during the rains.

Dorotea hated to see the courtyard in such a terrible condition and had demanded the caretaker be fired on the spot the moment she arrived at the house. Don Murillo grudgingly acceded to his sister's dictate, relieving the caretaker of his duties. The old man departed, but not without grumbling about the wealthy and their lack of grace and the nature of an old woman for whom the milk of human kindness had soured long ago.

Winter gardens reminded Dorotea of her loss, of her late husband's passing. He had left her alone in the world save for her brother, with whom she shared a common grief. Dorotea had planned on their suffering together, striving to make a life as best they could, nurturing each other through the rough days. Esperanza had ruined everything. Dorotea never expected her husband to marry again. These days, Murillo was hardly in mourning. It was shameful.

The widow was convinced this flirtatious little house servant had bewitched Murillo. It galled Dorotea that she could not make him see the light. But maybe tonight . . .

"Is that my wife?" asked Don Murillo, hearing the back door open and shut. The ranchero was enjoying a well-deserved pipe. He was seated in a handsomely appointed wing-backed chair in the sitting room of his house on the Calle Dolorosa. Flames danced in the fireplace, greedily consuming the pecan wood logs. He was alone in the house and therefore alerted by every sound.

The front room was much like the rest of the house, open and airy, sunlit during the day with long, wide windows to capture the summer breezes and thick white-washed walls adorned with multicolored blankets and wood carvings depicting moments from the life of

Christ. A red oak staircase in the center of the house led to the bedrooms upstairs.

A dining room took up the entire north wing of the hacienda. The front room and study had been built on the south side and caught a great deal of sunlight during the day. Pantries and cabinets lined the hall. A door at the rear opened onto the winter kitchen with its stone hearth, great oaken table, and shelves of clay roasters and cast-iron cook pots.

Dorotea Saldevar y Marquez had entered the house through the kitchen while Chuy dismissed his companion, following the woman into the kitchen. The *segundo* took a chair near a carving table, poured himself a glass of tequila, and filled a plate with tortillas, peppery rice, and beans that had been left warming by the fire.

Dorotea gathered up a previously prepared tray of *pan dulce* and a pot of coffee to offset the sweetness of the pastries. She carried them down the hall and into the sitting room, where Don Murillo waited.

"Did you hear? I called out."

The widow marched to the nearest end table and set down the platter. The sweet breads were fresh from the oven, their golden crusts drizzled with a glaze made from honey, Madeira, and brown sugar.

"She is with Wallace," Dorotea matter-of-factly said.

Outside the walls of the hacienda, from the Calle de Calabosa and the Plaza de las Islas at the center of town all the way to the banks of the river, a celebration was well under way. The sound of laughter and music from a band of wandering mariachis drifted in through the open window overlooking the Calle Dolorosa. A troupe of singing youngsters hurried past the narrow drive in the front of the hacienda and vanished down the street, searching for romance or mischief or a little of both.

"Good. A little gaiety will do her some good."

"I came home to take care of you," Dorotea said.

"You shouldn't have. Go on and enjoy yourself. Dance. If not for yourself, for me." He indicated his bandaged leg. "I fear my dancing days are done. One of General Cos's grenadiers has seen to that."

"Gracias. I will refrain from making a fool of myself," Dorotea coldly replied. She took a chair by the fire, served her brother a cup of coffee and one of the honey-glazed bread rolls, then settled herself in the warmth of the firelight. "Now if only you would do the same."

"You have a waspish tongue, dear sister."

"I am only trying to protect you. Do you not understand? Esperanza is alone with William Wallace. And I have seen the way he looks at her."

"Of course," said Don Murillo. "So have I." The old man sighed and settled back in his chair. "Señor Wallace is in love with my wife." Don Murillo took a sip of his coffee, puffed on his pipe, listened to the sound of crackling embers in the fireplace. A fragrant trail of smoke curled upward from the bowl. Coffee, tobacco, and a warm place by a fire were life's real pleasures. He cleared his throat and stared at the flames. There was an answer somewhere in this simplicity, but men were too busy to ever notice. "He loves her. That is why I know she is safe with him. William would do nothing to dishonor her. Or me."

They kissed in the shadows, out of the glare of the luminarias. One moment they were talking, and the next their lips met and they embraced. William held her close so as to feel the pressure of her round breasts pressing against his shirt; passion rose like a fever in the blood. He burned. Burned. It consumed him. And she was all . . . too . . . willing . . .

"William?"

Her voice shattered the fantasy. The big man blinked and brushed his red hair back from his features, his scalp moist with sweat. How long had she been talking to him? *What a fool I am.*

They were standing on the fringe of the Plaza de las Armas not far from the infirmary. Around them, merchants and customers were haggling over the price of trade goods. Strolling mariachis played cheerfully upon their guitars and trumpets; troubadours sang of love and brave deeds and the joys of life.

"What on earth were you thinking of?" Esperanza asked. She held up her hand. "No, don't tell me. I can just imagine."

"I hope not," Wallace stammered beneath his breath, but she didn't hear.

"If I know Big Foot Wallace you were picturing the trails that crisscross the border country to the south and convincing yourself that you alone should be the one to scout the Rio Grande in case General Cos chooses to break his word."

His cheeks colored. William breathed a sigh of relief. He wasn't about to tell her the truth. "You have guessed it."

"I read you like a book," Esperanza chuckled. "I don't even need the cards." She had a fine laugh, a sweet laugh, like music, if a rippling creek is music, or wind in the buffalo grass, or cries of a mourning dove homeward bound against a gold dust sky. Her laugh was music. She was natural and good, and there was a sense of truth about her made all the more appealing by the fact that she seemed utterly oblivious to her own charm.

Esperanza's eyes twinkled as she watched a sultry señorita begin to dance seductively around a fire pit, much to the enjoyment of the men who began to gather around the dancer, cheering and eager to be teased. Elsewhere, a couple sauntered past, obviously in love and standing so close together they cast one shadow upon the stone path. Esperanza looked up and caught William staring at her. Color crept to her cheeks. For a brief second he had lowered his guard, allowing her to glimpse the desire lurking behind the emerald chips that were his eyes.

"Why did you want me to be with you?" she asked. Suddenly she had a gnawing tightness deep in her gut. It was dangerous to be here with him, for she sensed a wildness in him, a raw recklessness that took her breath away, just to be this close, within arm's reach.

"Why did you come?" asked William, countering the question with one of his own. It was a way of stalling for time. He reached up to fidget with his scarf and found he'd lost it, probably among the rubble that used to be the Casa del Oro Hotel. Well then, let it be. He had no desire to risk Mama Gavia's wrath. But Esperanza's question still remained, like a lantern hung in the air between them, shedding light on those emotions and desires best left undisturbed. How much could he tell her? How much did he understand his own motives?

For the moment, he looked none the worse for the day's events. William had discarded his torn, singed clothes for woolen pants, boots of Spanish leather, and a shirt of brushed buckskin. A wide leather belt circled his waist, holding in place the pair of lethal knives with which he had forged a reputation. But his knuckles were burned and scraped, and beneath his fresh clothes his torso was streaked with cuts and patched with bruises. As he stood on the edge of the plaza, the firelight lent an almost sinister look to his features, revealing a dark side that one day he would want to forget. War did that to a man. Revolutions aren't made with rosewater.

"Being with you is a way of putting this day behind me. Look at them dancing where the blood has hardly had time to dry upon the earth."

Esperanza grew quiet. She shrank against him, recoiling from the image. William shook his head, closed his eyes for a moment, then put an arm around her and steadied himself. He wanted her. Then and there. And the devil take the consequences. To make love to her was to find life, to reaffirm some truth other than a day fit for dying. When she reached up and touched his face he looked at her and realized she was willing . . . waiting . . . in that moment of need, a gift for the taking.

My God . . . my God. . . . What was happening? One wrong step and his future would be written in the ruins of a dishonored friendship. He loved her. Always had, always would. And the love showed him the way.

"I had better bring you home." He barely got the words out.

She nodded.

But the look in her eyes left him weak in the knees. Maybe he'd curse himself all his days. But he would enter his house justified. Wallace offered his arm. She accepted. And with the utmost propriety, he walked the lady home. Neither of them spoke. It was for the best.

Lanterns were lit above the front door; an amber glow melted through the shuttered windows. He opened the wrought-iron gate and accompanied Esperanza across the front courtyard and up to the front door of the hacienda. She offered her hand and he bowed and brushed a kiss over the back of her hand. Her fingers tightened in his grasp. She leaned forward and whispered, "I would have gone with you."

"I know," Wallace said. And then he vanished into the night.

Esperanza headed straight across the foyer and had started up the stairs when her husband called to her from the study off to the side. She retraced her steps and entered the study, the presence of Don Murillo announced by the aroma of tobacco and coffee.

"My dear, I thought you would be enjoying the celebration."

"A poor showing without you," Esperanza said, crossing to his side and brushing his forehead with a kiss.

Dorotea cleared her throat. She was seated across from her brother, mouth downturned, her expression one of complete displeasure. "I have seen to your husband's wound and changed the bandage."

"What would we do without you?" Esperanza asked.

"It was the least I could do."

"Husband, shall I help you to bed?"

Don Murillo gently brushed his wife's hand away. "No no, I think I may just sleep down here. This chair is comfortable. And I have my books, my sweet bread, tobacco, everything I require. Go on to your room, my dear. But where is William? I thought you might bring him here. We have an extra room."

Dorotea choked on her coffee. She had to set the cup and saucer aside while she cleared her lungs. Esperanza hurried to her side and began to slap the older woman on the back.

"Leave me alone. Quit pummeling me, for heaven's sake!"

"See what you've done, Husband. Nearly ruined her night. Don't worry; Señor Wallace had business elsewhere tonight." She knelt by her husband. "I shall go to bed if there is nothing you need."

"Only the joy you bring me," Don Murillo told her. "I would dry up and blow away without you in my life, little one." He took her hand and kissed it. How cold her fingers felt to his lips.

Esperanza excused herself and hurried from the room before the color creeping up her cheeks gave her away. She hurried up the stairs and darted down the hall to the master bedroom, overlooking the front courtyard. She walked past the massive four-poster bed, avoiding her reflection in the mirrored vanity, stepped around a chiffonier, and opened the French doors. A cold breeze rushed in to the replace the warmth as the young woman stepped out on the balcony and leaned against the wrought-iron railing, gulping the cold night air while trying to will away the emotions warring in her heart.

"Oh, God," she whispered. "Help me. Please help me."

"You can't fool me," her sister-in-law's voice drifted out from the room's interior.

"Go away."

"My brother is old and blind when it comes to a pretty cheek." Dorotea seemed to glide forward, her harsh features leaning forward, back curved, chin pointed and leading the way, her physique accusatory. "He was blind to you, but I am not."

"Leave."

"Not until I have said my piece."

"No. I won't hear you." Esperanza brushed past the woman and walked to the table. Dorotea followed her, but the younger woman brought her up short, confronting her with the deck of cards.

"Stay then, and know your destiny. Draw a card. No? I shall draw it for you."

"I will have none of this," Dorotea protested. She dreaded the cards and had no desire to learn what the future held for her.

"What is this?" Esperanza pulled a card. "Muerte?"

"No. You are a witch. Do not speak of this. I will not hear it." Dorotea beat a hasty treat from the room, leaving Esperanza triumphant. She looked at the card in her hands, a gay little jester in dark green tights and a shirt embroidered with the moon and stars juggling seven cups, keeping them all airborne. Hardly death . . . but a bluff was as good as a pat hand.

Esperanza sat on the featherbed, her weight sinking into the covers. She stood and closed the doors, but not before checking one last time, just in case William had decided to wait below in the courtyard. She was both disappointed and relieved to find him gone. All that stirred below were dry leaves in moonlight, the husks of flowers, and dreams that could never be.

A voice, subtle, whispering on the fringe of his thoughts, drew William Wallace from Don Murillo's door and lured him down the Calle Dolorosa, the Road of Sorrow. He followed the voice beyond the warmth of the lantern-lit streets and the reassuring crush of bodies, past people who knew him, called to him by name and handed him a bottle of tequila. The revelers were oblivious to his troubled heart. They laughed and drank and made love and danced and saw the future as a bright array of bold successes. Their good will couldn't hold him.

The tequila seemed to help. It was the good stuff, with a caterpillar preserved by the alcohol floating in the bottom of the bottle. He drank it straight, with a lick of salt and a bite of lemon until both ran out.

Wallace stumbled through town as one entranced, images of a woman floating on the black sea of his thoughts. Then the voice called and chased all other regrets from his mind. He crossed the Rio San Antonio de Padua and gravely approached the silent, imposing, broken battlements of the Alamo, abandoned by all but the keening wind.

"William . . ."

The voice again, familiar, where . . . who? The blood ran cold in his veins. He stared at the empty bottle in his hands, glowered at its betrayal, empty indeed! He tossed the bottle aside. The sound of it shattering on the stones was enough to wake the dead.

"William . . ."

Wallace dismounted and left his horse by the main gate and walked inside. The great door creaked on its rusting hinges as he shoved it open.

"Samuel?" he whispered.

A north breeze stirred, caused him to shiver despite the warmth of the buckskin against his flesh. The mission was a motley collection of low-roofed barracks, a main church with an arched battlement, another two-storied adobe brick building that had once housed the priests, and a low wall that connected the barracks. There were artillery placements, stockade redoubts erected at the corners to defend the walls. A powder magazine had been built by the former occupants and set in the center of the main compound near the well. A twig cracked and Wallace spun about, dropping a hand to Bonechucker's hilt.

A coyote scampered across the parade ground and darted under a two-wheeled cart. Come the morning the critter would have to hand the place over to Travis and the militia. But tonight the little predator was the only commandant.

Wallace closed his eyes and slumped against the wall of the powder magazine, his weight bearing him down. Then, unwilling to yield, he forced himself to stand erect, squared his shoulders, and wiped the perspiration from his face that formed despite the coolness of the night.

"All right, you phantoms, out with you; I'm ready for you. Come on!" He drew both the dirk and short sword, Old Butch and Bonechucker, and slashed at the night shadows. The air swelled with the sounds of battle, the screams of the dying, the cannon's roar and the rattle of rifle fire, the clash of steel bayonets, hunting knives, clubbing rifles, and tomahawks. Texicans were fighting tooth and nail around him, the air thick with smoke and fire and the ground running red . . .

"Señor Wallace?"

Was this the ghost at last materializing to accuse him? All these years his brother's spirit had wandered aimlessly and unavenged. Wallace had set vengeance aside for a dream of empire, a kingdom of rolling prairie, of bright rivers and limitless horizons, of a big sky, this beautiful country, this Texas.

His eyes loomed large as the figure cautiously approached. "Señor Wallace, it is me."

"Roberto?"

"Sí, my friend. I came to find you. My father and I were worried about you."

"Jesus worries too much."

"Come with me," Roberto said. "Leave this place. There is the stink of death here." Young Zavala glanced down at the knives pointed at him and breathed a sigh of relief when Wallace returned them to his belt.

"Your father is a good man," Wallace declared. "And a damn fine blacksmith." His speech was slurred, and he wondered if he was making any sense. Too many emotions this night, too many shades of right and wrong. What was a man to do? Why try to make sense of it? "At night all cats are gray," he told Zavala. Then with Roberto at his side he walked out of the Alamo, leaving the tequila-fueled images of life and death behind in the shadows. He turned and for a brief second thought he spied another shape watching him, diaphanous, shifting. Yes, it was him, his brother; it could only be him. And his lips were moving. A warning?

"What?" Suddenly Wallace had a premonition that something terrible was about to happen, disaster was closing in on them. He saw dying men, a terrible battle, hand-to-hand fighting, a death struggle. Then the image was gone and so was its messenger. "Wait, Samuel! I don't understand."

His outburst startled Roberto, who blessed himself

and kissed the image of the Blessed Virgin Mary stamped on the holy medal dangling against his chest.

"Samuel! What are you trying to say?" William shouted.

Zavala searched the moonlit mission for any other sign of life.

The two men were alone here. Alone. Whatever Wallace saw waited in the heart of darkness.

FOR A WHILE THINGS SETTLED DOWN IN TEXAS. The military courts were gone. In their place, Don Murillo Saldevar as the alcalde of San Antonio governed wisely and fairly. The Texicans trusted him. Stephen Austin recognized his limitations as a soldier and did not object when Sam Houston got himself appointed commander of the Texas Militia, a paltry little force bivouacked over by San Felipe, near the Big Thicket.

Just as Esperanza had predicted, William "Big Foot" Wallace volunteered to be the eyes and ears of Houston's militia and stood ready to sound the alarm at the first sign of an enemy's approach. Throughout the winter, he ranged those borderlands—sometimes alone, other times with a trusted compadre—and followed the Rio Grande always searching the skyline for a telltale wisp of dust stirred by an advancing column of men. It wasn't long before his patience and perseverance were rewarded.

Now some folk claim Antonio Lopez de Santa Anna was a great general. He was wily and arrogant, true enough, and no man was ever more convinced of his destiny, more confident of his own invincibility. He reached Texas in mid-February and crossed the Rio Grande at Presidio. It was a glorious sight; five thousand lancers, dragoons, artillery, grenadiers, and infantry who had crushed a revolt in Zacatecas, broken the back of a revolution in Coahuila, now had come to Texas to restore order and destroy anyone who stood in their path.

William Wallace was there to welcome them....

21

---◆---

"WELCOME TO TEXAS,
YOU SON OF A BITCH!"

Wallace had President Santa Anna dead in his sights.
Then a drop of moisture seeped into the corner of William's eye and he blinked and rubbed it clear. He balanced the rifle on a tooth-shaped outcropping of granite,
licked his thumb, and moistened the sight at the end of
the barrel.

"*Mi amigo,* what are you fixing to do?" Roberto Zavala nervously asked, crouching alongside the big Texican.

"Doesn't seem right ol' Santa Anna should march all
this way and not receive a proper greeting." William
adjusted his sombrero to shield his eyes from the glare
of the sun overhead. Despite the chill wind, heat waves
danced off the arid landscape. Save for the river itself
and the trees nurtured by its proximity, this was a place
of dry, harsh beauty. Even the column of men strung out
along the Camino Real was dwarfed by the immensity
of the terrain.

"That's an impossible shot from here," Roberto observed.

"You're right," William said with a wink. He glanced
back at the column. Santa Anna had taken the lead and
not bothered to post any skirmishers as he forded the
river. The general expected no trouble and had turned
the crossing into a ceremonial advance, hoping to inspire

his troops. "You stay here; I'll be back directly."

"Have you lost your senses?"

Wallace jabbed a thumb in the direction of the horses they had ground-tethered in a dry wash. "Wait for me down in that gully, and when you see me come running don't dally." He wiped his forearm across his face, dry-swallowed, then checked his rifle. The weapon was loaded and primed. Both men were as careworn and weathered-looking as the boots they wore. Their features were dust-caked, crow's-feet stretched around their eyes from squinting into the sun—hard faces, hardened hearts.

As Wallace stalked off across the uneven terrain, a spyglass in his hand, his thoughts wandered back to the day he had volunteered to ride patrol throughout the winter months. It had been a difficult decision, keeping a respectful distance from San Antonio and Esperanza Saldevar. But life was easier this way. Being in love with another man's wife sure complicated things. Mad Jack would say, "A wise man knows when to keep his distance," and the old sea dog would be right.

With Roberto Zavala at his side, Wallace crisscrossed the roads leading up from old Mexico. When their supplies ran low the two men trapped and lived off the land, hunting antelope, wild turkey, and white-tailed deer when the bacon and salt pork were gone. Texas winter brought days of bright sunlight and mellow temperatures, interspersed with a week or two of freezing temperatures when a blue norther struck and lashed the deserted hills with wind and rain and ice pellets that stung like buckshot. But Wallace was the kind of man born without an ounce of quit in him, so he endured. And Roberto was not about to abandon him.

However, with only enough coffee left for a couple of days and looking forward to their third evening meal of fried rattlesnake and boiled jicama root, the two men reached a mutual understanding and had just decided to start back for San Antonio when they spied a column of dust spiraling up against the hard blue sky.

A herd of buffalo or an approaching army? Wallace and Zavala forgot about their dwindling supplies and tracked the dust to its source. William scrambled up a steep incline of loose shale and, removing his sombrero, eased the spyglass over the edge of a limestone ridge overlooking the Rio Grande. Before him was just about the prettiest army the big man had ever seen.

The Otaxaca Regiment took the lead in their white tunics and blue trousers. The Zacatecas Regulars, in red coats and white trousers, came next, followed by the Coahuila Brigade in blue tunics and faded red britches. Mounted dragoons garbed in the red-and-black uniforms of Santa Anna's personal guard surrounded the general. A formidable troop of hard-riding lancers in green coats, white pants tucked into thigh-high black boots, and brass helmets with horsehair plumes scouted the perimeter. Gen. Antonio Lopez de Santa Anna rode at the center of all this activity. He was resplendent in a scarlet-and-gold tunic, dark blue trousers stitched with silver thread, medals gleaming upon his chest, and on his head a magnificent *chapeau bras,* a broad black hat embroidered with gold thread, upturned at the sides, and crowned with a thick presentation of white plumage.

Wallace followed a deer trail that led up through some loose shale to the top of a bluff several hundred feet closer to the column of soldiers snaking along the south bank of the Rio Grande. The column crossed the muddy expanse at its low point and threaded their way north into the golden hills. Wallace brought out his spyglass and focused on the man in the lead. *El presidente*'s image filled the eyepiece. An arrogant, forceful man of average height, his black hair was brushed forward to conceal a receding hairline. Confidence radiated from

him like warmth from the sun and spread to the men
under his command.

Wallace shifted his focus, played the lens across the
faces of the men marching toward him. "Cos," he muttered beneath his breath as the general's combative image materialized out of the dust. And there was
Bradburn, looking haggard and uncomfortable, his great
bulk astride a mouse brown dun. William wasn't surprised. The two men had taken an oath on their honor
never to return to Texas. It seemed honor was in scarce
supply south of the Rio Grande.

A flash of sunlight caught Wallace's attention, and
once again he swept the ranks and was forced to squint
against the glare of the sunlight on the tips of the lances
as a troop of cavalry forded the river and plunged
through the sluggish waters and up the north embankment. William thought he recognized the uniforms and
turned his spyglass on them.

The muscles along his jawline began to twitch; his
mouth went dry as he recognized the officer directing
the horsemen to take the point and fan out in several
directions. The features were unmistakable, even though
they were partly concealed by his horsehair-plumed
brass helmet. Wallace's jaw dropped. The officer's name
rolled off his tongue as easily as a muttered curse. "Juan
Diego Guadiz." Even as he spoke the words, the man
rode out of range and disappeared behind an embankment. William heard his brother's ghost whisper in his
ear, *And now you know . . .*"

Wallace set the spyglass aside and shouldered his rifle. The gunshot rang out across the landscape, echoed
off the rugged walls, repeated like a withering volley of
gunshots. Santa Anna's pride and joy, his beloved,
imperial-looking hat, was blown from his head and
ripped apart by the impact of the rifle ball and landed
beneath the iron-shod hooves of the horses behind him,

who proceeded to trample the remains into a shapeless mass. The general jerked backward as if he had been hit and slid from the saddle, landing on his rump in the dirt. He clutched his tunic, half-expecting to see blood spurting from a wound, then scrambled to his feet, tripped over his saber, and fell face forward, landing in a most undignified position.

"Welcome to Texas, you son of a bitch!" Wallace shouted, standing atop the ridge. His voice rang out across the brakes, shouted from the heart, from the violence of his memories. He spun on his heels and cradling his rifle trotted downslope, slipping in the shale, steadying himself with the butt of his rifle, scrambling, twisting, reaching solid ground. He stopped to catch his breath, then straightened and closed his eyes and roared out, "Guadiz!"

The name exploded from the depths of his soul, the cry of a man in torment, enraged as the memories and the guilt flooded back. His brother's murderer, up from the south and out of the past. William wanted to stay. But now wasn't the time or place. To linger was to court disaster—he had business elsewhere. The people in San Antonio must be warned. Santa Anna's army was too big to resist. Texas was going to need a lot more volunteers. There were some hard days ahead.

He had to run now. Run from Guadiz as he had before. *No, it isn't the same*, William told himself. *I am a different man. This is my country, my land; Juan Diego Guadiz is the stranger. And when the time comes, no army on earth will spare him a day of reckoning.*

Wallace could imagine the commotion surrounding Santa Anna as the troops hurried forward to protect him. The dragoons and lancers must be scouring the hills in search of the sniper. The image quickened his pace, and it wasn't long before he scurried along the arroyo and arrived alongside Roberto Zavala.

"The way I see it, if Santa Anna wants to be president of Texas he's got to run for the office just like everyone else!" Wallace breathlessly exclaimed, grabbing the reins from Zavala.

The younger man looked perplexed. "I heard the shot." Zavala asked, "What happened to the general? Did you 'elect' him?"

"No." A smile of grim amusement flitted across Wallace's face as he pictured Santa Anna, his hat shot away, panicked, fumbling with the saber and landing facedown in the dirt. "But I nominated him pretty good."

Santa Anna warmed himself by the fire in front of his tent and took comfort in the fact that his army was across the river and secure for the night. He took comfort in the skill of his officers and the morale of his men, comfort in the warmth of the fire, the meal his servant had prepared, the French brandy gleaming coppery gold in the crystal decanter on the walnut table next to his camp chair. It was good brandy, its bouquet so intense that the mere act of inhaling its aroma left a taste on the palate. These things were good and appeased him. The general found solace in the knowledge that he commanded the most formidable host in all of Texas and that he had never known defeat. He was proud of himself and all that he attained, and if anyone mentioned the incident along the riverbank and the indignity he had suffered at the hands of an unknown assailant the general would have the fool shot.

"Come, Paloma; drink to your brother's health. He should be back soon and with good news to report," said Santa Anna to the woman seated by the fire. He leaned forward and poured a measure of brandy for Juan Diego's twin sister. His gaze roamed her lithe body, barely concealed by the vaquero's jacket and tight breeches. He envisioned running his fingers through her black hair that was gathered back in a tight bun and concealed beneath an ocher bandanna. If she hadn't been the niece of his old friend and supporter, the governor of Veracruz, Santa Anna would have ordered her to his bed long ago. Alas, this one would have to come willingly. Well, no matter; time was in his favor. After all, he was *el presidente.* What woman could resist him?

General Cos cleared his throat and then held out his plate as the president's servant began to serve the dinner—catfish braised in butter, peppers and rice, frijoles, tortillas fried crisp and drizzled with honey. The air was permeated with the aroma of the cook fires radiating out in a wheel-like pattern from the general's tent—so many pockets of fire that it seemed as if the hillsides and riverbank, like the obsidian sky overhead, were strewn with stars. The common soldiers were only too glad to make a meal of beans and tortillas with a few links of chorizo sausage fried up for good measure to spice up a cold night.

"Speak up, Martin; what is on your mind?"

Cos considered his options and tried to make the best of a bad situation. He wasn't about to address the sniper, at least not directly. He glanced in Bradburn's direction. The rotund Englishman was wolfing down the food as if it were his last meal on earth. He glanced up from his plate when he sensed Cos staring at him.

"John and I are concerned by what has happened," Cos said.

The blood drained from Santa Anna's features, and his expression grew stern. Bradburn appeared horrified that his name had been dragged into the discussion. He could see no benefit in a confrontation with the president of Mexico. Santa Anna was already thin-skinned when it came to his reputation.

"What do you mean?"

"We have lost the element of surprise."

Santa Anna stood and looked around him at the troops fanned out along banks of the Rio Grande. His breath clouded the air with every exhalation. The temperature was falling as the barren hills released their warmth to the cloudless sky. The moon rose behind a vast array of broken ridges and the spiny supplications of the ocotillo cacti that grew in rich profusion in the arroyos and dotted the slopes.

"Look about you," he addressed his brother-in-law. "What do you see?"

Bradburn rose to the occasion and interjected a remark: "An invincible army."

Santa Anna nodded, pleased. "Precisely," he replied. Cos glared at the Englishman, but Santa Anna clapped Bradburn on the back. "You are a perceptive man. When I drive the rabble out of San Antonio, perhaps I shall make you alcalde."

That had been Cos's position along with governor. The general decided to repair the damage. "I only mention this in case you might want me to lead a force of dragoons and lancers and storm San Antonio and occupy the town before you get there."

"Well done," Santa Anna chuckled. "You are a brave man after all, Martin. But that will not be necessary. I intend to arrive in full force. I want to impress these Texicans . . . before I kill them." A disheartened foe was a beaten one. "Let them see us. Let them watch us sweep toward them like an oncoming tide."

"Some of these Texicans are a bold lot. Don Murillo Saldevar, Sam Houston, Stephen Austin, and more especially the ruffian William Wallace," said Bradburn, reeling off the names of his enemies. "Men like him are not the panicking kind." He had his own agenda in this and wanted to be certain his enemies did not escape Santa Anna's wrath.

"Wallace?" Paloma said, "Saldevar? . . . The names

are familiar. There is a woman, *Elle anda en las sombra*, a shadow walker with her cards."

"Don Murillo's wife," Bradburn told her, his tongue moistening his lips. Now there was a dessert he intended to sample. "You know them, Señorita Guadiz?"

"Our paths have crossed," Paloma replied, shivering.

"Here, my dear; take my coat," Santa Anna purred, draping his medal-bedecked coat over the woman's shoulders. But the cold she felt was the chill hand of fate, and the only protection against that was the reassuring presence of the pistol tucked in her belt and the knowledge that her brother was without peer with pistol or blade.

"You are most kind, señor," she said. "And do not worry, General Cos. Men like my brother, Colonel Guadiz, are not so much worried of being watched but that our enemy might not stand and fight. We have chased some of these rascals before." Paloma took a sip of brandy. The warmth spread to her limbs, and she closed her eyes in satisfaction. At that moment a commotion erupted at the perimeter of the encampment, and word soon arrived that the lancers had returned. Moments later, a scowling Juan Diego approached the general's tent. He nodded to the men, glanced in his sister's direction and shook his head, then removed his brass helmet with its horsehair plume and tucked it under his arm and saluted Santa Anna.

"Excuse my intrusion, Your Excellency, but with darkness we lost the trail. There were two men, though. They ran like rabbits before us. And their horses were in better shape than ours. We lost them on the Camino Real. No doubt we will find them again in San Antonio."

Santa Anna frowned and his lips drew tight. The muscle along his jaw began to twitch.

"Then we shall deal with them later," Paloma spoke

up, defusing the situation. "Victory is best when it is savored."

Santa Anna glanced in her direction, slowly smiled, then stood and indicated the food set out for their enjoyment. "Come and eat, my gallant colonel."

"*Gracias,* but I must see to my men first," Guadiz said.

"I will walk with you," Paloma interjected. The woman set her food aside and, excusing herself, hurried to her brother's side as he headed back through the camp.

Burly old Sgt. Cayetano Obregon emerged from the shadows and fell in step behind the twins. "Don't suppose you could bring along some of that brandy, ma'am?"

Paloma glanced over her shoulder, then, reaching inside her tunic, removed a small silver flask she had surreptitiously filled from Santa Anna's own decanter while the general was occupied with his meal. She tossed the flask into the sergeant's outstretched hands.

"Bless you, señorita. This will soothe these old bones of mine."

"I am surprised you can feel those 'old bones' through all the layers of fat."

Obregon muttered beneath his breath. And yet staring down at the flask, he could afford to be forgiving. At Diego's command he hurried on ahead while the twins made their way toward the edge of camp, away from the glare of the campfires. Alone at last, Diego slowed his pace until they ambled side by side across the moonlit landscape. Coyotes howled in the distance.

"What is it, Paloma? . . . What mischief are you about?"

"Must I have news just because I wish to be with my brother?" the woman softly laughed.

Their boots made a crunching sound in the loose

rocks underfoot. His saber slapped against his thigh as he walked. Juan Diego was fiercely handsome. War had aged him, tested the bonds his sister used to "guide" him. He was more direct now and given to going his own way . . . until the headaches returned, and then only she could ease the pain.

"William Wallace . . . do you remember?"

Diego stopped and looked at her, oblivious to the impressive array of soldiers displayed before them. Many of the infantrymen had their wives and children living with them in their tents. To some it might have seemed odd to find children scampering and playing among the stacked muskets, saddles and lances, caissons and artillery. To these men, war was their occupation and the army was their home. It was the way of things.

"Ah, the *norte americano*," Guadiz said, not bothering to mask his contempt. "El Destripedor Rojo. Such a meddlesome bastard. Too bad he escaped. I would have liked to have had him at sword's point."

Paloma Turcios Guadiz grinned. Did she ever have news for him!

22

"NONE OF US ARE LOOKING TO BE MARTYRS."

There are no simple "good-byes" in a time of revolution. Each separation carries the threat of permanence. Don Murillo tried not to think of such things as he paced the sitting room and waited for Chuy Montoya to bring his carriage around to the front of the hacienda. The room was charged with tension as the landowner and his wife vied with each other over who should stay and who must leave.

"The first Señora Saldevar did as I ordered. Why must you be so stubborn?" Don Murillo blurted out. He might as well have spent the last few hours arguing with the wall for all the success he was having.

"Because I am not the first Señora Saldevar," Esperanza flatly replied.

"She knew her place."

"So do I," the young woman retorted, cheeks flushed, her black eyes bold, her mouth firm with resolve. She wore her riding clothes, a warm woolen dress of leaf green velour and high-buttoned boots. "But seeing as you refuse to bring me with you into the Alamo Mission, I shall stay here until the conflict is resolved. Then we will return to San Felipe together."

Don Murillo threw his hands in the air and turned his back on her. He walked across the room and stood leaning on the hearth. He glanced around and saw Dorotea tentatively position herself in the doorway. She seemed reluctant to intrude.

"Sister, come and talk some sense into my wife," said Don Murillo.

Esperanza prepared herself for another onslaught. She was up to it. No one was going to change her mind. On this matter she was resolute. However, today Dorotea was full of surprises.

"I, too, will remain," she said. "If it is your right to go, then it is ours to stay."

Esperanza couldn't believe her own ears. Dorotea had never taken her side in anything. Ever since the marriage, Dorotea had been at odds with her sister-in-law. There had been no common ground. Now, all of a sudden, she was supporting Esperanza. It was becoming a day of "first."

Don Murillo sighed, overwhelmed by the combined forces arrayed against him. Two stubborn women made a united front, which was two more than any man should ever have to confront. "I stand defeated. Stay. Both of you. Though it goes against my better judgment."

"I have prepared a basket of tortillas and *barbacoa*," Dorotea added, sensing the matter was settled. She had spent the entire morning in the kitchen, preparing coffee, chorizo, and eggs. It was the way she took her mind off her worries. The widow held up a woven basket covered with a small cloth to keep the contents warm. She hated this struggle, wanted no part of a revolution, and thought her brother rash and even foolish to jeopardize all he held dear. He was a man of substance with so much to lose.

"Put it on the floor of the carriage," said Don Murillo. "Chuy's bringing it around front."

"As you wish," Dorotea replied, her features softened by concern for her brother's safety. Her black dress rustled as she headed for the front of the house and vanished through the front door.

Esperanza allowed her gaze to drift across the bookshelves. All of this learning but no answers other than what she felt to be true in her heart.

Don Murillo stoked the log in the fireplace until flames danced along its gray-black bark. "Why are you doing this?"

"It is my duty, my privilege," she replied. "Even a servant can have a sense of honor."

He started to reprimand her, then reconsidered. He was tired of arguing, if indeed these were the final moments. "Well then, it is time," he tenderly said. In his ruffled shirt, brocaded vest, waistcoat, and flat-crowned hat, the landowner looked as if he were on his way to the theater instead of a war. Only the brace of pistols thrust in his belt belied the image. It was a scene being repeated in varying degrees throughout the town. Men were kissing their loved ones, stealing one last embrace, doing what must be done in a time of conflict and conflagration.

He took her in his arms and held her close, kissed her willing mouth, breathed in the smell of her, memorized the feel of her in his arms. He might need a memory of warmth in the days to come.

"I read the cards last night, while you slept," she said, her cheek against his neck. He felt a tear moisten his flesh. Had she glimpsed his fate? Tears weren't a good sign.

"I do not wish to know," he quickly stated. "Dust is our destiny. If not now, then it will be." He brushed a strand of hair back from her moist cheek. "If that tear is for me, then I am happy."

"Who else would it be for?"

"I know you care for me," he said. "But you are

young and in the fullness of your years. I would never have blamed you if—"

She put her fingers to his lips. "No. Do not say it." Her eyes were full and moist. "Mi amor," she said. And meant it.

A straggling procession of wagons and mules loaded down with kegs of gunpowder, round shot, food, water barrels, and the last of the medical supplies hurtled up the Calle de la Mission, kicking up clods of dirt and a dusty haze that trickled into the cold blue sky.

Seated astride a sturdy mustang, William Wallace skirted the supply line and galloped on ahead to the Alamo. Sentries on the wall hailed the big man as he approached, but the gate failed to open.

A soldier perched squarely above the gate called out, "Halt! Who goes there?" and went so far as to brandish his rifle.

William reined in his mount and, shading his eyes, glared up at the man above. "Is that you, Mr. Kania?"

"Sure is!" the shopkeeper shouted down.

"Then you know me."

"Orders are orders. Colonel Travis said I was to stop anyone from entering without they give the proper word of passage. You're supposed to say it."

William slipped one of the pistols from his belt, cocked it, and drew a bead on the sentry. "How about I just shoot you off that damn wall?"

"That'll do!" the shopkeeper called down. "Come on through."

Wallace rode on into the compound, looked about for Bill Travis, and found him overseeing the last-minute placement of a twelve-pounder cannon atop a corner redoubt.

"I want this gun to be able to sweep the road!" he

called out. "But we also need to be able to protect the main gate should it be breached."

A cold north wind hounded the Texicans as they used every minute to bolster the defenses of the makeshift fort. Time was precious. Columns of swiftly riding dragoons, sent ahead by Santa Anna, were reported to be advancing on the town. Although Wallace had yet to engage a Mexican patrol, he had heard what sounded like gunfire reverberate in the foothills upriver.

A party of Tennesseans led by David Crockett had skirmished with a troop of Mexican cavalry two days' ride from San Antonio. Though only numbering a couple of dozen men, Crockett and his "Smoky Mountain boys" had acquitted themselves with distinction and sent the patrols scurrying to safety. Wallace had taken an instant liking to Crockett and found him a welcome addition to the garrison.

As William walked his mustang across the parade ground, he marveled at what Travis had accomplished. Over the course of the past couple of months the lawyer had proved himself to be a capable officer and engineer. Redoubts had been strengthened; sections of crumbling adobe wall had been reinforced with brick and timbers. He had molded the defenders into a real military unit, much to the chagrin of Bowie and the more vocal volunteers who didn't take kindly to rank and protocol and were accustomed to doing what they pleased when they pleased.

"Wallace, thank heavens you're here!" Travis exclaimed, scrambling down from the redoubt. The lawyer's once smooth, graceful hands were calloused and begrimed. His blue coat was smudged with dirt, the red sash about his waist faded and streaked with mud. His boots were spattered and scuffed.

Wallace's gaze swept over the walls and the mismatched group of defenders who intended to defy an army that outnumbered them twenty-five to one. Mad Jack would have never stood for it. A freebooter never bucked the odds. He could imagine the old sea dog arguing they ought to slash and run and live to fight another day. But the men here were full of ideals, proud and ornery, and convinced they followed a noble cause. *There isn't a pirate among them,* Wallace thought, *and more's the pity.* A premonition of disaster had a strong hold on him.

Three days ago he had ridden in from the borderlands with word of Santa Anna's approaching army. Within hours the entire populace had heard the news. What followed was a night of endless-seeming debate that ended with Travis ordering the militia into the Alamo.

Jim Bowie, cantakerous as ever, retired to one of the town's many cantinas and had not been seen since. Meanwhile the townspeople waited, many of them unsure where their loyalties lay. The euphoria of independence had begun to wear off the closer Santa Anna came.

"I begged, borrowed, and outright stole all the powder and shot in the town," the big man said, jabbing a thumb in the direction of the wagons. "I figured you'd find a use for it."

"Yes indeed," Travis replied. Despite the dust and his weary countenance, he remained a dark and dashing figure, like someone's aristocratic son playing at war, caught up in the romance of the struggle. "I know you think this is a foolish gamble. Santa Anna commands a vastly superior force."

"I've little stomach for a stand-up fight. At least not until Santa Anna gets whittled down to size. You'll feel the same way once you see what we are up against."

Travis cleared his throat and removed a folded piece of parchment from his vest. "I just received a dispatch from the volunteers over in Goliad. They're on the way to join us. Once they arrive we can make a real fight of it. And Stephen Austin writes that volunteers are coming in every day and joining Houston's army. But Sam's going to need us to buy him some time while he whips his command into shape."

Wallace considered the young colonel's arguments. He didn't mind risking his neck; he just wanted it to be for good reason. "I reckon we can slow General Santa Anna and maybe even give him a bloody nose. I'm game. Just so long as you know when it's time to turn Mother's picture to the wall and make a run for it," Wallace told him. "And live to fight another day."

"We understand each other. None of us are looking to be martyrs." Travis glanced about to check if anyone else was within earshot. He lowered his voice. "Perhaps you could find Colonel Bowie. I sent that Crockett fellow after him, but I fear whiskey has a similar hold on the Tennessean."

"I'll run them to cover," William said. "Don't judge Bowie too harshly. Keep in mind he will do his part when the time comes." He touched the brim of his sombrero as a gesture of farewell, turned his mount, and started back through the main gate. He waited for a pair of wagons to ease through, then rode through the arched entrance and headed for town.

Wallace had only gone a few hundred yards when he recognized Don Murillo's carriage rumbling across the bridge, breaking from the emerald shadows beneath the trees, and rolling toward him up the mission road. William couldn't help himself. He had to check to see whether the carriage held one person or two. He glimpsed the *haciendado* alone in the carnage, shielded from the north wind by a black leather frame. The carriage was pulled by a dappled stallion with white stockings and a blazed face. Chuy Montoya rode a few paces behind the carriage. The remainder of the vaqueros either had been dispatched to East Texas or were already within the walls of the Alamo. The *segundo* sat slouched in the saddle, a quirt dangling from his wrist. He was a man of few words but direct action.

Wallace cut across the road and intersected the carriage. He removed his sombrero out of deference and respect for the older man. The air turned brisk with every gust that tousled Wallace's unruly mane.

"Good afternoon, Señor Saldevar."

"Well now, I think I recognize the red hair. Yes, by heaven, it is William Wallace. You have been too long a stranger, my friend."

"I hoped you and your wife might return to San Felipe before the trouble starts."

"Too late. It's begun. However, I believe I have earned the right to join Colonel Travis at the Alamo. Chuy and I cannot allow you and the others to have all the fun," said Don Murillo. "Then again, once he arrives, perhaps Santa Anna can be made to listen to reason."

"Only at gunpoint," William replied. "The man I saw crossing the Rio Grande looked about as reasonable as a starved panther. Roberto Zavala would tell you the same thing, but I sent him back to San Felipe to help look after his family."

"A wise move. I wish I could convince Esperanza to wait for me in East Texas. But she refuses to leave San Antonio as long as I am here. Although Santa Anna is not the kind of man to make war on women and children, still I am worried. Perhaps *you* could talk some sense into her, persuade her to take my sister and return to our ranch up north. She is especially fond of you. Stop by my house and reason with her."

"I don't rightly see how I would succeed where you failed, Don Murillo," William said, uncomfortable with the subject.

"I am old, not blind. Who can we be honest with, if

not with our friends?" Don Murillo leaned forward, his
features in sunlight. He brushed a hand through his thick
white hair, then scratched at his neatly trimmed beard.
"You and I both know she might listen to you, my young
friend."

Wallace lifted his eyes to the hills. Before the day
was out they might be lined with troops. Now was hardly
the time or place for this moment of truth. What did the
haciendado suspect? Since the night when William had
almost succumbed to temptation he had kept his distance
from the Road of Sorrow and the house of Saldevar.
"Don Murillo, I hope that you know I have never betrayed our friendship."

"Of course," Don Murillo replied. "I have never
thought otherwise. That is why you have always been
welcome under my roof, despite the fact that you are in
love with my wife."

"I have to find Bowie," William said, eager to change
the subject. He returned the sombrero to its proper place.
The broad brim shielded his features from the bold glare
of winter sunlight. "If you will excuse me, sir—"

"Vaya con Dios," Don Murillo replied. At a flick of
the reins the stallion started forward. The carriage rolled
off in the direction of the mission, following the last of
the freight wagons through the gate.

"You need help with Bowie?" Chuy asked as he rode
past.

Wallace shook his head no. "Watch out for Señor
Saldevar," he told the *segundo*.

"Always," Montoya replied.

A half hour later, after making inquiries at two other
saloons and the local bordello, Wallace dismounted in
front of Rita's Cantina and knew exactly who he would
find inside. He stood in the middle of Calle de Soledad
on the north edge of town and took a moment to peruse

the deserted-looking array of houses and storefronts. He was being watched. Townsmen and their families were hiding behind those bolted doors and shuttered windows. William could taste the fear. It was bitter on the tongue.

A pack of dogs started barking on the north edge of town. Something had alerted the animals, but the source remained unseen. The pair of horses tethered in front of Rita's ignored the dogs. Wallace recognized the geldings. One belonged to David Crockett. That figured. Bowie hated to drink alone.

"Are you planning on going in there?" David Crockett asked, rounding the corner of the cantina. Middle-aged, average in height, stocky, with muscular forearms and an infectious grin, Crockett and his Tennesseans had only been in town a few days, but already the man had a friend in William. Who couldn't like him? He'd been an Indian fighter, a congressman, a river brawler; he spun a good yarn and was a marksman without peer. " 'Cause I'd sooner wrassle a bear and dip my ass naked in a honey tree than take a bottle of whiskey away from the likes of Jim Bowie when he's on a drunk." In his black frock coat and gray woolen trousers tucked into his calf-high boots, Crockett might have passed for a preacher save' for the beaver hat he favored, with an eagle feather tucked in the brim.

"So you've been waiting him out?"

"I haven't been able to come up with a better plan," Crockett said.

"You have to know how to talk to him. That's all." William walked across the street to a horse trough and nearby well. He removed the bucket from its rope and dipped the bucket into the trough. Wallace headed straight for the front door of the cantina. "I'll be back directly."

He disappeared inside. A few seconds of stillness ticked past broken only by a dog barking and the lazy whir of cabin bees overhead near the roofline. Suddenly Crockett heard a loud splash and an even louder howl of indignation. Moments later William hurled through the front door followed by Bowie, big and snarling and rawboned, soaked to the skin, his shaggy brown hair and sideburns plastered to his skull.

"Wallace! You son of a bitch!" He lunged at the Texican, who darted out of harm's way. Bowie crashed into the side of the building, staggered back, and noticed his audience. "Howdy, Crockett. Did you come by to drink with me? Good. I'll be just a minute. I got to kill me that redheaded bastard."

"Are you certain we can spare him?" Crockett asked.

"What's that supposed to mean?" Bowie replied, drying his grizzled features on the sleeve of his shirt, which was already soaked to begin with.

"We might be needing the younker," Crockett said.

"For target practice, maybe."

"No, to help us with them." Crockett was looking past Bowie, his steady stare focused on something up the street. Bowie lurched about, rubbed his eyes, growled. He stepped around Wallace, who had his back to the knife fighter. Bowie managed to focus on the smartly uniformed Mexican dragoons watching them from the edge of town, about a hundred yards up the street, where the grassland began.

The patrol's scarlet tunics and horsehair helmets shimmered in the sunlight.

"Who the hell invited them to the party?" Bowie grumbled.

The patrol loosed a volley in the direction of the three men. Puffs of black smoke and orange flame spewed from their carbines, the short-barreled rifles favored by Santa Anna's mounted troops. The rumble of the guns reverberated down the street.

"Looks like they're playing your favorite song," Wallace said, swinging up into the saddle. Crockett and Bowie weren't far behind.

"I don't think I want to stay for the dance," Bowie declared. He darted back inside the cantina only to re-emerge with a pair of rifles. Crockett had his own. Bowie tossed a rifle to Wallace. "Try one of these. It'll reach further than those pistols of yours."

Wallace caught the long rifle in midair. "Maybe we can get them to lower their guns and palaver with us."

The dragoons charged, rifles blazing, sabers flashing in the sunlight.

"Then again, maybe not," he added.

Crockett fired. The unexpected boom of his rifle made Wallace jump. One of the dragoons tossed his carbine into the air, clutched his chest, and pitched from horseback. He crashed through a hitching post and rolled onto his side, where he stuck, propped against the wood. The patrol charged them. Wallace and Bowie glanced at each other and then raised their rifles. They fired in unison. Two more of the dragoons dropped from horseback, bounced off the hard-packed earth, their bodies rolling over in the street, arms and legs flailing wildly until they came to rest upon the hard ground. They'd ridden a long way to die.

"Mine hit the ground first," Bowie boasted.

"Mine rode the taller horse," Wallace countered.

"Like hell!" Bowie growled.

Lead slugs fanned the air, thudding into the dirt around them. An olla dangling near the front door of the cantina exploded into a thousand shards, spraying water everywhere. Slugs glanced off the earth and ricocheted off porch supports and thudded into shuttered windows. "Maybe you two ought to settle your differences later," Crockett suggested.

"Works for me," Wallace said, pointing the mustang toward the river and the mission fortress beyond. The mustang was born to run. William leaned forward in the saddle and gave the animal his lead. But Bowie and Crockett weren't far behind.

The three men plunged through the river, forded the shallows, fought their way up the opposite bank and out onto the clearing and the open plain, all the while running a gauntlet of gun smoke.

From his vantage point atop the gate, Pvt. Robert Kania, the storekeeper, saw the three horsemen riding flat out across the meadow and turning onto the mission road. He grabbed a spyglass and studied the riders being pursued by the patrol until he recognized the big man with the long red hair streaming in the wind, his sombrero dangling between his shoulder blades from the thong about his throat. He remembered Wallace's earlier admonition.

"Close the gate?" a man said from below.

"Hell, no!"

Travis and Don Murillo hurried up to the redoubt with Chuy Montoya right alongside them. "It's Wallace. And he's bringing Bowie and Crockett," Travis said.

To the rear of the three men, the dragoons fanned out across the grassland and tried to cut the three off from the mission.

Within the Alamo, the Texicans were flocking to the walls eager to catch a glimpse of the action. Travis ordered covering fire laid down, and several marksmen stationed above the gate alongside Kania opened fire. Don Murillo suggested a taste of the nine-pounder might give the Mexican patrol something to think about. Under his direction a crew swiftly prepared the gun. Saldevar corrected the elevation and then touched a firebrand to the priming powder. The cannon bellowed and sent a round shot over the heads of the three Texicans. It landed with a thud and exploded a few yards in front of the dragoons. Horses shied and reared and tossed several of their riders, including the officer in charge, onto the ground.

A cheer went up from the men on the wall. The dragoons halted their mounts and began to mill about while the captain and his subordinates recovered their horses. The marksmen on the mission walls continued to pepper the hapless dragoons with gunfire that left another couple of men writhing with flesh wounds. It wasn't long before the Mexican patrol abandoned the chase and withdrew beyond the range of the Texicans' long rifles.

Minutes later, Wallace won the race, dashing through the gate into the makeshift fortress. Bowie and Crockett weren't far behind. The defenders crowded around the three men and clapped them on the back. Someone produced a jug of whiskey that got passed around and drained. Wallace waved to Kania. The storekeeper nodded and shouted down for a pair of sentries below him to close the gate.

"Welcome, gentlemen!" Travis called out from the redoubt. "You're safe now."

Wallace looked around at the pitifully small force of Texicans occupying the mission and couldn't help but compare them to the army he knew was just over the horizon. Safe. More like trapped. But damn if he wasn't in good company.

23

"SOONER OR LATER WE ALL ANSWER FOR OUR DEEDS."

Esperanza and Dorotea stood on the balcony of the hacienda and watched the advance guard of Santa Anna's army file through the street. A brown haze settled over the town, limiting the visibility. Even from the balcony they could only see for a few blocks. The noise was ominous—tramping feet, jangle of harness, officers barking their orders to the enlisted men. Row after row of infantry passed along the Calle Dolorosa, their bayonets gleaming in the sun. Long lines of mule-drawn supply wagons followed the foot soldiers. And from the sound of things, provisions were being confiscated at every shop. It was only a matter of time before the Saldevar hacienda was approached. The women watched that dreadful parade of dragoons, lancers, and infantry throughout the afternoon. Eventually the dust churned up by the army became unbearable, and the women sought respite within the hacienda.

Dorotea began to pace the front sitting room, her hands fidgeting with a lace kerchief, her mouth a grim slash that made her seem all the more severe. Esperanza retired to the kitchen and hung a kettle over the fire. Dorotea sought her out.

"I have behaved badly toward you," she said, as if making an announcement. The older woman glanced down at her trembling hands and clasped them together for strength. "I was afraid you would put me out of the house, turn my brother against me. I had nowhere else to go."

Esperanza crossed the kitchen and handed the woman a loaf of crusty bread. "We shall have some with our coffee." Dorotea realized that by her actions Esperanza was telling her that no apologies were necessary. Dorotea had just begun to slice some bread when someone began to hammer at the front door. She dropped the knife and placed her hand to her lips to stifle her own outcry. Esperanza rose from the table and hurried toward the front of the house. She managed to unbolt the door before the soldiers hammered it loose from its hinges with their rifle butts.

Esperanza threw a shawl around her shoulders and stepped outside. The soldiers retreated a few paces and allowed her to confront an old acquaintance, Col. Juan Diego Guadiz. The officer remained in the street, flanked by a detachment of dragoons—impassive men in dark green waistcoats and horsehair-plumed hats, sabers rattling at their sides as they awaited the colonel's orders.

Paloma Guadiz, imperiously erect, lithe and dangerous, dressed as a vaquero, folded her slender hands across the pommel of her silver-embossed saddle. Her dun gelding shook his head and chewed the bit in his mouth. The horse was eager to keep moving. Diego's sister maneuvered her way out of her brother's shadow, smiled, and touched her braided quirt to the brim of her hat. Esperanza had never seen such cold eyes in another person. Even Juan Diego, for all his arrogance, paled in comparison. Esperanza shivered despite herself and dug deeper into her shawl.

Two of the dragoons parted and allowed John Bradburn to dismount and approach the woman in the doorway. The former alcalde bowed and removed his hat, revealing his sunburned scalp and wispy strands of hair. His thick features positively beamed.

"*Buenos tardes, señora,*" Bradburn said. "Well now, this is splendid. Simply splendid."

Esperanza ignored the Englishman, whom she considered a lackey, and gave her attention to Juan Diego. The colonel glanced at his sergeant, Cayetano Obregon, and the brute grinned and dismounted with Guadiz and followed him over to the woman. Bradburn was shunted out of the way and left, scowling at the intrusion. Whatever ideas he had been entertaining were of no importance to Juan Diego and his sister. Obregon walked past Esperanza and, using his carbine for a lever, pried loose one of the shutters and peered into the house. He looked back and shrugged. Paloma walked her mount forward and allowed the gelding to crowd Esperanza.

"Where are your husband and the *norte americano,* Wallace?" asked Juan Diego.

Esperanza said nothing. Guadiz repeated the question. Still, Esperanza refused to answer him. Paloma leaned down and lashed the woman across the face with the quirt. Don Murillo's wife staggered back from the blow. The braided rawhide left an ugly welt from the corner of Esperanza's eye to the base of her neck.

"Answer my brother when he speaks to you," Paloma snapped.

Esperanza glared at the woman. Paloma raised the quirt yet again. Esperanza knelt as if cowering, dug her fingers beneath the roots of a prickly pear cactus that had sprouted up through the dry earth, tore a pad free, and, ignoring the barbs in her own hand, slapped the cactus against the gelding's belly. The animal leaped away, arched his back, and began to violently buck and paw the air. Paloma could not remain in the saddle. The gelding sent the woman sprawling, much to the muted amusement of some of the dragoons. Juan Diego's sister staggered to her feet and dragged a pistol from her belt.

"No," Guadiz said, hurrying to intervene before she ruined his plans. He stepped into the line of fire, turned his back on his sister, and offered his hand to Esperanza.

The woman stood unaided. Blood trickled from the corner of her mouth. He advanced on her and Esperanza gave ground until the back of her skull slapped against the wall of the house. She could go no farther.

"I have another way of making you talk. Shall I show you?" He leaned forward and licked the trail of blood from her chin. His left hand crept up to grope her breast. The horsemen in the street exchanged glances and wondered just how much they were going to be able to see. Any one of them would have gladly exchanged places with their colonel.

Esperanza closed her eyes and forced herself not to feel what was about to happen. She would not give the soldiers the pleasure of seeing her cooperate, even if it meant sacrificing . . . everything.

"Don Murillo and William Wallace are in the mission!" Dorotea blurted out from the doorway. "*Por favor,* leave her alone!" Her cheeks were streaked with tears. She could bear it no longer. Esperanza's silence was a gallant gesture, but it had to be stopped. Dorotea knew her brother would never forgive her if she allowed this to happen.

Juan Diego nodded and stepped back. "Well now, that wasn't so difficult." He winked at Cayetano Obregon. "Personally, I was counting on a little more stubbornness. Too bad." He turned back toward the señora.

Esperanza spit in his face.

Obregon gasped and retreated a few paces. He did not want to be in harm's way when Guadiz exploded in a violent rage. Dorotea, who had tried to see Esperanza spared punishment, looked physically ill.

Juan Diego wiped the spittle from his forehead and

cheek with a silk kerchief. "Five years is a long time. Perhaps you have forgotten who I am."

"I know you," Esperanza said.

"Good." He held the kerchief up to her face, crumpled the fabric into his fist, and dropped it at her feet. "Then you know you will answer for this insult."

"Sooner or later we all answer for our deeds," she remarked.

Juan Diego looked over at his sergeant. "Take her inside. Deploy the men about the house. There is a walled garden out back. If anyone tries to visit Señora Saldevar, kill him and bring me his head. And be on your guard. I will be back to check on her." Juan Diego swung about and walked back to his horse. "She is not to be harmed. At least, not yet."

"Now see here. Why don't I remain with these ladies? I daresay your behavior is hardly appropriate," Bradford said. The Englishman had entertained his own ideas of occupying Esperanza's time. He firmly believed in his ability to charm his way into her affections.

"You will come with me."

"Why? I am no soldier."

"No, but Santa Anna wants you to learn. He has no use for an Englishman anymore. The *norte americanos* no longer think of you as one of their own." Guadiz enjoyed watching the man squirm. "I shall place you with the pickets, at the front, where you can watch your compadres. I wonder if they will have your courage?"

Bradburn paled at the notion. He had not fired a gun in anger in years. Now he was being thrust into the middle of a war. Guadiz was mocking him. In that moment, Bradburn began to feel something he hadn't experienced in a long time. Shame.

"I shall remain at the hacienda," Paloma announced. "I am tired and would like to wash the dust from my limbs."

A look of alarm flashed across her brother's face. Paloma wore an expression of innocence that didn't fool him for a second. "Paloma . . ." He had his own plans for the wife of a traitor.

"She has nothing to fear from me. Trained servants are difficult to find," Paloma told him. "Now go. And be careful, *hermano*. Everything will be well." The woman motioned for Obregon to accompany her. The brutish sergeant looked toward Juan Diego, who nodded his permission. The burly soldier fell in step behind Paloma as she sauntered toward the front of the hacienda, paused briefly in the doorway, then looked back at Esperanza, who cradled her injured hand. "Hurry along, señora. A servant once, a servant you shall be again."

24

"I'LL PLAY 'EM AS THEY LAY."

Stand aside! Lay a hand on me and I'll keelhaul you!"
Mad Jack bellowed as the sentries outside the cabin on
a knoll overlooking the Brazos tried to intercept him.
The soldiers were Mississippi volunteers, recently arrived, and they didn't know Mad Jack Flambeau from
the man in the moon. But they heard the commotion as
he blundered through the camp, a mongrel dog at his
side and both of them snapping at the soldiers around
them. It was a toss-up who growled the loudest. The dog
bared his teeth at anyone who tried to approach him.
Flambeau wielded a cutlass with the expertise of one
familiar with the blade.

"General Houston and Mr. Austin left strict orders
they wasn't to be disturbed," one of the sentries tried to
explain. He brought up his rifle across his chest to block
the intruder. The volunteer had never seen a pirate, but
this cantankerous old-timer sure looked the part.

Flambeau was dressed all in black save for a yellow
scarf to cover his shaved skull. A gold ring glinted in
one ear; a black patch covered one eye. He was wrinkled
and wiry and looked tough as whipcord.

Several other sentries hurried forward. Lucky stopped
them in their tracks with a guttural snarl; saliva dripped
from his scarred muzzle. Mad Jack swung the cutlass

over his head. Come heaven or high water he was getting
past the guards.

"Ready yourselves, my buckoes. I'm the Butcher of
Barbados, the Scourge of the Antilles. Trim your sails
and rig for boarding; there's a man coming your way!"
Flambeau charged the sentries, who balked at the onslaught and might have dashed from harm's way, but
just then the door opened and a tall, powerfully muscled
figure loomed in the doorway.

"What the hell is going on out here?" Sam Houston
stepped out into daylight, squinted against the glare, and
then recognized the buccaneer. "Mad Jack . . . where did
you come from?"

"The Flying Jib, where else?" Flambeau said, lowering the cutlass. "I came over with Jesus and Roberto and
the boys from town." He stabbed the cutlass into the
dirt. "I aim to talk with you. And Austin if he's in yonder."

"I'm here, you old sea dog!" Austin called out, standing in the doorway. "Come inside and have a drink. Our
general is buying. He's got real Tennessee sipping whiskey."

Houston glowered, but he waved a hand toward the
cabin. "We don't have the time. Austin and I are pretty
busy—"

"Make time. It won't take me long to speak my
piece," said Mad Jack.

"What the hell. Join us," Houston replied. He glanced
around at the encampment. Over six hundred men had
answered the call to arms. And more were crossing the
border from the United States every day, lured by the
notion of a good fight and Texas's struggle for liberty.

Mad Jack kept his counsel until the door to the cabin
was closed; then he turned on the two leaders of the
revolution and, ignoring the whiskey set before him, dug

his knuckles into the tabletop and the draft documents Austin had been laboring over.

"I heard dispatch riders had been arriving."

"Some," replied Houston.

"Santa Anna's got the Alamo surrounded. Been that way for days now."

Houston glanced aside at Austin, then nodded. "For the better part of a week."

"Then what are you doing hiding out up here? You ought to be marching to San Antonio right now. Just give the word."

"It isn't that simple," Houston told the older man.

"Santa Anna has an army larger than anything we can put in the field. We simply aren't ready to confront him. Wallace, Don Murillo, Bowie, and the other men can't take the general on." Mad Jack glared at the men until they both shifted uncomfortably before him.

Finally Austin broke the silence. "Yes." He looked at Houston for support. "We know what we're doing, Jack."

"*Mon Dieu,* that makes it even worse."

"I need time to turn this bunch into an army," Houston said. He walked to the windows, leaned on the sill, and studied the tents among the trees; a canopy of branches dispersed the sunlight in slanted rays of molten gold. They had come to fight, were ready to march at the drop of a hat, but not yet, not now. He wanted them good and mad, so crazed for battle as to be able to overwhelm a superior force. "Look at them. Farmers, shopkeepers, trappers, riverboat men. I won't throw them at Santa Anna until they have a chance to defeat him."

"And meanwhile, the men at the Alamo can fight and die to buy you that time."

Houston turned back and looked at Flambeau. "I didn't like the cut, but that's the way the cards were dealt. I'll play 'em as they lay."

"Why don't you come with me, Captain Flambeau?" Austin said. "I am leaving tonight for the coast. We're setting up a provisional government for the Republic of Texas and drawing up the articles and such with the representatives from the colonies. It ought to be safe on the coast. We'll have time to complete our work."

Mad Jack Flambeau spun around as if struck. Some things were beyond his control. But not everything. His reply spoke for the living and for those about to die.

"I didn't come here to be safe."

25

"... NO QUARTER ..."

William Wallace rode out of the Alamo on the fifth of March in broad daylight amid a calm made all the more terrible after twelve days of siege. The army surrounding the fortress had announced each morning with a barrage that lasted until the defenders with their long rifles sighted in on the artillery crews and began to pick them off. Then the cannons would be drawn out of range for the day only to be relocated under cover of darkness and positioned for the next morning's barrage.

Bill Travis should have ridden out to meet with the Mexican officer under a flag of truce. But Wallace had recognized the man beneath the white flag and received permission to meet with the envoy in Travis's place. Of course, if William had mentioned the officer bearing the flag of truce had murdered Samuel Wallace, Travis might have thought twice before allowing "Big Foot" to represent the defenders.

Once he was clear of the gate and fifty or sixty yards from the mission, William glanced over his shoulder at the besieged garrison. He was shocked by what he saw. The mission walls were pockmarked and crumbling from the pounding they had endured. The makeshift fort seemed small, even paltry, compared to the vast array of soldiers surrounding its ravaged battlements. And yet the Alamo's defenders waved to him with their hats and lifted their rifles in defiance.

After twelve days of being pummeled by Santa Anna's artillery, of staring at the columns of Mexican infantrymen parading in the distance whose camps completely ringed the mission, of knowing in their hearts that they were hopelessly outnumbered and it was only a matter of time before the final attack, the Texicans could still muster a show of defiance. Cornered, they continued to bare their fangs and await the inevitable.

"Once again our paths cross. For the last time, I think," Juan Diego said, riding up to confront the Texican.

"I wouldn't be so sure," Wallace replied suppressing the urge to lunge at the man despite the flag of truce. "Looking through my spyglass, I see Santa Anna hasn't found himself another hat."

"Then it was you at the river," said Guadiz. "I might have known. You have a way of being where you are not wanted."

"A time is coming when you will no longer have to worry about it," Wallace told him.

Guadiz chuckled. "Señor, are you threatening me? You are in no position to do anything of the kind. Although such talk costs you nothing. Maybe it even gives you courage to face what will come. His Excellency the President offers you one last chance to surrender and place yourself at his mercy. It is a more generous offer than you deserve. I think he will even allow some of you to live." Guadiz shrugged. "What is your reply?"

"You should not have come to Texas," William told him. "Because you will never leave it."

"You have been a thorn in my side. But I shall pluck you out." Guadiz stroked his carefully trimmed goatee. "Not so the beautiful wife of Don Murillo. I find her company most refreshing. Tell the *haciendado* my sister and I are enjoying his hospitality. Too bad he cannot join us."

Wallace's blood went cold; his skin paled as he struggled to keep his features impassive. "If you harm her—"

"Harm? Come now. Esperanza is a most efficient servant. But then, she had years of practice before seducing that randy old peccary, Saldevar. Now she is back where she belongs . . . on her knees!"

"You are a bastard," Wallace growled. "Are you without shame?"

"Of course not," Diego said. "Why, I shall see her a merry widow, mark my words." Guadiz smiled broadly, showing off his white, even teeth. The colonel of lancers steadied his horse. Thunderheads were building on the western horizon. But "if" and "when" the rain might come was anyone's guess. He gestured with the pole bearing the white flag, fluttering in the breeze, and jabbed it at Wallace's chest. "I will have your answer. Surrender and save some lives. Tomorrow the bugles will play 'De Guello,' no quarter, and all will be put to the sword." He tapped Wallace once again. "What is your reply?"

Wallace's hand was a blur as he slipped Bonechucker from its sheath; cold steel flashed in the sunlight and severed the pole, dropping the white flag in the dirt beneath the iron-shod hooves of his mustang. Guadiz almost fell out of the saddle as he jerked backward to avoid what he thought was a killing thrust. He stared blankly at the truncated shaft still gripped in his hand. It took him a moment to realize he was still alive and not gushing blood.

"Next time," Wallace warned him.

A cheer rose from the walls of the Alamo. The men there did not realize what was happening; they only knew William Wallace had saved face in a most dramatic fashion. Guadiz scowled and whirled his horse about and galloped back the way he had come. William took his time, allowing Juan Diego to be first to reach the ranks of his command.

The moment Guadiz was safe he ordered the troops around him to open fire on the Texican. A column of dragoons trotted forward until they had the range, then loosed a volley in William's direction while he was still outside the walls. The big man refused to dash for cover as geysers of dirt erupted all around him. A few well-placed shots even tugged at the sleeve of his shirt. He kept his back contemptuously turned to his enemy as if daring them to take their best shots. A cheer rose up from the Alamo as he high-stepped the mustang right on through the front gate. He wondered if Bowie, Kania, Crockett, and the others would still be cheering when they heard the terms of surrender and Santa Anna's threat of *de guello*. No prisoners.

Now the men in the Alamo had no other course but to fight to the death.

26

"I NEED A KILLER THIS NIGHT."

To the People of Texas and all Americans in the World.
Fellow Citizens and Compatriots—I am besieged by a thousand or more of the Mexicans under Santa Anna. I have sustained a continual bombardment & cannonade for 24 hours & have not lost a man.

William ducked inside the church as another explosive shell blew a grave-size crater in the plaza. Travis's headquarters were just inside the door, to the left and nestled against the north wall dangerously close to the powder magazine. Wallace instinctively ducked as the ground shook and dust came raining down on everyone and everything within a thirty-foot diameter.

Travis was seated at a weathered old desk, an oil lamp gallantly attempting to dispel the gloom. A draft of a letter lay before him on the desktop, an inkstand and quill nib close by. Twelve days of siege had sapped the youth from the colonel's once-boyish features. His eyes were sunken and hollow-looking, his flesh drawn taut over prominent cheekbones. But there was determination in his voice. He was bent, not broken.

"Look at you," he said, appraising the big redheaded man whose great bulky presence crowded the room. By heaven, a titan walked among them this night. "The more desperate our situation becomes, the stronger you seem. What is it with you Wallaces? Do you revel in this?"

"A fight is coming. So be it. Whether I live or die, I swear Santa Anna will rue the day before it is done."

"Indeed he shall," Travis said. "But you will have a different role to play in the general's fate."

"Colonel, I'm a simple man. That's why I leave all this talk of governments and ranking to you and Austin and Houston, folks it matters to. I deal with things head-on, with either my word or these knives at my side."

"And God bless you for it," Travis said. "Yours is the greater strength, and that is what you will need to carry you beyond the lines tonight. Strength, a fast horse, and plenty of luck."

"Why would I leave?" Wallace asked, frowning.

"Because I asked you to," Travis said. "Carry this letter out of here. Find Houston and the rest of the army. Tell them what happened."

"I can't ride out, not now. I have the right to—"

"Die with the rest of us, of course you have, and then some. But what I ask is more important. This letter is the voice of every man here. Don't get me wrong. You were outside today with the officer and the flag of truce; you could see how tight the noose is drawn. Chances are you'll never get past the first line of skirmishers. But if anyone can, it's you."

"There are other men, smaller, faster," Wallace blurted out.

"I don't need speed. I need a man who can ride, yes, but also a man who can fight like the devil, who will carve his way through Santa Anna's lines if necessary." Travis poured a small glass of whiskey for himself and one for his guest. "I need a killer this night. I need El Destripedor Rojo." He raised his glass in salute. Wallace shook his head.

"In this letter I tried to speak for all of us. Carry it out to the rest of Texas. Let that be our triumph. Years hence, when men of good will are forced to buck the odds and make a desperate stand against tyranny, let them say, 'Remember the Alamo,' and take heart." Travis leaned forward, resolute, willing to accept his destiny and the sacrifice it entailed.

Wallace closed his eyes, shook his head, reached for the drink, and then took up the letter. The whiskey burned his throat, but he hardly noticed. His eyes began to water. He wiped them on his sleeve. He turned and left the way he had entered, forgetting to salute.

Travis didn't call him back.

THE ENEMY HAS DEMANDED A SURRENDER AT DIS-CRETION; OTHERWISE THE GARRISON ARE TO BE PUT TO THE SWORD, IF THE FORT IS TAKEN ... I SHALL NEVER SURRENDER OR RETREAT.

Don Murillo, Chuy Montoya, and Jim Bowie found Wallace in the corral. The big man had already saddled his mustang and was tightening the cinch. The ground trembled as another pair of shells landed in the plaza; another round exploded against the eastern wall where the adobe was at its thickest. The Mexican gunners could shoot another month and that battlement wouldn't be breached.

"So you're going out," Bowie said. "That damn law-yer talked you into suicide."

Another shell burst flared against the night sky and peppered the hard earth with fragments of iron, causing them all to duck.

"Yeah. I suppose I ought to stay here where it's safe."

"Maybe so, but at least we have good company. There's only you and the night outside these walls." Bowie shrugged. "Guess it's your call. You told me once, 'This is Texas. If a man wants to get himself killed, he's come to the right place.' " Bowie extended his right arm. "You sure called it."

."I'll be seeing you," Wallace said, shaking hands.

"Stay low and don't stop to smell the wildflowers," replied Bowie. "Too bad we never found out who was the better man." He patted the knife at his side.

"Hell, Jim, it was you all along," Wallace said.

"Sure thing," Bowie chuckled. He trotted off in the direction of the east barracks.

Don Murillo watched him leave and added, "There goes a man."

"Sí," Wallace replied. "Much man. Like you, *padrone*."

"There are no cowards within these walls," Don Murillo said. "Chuy, keep close or one of those stray rounds will part your hair."

"I will keep my sombrero on." Chuy grinned.

"I reckon the entire garrison knows I am going out," Wallace grumbled.

"Yes, and none of them envy you," said the landowner. Wallace had kept Guadiz's comments to himself. As far as Don Murillo was concerned, Esperanza was safe and well. It was the least Wallace could do to ease the older man's burden. Don Murillo reached in the pocket of his frock coat and handed Wallace a small oilskin packet.

"It is a Bible. I have written in it, on the front page. Perhaps you will . . . deliver it to Esperanza for me." He cleared his throat and struggled to continue. "If I am unable to. And if, it is no problem."

Wallace accepted the packet and placed it inside his shirt, next to his heart. "I shall give it back to you one day and you can hand it to her yourself."

"Of course," Don Murillo said. Neither of them believed that for a second.

Wallace removed his hat out of respect for the white-haired *haciendado* who had joined the cause and sacrificed everything for freedom. He hoped the colonists remembered. He hoped Texas remembered.

Don Murillo looked up at the stars, like diamonds flung against the black velvet canopy of night. The ground shook. Would the bombardment never end? Beauty and death, bound inextricably by fate. There was a terrible truth here; if he looked long enough he might just figure it out. Maybe tomorrow . . . He wanted to ask Wallace to watch over Esperanza, to be her friend, to protect her if the worst happened. But the words would not come, not that they were necessary. After all, this was William Wallace. And some things were understood.

The three men skirted the corral, avoided the main plaza, and hugged the barracks wall as they made their way to a side gate where Ken Kania and a handful of the original colonists waited to shake Wallace's hand. The big man greeted them like old friends. The words were few, the farewells heartfelt and laced with humor. The defenders quickly returned to their positions on the battlements. Tomorrow they had a date with destiny. This was William's night. On his word, Chuy Montoya unlatched and opened the gate.

Don Murillo patted Wallace on the shoulder. William took a deep breath and hurried down the passage between the church and the barrack. As he approached Montoya, the *segundo* whispered, "Go with God." And when William had vanished into the night and Montoya had closed and barred the door the *segundo* could be heard to add, "And I don't envy God."

THEN I CALL ON YOU IN THE NAME OF LIBERTY, OF PATRIOTISM & EVERYTHING DEAR TO THE

AMERICAN CHARACTER, TO COME TO OUR AID
WITH ALL DISPATCH.

Men crowded the battlements. They searched the Mexican lines for movement, for any indication that Wallace
had been discovered. Bright fires burned on the plain,
ringed the fortress, blazed against the line of trees where
the waters of the San Antonio River flowed sweet and
clear. Campfires beyond the river flanked the road to
town, the Camino Real. How could any man hope to run
a gauntlet of such magnitude and survive? The cannonade had momentarily abated; the stillness that followed
was damn near intolerable.

"Listen to that," one of the men muttered. Not a
sound, nothing stirred, no dark wing or scurrying rodent,
not a gnat or jackrabbit. "Loud, ain't it?"

Everyone agreed, but no one spoke.

"I think he made it, *padrone.*"

"He'll make it, if his horse is fast enough," Bowie said.
"And if them guards have been drinking. We could have
used some of Mad Jack's home brew to spike the wells."

"They'd have to move the town," Kania commented.
He had come to Texas to open a store. Now a place in
history had been thrust upon him. He wondered if the
men around him were frightened. He was. But he would
see this through. "And dam the river."

The men on the wall chuckled. The shopkeeper
straightened a little, squared his shoulders. He had been
accepted as an equal by men of action. And though his
hands were sweaty and his mouth dry, he felt proud.

In San Antonio, in the house of Saldevar, Juan Diego
sighed with pleasure as Paloma's fingers massaged his
temples, easing the sudden spasms that threatened to
bring him down. She hovered over her brother like a
fallen guardian angel, the two of them in the study,

among the books, wood desk, and wing-backed chairs, one of which Guadiz had chosen to sit in while his sister tended his needs. Orange flames from the hearth cast a host of dancing wraithlike shadows upon the bare walls and bookshelves. His gut rumbled.

"What's taking her so long?"

"Shall I see?"

"No. Stay here." He reached up to pat her hand. "I spoke to him today, that damned *norte americano*. The pirate's whelp, Wallace."

A sudden intake of air, Esperanza tried to stifle her gasp. Guadiz glanced around his sister and caught sight of her in the doorway. "Food at last." He waved her in. "So you are interested in the redhaired one. I have always felt like I know him, yet I do not think I have ever seen him before." His cruel eyes undressed her as she carried a platter of beans and tortillas and a jug of whiskey to the desk. In his mind he peeled away the peasant blouse and skirt she wore and imagined every appealing curve of flesh. "But you like this man, very much I think. Does your husband know? Perhaps he even has given his blessing. After all, Don Murillo is an old man to have taken such a young wife. Does Wallace make up for what is lacking in your marriage bed?"

"Here is your food," Esperanza said, unwilling to play his game or to be baited into humiliation.

"I could take you, here and now, drag you upstairs by your hair, and have my way with you," Juan Diego warned. "It is a tempting notion." Paloma's fingers dug into his scalp. He yelped and brushed her hand away. Now that the pain had subsided he enjoyed arousing his sister's jealous nature. He returned his attention to the señora. "Who could stop me?"

"I see beyond seeing. I hear while others merely listen. I am 'She who walks in shadows,' the path that lies between the darkness and the light. The powers of both dwelt in my mother and now in me."

"I am no peon. Do not seek to frighten me."

"I say what is." Esperanza spoke quietly, yet her voice seemed to fill the room. It whirled about the twins like dead leaves in a gust of wind. Her eyes began to bore into Guadiz, who began to shift uncomfortably in his chair by the hearth. "I bend to your will, but I do not break. Touch me and I will summon the 'haunter of the dark,' for he is the bearer of lost souls; he is *muerte*. And this will be my curse. Your manhood will shrivel and rot away, then your bowels and gut, then at last your heart. And you, Señorita Guadiz, will experience all the pain you have caused, your own bitterness will eat your flesh, and your tears will scald you."

Standing before them, with the firelight transforming her comely features into a lurid orange mask, Juan Diego was tempted to believe this woman. Chancing a scratched cheek was one thing; risking the wrath of some demon called the haunter of the dark was an entirely different matter. She wasn't the only beauty in town.

"Go on. Get out of here. You may be 'She who walks in shadows,' but tomorrow you will be just another widow." Guadiz laughed aloud. "What do you think of that?"

Esperanza paused in the doorway. Again she refused to be goaded into hysterics. "My husband is ready to die," she said. "Are you?" She continued down the hall, encountering Dorotea in her nightdress, who had followed her and been listening from a distance. Esperanza took her sister-in-law by the arm and led her to the back of the hacienda. The two women retired together to the servants' room, a small but adequate chamber with a featherbed on a brass frame, a hand-hewn dresser, and a washbasin. Years ago, Esperanza had shared this same room with her mother, but those were in the days of the first Señora Saldevar, a woman of culture and civility, fair but rarely familiar with her servants. Safe within the room, Dorotea sat on one side of the bed while Esperanza prepared herself for the evening. She removed her clothes and slipped into a warm cotton gown that fastened at her neck with tiny white satin bows and hung to the floor.

She eased into bed and slowly relaxed against the pillow. The bed shook as Dorotea did the same. Don Murillo's sister leaned up on her elbow and turned the lamp down low, then lay back in bed, adjusting her lace cap and tying it under her chin. The older woman tried to rest, but curiosity got the better of her.

"I overheard you," she said. "What you said about forces of light and darkness and walking the path between and having the power to summon the 'haunter of the dark.' Do you really believe that?"

"What's important is that Juan Diego believes," Esperanza replied. She was about to elaborate when gunshots rattled in the distance on the edge of town. Both women sat upright, listening. Dorotea blessed herself. Both women began to pray.

Gunfire erupted along the picket lines to the south of the mission. From his vantage point on the redoubt Don Murillo clutched at the stone wall. Rifles, pistols, musket fire bloomed in deadly profusion along the perimeter of the besieging troops, one patrol exchanging shots with another, both parties spooked into this lethal exchange by the horseman charging through their midst and into the trees.

"Ride, *hombre, ride!*" shouted Chuy.

"Cut your way through!" Bowie added.

A whole chorus of cries rippled along the wall; the defenders cheered and chanted, "Wallace," as the intensity of the gunfire increased. From a distance it appeared he had alerted the entire camp to his presence. Sentries, made nervous by previous incursions from the fort, continued to take potshots into the night until their officers arrived on the scene. For several long minutes a full-scale battle raged. Then it stopped as quickly as it began. An ominous silence returned.

"He made it," Bowie muttered. Not because he knew any more than anyone else, but because it had to be true. It simply had to be . . .

John Bradburn stood away from the fire at the camp site. He did not wish to present too easy a target. However, a man of his size was hardly going to dodge out of harm's way. The other two sentries, a pair of unpleasant miscreants from Veracruz, had also recognized the sound of a horse approaching them from under the cover of the cotton woods. The gunfire that lit the night had died. Here on the banks of the Rio San Antonio, the pickets felt especially vulnerable. There was no one behind them. They were isolated. However, being an afterthought in Santa Anna's army did have its rewards. A man might sneak away and sit out a fight and have no one the wiser. But some days, despite a man's best efforts, trouble had a way of riding unbidden into camp.

"I hear something," one of the sentries muttered. He had eyes like a cat but the heart of a coward for whom a life in the military had been a choice between eating and starving to death. His companion was equally skittish and a slave to pulque, which was about the only drink he could afford. Throughout the siege, Bradburn had rarely seen either of his companions sober. In turn, they were continually mocking the Englishman and making life miserable for him.

Juan Diego Guadiz had certainly not placed the Englishman with the cream of Santa Anna's troops. Bradburn had the distinct impression when it came to frontal assault on the Alamo that men like these, including himself, would be leading the advance. In his own way he had begun to envy the men besieged within the Alamo's crumbling walls. At least they were standing for something. Their deaths would have meaning . . . and, in some small way, nobility.

"Look, there!" Cat-Eyes whispered. Bradburn felt as if chips of ice were melting the length of his backbone. His hands were trembling. It was becoming hard to breathe. Suddenly a man on horseback materialized out of the gloom. He was big, overgrown, his mustang ambling forward at a lazy pace. The big man's shoulders were slumped, his body leaned forward across his saddle pommel, long arms hanging loose at his side along the folds of his serape, head tilted down, his wide-brimmed sombrero concealing his features.

"Is he dead?" Bradburn hissed. He knew of only one man that big in all of Texas. Sweat beaded Bradburn's forehead and rolled down the folds of fat around his neck. He raised the shotgun and held it across his chest. The other two men cocked and primed their rifles and started forward.

"Looks like it!" Cat-Eyes exclaimed, suddenly finding his courage when confronted by a dead man.

"Dead as a slug on hot iron," the drunkard said, wiping his mouth on the sleeve of his soiled uniform. "He might have something of value."

"I seen the boots," Cat-Eyes said. "They're big ones."

"If he has a watch it's mine."

"Not if I find it first."

"Keep your distance, English," the drunkard warned.

The two men swooped down on their prize like vultures on a ripe feast. They ran up to either side of the slumped figure, each man anxious to be the one who dragged the rider out of the saddle. Suddenly the rider's arms rose to either side. He held a pistol in each hand.

He fired them both almost simultaneously, shooting Cat-Eyes through the chest and drilling his companion between the eyes. Cat-Eyes was blown backward into the river. The drunkard slammed into the embankments and slid down until his knees buckled and he rolled over on his side, already dead.

The horseman drew closer until the big man's shadow fell across Bradburn, who stood with his shotgun cocked and ready and aimed at the center of the rider's serape. The man lifted his head. Eyes blazing like green fire seemed to look right through the former alcalde. The smell of blood was in the air. All Bradburn needed to do was squeeze the trigger and cut the rider in half and earn the respect of Guadiz once more.

He lowered the shotgun and stood aside. It had been a long time since he had done something he could actually feel good about. Maybe this was a start. He watched the horseman pass by, a hard rider on a long and desperate journey.

John Bradburn walked across the clearing, kicked dirt on his campfire until nothing remained but a faint wisp of smoke. He dragged the remaining body from the riverbank and rolled it into the Rio San Antonio de Padua. Then he caught up the reins of his own mount, saddled the animal, and led him across the river. Someone hailed his camp, uncertain where it was. Bradburn refrained from answering. He climbed the opposite bank and settled into the saddle.

Maybe it was time to leave Texas.

Wallace started to slip from the saddle. He willed himself upright. His skull throbbed. His face felt hard and sticky. Numbness was creeping along his shoulder and down his arm. Blood continued to ooze from a hole in his thigh. He fumbled for his powder horn, sprinkled the hard black granules into the wound. Where were his pistols? He had dropped them. Damn. But there was still flint. Funny, the way the sentry had allowed him to ride past. The Mexican had looked a hell of a lot like John Bradburn. Wallace found his flint and a striker, held the stone over his wound, and struck it twice. The sparks settled on the gunpowder, igniting it in a flash that startled the mustang and started him trotting forward.

The pain nearly pushed the wounded man over the edge. It exploded inside his skull and coursed through his veins like brimstone. But the wound was cauterized. Wallace reined in his mount at the edge of a thicket of live oaks. He waited, listening for the sounds of pursuit, and heard the night wind moaning in the branches, the distant cry of a coyote, the beating of his own brave heart.

He was dying. But he had a choice. Face it here or ride.

Boldly ride.

I AM DETERMINED TO SUSTAIN MYSELF AS LONG AS POSSIBLE & DIE LIKE A SOLDIER WHO NEVER FORGETS WHAT IS DUE TO HIS OWN HONOR & THAT OF HIS COUNTRY—VICTORY OR DEATH.
                                        —WILLIAM B. TRAVIS

27

"TELL THEM TO REMEMBER THE ALAMO."

The bugles sounded a few hours after morning. From every camp the discordant notes blared the ominous strains of "De Guello." Across the dry and dusty plain surrounding the beleaguered mission, the grim warning drifted on the wind. The thunderheads of the previous day had drifted off to the northeast, leaving the land here forsaken and the wildflowers to struggle on their own.

Don Murillo had not slept. If this was to be his last night and day on earth, he wanted to see it all, the beauty of the stars, the wonder of moonlight, the glorious promise of a sunrise that gave him hope that whatever happened today was not the end.

Chuy Montoya lit the last of the cigarillos he'd been saving. From the number of troops that Santa Anna was about to hurl against them, he decided this might be as good time as any. He inhaled deeply; his brown eyelids became slits as he allowed the silken strands of smoke to curl over his tongue before he slowly exhaled. The *segundo* took a final drag and then flicked the stub over the wall. He raised his rifle and sighted on the ranks of soldiers marching across the prairie.

"Well, old friend, I should like to be fishing down by the banks of the Brazos right now," Don Murillo said at his side. The *haciendado* had armed himself with a pair of dueling pistols. His rifle was a finely tooled weapon of English design.

"*Sí, padrone,* as in the old days, with a bottle of tequila, plenty of food, and maybe a beautiful señorita or two for company."

Don Murillo chuckled. The two men had sowed their share of wild oats in their youths. "Those were salty days," the *haciendado* agreed, and didn't regret a one of them.

Travis walked up alongside Saldevar and his vaquero. "They're coming at us from all sides," he said. "I guess we must have Santa Anna worried."

Don Murillo glanced around. Travis was right. Column after column of soldiers, with flags flying and bayonets gleaming in the sunlight, converged upon every wall of the mission. The Mexican artillery opened up on the walls for the last time, firing over the heads of the assault troops. The earth itself seemed to tremble as the Alamo's cannons returned the fire, dueling at first with the Mexican guns, then turning their attention to the advancing lines.

Don Murillo and Chuy fired as one, joining the rest of the men along the walls. Out on the plain, the soldiers died in droves. Men clutched at themselves or clawed the air, then fell writhing on the hard earth. More soldiers took their places, and then they, too, died. And still others filled their ranks. And if the Mexican infantry wavered, the cavalry was right behind them, sabers drawn, prepared to cut down any foot soldier who failed to do his duty.

Before long, the plains were littered with the dead and dying. And still the officers pressed the attack, willing to accept this wholesale slaughter because the Alamo must fall and its defenders must be put to the sword. To fail meant disgrace and execution.

Time lost its meaning for the men on the walls. Don

Murillo loaded and fired and loaded and fired, repeating the process until his rifle was almost too hot to touch. So much death. The whole affair sickened him. There had to be a better way for men to settle their differences. Ladders were set against the wall of the redoubt, and the men below hurriedly began to climb. The defenders used their rifle butts to shove the ladders free and send the soldiers tumbling back to the ground.

Don Murillo was practically deaf now, and he no longer reacted to the cannon firing next to him. The powder smoke was thick enough to cut with a knife. Somehow above the din he heard Travis yell out an order for everyone to help train the nine-pounder cannon on the main gate. Don Murillo and Chuy numbly joined the other men on the rampart in manhandling the nine-pounder into place just as the main gate exploded, flinging jagged chunks of timber and twisted iron into the air.

Troops surged through the opening. The cannon roared as it emptied a load of grapeshot into the solders massed at the entrance. The results were terrible to behold. Solid shot tore through flesh and bone, savaging the ranks of the soldiers and momentarily stalling the attack. But the press of soldiers was too great. The dead and wounded were trampled underfoot. The men on the redoubt opened up with their rifles and pistols.

While reloading, Don Murillo quickly appraised the rest of the mission. A section of one wall had collapsed. He thought he saw Crockett and his men being engulfed by wave after wave of soldiers. Mexican cavalry charged through the breach in the west wall and were carving their way into the plaza at a terrible cost to horse and rider.

"Padrone!"

Don Murillo rammed another load home, then looked around at the *segundo*.

Chuy Montoya was staring down at the front of his shirt. A crimson stain spread across the chest. "I'm sorry," Montoya said, as if apologizing for letting the *haciendado* down in some way. A trickle of blood formed at the corner of his mouth and trickled down his chin. He drew a pistol and his knife, turned and stepped over the edge of the redoubt, and was lost from sight.

"No!" Don Murillo shouted in vain.

Another explosion shook the redoubt and knocked him backward against the wall. The world spun crazily, colors mingled in a savage kaleidoscope of sound and fury. For a moment he lost consciousness; then Don Murillo rose from the dust, shoving himself free of the wall. The nine-pounder lay on its side, one wheel spinning, the other broken into fragments. Two men stood at the base of the ramp, Bill Travis and Ken Kania, a lawyer and a shopkeeper, fighting side by side. The gallant Travis battled against half a dozen men with his saber, mortally wounding two of them and forcing the remaining soldiers to retreat until a grenadier ran up from his blind side and fired a musket into his skull, spattering a nearby wall with a grisly mist. Travis died instantly, toppling forward like an overturned statue. But the humble little shopkeeper, like the other Texicans in the plaza, fought on with a ferocity and desperation that gave him almost superhuman strength. Kania emptied his guns into the soldiers surrounding him, then took up the nine-pounder's ramrod and used it to club any man who dared come within reach. And when the ramrod shattered, the shopkeeper leaped onto the nearest soldier, ignoring the musket balls plowing into his torso, and dragged him to the ground and choked him to death, when, bleeding from a dozen wounds, Kania himself slumped forward and died also.

Don Murillo glimpsed movement out of the corner of his eye and turned, bringing his dueling pistol to bear on a soldier who had just scaled the wall behind him. The soldier, on seeing the white-haired *haciendado,* brought his musket up and squeezed the trigger. Nothing happened. He stood there with the tip of his bayonet a good six feet from his intended victim and stared into the muzzle of Don Murillo's weapon and knew he was as good as dead.

Don Murillo could see his adversary looked no older than sixteen or seventeen. He wore his fear like a mask of inexperience. For a brief moment the old man and the brown-faced youth stared at each other. Then Don Murillo slowly turned the gun aside, sparing the life of his assailant. The soldier lunged forward and buried his bayonet in Saldevar's chest. Don Murillo gasped, his features contorted as he slid off the iron barb and sank against the wall.

There was a look of inexpressible sorrow in his eyes. Then nothing at all.

A somber procession of women and old men made their way along the mission road in the waning daylight. The din of battle had long since faded. All that remained was the grieving, the moans of the dying, the crackle of flames, the stench of cauterized wounds, and women in black veils like ravens, hovering among the dead.

Dorotea gasped and shrank back against the woman at her side. Esperanza placed an arm around her sister-in-law's bony shoulders. "Courage," she whispered. "Perhaps you should remain here."

"No. I must—"

"Very well," Esperanza replied. The two women continued across the river, wading through the shallows and glancing from right to left, unable to take their eyes off the wounded and dying that crowded the riverbank. Voices called out in the fading light; prayers and pleas for pity drifted up into the purpling sky. Esperanza could not hate them, but she was moved to anger at the nature of men like Santa Anna and Juan Diego, who were willing to waste so many lives.

Many of the officers she passed looked stunned. No one had expected the defenders of the Alamo to put up such a vicious resistance. No one had been prepared for the losses. She heard two lieutenants arguing between themselves as the women marched past on their sad journey along the mission road.

"They fought like trapped animals."

"More than a thousand are dead. May God have mercy on their souls."

"And soon we will march north to destroy the rest of their army."

"At what cost? I want no part of these Texicans. They are devils."

The officers receded into the night. The procession continued up through the trees and out onto the plain. The people from town could see for themselves what had transpired earlier in the day. The column of women halted in their tracks, struck by the enormity of the scene.

Flames continued to burn within the battered walls and crumbled battlements. Before the shattered remains of the front gate, a troop of lancers led by Juan Diego awaited the arrival of the friends and loved ones of the "devils" that had defended the Alamo.

Esperanza quickened her pace, her heart-pounding in her chest. She had known it would end like this—second sight, a premonition of disaster, her mother's gift, had become a curse. She had glimpsed her husband's fate in the shadows and wanted to warn him, but Don Murillo would have taken his place with the rest of the Texicans despite her objections. Honor was stronger than death. And William, had he shared the same fate? Or were there prisoners, anyone to possibly ransom from a firing squad? If her worst fears came to pass, at least she could give them a Christian burial.

Them?

Yes, may God forgive her. The man she loved, the man she was forbidden to love. She held both in her heart. So be it.

Esperanza passed the other women, drawn by the grim possibilities awaiting at the gate. She took the lead across the killing fields littered with the wrecked remains of the assault. Cannons blasted off their carriages, the dead who had yet to be gathered and taken to the rear, sections of ladders, dropped muskets, bloodstained hats, none held any meaning for her now. All that mattered was what awaited within the ruined battlements; all that mattered was what she dreaded more than anything else in the world to find.

Juan Diego waited astride his charger, blocking the entrance. Behind him, Paloma kept more to the shadows. Even her iron resolve seemed shaken by the slaughter she had witnessed this day. Not so her brother, Juan Diego likened the mayhem to a great victory.

"Welcome, señora," he said. "Welcome," he repeated to the straggling procession. "No doubt you have come to honor these traitors and insurrectionists. I will not stop you. My men are eager to help you bury your dead. Then our illustrious president, General Antonio Lopez de Santa Anna, has given you permission to leave San Antonio. Go where you will."

He waved a hand in the direction of his mounted command. The troops parted; his own charger sidestepped. Juan Diego removed his brass-and-leather helmet, sweeping its black plume across his chest in a mocking salute. He dismounted as Esperanza bolted past him and through the gate.

She was the first to enter the ruined mission. The first to be branded by sights and smells that left an indelible imprint of revulsion and grief upon her mind and heart. Everything . . .

Everything within the walls and including the walls was either shattered, charred, or pockmarked with bullet holes. The ground was patched and horribly moist. Those battlements still standing were splashed with hues of red and crimson that darkened as the stains dried.

But the most terrible sight of all dominated the center of the plaza, where a long, wide hole had been dug in the dark and bloody ground. The bodies of the defenders had been unceremoniously tossed into the pit and set afire. All that remained were charred broken bones and bits of clothing that had survived the flames—brass buttons, the twisted frames of spectacles, a glass flask, a snuff case, the seared leather cover from a Bible.

Many of the women began to weep openly; many fell to the ground, Dorotea among them, and doubled over retching and sobbing. Esperanza stood and held back what was in her heart. She would not give her husband's killers the satisfaction of seeing her break. Then Juan Diego drew close to her.

"You may leave here, tomorrow, the next day; you are free to go." The flames of destruction continued to gleam in his arrogant expression. "Find this General Houston and the rest of his little army and tell them we are coming. Tell them what you have seen here. Tell them to remember the Alamo."

Esperanza met his gaze, her eyes deep beyond his understanding, strong beyond his suspicions. And in a calm, even voice, without a hint of the torment and sorrow raging in her soul, she replied, "I will."

28

"THE BIBLE IS FOR SEÑORA SALDEVAR."

Papa, look at me. This is no work for a lady," Isabel Zavala complained, holding out her soot-stained hands. Ashes had worked their way under her fingernails, much to her horror. Living in a tent and trailing along with Gen. Sam Houston didn't have to stop a girl from looking nice.

"What lady?" Jesus Zavala asked, wildly looking about. "Where is the grand lady?" He stared down at the coals. "Pump the bellows for your father."

"Why can't Roberto do it?"

"Because he must scout for General Houston."

"I could scout."

"You'd get lost." Jesus lifted the horseshoe out of its bed of coals. It still needed heating. "Now work."

Valentina emerged from their house and hurried across the alley to the blacksmith shop where her husband had plied his trade for more years than she cared to count. She had matured into a round, pleasant woman whose bubbly personality reflected her zest for life. She had packed a substantial basket with cold chicken, tortillas, strips of peppered beef, and a jar of salsa spicy enough to make the devil sweat.

"Mama, tell Father I shouldn't be doing such work," Isabel complained. "What if my friends should see me?"

"What friends? We are the last people in San Felipe,"

Valentina observed. Most of the inhabitants had brought their families into Houston's encampment farther down the Brazos. There was word that Comanche raiding parties were using the current conflict to raid settlements whose able-bodied men had joined the militia to fight Santa Anna. To that end, by the tenth of March San Felipe had been reduced to a ghost town. At the last minute of their departure, one of Zavala's horses had thrown a shoe. The blacksmith had unhitched one of the geldings from his wagon and brought the animal into the front of the shop.

Isabel continued to complain as she pumped the bellows to stoke the fire in the coals. When the iron was glowing red-hot, Jesus removed it from the coals and placed it on an anvil and began to hammer the metal into shape. "Go on then; off with you," Zavala told his daughter. "But don't wander far. I will be finished here in a few minutes."

Isabel squealed in relief and raced off into the cool exterior of the street, where there was a breeze and no bank of coals in forge. Valentina was content to watch her husband ply his trade. She enjoyed the skill he used in tempering iron and bending it to his will. There was music in the iron as it rang out with each strike of the mallet.

"Our daughter is growing up," she said.

"Too quickly. Woman, where does the time go?"

"I don't know," Valentina said, bemused. "I thought *you* were counting." She sighed. "First our son and now our daughter. She will be bringing home a young man before long."

"And I will take my hammer and temper the resolve of each young man who presents himself."

Jesus dunked the glowing red horseshoe into a bucket of water. Steam exploded in his face while the surface of the water bubbled for a few seconds until the metal cooled. He brought the iron shoe over to the gelding and began to shoe the animal while he enjoyed a bait of oats. A few minutes later Jesus had finished the task, smoothing the edges of the horseshoe with a metal file, and returned his tools to the box beneath the bench seat in the freight wagon.

"You know, I have piled a nice bed of hay in the back stall. We could go back there and pretend we are sneaking off at night under the nose of your father." He reached down and patted his wife's ample derriere. Valentina laughed and slapped his hand away. He reached for the other cheek, and she danced out of his grasp, but not too far.

"Now see here. What if Isabel should come in?" his wife protested. But he could tell her resolve was weakening. Jesus persisted, confident he would wear her down. It was a beautiful day in March, the birds were singing, trees were budding out, and the first green shoots of new grass were forcing their way up through the sandy soil.

"She won't set foot in here again for fear I might put her to work," Jesus said. They laughed together, and for a few brief moments the tension of the past week drained away. Flirting with his wife, teasing her, helped to maintain the blacksmith's sanity in this time of trial and sacrifice.

Zavala lifted his wife in his arms.

"Be careful, you silly man, or you will hurt your back and you will not be able to parade back and forth for General Houston."

"More's the pity," said Zavala. "All the more reason I should ravish you upon the straw. Oh. . . . oh." A catch at the small of his back warned him to put her down. He obeyed the pain but continued to embrace her.

Valentina glanced toward the front door, then nodded and led her husband toward the rear of the stable. She liked him like this, smelling of ash and iron, his muscles swollen and glistening, like some animal, *her* animal. But their foreplay had not gone much beyond an initial caress when they heard Isabel scream.

Zavala was out of the stall and charging up the aisle. He paused long enough to grab his rifle, powder, and shot, then plunged forward into the street. Valentina wasn't far behind, moving with surprising quickness, her lustful thoughts replaced with images of howling Comanche chasing her daughter down the deserted streets of the town.

"Papa! Mama! Come quickly!"

Jesus Zavala charged into the plaza, rifle ready, his temper as hot as his forge. Anyone attempting to harm his daughter was going to have a hard death. The blacksmith rounded the corner of the street and bolted past the abandoned stalls, finding his daughter standing in front of a worn-out nag, a hulking, corpselike figure slumped forward in the saddle. Jesus knew his horses. He knew the mustang, though the poor beast had been ridden nearly to death. And he knew the rider; at least he thought he did.

Behind the blacksmith, Valentina gasped and blessed herself. "Madre de Dios," she whispered. "Can it be him?"

"I think so," Jesus replied.

"Papá . . ."

"Yes, daughter, I am here," Jesus said, walking across the plaza to stand alongside the unnerved young girl. Then he discovered why she had reacted with such alarm. The man on horseback was covered with blood; the flanks of the mustang were stained with crimson patches. The serape the man wore was torn and bullet-riddled. There was a hole in his thigh. The wound looked burned and black and ugly.

Jesus gingerly drew closer to the mustang. The horse

was too weary to shy away. Jesus craned his head down to peer beneath the sombrero. "Señor Wallace, is that you? Are you alive?"

The man stirred, tilted his head; the sombrero fell away. Isabel stifled a scream at the sight. The man's face was a red mask. Blood was caked around a puckered scalp wound where a pistol ball had glanced off his skull and left a tattered furrow of flesh from his temple to well above his right ear.

Jesus marveled at how the man even managed to sit a horse, then noticed that Wallace had lashed himself to the saddle, tying his left hand to the pommel and passing the rope around his legs and waist and the mustang's neck.

William fumbled inside his shirt and removed the oil-skin packet containing Don Murillo's Bible and the letter Col. Bill Travis had written to a world beyond the beleaguered walls of the Alamo.

"For General Houston," the big man said in a rasping barely audible voice. "The Bible is for Señora Saldevar."

"Yes, my friend," Jesus replied taking them out of Wallace's hand.

William looked around and saw that Valentina and Isabel were weeping, but he couldn't spare the time to worry about it. He needed to get back to the Alamo. But maybe . . . just maybe . . . he ought to rest, for a minute or two. The ropes no longer held him; they snapped beneath his weight. Zavala rushed to support him. He lowered Wallace to the ground.

"Samuel, am I dead?"

His brother's ghost shrugged. "Maybe. Wait and see."

29

". . . YOU ARE GOING TO LIVE."

Dreams and dying and rising to life again. Wallace burns and Isabel places a cool compress on his forehead. He thrashes about in his delirium and Mad Jack is there with a calming word, and when that doesn't work, Roberto and Jesus restrain him. He hears Mad Jack say, "It's for your own good, lad. You're among friends now."

Valentina spoon-feeds him, sometimes Henneke, who regales him with one bawdy tale after another. But Mad Jack and Roberto Zavala are never far. They talk to him as if he is still among the living. Once Houston comes by, big and rangy, but he looks tired and he bears bad news.

"Folks have been drifting in from San Antonio. The Alamo has fallen. Travis, Bowie, Señor Saldevar, they're all dead. All hundred and eighty. They died to a man. The general went and burned the bodies and scattered the bones. Reckon he's trying to scare us. Heal up, Will. I need you. Texas needs you."

Wallace starts to correct him. But he cannot speak; the words won't come. He sleeps and wakes or thinks he does and finds Samuel standing next to his bed, but the ghost has always been with him. Who is that behind you? Faint shimmering shifting shapes. Is it Don Mu-

rillo, Chuy Montoya, Bill Travis, Bowie? . . . I should have been with you.

"Have you come for me?" Wallace says. My God, is that my voice?

Then Samuel and the faces behind him drift apart like bayou mist at sunup. There is a roaring in his ears, the light fails, and he drifts upon a dark and troubled sea. He hears moaning, the siren call of dying men. He is caught in the rush of a violent whirlpool from which he cannot struggle free. Thunder resonates like an artillery barrage; lightning crashes; the dead and the dying call him by name. "William Wallace, we own you now." *He cries out and a slender coppery hand reaches down through the shadow of death and catches hold of him.*

He hears his name, whispered, holding him fast against the maelstrom, refusing to let him be swept away. Esperanza? Is he dead at last and creating his own heaven? Her touch soothes him, eases his fears. He sleeps and wakes and she is there. He closes his eyes, waits, then opens them again.

Esperanza was there, bathed in the sunlight that streamed in through an opening in the tent, the luster of her raven black tresses muted by a veil of black lace. She leaned forward and placed her hand on his forehead, looked him squarely in the eye, and told him, "William Wallace, you are going to live."

And so he did.

30

"BURN EVERYTHING!"

San Felipe was burning. Black smoke rose upward into the April sky. On the first of the month the market should have been crowded with townspeople and farmers in for supplies or the plain socializing aspect of a trip into town. *Mamacitas* would be keeping a watch over their ripe and willing daughters while the young men from town and the vaqueros from the ranches vied with one another hoping to catch the attention of the prettiest señorita. On another day, *haciendados* and hardscrabble farmers might have met to exchange news about crops; wives would have gathered for quilting and gossip. The first week of April had always brought a spring fandango. The hotels should have been crowded with guests, folks gathered for a town meeting. Not this year and, perhaps, never again.

"I built that shop with my own two hands," said Jesus Zavala, sitting astride his horse on a wooded knoll overlooking the town. Flames devoured the wooden shingle roof of the livery stable, feasted on the blacksmith shop, and gorged themselves on the interior of his hacienda. The adobe walls might remain, but they would house nothing but charred memories.

"There goes the Flying Jib," said Austin. He had ridden up from the coast to ascertain the condition of the army in the wake of the Alamo's destruction, but he stayed to scout the vicinity, ignoring every word of caution. He had wanted to see for himself, but he wasn't expecting such a show. Half a dozen other riders waited, downcast, frustrated by the fact that they were too few in number to rush to the town's defense. The tension of the past weeks was plainly evident in their hardened features. Their rage continued to build, souring their dispositions, leaving them on edge while at the same time despondent. Everything they had worked for was up in smoke.

"We can build again," Jesus said. "Santa Anna hasn't won yet."

"If men like Bowie and Crockett couldn't stop them, what chance do we have?"

"What are you saying?" growled the blacksmith. "Madre de Dios. They made the sacrifice and now we must crawl to Santa Anna on our hands and knees and beg forgiveness. Not I. Not while I can walk and speak and fight."

"Talk like that and you'll make a good governor," Austin said.

"I am a blacksmith. It is all I want to be. No, one thing more. I want to be free. And if some of you won't fight, then get on down there and ask Colonel Guadiz for mercy. He will show you salvation at the point of a lance."

"I didn't say I wouldn't fight," one of the other Texicans muttered. He was a thickset man of average height and a plodding demeanor.

"I've seen enough," Austin remarked. "We had better warn Houston."

"So he can tell us to retreat again," another of the group grumbled

"Santa Anna couldn't kill Big Foot Wallace," Jesus said. He was proud to have been the one to have brought the big Texican into camp.

"Thank God," Austin said. It had been touch-and-go for a while. But Esperanza along with Dorotea had nursed him back to health. He had a notion Texas was going to need all the legends it could get.

Juan Diego galloped his horse down the Calle Nicholas Bravo, through the center of town until he came to Commerce Square, the central plaza and heart of the settlement. Flames leaped from every building. The heat was near unbearable. Before the end of the day San Felipe would be reduced to cinders. It would be no more than a blackened memory among the piney woods.

Cayetano Obregon galloped up to the Whiteside Hotel and hurled a firebrand through the front window and tossed another onto the porch. The sergeant was never any happier than when he could be involved in a bit of mayhem.

Paloma seemed to materialize out of the smoke and rode up alongside her brother. She kept her nose and mouth covered with a bandanna, to filter out some of the smoke and help her breathe.

"This is a bad move!" she complained, shouting to be heard above the roar of the flames. "I fear this will work against us." The roof of the hotel collapsed and sent a column of sparks jetting toward the sky. "I don't think this will frighten the Texicans. I think it will make them furious."

"It will break their spirits; you'll see," said Juan Diego.

Another building burst into flames, the meetinghouse across from the plaza. It was fitting that it should succumb to the fire, Guadiz thought. The seeds of insurrection had been sown within those walls. "Let these flames scour the last vestiges of rebellion from the land," said Juan Diego. Were they being watched? He hoped so. "You will all perish!" he shouted, walking his mount out of the smoke and into full view of the surrounding trees. "There is nowhere you can hide we cannot find you. *Norte americanos*, go back where you came from! This is our land. All we will give you is enough to bury you in." Juan Diego liked the way he sounded. Santa Anna was already hinting there would be a new governor of Texas. Why not a man like Juan Diego Guadiz?

"When do we stop, Colonel?" A lancer rode up. His cheeks were blackened, but his eyes were game.

"Burn everything!"

"Retreat?" Wallace said, hobbling over toward Sam Houston. "After what Guadiz has done to San Felipe? You cannot be serious, General." The big man looked more like a casualty then a willing soldier. His skull was bandaged; another held a compress to his side. He needed a crutch to walk while the bullet wound in his thigh healed. But he was alive and growing stronger by the day. The soldiers and their families in camp watched him regain his strength and took heart. "Give me a horse and a dozen men. I'll drive him out."

"This army is more important than a town," Houston replied, glowering down from horseback. Saracen, his white stallion, pawed the ground. "Buildings can be rebuilt. I cannot afford to lose a man. Caution is the better part of valor."

"Stephen, are you gonna abide by this?" As Houston departed, Wallace turned toward the only other man who might outrank the Tennessean.

Austin shrugged. "He's the general. Trust him, William." Austin stepped around his own gelding and placed his hand on Wallace's shoulder. The two men stood on the edge of the encampment, a half-day march from Santa Anna's columns. More than a thousand men had heeded Houston's call. Many of the volunteers brought their families, a wise move judging by the fate of San

Felipe. The Texicans were anxious to take on the general despite his overwhelming numbers. Maybe Houston was right. The longer he held his men back, the angrier and downright meaner they became. He might just be delaying to even the odds. When the battle came, it was going to be no picnic.

Santa Anna was pursuing a scorched earth policy even as he attempted to close in and engage Houston's army. And there was nothing anyone could do to stop him.

"Keep healing, Will. Sam will need a good scout. And give him your trust. He may be a bit of a blowhard when it comes to speeches, but he's a good man." Austin climbed into the saddle.

"Why don't you come with us?" Wallace said.

"No, old friend. It is back to the coast for me. The representatives are still attempting to draft a constitution. I need to be there." Austin placed a hand on the saddle horn and then looked around the clearing at the colonists and volunteers who had all come together to fight for liberty. "I never meant for this to happen, for the Alamo, all those deaths. And look at you."

"What the devil's the matter with me?" Wallace said, peering out from his bandaged skull. "Just a few nicks and bruises."

"Hardly even scratches," Austin replied with a grin. He indicated the colonists. "They believe in you, like it or not. Let them see you, my friend. Houston may be leading them, but they'll find their courage in you. You're Big Foot Wallace. There isn't a man who wouldn't follow you." Austin shook his hand. "Good luck. To all of us."

William watched his friend ride off along the south road. He did not envy Austin's task, putting the dream and aspirations into a foundation of words to build a republic upon. He hobbled back the way he had come, pausing by Mad Jack's camp to see how the freebooter was holding up. The pirate was inconsolable over the loss of the Flying Jib. All that wonderful whiskey and tequila, not to mention kegs of his home brew.

William decided to continue on through the camp, determined to walk the stiffness out of his leg. The blow to his skull had not impaired any of his faculties save that he had no memory of the nights and days when he hovered between life and death. But he could vividly recall seeing Esperanza and feeling her healing touch and the way she admonished him to live. He glanced over at her campsite and was tempted to approach her. But the time wasn't right. The death of Don Murillo poisoned the air between them. He wondered if it would always be that way.

His leg started to ache, but he forced himself to keep moving, to walk through the pain. He had to heal. Another battle was taking shape and he wasn't about to miss it, no sir, not this time. William hated being unable to ride to the sound of the guns. But here was at least some small part he could play, to make the bitter pill of another retreat easier to stomach. If his presence offered encouragement, then he'd walk till he dropped.

31

"TELL GUADIZ I WILL BE WAITING FOR HIM."

It was the twentieth of April, and the man watching Santa Anna lead his army into Buffalo Bayou was no stranger to the land. William Wallace had prowled these marshes many times. He knew where the ground was firm and made a good campsite, where the land was treacherous and quicksand waited to consume the unwary.

Mad Jack Flambeau had no use for the place. He cursed the oppressive air, the snakes, and gnats and mosquitoes. He slapped the back of his neck and with a scarf wiped the blood of whatever had bitten him from the palm of his hand. His loose gray shirt was patched with moisture. But the checkered bandanna covering his smooth hairless skull kept the sweat from stinging his good eye.

"Why don't you just go down there and tell those lancers where we are?" Wallace muttered. He had healed slow and steady since riding into San Felipe, more dead than alive and bearing the last letter from the Alamo. His recovery had been nothing short of miraculous. But then, he'd been tended by a ministering angel, in the person of Señora Saldevar.

Throughout the long weeks following the deaths of so many friends and loved ones—Don Murillo, Bill Travis, Jim Bowie, and the rest of the gallant defenders—it cheered the Texicans to see Big Foot Wallace up and about. If Santa Anna's whole army couldn't kill him, then there might yet be hope. The band of volunteers, under the command of Sam Houston, regrouped and prepared themselves for the final battle that would win them "victory or death."

William swept his spyglass across the faces of the infantry. The soldiers looked more than a little weary from the rigors of the campaign. They were apprehensive, too. The infantry obviously preferred the dry hills of West Texas to splashing through hedges of spike moss that might conceal an alligator or sloshing across shallow pools of stagnant, snake-infested waters whose flat green surfaces were choked with mosquito fern, spangles, and lily pads.

Wallace had learned the value of patience. He ignored the mosquitoes and gnats that made life miserable for the Mexican troops. He was leaner now, his eyes harder, his flesh seared and scarred like his soul. War had marked him, marked them all. Maybe there would come a day for softness, if Santa Anna didn't kill them first. And it wasn't for the general's lack of trying. But each and every time *el presidente* tried to close with Houston's force, the Texicans would retreat deeper and deeper into the bayous. Who could blame Houston for "this runaway scrape"? Though Santa Anna had lost a third of his army during the assault on the Alamo, his troops still outnumbered Houston's force two to one.

"Oh hell, they can't hear nothing," Mad Jack said. "And I don't need none of your sass, *mon ami*. Don't you forget who taught you everything you know, eh."

Wallace tossed the old sea dog a twist of tobacco. "Chew on that instead of my ears," he muttered.

The freebooter looked incensed. But a good plug of tobacco was worth the trouble. He shrugged and bit a chunk off the twist and tucked the rest in his pocket. He decided to keep his opinions to himself. It was the younger man's loss.

"Look over yonder," William said, pointing and passing the spyglass over to Mad Jack. "Can you see?"

"Of course. I told you my good light's cleared up. I can see fine now," said the freebooter. He used the spyglass. "What am I looking at?"

"The cannons. Santa Anna's artillery," Wallace replied.

Mad Jack surveyed the columns of men and horses laboring in the humid air. "But there aren't any."

"That's what I mean!" Wallace quietly exclaimed. "The ground's too soft. Santa Anna has abandoned his cannons. Houston will want to hear that. Now maybe we can stand and fight for a change." William noticed that several patrols of dragoons were ranging ahead of the column. Santa Anna wanted no surprises like the one he had experienced crossing the Rio Grande. The big man grinned. He could use this. Four lancers were riding directly toward the grove of cedars where William and Mad Jack had concealed themselves. The trail was narrow past these trees, bordered by marsh. The men would have to cut through right where he knelt and continue on beneath a stand of old-growth willows whose moss-draped branches provided just the concealment he required.

The two men crept back to their horses; Wallace returned the spyglass to a leather case hung from the saddle horn. He swung aboard a hammerhead roan, while Mad Jack favored an even-tempered mare with a sweet disposition.

"Head on back to camp. I'll catch up."

"Roberto warned me about you." Mad Jack scowled. "Santa Anna is beyond your reach." He glared disapprovingly at the big man. But William Wallace was immune to his old friend's stare. He removed the cartridge belt slung across his chest. He glanced over at the tree he intended to climb and then lost his shirt as well. There was no sense in tearing up his clothes. His bronze torso was leaner than usual, but long-limbed and still powerful. His dark brown woolen pants would blend in with the foliage. His belly was hard. A jagged line of scar tissue ran along his side, above the wide leather belt that held his knives and a brace of pistols.

"Santa Anna can wait. My concern is with another."

Mad Jack shook his head. "I will not leave without you. Look what happened the last time I let you go off on your lonesome." He indicated the furrowed flesh that ran along William's scalp line and formed a scar behind his right ear where the ridged flesh disappeared beneath his shaggy red mane. "No. Someone's got to stay around to sew you up."

Four lancers rode two abreast along a faintly discernible deer trail that cut through the marshland. Cedar, live oak, sweet gum, and willow trees overshadowed the trail, forming a canopy of intersecting branches thick with vines and Spanish moss. Leafy ferns and the spongy soil underfoot served to muffle the sound and lent an eerie quality to the scene. With the advancing army screened from sight by the foliage, the men of the patrol felt quite alone. The dragoons rode on through the emerald gloom, sweating and uncomfortable in their green coats and tight breeches, their brass helmets like miniature ovens. They were anxious to be out of bayou country and East Texas. With every twist and turn in the trail the soldiers scoured the terrain, watching the overgrown path for alligators and water moccasins. The scouts never knew they were in danger until it was too late.

Wallace dropped from the branches of a moss-draped cottonwood and landed on the rump of one horse, knocked the rider senseless with the flat of Bone-

chucker's blade, tossed the unconscious man aside where
he rolled into a patch of spike moss. Wallace's left hand
shot out, and he plunged Old Butch into the side of the
lancer next to him on the path. The slender blade slid
under the soldier's ribs. The man groaned and dropped
his lance, slid from the saddle, and, clutching his side,
started running down the path, back toward the safety of
the main column.

A few yards up the trail, the other two lancers heard
the commotion and turned their mounts in an attempt to
face their attacker. Mad Jack waited until their backs
were turned, then came riding at a gallop along the trail
and, swinging his rifle like a club, dropped one of the
two remaining soldiers with a well-timed hit.

Wallace spurred his stolen mount forward and leaped
from the saddle as the remaining lancer grabbed for a
saddle pistol and tried to fire off a warning shot. Wallace
batted the firearm from the soldier's hand and dragged
him from horseback and flung the man to the ground.
Then Wallace lunged forward and landed on the man's
chest, pinning his shoulders. The lancer was young and
stared with eyes wide as he beheld his death in the form
of a wild red-maned giant with a pair of knives made
for bloodletting. But the killing blow never fell.

"Is Colonel Guadiz with you?"

"I will never give you the satisfaction of an answer."

"Then I will give you the satisfaction of dying for
your principles." Wallace raised the short sword and prepared to plunge it into the soldier's throat.

"Wait!" The soldier winced and struggled in vain to
free himself. "Colonel Guadiz leads us. He is a very
brave man."

"Give him this message," Wallace said. He twirled
the heavy weapon and then, at the last second, before it
flew from his grasp, plunged it into the mud inches from
the lancer's head. The young soldier gave a startled yelp,

closed his eyes, then realized he was still alive. The weight left his chest. By the time the lancer struggled to his feet Wallace was astride the roan.

"What message?"

"Tell him what you have seen. Tell Guadiz I will be waiting for him."

"Who are you?" the lancer gasped.

"A ghost," Wallace said, red hair streaming on the fetid breeze as he galloped into the heart of the bayou.

32

"YOU GO TO HELL!"

Night came to Buffalo Bayou, hung the sky with robes of royal purple clouds, tinged them with gold, then seeded their domain with deeper hues of burnished copper, cobalt, black. Night settled softly, velvet smooth, over the marshes and shrouded the trees. Fireflies danced and flirted with the dark. Out beyond the firelight, eyes like copper coins nudged above the surface of the water as gators drifted past, blank and cold and ruthlessly efficient.

Wallace, standing alongside Sam Houston at the earthenworks the Texicans had thrown together over the course of a couple of days, folded his hands together and rested his chin on his forearms. With the bayou on three sides, the Texicans were trapped.

"Well, Sam, I reckon we won't run away from this fight."

The two men stood watching the Mexican troops bivouac for the night. The soldiers had begun filing in late in the afternoon, a slow-moving force guarded against an attack by the steady movement of the dragoons and lancers patrolling the perimeter.

"I suppose this looks familiar to you," Houston remarked. He was a large man, but he had to look up to William, who towered over him by several inches.

"Too familiar," Wallace replied. The similarities were

unsettling. With Austin on the coast, this was the last stand for the fledgling republic. The hour was at hand.

"Walk among the troops, let me know how they are feeling?"

"Hell, Sam, I can tell you right now. The boys are tired of running away, tired of being told they can't measure up to 'regular' troops. They're madder 'n a June bug on a match."

"Good," Sam replied.

"And there sure as the devil is only one way out of this predicament and that's straight through Santa Anna."

"Yep," Houston chuckled. "We're trapped."

William glanced aside at the general. "So are the women and children." Almost a thousand men, many with their families, were encamped behind this line of makeshift earthworks and overturned freight wagons. It was hardly a sight to strike fear in the heart of Santa Anna or any of his troops. But perhaps that was to the good.

"A man will fight even harder when his family's in danger," Houston said.

"General Houston, you're a hard man."

"So I've been told."

William Wallace was too restless to sleep. With the Mexican army besieging them, and the chance of dying soon, each moment was precious to him. So he walked throughout the encampment, and every few hundred feet or so he heard someone call out, "Big Foot Wallace!" as he passed, and children in homespun clothes would run up to him and take his hand and walk with him for a spell until he sent them back to their parents.

He passed the Zavalas' campsite and paused to pass a few minutes with Jesus and thank him once again for his help. Valentina embraced him and called him her other son, which brought a grin to Roberto's face.

"Be careful, Will; now there will be someone else to help around the forge."

"Gladly," William grinned.

He continued his rounds, and while he walked he took a whetstone to the blade of his knife and honed the edge. The grind of the stone on steel made an ominous sound as he walked.

William gingerly approached Esperanza's campfire and found it tended by Dorotea. Don Murillo's sister had lost much of her "vinegar" nature.

"Will you have some coffee, Mr. Wallace?" she asked, tapping a pot near a stack of freshly baked tortillas. "Stay and eat."

"I'm not hungry for much. But Mad Jack might be along later." He glanced around the immediate vicinity.

"She's down by the bayou," Dorotea told him.

"Thank you," William said. He turned to leave, then looked around at the old woman. "Señora, your brother was a fine man. It was an honor to know him. I shall never forget his kindness and generosity . . . and his sacrifice."

She nodded. "My brother was also a fine judge of character, a quality I was too vain to appreciate until now." She sighed. "Murillo prided himself on recognizing the good in a man. He thought highly of you and valued your friendship. I hope you will allow me to do the same."

"It would be my pleasure," Wallace said with a bow. He left the circle of light and ambled down to the water's edge, where the moon cast its silver reflection upon the still waters, a floating silver disk upon a somber sea. Esperanza was there, her widow's mantle concealing her features. She turned as Wallace approached.

"If you'd rather be alone—"

"Stay," she said. "No one would rather be alone. They

just are and make the best of it with self-deception and mirrors."

Wallace stood alongside her, behind them a crescent of campfires, families bedding down for the evening, gathering their children, worrying about the future, quarreling, making up, speculating on what the morrow would bring. Memories of disaster and tragedy manifested in the mighty army confronting them. It was a chorus of life, of an age-old struggle for freedom. It was a fight he was born to from his forebears who had driven the English out of Scotland and battled them again in the New World when Thirteen Colonies defied the Crown and won their independence. And now it was his turn to carry the mantle. Cry, "liberty!" and a Wallace had to answer the call.

"He knew I loved you," she said. Esperanza glanced down at the Bible in her hands. "And he forgave me." She shook her head. "Poor silly man . . . noble fool. He deserved better than a servant girl who married him to escape her servitude."

"No," Wallace told her. "He deserved you, because you made him happy. Because loving you made him whole again." He reached out and took her hand in his. "I was dying and you told me to live. You brought me back, healed me." He reached down and stroked her long black hair, found a silken strand beneath the black lace veil, like gossamer to his touch. His movements were uncommonly tender for one of such size and power. "You are good and true and I have loved you from the moment I first saw you, in the governor's garden. Fate brought us together and placed another man between us."

"He is still between us."

"And it may always be so," Wallace said. "But my life is richer for the love in my heart. And so was your husband's." He lifted her hand and brought it to his lips, tenderly kissed it, then lowered it to her side. And took his leave.

"Paloma! Paloma! Where are you?" Juan Diego bolted upright in his tent. He thrashed about as something glided toward him from the shadows. He recognized his sister by her touch, heard her soothing voice, her fingers massaging the pain from his temple.

"There . . . there, *mi hermano*. Be still. The men must not hear you."

"Who is he? Why doesn't he die?" Juan Diego was covered with sweat, his nightshirt stuck to his chest.

The tent flap opened and Cayetano Obregon shoved his head inside. "You all right, Colonel?"

"Yes, he is fine!" Paloma snapped. "My brother is tired, like all the others. He needs to rest. A good day's rest. Leave us alone."

The sergeant did not like taking orders from a woman, but he was not about to argue with this one. He disappeared, allowing the flap to drop into place.

"He was here, right here in the tent."

"A dream," said Paloma. "Nothing more. I warned you about the tequila."

"Give me more."

"Juan . . . no."

He shoved her aside and felt around in the darkness until he found the bottle. He raised it, sloshed the contents.

"The answer isn't there," Paloma said. "But across the meadow. He's waiting for you."

Juan Diego cursed and tossed the bottle aside. He ran a hand though his hair. He was dripping with sweat. "Why doesn't he die? What kind of man is he?"

"The kind you must kill yourself," Paloma replied, still on her knees.

"Yes," Juan Diego replied. It made sense. No man

was his equal with the blade. Let the redhaired *norte americano* perish by the sword. Guadiz liked that. He sat back on his camp bed. Paloma resumed her ministrations; the throbbing in his skull began to ease. "What would I do without you?" He made a purring sound deep in his throat like a big cat. He leaned against Paloma's breast, felt the rise and fall of her chest as she breathed. He closed his eyes while she drew the pain out of his body.

Paloma replied, "Without me, you would be——"

"Lost," her brother finished. Before long he was asleep. Paloma gently eased him down onto his bed and then returned to her own side of the partitioned tent.

It galled her. She had the courage and the cleverness. But she lived in a man's world. And a woman, even one as resourceful as herself, could only hope to stand in the shadows. Juan Diego was a colonel, the dashing leader of his troops. And with her to guide him, her brother was certain to rise in Santa Anna's government. Why, there was even talk of a governorship after this campaign. She longed for a world where she might achieve power on her own, without having to rely on the whims of a man. But no such place existed for her. So she must rely on her brother and the influence she wielded.

She closed her eyes and soon drifted into sleep, a woman without worries, confident her star was in ascendance and never suspecting there could be a fall from grace.

"His troops must have scouted us. Santa Anna probably knows how many of us he's got to fight," Mad Jack grumbled, nursing a cup of coffee Henneke had prepared for him. "Woman, you forgot the salt." He shook his head in dismay. "How many times have I told you to add a pinch of salt? It cuts the bitterness."

The woman ignored him and finished scraping the last

of the food into the fire. When she had cleaned the plates and stacked them away, Henneke yawned and made a show of being tired. She eventually became disgusted with the Frenchman's seeming indifference and retired to their tent near the fire. Lucky bestirred himself from the shadows and stretched out across the entrance. In Wallace's absence the hound had adopted the tavern keeper, knowing full well he could always count on Henneke for the best table scraps in town.

The freebooter shrugged and rubbed the back of his neck. A storm was brewing. He glanced toward the Mexican encampment. Sacre bleu! What a storm. He looked across the fire at Wallace. The big man knelt near the coals and sat back on his heels while he honed the blades of his knives. Old Butch and Bonechucker had a job to do. The hour was at hand.

"It took Santa Anna most of the day to bring his troops up."

"They'll rest tonight, sleep late tomorrow maybe," Wallace said.

"I wish Austin were here," Mad Jack stated. "But I reckon it's important he stays out of harm's way and sets up the provisions of government in case we all don't get killed mañana."

"I wish a lot of people were here," Wallace said, remembering Don Murillo, Chuy, Travis, Bowie, even Crockett, whom he had barely known. Good men, all, and heaven's worthy allies. He hoped there was some kind of Valhalla for heroes such as these.

Mad Jack circled the fire and squatted down alongside Wallace. He took the dirk and checked the blade. It was honed to a razor's edge. He ran the blade along his forearm and shaved it clean.

"You wear them well, lad."

"Listen, you old pirate, perhaps when the fighting starts you ought to keep clear. No matter what you say,

I think your lights aren't what they used to be."

Mad Jack reddened at the suggestion he should remain with the women. "You go to hell!" he blurted out. The Frenchman rounded the fire and returned to his tent. He paused at the flap before ducking inside and looking back at the man he loved like a son, adding, "And I'll see *you* there."

33

"WHO ARE YOU?"

It was late morning, the twenty-first day of April. The sun traced its hazy lazy arc across the sky, bathed the land in a golden glow that the moist grasses captured and sent deep into the nourishing earth. There was a feeling in the air, a promise of a warm spring day when trees bud and flowers bloom and the great green fuse of rebirth ripples through the land. It would have been a day to celebrate life, except for William Wallace, standing tall and proud and quite alone in the field between two armies, his knives drawn, his whole being focused on the task before him.

Word spread quickly through the camp, passed along by runners from cookfire to tent, and soon it seemed every man, woman, and child crowded the breastworks to watch the strange sight of that solitary figure standing alone in the meadow, about thirty feet beyond the Texican lines, in full view of the Mexican encampment. But no one across the way had yet to raise an alarm. The sentries, exhausted from their efforts the day before, were asleep at their posts.

The crowd of Texicans parted for Sam Houston, who stared dumbfounded at the frontiersman. "What in heaven's name?" He turned, spied Mad Jack and Roberto, and asked them to bring Wallace back to the encampment. Esperanza arrived at the makeshift fortifications and gasped in horror at the sight of William standing within range of the Mexican sharpshooters. She caught Flambeau by the arm.

"What's the matter with him? How long has he been standing there?"

"I left him sharpening his knives. Last night," Mad Jack said. "I guess he got a good edge on them and needed something else to do." He followed Roberto over the mounded dirt and trotted across the long grass to stand at Wallace's side.

It was quiet out here in the field. The birds had ceased their chirping. Even the insects seemed to be avoiding the clearing. This was old country, Wallace reflected, and treacherous, but with a primal beauty all of its own. Of course, standing here in plain sight of Santa Anna's guns was hardly the way to appreciate the season.

"Amigo?" Roberto Zavala said, cautiously drawing near. "What are you doing? Santa Anna has enough marksmen to fill you full of lead."

"Reckon they're asleep. The whole camp hasn't stirred." Wallace carried no rifle or pistol. But the short sword, Bonechucker, gleamed in his right hand, and in his left Old Butch, slender and deadly. The blades were thirsty. And Wallace was through running. It was time.

He untied the scarf about his neck; the breeze carried it back toward the Texican camp. His left leg was throbbing, the legacy of the wound he had suffered a month earlier. But the pain would leave as soon as he started to move. "I think I'll take me a walk over there," he said, with a look in Mad Jack's direction. "What do you say, old man? Have you got one more broadside in you?"

The buccaneer nodded and began to prime the flint-lock pistols dangling from a belt he wore draped across his shoulder. "I should like my coat," the freebooter said. He preferred to be completely dressed for battle. His ruffled black shirt smelled of Henneke's rosewater. Well, at least he'd die fragrant.

"You both are loco," Roberto said. Then he shrugged. "I guess I am crazy, too." Roberto ran back to the fortifications and told one of the men to hand him a rifle, powder, and shot.

Sam Houston was becoming more flustered with every passing minute. He shoved his way along the earthenworks. "Zavala? I wanted you to bring him in."

"No offense, General Sam, but Señor Wallace has other ideas. And I'm not about to try and stop him."

"What do you mean?"

"I mean William Wallace ain't running anymore. He's taking a walk over yonder. And I'm going with him. Mad Jack, too."

"And me!" Jesus Zavala called out, joining his son. He scrambled over the fortification.

"I'll come along," Robert Kania spoke up. He had a father to avenge. Now was as good a day as any.

Wallace remained, sunlight warming his face—the beauty of the world transfixed him; ghosts whispered in his mind. He closed his eyes and relived a moment on the Mexican coast, below Veracruz, after the storm and the shipwreck, when he stood with Samuel and for one brief moment the two brothers gloried in being alive with the sea at their backs and all their dreams before them. Juan Diego Guadiz had ended all that. It was time to set the matter straight. For Samuel, for Don Murillo, and for all the rest.

A breeze ruffled Wallace's open shirt, dried the moisture on his sculpted chest, tugged at his long red hair that looked like a crown of fire. He glanced over his shoulder and was startled to see he was no longer alone in the meadow. William had been joined by nearly a thousand men who had formed a few paces behind him and arranged themselves along the front of the earthenworks. He spied Esperanza; the woman had climbed a wagon so that he might see her. She had retrieved his scarf and held it over her head like a banner, raised aloft as if to salute him. Behind the lines, Sam Houston had ordered his white charger saddled and brought forward.

Wallace didn't feel like waiting. "Remember the Alamo," he said. And started forward.

The phrase was passed from man to man, echoed like a somber benediction repeated again and again, up and down the line, growing in strength and intensity and volume. Rage was their fuel. It welled in their breasts, put steel in their backbones, billowed over in a rising tide of hatred as the Mexican lines drew closer and closer. Wallace led the Texicans over the makeshift breastworks and awakened the dozing guards just long enough to kill them.

"Remember the Alamo!"

And now the weary Mexicans struggled out of their tents and stumbled toward their stacked muskets only to be cut down in a withering volley from the Texicans' rifles. Dragoons and lancers staggered into the sunlight and tried to chase down their horses, then abandoned the effort in an attempt to repel the attack and fight on foot. More than a hundred men tried to form a skirmish line. Jesus Zavala and the townspeople of San Felipe smashed into them, firing at point-blank range, shattering their ranks, clubbing, clawing, hacking with tomahawks and hunting knives. Pistols at close range took their toll. The attackers fired and reloaded on the run. There was no stopping them. By the time Sam Houston astride Saracen galloped into the Mexican camp the issue had already been decided.

"Remember the Alamo!" rang out above the din, a terrible battle cry that meant no quarter. Rage unleashed. Men were driven berserk, their full fury at last unleashed. And none was more deadly than the redheaded demon in their midst.

Wallace darted and slashed and lunged and stabbed. Men died before him. They never had a chance. He was like some force of nature, unstoppable, immune to the efforts of mere mortals. Musket balls thick as hornets nipped at his clothing; bayonets and lances sought him out. But his blades of steel carved a bloody path through the camp.

"Guadiz!" he cried out. "Guadiz!" his voice boomed. A familiar face flashed before him, the brute ugly Sergeant Obregon. "I see you still wear my brand!" Wallace shouted.

Cayetano Obregon touched the red streak of scar tissue disfiguring his cheek. The man was shirtless, his chest, gut, and shoulders black with matted hair. Recognizing Wallace, Obregon could no longer contain himself. He grabbed a ten-foot lance from the ground, trained the broad iron point at Wallace, and charged forward. William chopped the weapon in half with a single swipe of Bonechucker's heavy blade. Obregon could not reverse his course. He swung the shaft at the knife fighter. Wallace closed in and stabbed left–right–left–right in rapid succession, driving Obregon backward with each thrust of those terrible weapons. Obregon's eyes widened, his chest red from shoulder to waist. He stumbled back, slipped in the mud, and collapsed in a patch of spike moss. A Texican ran past, caved in the sergeant's skull with the butt of his rifle, and charged off after another victim.

Obregon was never far from Guadiz. An inner voice told Wallace to look to the right. He obeyed his instinct and came face-to-face with Juan Diego. The mortal enemies spied each other through the drifting haze of powder smoke.

Guadiz raised his pistol and snapped off a shot. A

colonist bolted in front of William and unwittingly saved the big man's life at the expense of his own. The wounded man staggered, clutched his side, cried out his mother's name, and sank to the ground.

Juan Diego cursed and tossed the pistol aside and drew his saber.

Wallace charged him. But it wasn't going to be that easy. At a signal from Guadiz half a dozen men rushed forward to intercept the big man. Wallace slashed the first soldier who came within striking distance, then caught his opponent by the front of his uniform and used him for a shield as two other soldiers lunged forward, thrusting their bayonets into their hapless *compadre*. With their muskets caught in the dead man's chest, Wallace leaped on his victims and slammed their skulls together, staggering the men. He whirled and dived to the ground as the remaining three dragoons fired a volley into their companions. The men drew their pistols and tried to bring them into play when a scarred old blue heeler leaped out of the acrid pall drifting over the meadow. The hound clamped his jaws around the first calf muscle he came to. Wallace leaped to his feet and was on them like a great cat. Old Butch and Bonechucker were his claws and fangs. He cut and jabbed. One man stumbled away, cradling his useless arm, blood pouring down his side, Lucky nipping at his heels. The other two died hard. They grabbed knives from their belts and attacked together. Wallace threw his dirk underhanded and skewered one man.

"Come on!" Wallace roared. The last soldier was too proud to run. No matter. Wallace would have caught him from behind. He grabbed the soldier by the throat and flung him to the ground and pinned him there, driving the short sword deep into his chest. When the man quit wriggling, Wallace withdrew the blade, retrieved the dirk, and started off after Juan Diego.

He spied the colonel making a dash for the trees. Guadiz had joined a rout that was already under way. Wallace's gaze swept the camp. Mexican soldiers were scattering in every direction, hounded by wild-eyed Texicans hell-bent on revenge. The slaughter was terrible. He noticed Sam Houston being helped down from horseback. The general was favoring his right ankle. A swirl of powder smoke obscured Wallace's vision. No matter. He had business elsewhere. He couldn't let Guadiz escape yet again.

As Wallace took off in pursuit of Juan Diego, his sister rose from the ground where she had been pretending to be dead. Paloma was dressed as a soldier, her hair bound beneath her cap, pistol and saber slung from her waist. She raised the pistol and drew a bead on Wallace's back. At this range she wasn't about to miss.

"With this I put an end to your torments, *mi hermano*," she muttered and squeezed the trigger. A cutlass blade batted the gun upward, and she fired harmlessly into the air. Paloma cursed and swung around to find herself face-to-face with Mad Jack Flambeau. The pirate looked possessed. His lips curled back and in that moment he was riding the seas once more, the scourge of the Caribbean, in a time when the decks ran red with blood and there was no mercy beneath the black flag.

Paloma did not like what she saw in the old man's expression. She retreated a step, swept the cap from her head to reveal her long hair. "Wait. I am a woman." Paloma never expected to die. No one ever does.

"I don't care," said the Butcher of Barbados and ran her through. He never gave the dying woman another thought but stepped over her body and looked for someone else to kill. He spied Roberto emerging from a tent, dragging a docile-looking peon who had probably been some officer's servant. Mad Jack thought the man looked familiar and hurried over to Zavala's side.

"Back off, Mad Jack. This man has surrendered. Besides, he is just a servant. He can do no one any harm. Let him get back home as best he can." Roberto motioned for the man to go.

Flambeau blocked the prisoner's path. He jabbed the cutlass against the peon's chest and forced the innocent-looking servant to stand back.

"Not him. You might want to escort him over to Houston."

"Why?" Roberto looked puzzled.

"Because, my lad, you have just captured *el presidente*."

Guadiz slogged through the swamp until he reached the San Jacinto, where he saw a number of the lancers he had commanded attempting to ford the river. He almost called out, but a commotion in the woods caused him to duck out of sight. Moments later an armed mob of Texicans came barreling out of the underbrush and arranged themselves along the riverbank.

They opened fire on the fleeing lancers. Juan Diego watched in horror as the soldiers pleaded for mercy only to be shot down in cold blood by men who had been pushed too far and couldn't stop the killing. Santa Anna's army had slaughtered their loved ones, burned their homes and villages. Now the chickens had come home to roost. It was the time for vengeance, and there would be no stopping the carnage until the last man had paid the price. So the soldiers died in the shallows, died wading in the channel, died crawling up the opposite bank, their bodies sliding down the muddy embankment.

Juan Diego crouched down behind the fallen timber and covered himself with several broadleaf ferns and waited until his limbs ached and he grew stiff, and then he continued to wait while the heat leached the moisture from his body and the flies and mosquitoes practically ate him alive. He remained in hiding until the gunfire ceased and the Texicans had tramped off through the woods. Only when it was quiet and still did he crawl forth and stagger to his feet, steadying himself with his saber.

The San Jacinto River ran red with blood. Bodies floated on the surface, drifted past like dull dead logs, men he had known and commanded, arms outstretched, facedown, half-submerged. The hell with them. He had business on the coast. There was always someone willing to sell a boat if the price was right. And he had a coin pouch sewn into the lining of his coat.

"His name was Samuel."

Juan Diego froze at the sound of the voice then slowly turned. William Wallace was standing about fifty feet away, half in shadow, half in light, knives gleaming, crimson-stained with a viscous smear. Guadiz walked out onto the riverbank where the ground was flat and firm and bordered by weeping willows. He did not understand the meaning behind the big man's remark, nor did he care. He pointed the saber at Wallace.

"And again you survive," he said. "You have lived a charmed life thus far. But it shall end with me."

Wallace started forward. He had said the name, alerted the man to his presence. That was enough. The time for talking had ended; retribution was long overdue. He covered the ground with the same long-legged gait of a man going about his job, unemotional now, the rage and lust in him spent; his only desire was to see justice done and appease his brother's restless spirit.

The two men warily circled each other. Juan Diego was the first to lunge forward; Wallace darted inside and feinted with Bonechucker, caught the saber and batted it up, then darted inside the man's guard and slashed his thigh. Guadiz yelped in pain and swung the saber in a vicious arc at Wallace's head.

William ducked beneath the blow and danced out of reach. His boot heels slipped in the mud and the big man went down. Guadiz charged in and slashed Wallace across the chest as he rolled out of harm's way. Juan Diego roared in triumph and closed in for the kill. William retreated, glanced down at his shirt and the superficial wound that hurt like the devil.

Guadiz stabbed and slashed and thrust. The blades clanged off one another. The crash of steel on steel echoed in the stillness. William's hands were a blur, thrust and parry, slash and stab, first one knife, then the other. Juan Diego tried in vain to match the knife fighter. He had the advantage of reach with his saber, but it didn't last long. With a clang and a snap, Bonechucker sliced through the saber, and a metal shard went flying through the air. Juan Diego staggered back, retreated down the riverbank, blood oozing from a dozen superficial wounds he just realized he had.

He was in pain now, and his left arm was suddenly numb and slick. "Diablo!" He grimaced. "Who are you!?" He could sense the big man closing on him. The colonel bided his time, cautioned himself. "Do you think I am finished? I am Juan Diego Guadiz. Ten men have I killed on the field of honor. I am Juan Diego." *Wait . . . wait . . . now turn and attack!* He spun around in midstride and hurled himself at the Texican. But his broken, jagged blade sawed away at nothing but empty air.

No! He was unprotected.

Yes! A flash of movement on his right as Wallace darted past. Something stung Juan Diego's neck. He stumbled forward off balance.

"In case you're wondering," Wallace said, "I just slit your throat."

Guadiz dropped the saber and collapsed, his legs buckled, and he sank backward. He heard the river, the rasp of his own breathing, the warmth of the blood as it seeped from the severed artery. He was dying. But he had to know why this man had plagued him and been his downfall.

"Who are you?" he managed to gasp.

Wallace knelt at his side. He held up a familiar card, one that held the likeness of a man, bathed in crimson flames and brandishing a lethal array of knives. Other blades littered the ground at his feet, thrust into the earth like so many grave markers. And Juan Diego remembered Esperanza's admonition, long ago. *"Draw the last card and see for yourself what must be overcome. Beware, though. Once it is drawn, the card can never be returned."*

"Who . . . are . . . you . . . ?"

Wallace placed the image on the dying man's face. "El Destripedor Rojo."

The Red Ripper.

34

⟦❦⟧

THE TEXICANS GAVE SANTA ANNA A CHOICE: *either sign the articles recognizing the sovereignty of the Republic of Texas or be handed over to Capt. Mad Jack Flambeau, the Butcher of Barbados, who threatened to nail His Excellency's pecker to a tree stump. El Presidente sprained his wrist grabbing for the nearest quill pen. By the time the ink dried, the Republic of Texas was born.*

Santa Anna returned to Mexico City in disgrace. A new San Felipe rose from the ashes of the old. Sam Houston got himself elected president. Stephen Austin, stung by what he considered the ingratitude of his former colonists, died a couple of years later, a bitter man mourned by his friends.

Esperanza Saldevar returned to her East Texas ranch, where she proved to be as smart and stubborn and resourceful as her late husband. Now and then on a soft summer evening she could be found keeping vigil on the balcony of the hacienda, her restless heart full of mystery and desire—alone with her memories and the whispering wind. It was rumored she eventually took a lover.

And what of William Wallace?

Listen up, old salt; I'm a mite dry, but I'll tell you this. Texas had a rough birth, and it didn't get any easier. Bandits from south of the border raided the early settlements and turned the Nueces Strip into a killing ground. Comanche war parties stormed out of the Staked Plains, looting and plundering without mercy. The howling wilderness needed a mighty big man to set things right.

But that's another story.

TURN THE PAGE
FOR A LOOK AHEAD
TO

Mad
Morgan

THE ELECTRIFYING NEW NOVEL FROM KERRY
NEWCOMB, NOW AVAILABLE IN HARDCOVER
FROM ST. MARTIN'S PRESS!

Black sky. Black bay. Black rage in the water.

Muscles strained as the swimmer sliced through the stygian sea, sweet smooth, with an economy of effort. Gauging the distance, he saved his strength, a talent learned in the fields where he'd cut cane, slick clean with one swipe of the hooked steel blade. After years of toil, the wicked tool had become an extension of his powerful arm. The plantations took their toll; bone and blood was the price of a hurried harvest. Still, he had refused to die. Years of harsh servitude that broke the spirits of lesser men tempered him. He was lean but powerful, his iron strength had been forged by slavery in the furnace of the Caribbean sun. Ridges of lurid white scar tissue marked his back and shoulders in the pale glare as he broke the sheltering sea, gulped air then dove again, sleek as a watersnake, fanged and deadly on its course. His captors had been liberal in their punishment over the years. A taste of "the cat" was every slave's lot from time to time.

How far now? Not very. Head for the stern. See there, the Jacob's ladder. And the bark is well lit. No doubt the men aboard will be celebrating the birthday of their king, just like the others.

He paused and treaded water and glanced back across the bay to the shore, aglow with lanterns—the streets of

Santiago were crowded with a happily inebriated populace. The birthday of the Spanish monarch was cause for celebration. The sounds of music and laughter drifted across the incoming tide, echoed to a lesser degree from the prison ship anchored offshore. He was one man alone, unnoticed, lost in the dark. No alarm preceded him. The carnival had masked his escape. And the watchmen who might have noticed his absence and raised an alert were beyond speaking.

Abelardo Montoya paced the poop deck, his back to the sea and his eyes on the harlots his compadres had brought from shore. The women were willing, obviously, and though plain as planks and broad in the beam, there wasn't one he wouldn't climb if given half a chance. Unfortunately, he had been assigned first watch by Sergeant Salas. Fate had decreed Salas and the other guards would play while Abelardo endured his lonely vigil, with naught but a heavy-bore Spanish musket to clutch in his grudging embrace. The guard stamped his feet and shook his head and tried to look away from the bark's gaily illuminated quarterdeck. Lanterns hung from the shrouds and along the ship's rail. Rum kegs had been tapped, tankards had been raised to toast the health of Carlos II, and now a solitary piper coaxed a merry tune to dispel the gloom. Abelardo knew he was only punishing himself by watching but he couldn't bring himself to turn his back on the revel below. He sighed, removed his tricorn hat and mopped the perspiration from his forehead and grizzled cheeks upon the sleeve of his faded pea-green coat. The *Dolorosa* wasn't a bad ship, just a prison ship, stripped of its armaments to make room belowdecks for the murderous sea scum they had captured on the island. Guarding prisoners was a boring, tedious job but one that had to be done by someone.

"Hang the lot and be done with it," the Spaniard muttered, his hungry gaze sweeping the quarterdeck below. The ship's company had been raiding the rum stocks for several hours now. Sergeant Salas was roaring drunk and the rest of the crew weren't in any better shape. There wasn't a steady hand aboard, save his own. Curse the sergeant. Salas and the others intended to have their fun till the morning hours. And why not? Captain Gomez would not bring the rest of the crew aboard until tomorrow afternoon, plenty of time to load the whores back into a longboat and point them toward shore. "Not before I sample their wares, I swear," Abelardo scowled. "Short straws," he muttered. "Always choose the damn short straw. That's my luck."

In the middle of his self-pity he heard the Jacob's ladder behind him at the ship's stern rattle against the rail, then something thumped the deck behind him. Abelardo turned, took a step back and stared slack-jawed at the ragged, half-naked apparition that had swung over the side and landed on the poop deck. "*Madre de Dios* . . . what has the sea coughed up? A slave from the cane fields?" Abelardo cocked his weapon. "You had a long swim to hell, amigo." The Spaniard centered the musket on the slave's brow, just below his sodden brown mane.

The slave lunged forward as the guard squeezed the trigger and batted the priming powder from the pan. The flintlock misfired and failed to discharge. Abelardo cursed and clubbed the slave with the gun butt, opening a gash on his cheek. The slave staggered back and dropped his own weapon, a cane-cutter. Abelardo kicked the curved blade out of the way, stepped in close and swung the musket a second time. The slave recovered and dodged the blow, rammed his head into the Spaniard's groin, and forced him back against the rail. Abelardo gasped, dropped the musket, and called out to his compadres in a hoarse voice. The slave wrapped his arms around the guard's legs and dragged him down. On the quarterdeck, the revel continued, its participants heedless of the struggle.

Abelardo slipped a dagger loose from his belt sheath and sliced his opponent's shoulder. The slave ignored the pain, caught the guard's wrist and twisted the weapon in the man's hand, forcing the lethal blade down toward its owner's chest. Abelardo twisted and fought but the slave would not let go. Overhead through a forest of masts, trimmed sails, and rigging, a single star appeared through a rent in the clouds and tried to cast its feeble reflection upon the bay. On the ship below, two men struggled soundlessly for their lives, muscles straining.

Abelardo watched in horror as the knife he held inexorably lowered to his own breast. He once again tried to shout to his companions. Even now they might save him. But the slave covered the Spaniard's mouth with his forearm, then with a violent and overpowering effort thrust the blade deep into the guard's torso. The blade glanced off a rib and sank home. Abelardo twisted and thrashed in one last effort to break loose. But his strength failed him. His killer's gray eyes searched the dying man's features, made a connection; the slave from the sea and his victim bound in silent communion for one last moment.

Gray eyes without mercy, bleak as a thunderhead. Look away. . . . look to the star in the rigging. See how it sparkles briefly, oh, briefly, then fades . . . to black.

The slave rolled onto his side, then lay on his back, gulping air, shoulder to shoulder with the dead man. After a short breather, he crawled across the deck and retrieved his cane-cutter, then, peering over the edge of the poop deck, counted six more guards. Though he ached from his exertions and was near exhausted, thoughts of surrender never entered his mind. His gaze shifted from the blade in his hand to the Spaniards below. *Six to one? Fair enough.*

Loose havoc, harry mercy. Be it now . . . or never. There was blood on the moon tonight, and no turning back.

Welcome the living dead: these men without hope, existing in filth, dying in misery below the quarterdeck of the Spanish bark *Dolorosa*. The prison ship rode at anchor a couple of hundred yards off the port of Santiago de Cuba. The imprisoned freebooters crowded in the gun deck were human cargo for the slave pens of Panama. These brethren of the Black Flag would have preferred a cleaner, quicker death. A firing squad, even dancing a jig at the end of a hangman's rope, had to be a better fate than what the Spaniards had in store for them. For men born to the sea, imprisonment and brutal servitude deep in the silver mines south of Panama would be a hellish ordeal.

On this humid, stifling night in the year 1660, the weary denizens belowdecks listened with a mixture of remorse and envy as their captors passed about flagons of rum and lifted their coarse voices in songs of celebration. Someone piped a tune for his drunken comrades. Half a dozen guards, unsteady on their feet, danced to the melody, swilled rum, sang and laughed and goodnaturedly vied with one another for the jaded favors of the whores who had been brought across the bay at no small expense to these soldiers.

Sir William Jolly licked his parched lips. His nostrils flared. He could smell the rum despite the stench of unwashed bodies surrounding him. Jolly was a squat, solid-built man. Stringy red hair hung to his shoulders, beads of sweat rolled along his grizzled jaw and brooding brow. At a glance he seemed almost a dullard, a thick-skulled seaman affecting the ragged attire of a gentleman. But even Jolly's captors had noted the deference accorded the disgraced aristocrat by his fellow prisoners. Jolly's past was a mix of conjecture and rumor. It was said the physician had fallen victim to a libertine existence. Drunkenness and gambling may have cost him his heritage, but the forty-year-old physician had found a true calling among the thieves and cutthroats of the Spanish Main.

"Doc?" muttered Israel Goodenough, emerging from the shadows. The tall, rail-thin gunner had to walk stoop-shouldered as he approached. His forehead showed a bruise where he'd recently forgotten his height and clipped the crossbeams with his skull. Israel raised a bony hand and gestured aft where the worse of their number lay in misery upon makeshift pallets of empty grain sacks.

Goodenough dry-swallowed, hoping to coax a little moisture up into his throat. The round knob of his Adam's apple bobbed in the leathery trough of his long neck. "It's Hiram James. The fever's on him again."

"And if he's lucky it will kill him this time," said Jolly, glancing in the direction as a pitiful, almost animalistic wail rose from the shadowy recesses of the ship's stern. The poor soul sounded like some wounded cur left to die in an alley. In contrast, coarse laughter drifted down through the barred grating in the quarter-deck that permitted the only fresh air to reach below. "There's nothing I can do. Without my herbs and tinctures . . ." Jolly shrugged and held up his hands in a gesture of uselessness. Droplets of sweat formed on the bulbous tip of his pocked, pinkish nose.

Listen to the revelry. The bloody curs . . .

Jolly turned his sad brown eyes upward as if he could pierce the oaken beams and observe his captors indulging their debauchery in the lantern light. "They've left but a skeleton crew, I wager," the physician muttered.

"*Sacre bleu.* It might as well be an army for all the good it does us," another of the brethren drily observed. Pierre Voisin was a bastard by birth and a thief by choice. His narrow features were seamed from his perpetual squint and burned dark from a life lived before the mast. "I once was prisoner of the Marathas, south of Bombay. The vizier, old Kanhojii Angria, boiled half our crew in oil. On my honor, he did; then threw 'em to the sharks. I tell you, *mes amis*, be glad these sons of bitches above us at least are Christian."

"Shackles are shackles," said Israel Goodenough. He took no comfort in Voisin's story. "Christians ain't got no lock on mercy. Thomas LeBishop carries the Savior's cross into battle and I never seen such a bloodletter as the Black Cleric." Stooping forward, the gunner kept pace with the physician as Jolly maneuvered his way among his miserable companions. The buccaneers outnumbered the Spaniards. But the iron chains clamped about their ankles and the stout oak door with its heavy iron bolt kept the prisoners from forcing their way topside and commandeering the vessel.

"LeBishop's a hard one," Jolly agreed, shadows and firelight flickering on his coarse features. "Tell us again, Voisin. How did you escape the heathens of Islam?"

"I didn't," the Frenchman replied, flashing a gap-toothed grin. "I got killed!"

Weak laughter filtered through the crowded confines of the gundeck. Bollica growled. The thirst was intolerable. But the last time the freebooters had cried out for water the guards had responded by urinating through the iron grate overhead. A few crusts of mealy bread and a bucket of slops that passed for gruel came infrequently at best. With any luck the men below would starve to death in their shackles before ever setting foot in a silver mine.

"I ain't eaten in so long my gut thinks my throat's been cut," muttered Israel Goodenough.

"That's the only way you'll escape this cursed boat," another man replied, limbs trembling, eyes gaunt, ribs showing through his flesh. "What say you, sawbones?"

William Jolly shook his head and began to pace in a tight circle, his chains rattling with every step. His companions close by growled in discomfort as they moved their shackled limbs out of his path. Jolly stopped and stared at the steps leading up to the bolted door. He raised his clenched fists and shook them at their unseen guards. "Listen to them, dancing on our graves. By heaven . . . if we only had them in our gunsights . . ."

"Heaven?" said Israel. "Your shadow won't ever fall there, William Jolly. It's a mite late to be calling on the angels." The gunner spoke with a sense of grim resolve. He hadn't lost hope quite yet, but the light was dimming fast.

Jolly continued to shake his fists, his mouth drew back in a grimace. This was his fault. Their schooner, *Red Warrant*, had run aground on the coast of Hispaniola, leaving them at the mercy of the Spanish forces. They had avoided capture for several days, but at last, starving and with their captain dead, Jolly had led the men in surrender, hoping to appeal to the mercy of the Spanish authorities. Alas, mercy was in short supply these days. Maybe they should have fought to the death. But he had a daughter in Port Royal. A nine-year-old girl who expected to see him again. He was the only family she had. He must get back to her, somehow, some way. "Nell," he softly whispered to himself. "I swear I shall never leave you again."

He slumped back amid his brethren. In the darkness back toward the stern, poor delirious Hiram James cried out for his sister. The hallucinations shifted: he called out for men to join him at the topgallants, he shouted for his comrades to cut away the sailcloth. "Watch your-selves, lads, they're using chain." His breathing grew more labored then rattled deep in his throat and ceased altogether.

"It's all over," someone called out.

"Good for him," Pierre Voisin disconsolately replied. "Should we grieve? *Je ne sais pas*. Why? At least he's free. Hell can be no worse." In the silence that followed the Frenchman's benediction, the buccaneers gloomily pondered the fate that awaited them all. In sharp contrast to their mood, the revel above continued unabated. The guards were celebrating as if there were no tomorrow. A scar-faced Spanish sergeant knelt upon the grate over-head, his bulk blocking out the pale moonlight appearing through the tattered clouds. Manuel Salas dragged his pewter tankard across the iron screen, taking care to spill some of the rum. Why not? There was plenty. He en-joyed taunting the prisoners. Animals like these were a constant threat to Spain's colonies in the New World. They deserved to suffer.

"What say you, thieves, murderers, you sons of bitches? The rum is sweet as mother's milk. Are you thirsty, my pretties?" One of the whores joined the ser-geant and began to pull on his coat. She was a round, heavyset mulatto, wide-eyed and unsteady on her feet. Salas whispered in her ear. The mulatto nodded and laughed, raised her skirt and presented herself to the pris-oners. "Feast your eyes," roared Salas. "For you'll never again enjoy a woman's favor." The sergeant grabbed her ample derriere, turned her about and buried his scarred face beneath the woman's rumpled skirts. The mulatto squealed in delight and rose up on her toes. A few mo-ments later the guard freed himself from her coffee-colored thighs and struggled to his feet. The curses rising from below amused him. He emptied the contents of the tankard onto the upturned faces. "Here you soulless scum, you *boucaniers*. Drink. Drink." Beneath the grate, several of the freebooters surged forward, struggling to place themselves beneath the trickle of rum. William Jolly bullied his way through the men, with Israel Good-enough and the Frenchman, Voisin, at his side. Sir William put an end to the altercation before it spread throughout the gundeck.

"What is this? Shall we give this jackal the satisfaction of watching us kill one another for a few drops of grog?!"

The prisoners surrounding Jolly grudgingly retreated, chains rattling as they shuffled back to their places. Salas hurled the tankard against the iron grate, cursed the physician in the darkness below and, grabbing the whore in his rough embrace, dragged her out of sight. Jolly and the others could hear him laughing above the din of his companions. Elsewhere on the deck a pistol shot rang out, followed by another. In celebration . . . ?

A few moments later the whore began to scream. The prisoners assumed she was being brutally taken by her paramour. Indeed, there wasn't a guard who seemed to be anything less than mean and dangerous. Suddenly Sergeant Salas landed facedown and covered the grate with his body.

"Has this bastard no shame?" said Israel Goodenough. "Will he go a'romping in bushy park right above us?" Droplets of moisture spattered into the hold.

"More rum," Israel muttered, catching a few droplets on his fingertips. Then he sniffed his fingers and stepped back from the spreading stain. "Blood?" The mulatto continued to scream as she ran across the deck and vaulted over the side of the ship. A mouthful of salt water stilled her cries.

William Jolly dipped his fingers in the moisture and nodded in confirmation. Now one and all recognized the unmistakable clatter of steel on steel. Bootheels drummed across the deck. A door slammed back on its hinges. A musket discharged. The commotion on deck intensified as the guards scrambled about. Someone cried out, *"Quien viené?!"* There were growls and groans, a cry of pain and a litany of curses, all in Spanish. Someone cried out in agony, his voice trailed off. The other prostitutes attempted to raise the alarm but the women were obviously frightened and desperate to be off the prison ship. This far out in the bay there was no one to hear them scream. Even a pistol shot failed to rouse the garrison ashore.

"Sacre bleu. What is happening?" Voisin muttered, echoing the concern of every man. He blessed himself.

Jolly shrugged. "Sounds like hell's come to the dance." He shook his head, stroked his broad rough chin, and moved to the steps leading up to the quarterdeck. The melee raged on. Another guard collapsed, moaning and writhing on the deck until he gagged and died. His companions lost heart and followed the prostitutes over the side of the boat. Their voices grew distant as they splashed and pawed the water, exhorting one another to swim for shore.

Then silence. The seconds crept past. They heard the pad of bare feet upon the quarterdeck as someone made their way past the grate. Upturned eyes followed the sound as it passed overhead then leveled toward the door at the head of the steps leading up from the gundeck. The iron bolt on the outside of the door shrieked like a banshee as it slid back. Next, the iron hinges offered protest as the door swung open and crashed against the deck. A wiry-looking figure outlined in silvery light appeared on the top step, then started down into the foul chamber. The slave moved with catlike grace; as if stalking prey, watchful . . . dangerous and ready to lash out. William Jolly squinted and rubbed his eyes. The stranger on the top steps brandished a wicked-looking cane-cutter in one hand, a ring of iron keys in the other. He was clad in torn breeches, damp and clinging to his powerful thighs from the long swim from shore. His torso was burned dark, his belly lean and corded with muscle. The collective gaze of the prisoners focused on the ring of iron keys dangling from the stranger's fingers.

"I intend to steal this ship," said the man on the steps. He looked to be no more than twenty, young and untried but resolute; he spoke softly, but with conviction, saying exactly what he meant. His gray eyes, tempered like the raw steel of the cruel blade in his fist, cast a spell over this collection of sea rogues. "I shall need a crew."

"Where are the guards?" Israel called out, voicing a question on everyone's mind.

"Some took their chances in the bay. The others . . ." The man on the steps raised his cane-cutter, its hooked blade spattered crimson.

"Who's with you?" another of the freebooters asked suspiciously. "You expect us to believe a jackanapes like yourself captured the *Dolorosa* on your lonesome?"

"Believe what you see," the stranger on the steps replied. Without further explanation, he tossed the keys into the hold. William Jolly made a perfect catch and with trembling hands began to fumble at the padlocks chaining the men to the deck underfoot. At last the ankle clamps fell away and he kicked free of the shackles and passed the keys to the outstretched hands of his companions. Jolly advanced on their benefactor, his great bulk looming over the younger man. This escaped slave was a sight, standing there half-naked, bleeding from several nasty-looking cuts, his shaggy shoulder-length brown hair framing his careworn features—for it was in the hard-edged lines of his face that slavery had marked him the most.

But the young man had single-handedly vanquished the Spaniards, taken the prison ship for his prize, and freed Jolly and his shipmates, one and all. The physician felt the breath of fate tickle his ear. Sir William was standing at the crossroads of all that had gone before, aware that his next decision determined the rest of his life, for better or ill. One thing he suspected: there would be no lack of adventure with this young man.

"By heaven, I'll serve with you. Never let it be said William Jolly forgets a good deed done his way."

"Aye, we're with you," Israel Goodenough exclaimed, rubbing his chafed limbs. He was grateful for a second chance. The newly freed buccaneers surged toward the steps. Jolly halted them with a wave of his hand.

"Lads, here be your captain. What say you?"

"*Mais oui.* I will follow the devil himself if he leads to freedom!" shouted Voisin. And the rough lot joined in with one accord, accepting the physician's decision to give their young benefactor a chance. He had proved a match for the Spaniards, whether he could fly the Black Flag and survive this unruly lot, only time would tell.

The stranger nodded and led the way up into the night air. William Jolly fell into step alongside the younger man. "Tell me, uh, Cap'n, what do you know of sailing a leaky bucket like this?"

"Not a damn thing," the escaped slave retorted. "That's why I need you." A wicked grin split his features. Once on deck, Jolly noted the dead Spaniards sprawled about the ship. Even a jaded old sea dog like himself was impressed. It was as if some terrible force of nature had swept down upon the guards and slayed them where they stood.

"Just who are you?" Sir William quietly asked, a note of unease in his tone. Their benefactor showed no regret for his actions, though he knelt and wiped his blade clean on the baggy coatsleeve of one of his victims.

"Henry Morgan."

Jolly shrugged. The name meant nothing. "You come from plantations ashore?" asked the physician, lighting a lantern. He held up the lamp and quietly appraised his new captain by the lamp's sallow glow.

Morgan nodded. "I was taken from my village in Wales and brought here, a long . . . long time ago." Music and laughter and the sounds of revelry drifted across the black bay. The port was draped in lantern light and the Spanish populace danced in the streets.

"Listen to them," Jolly said. "No one can hold a candle to a Spaniard for celebrating. And when it comes to religion, them's the saintliest sons of bitches I know, that is, when they aren't starving our poor families to death or hanging our kinsmen. Do you be a God-fearin' man, Henry Morgan?"

And for the first time Morgan smiled. But his humor was carved in ice and his storm-gray eyes narrowed and flashed.

"I shall follow only two commandments," said Morgan. " 'Get mad.' " His fierce gaze flared like a lit fuse. " 'Get even.' "

Jolly shivered in the warm, humid sea breeze ruffling the square-rigged sails overhead.

Morgan experienced a flash of memory, his thoughts reached back seven years to Swansea, a settlement on the coast of Wales, a quiet little port engulfed in flames and at the mercy of Spanish raiders. In his mind's eye he watched Welsh men and boys shackled and led away to be chained in the hold of a Spanish raider and carried off to the Caribbean. The rest was a blur of servitude and grueling toil. But Henry Morgan was free now, free to seek his fortune, to roam the Spanish Main. He'd leave Santiago de Cuba far richer than he came, with a ship and a crew. And an unquenchable thirst for retribution.

"What are they celebrating?" Israel asked in a deep

voice. He approached from amidships, the tall man folding his arms across his bony chest as he paused to stare off toward shore.

Morgan's ominous reply cut quick as a cutlass, unsheathed from some secret place where the hurt ran deep. "It is the last night of peace."